AmaranthA

4/11/2021

Dear Hannah,
  enjoy this adventure
& your stay in Amarantha
...it's like a second home
  to me, so be my guest!
  Warm wishes,

Jenn ♥

AmaranthA

E. R. Traina

Translated by Marinella Mezzanotte

KURUMURU
BOOKS

First published 2021 by Kurumuru Books
17 Trafford Road, Norwich NR1 2QW
www.kurumurubooks.com

ISBN 978-1-7399890-0-2

A CIP catalogue record for this book is available from the British Library.

Typeset by Kurumuru Books LLP, Norwich.

Printed and bound in Great Britain by Clays Ltd, Elcograf S.p.A.

Visit www.kurumurubooks.com to read more about our books and how to buy them.
You will also find extra features, author interviews, and news of upcoming author
events. You can also sign up to our newsletter to be the first to hear about new releases.

To all Daineﬁns and Kolymbas,

mine and yours and ours.

8

To all the translators who

kept going in 2020.

A Note To The Reader

This book has an accompanying soundtrack (composed by E. R. Traina) to supplement the story.

It's free to listen to, so if you would like to listen along, please visit kurumurubooks.com/amarantha-soundtrack. You can also download the music at: www.amarantha.land

Keep an eye out for the 𝄞 icon at the top of a page.

It will let you know when there's a song that goes with that part of the story.

Chapter 1

'The Queen is dead.'

How I longed for everyone to stop repeating that.

I drifted along the castle corridors, followed by the whispers of those who had worked in the castle their entire lives – and all of mine too. I had lost count of the days since Mother's death, and still the whispering never ceased. I'd turn around, but find no one behind me. Perhaps it was only my imagination, or the castle itself expressing its disbelief.

I could no longer speak.

I simply moved from place to place. It was important not to remain still for too long, because there were only so many sympathetic looks my pride could take. Besides, I didn't want to be found by my father or my twin brother Sonni; they both had enough on their minds without discovering that my voice had suddenly disappeared. Luckily, my older brother Anur was always easy to avoid.

As I roamed the outside world, I roamed my thoughts too, avoiding painful questions. My mind was too busy producing whispers and nightmares – and thoughts I'd never imagined myself capable of. When your mother is senselessly murdered, the best you can hope for is that soon, you too will be closing your eyes for the last time.

Of course, that didn't happen. Neither for me nor for the rest of my family. We continued to exist. And in the first few days after her murder, we all kept to ourselves. I had no idea what my father and brothers were doing from the moment of waking to when they collapsed into exhausted sleep. At times, as I wandered the ancient stone corridors, I was brought to a halt by scenes I knew I shouldn't be witnessing, like Father sitting in Mother's armchair with his head in his hands and the last dress she ever wore cradled in his lap.

Or a rare wraith-like glimpse of Sonni, who roamed the castle too, but without the frenzy that characterised my every movement. He walked lightly, noiselessly, as though the flagstones themselves had softened out of respect for a kingdom in mourning. I saw myself reflected in Sonni, recognising the dark circles under his eyes, the pallor of his face and hands. We shared the signs of grief just as we had shared everything since the March morning we were ushered into the world. The same brown curls, the shape of our hands. The button nose inherited from Father, the mouth turned down at the corners as if in a permanent sulk. We were alike with the exception of the colour of our eyes. But only in appearance, as Dainefin – the Priestess – was fond of reminding us. We were as unique as snowflakes. And just as white and frozen now.

Dainefin was the only one who, instead of disappearing in her grief, had rolled up her sleeves and was trying to pick up the pieces of our family. The rumourmongers had wasted little time in setting their sights on her. Who else would have had motive to kill Queen Levith, beloved by all? They said jealousy must have got the better of the Priestess and clouded her heart. Not for a second did I allow that doubt to become rooted in my mind. But others did.

I know it's what Anur thought. My older brother had kept himself out of sight, shut away in his room, protected by a screen of hostility. One day though, I saw him come across the Priestess on the staircase. Dainefin looked as if she were about to say something, but Anur's eyes . . . no, not only his eyes, but every fibre of his body screamed its judgement of her: guilty.

Dainefin didn't defend herself; her thoughts were elsewhere. Most of her time was taken up by my father. His Consuls would wait for hours in the Council Room, until Dainefin went to collect him from the royal bedchamber. When she addressed him, she would only hazard a few short words at a time: 'Your Majesty, take courage.' 'You are expected.' 'It is time.' On good days, my father would divert his eyes from the void he'd been gazing into, and follow her with a sigh. On bad ones, anything that interrupted his mourning triggered an eruption: smashed mirrors, clothes strewn on the floors and overturned furniture that would be left untouched for days, bearing witness to the moment his pain had become irrepressible.

I would sometimes catch a glimpse of his room and

marvel at the chaos reigning there. I pictured the day my father's rage would pour out over the person who had destroyed our family, if we ever found out who they were. I would only linger at the door for a few seconds, terrified of running into someone and being obliged to share the weight of tragedy. Death, after all, takes each of us individually. And when it takes the one we love most in the world, we end up having to deal with it alone.

Naturally, I felt for Dainefin. The Priestess always had an answer to every problem; she was doing her utmost to hide any weakness on her part while keeping all of us going. And we kept rejecting her: Father with his violence, Anur with his hatred, Sonni and me with our absence.

I had kept myself from Sonni too, even though I knew he needed me by his side. In all our seventeen years, nothing had ever come between us. I needed him, but I couldn't explain what had happened to my voice.

After over three weeks of seclusion, hiding in corners of the castle, the inevitable happened. Sonni found me in the library, one of the rooms where I was most likely to pause on my restless wanderings, finding comfort in the dusty rugs and tapestries, and in the fire, lit by a thoughtful servant. I couldn't concentrate for long enough to find distraction in any of the volumes, I simply found relief in the beauty surrounding me: the marble decorations on the mantelpiece, the frescoed ceiling depicting myths from the Old World, the never-ending rows of neatly shelved books.

'Lyria, we have to talk, you can't keep avoiding me,' Sonni said as he came up to me.

As if I didn't know that. I wished for nothing else. But I couldn't.

Since Mother's death, something had changed. I felt as if each of my thoughts were choking to death before they were fully formed. I felt the desperation rising inside of me, bursting out to communicate with him but—

I can't! I thought in despair.

He recoiled as if I'd shouted, but no sound had come out of my mouth.

'How did you do that?' he demanded.

I don't know.

Again, it was as if my emotions were slamming into him, and as much as I tried to hold them back, I couldn't. I saw him searching my face for a clue to what had just happened.

'Ly, you're scaring me. Say something. Anything.'

I can't. I looked away, unable to meet his pleading gaze.

Sonni sat down next to me on the rug by the dying fire. My eyes were burning from gazing into the flames too long. He wrapped his arm around my shoulders and made to lay his head in the hollow of my neck, only to draw back and surreptitiously dry a few tears. This was the first time he'd ever cried in front of me, perhaps the first time he'd wept at all since he was a child. The thought of Sonni and me as children caught me off guard. Every childhood memory had a little of our mother in it.

Forgive me, Sonni. I really can't.

He jerked away from me and stared intently into my eyes as if waiting for it to happen again. Then his face fell: we must have both imagined it.

'I didn't want to talk to anyone either at first. Not even you,' he said.

I opened my mouth to try to respond, and once more Sonni experienced my frustration on his own skin.

I swear I can't. I want to speak, but I can't!

I was pushing, pushing with all my might. But the words wouldn't come out. No signal was reaching my vocal chords, while the muscles around my eyes were working twice as hard. Everything I wanted to say at that moment spilled out in a flood of tears; in my head, a crazed drum was beating harder and harder.

'You really can't,' he gasped.

I shook my head. It was the only thing I could do.

'But how . . . ' The question died on his lips.

How did I fill him with my own frustration, infinite sadness, and guilt? I didn't know either. Since the day our mother died, I had been living inside a bubble of emotion, my own feelings orbiting around me, ready to possess anyone who crossed my path.

But Sonni didn't shy away. He moved even closer to me, squeezing my arms.

'Are you scared?'

He didn't need me to nod. It was all there. He didn't even need to listen – he was forced to feel everything, whether he liked it or not. Not least the question I wanted to banish at all costs because it would shift the attention from her to me.

What do I do now?

Sonni looked distressed, his gaze shifting as if the thoughts he was chasing were slipping away. I felt stupid. I should never have let him near me. I should have slammed the library doors in his face.

'Are you ill?'

Yes.

Panic came knocking: I had just admitted to Sonni what I hadn't yet admitted to myself. I could feel my heart thundering in my chest, pulsing in my wrists, in my stomach. The river inside me had burst its banks; I couldn't hold myself back any longer.

'Does Dainefin know?'

I shook my head. Dainefin was the last person I wanted to see. She would take the whole thing too seriously, turn it into a problem to be solved. I didn't want to be anybody's problem. I only wanted to be left alone.

'She'd know what to do. Don't you—?'

I don't want anybody's help.

Sonni was speaking to me as if he'd forgotten I couldn't answer aloud. Still, he seemed on the verge of guessing what the problem was, what I was so worried about. It was the first time I'd been so physically close to another human being since Mother's death, and I was shocked by how accurate my fears had turned out to be. I was a bundle of raw, uncontrolled emotion.

Just then, the thought flashed through my mind that maybe things weren't quite like that. I was forgetting that this wasn't just anyone next to me. It was my twin. We had always had a special connection; perhaps it had simply become intensified.

My brother didn't see it the same way.

'No, Ly. Being near you feels... weird.'

His words ran me through like a sword.

Please go away!

He hesitated, but nodded and left me. I returned my gaze to the embers in front of me, until the last spark went out in a wisp of smoke.

The hearth was cold, the library in near darkness. There was a knock on the door.

Dainefin didn't wait for my reply, she opened the door and hurried over to me. I made room for her on the rug, knowing no amount of annoyance would convince her to leave me alone.

The Priestess sat on her heels, in the position she alone was able to hold for incredibly long stretches of time. For all her efforts at composure, her eyes betrayed her attempt to read me. She was collecting clues and matching them to the immense catalogue of knowledge she had built up over a lifetime.

Dainefin had spent the last seventeen years at court, first as tutor to Sonni and me, then as Consul to my father, King Uriel. She was the only woman on the Council.

Everything about Dainefin gave the impression that she was not from the capital. She was unique in every way. Her striking features and complexion as dark as chestnut honey drew attention wherever she went. She had large, bottomless black eyes. Over all the years she had lived at court, her hair had never changed colour; not a single white hair had appeared in her thick, dark amber mane.

The way she told it, she'd been born in Shamabat, a fishing village in the south of the continent. Her first job had been in a typographer's studio, and she'd worked there for a few years, teaching the village children to read and write in her spare time. When she'd heard that the King and Queen were expecting twins, she had travelled to the royal capital and offered herself as our governess. And that was that.

But Dainefin didn't strike me as someone who'd spent her youth in a typographer's basement – in a fishing village of all places. She gave the impression of having travelled far and wide, of having lived every possible life. She knew everything there was to know. She could do everything, from alleviating Father's migraines to working out the best time for sowing wheat and barley. Whenever I pointed out that something in her life didn't quite add up, she would answer that none of the things she knew were a credit to her, but rather to the authors of the books she had read and memorised. I suspected that to be a modest half-truth. One of many.

Dainefin was extremely moral. There were days when I was exasperated by her goodness. That day in the library, for example, her sympathy made me want to run away.

I saw panic cloud her eyes. It was the first time I'd ever seen her look afraid. There were two possibilities:

she either had no clue whatsoever why I couldn't speak, or she knew very well what was happening to me.

'We must set off right away,' she said. 'Tomorrow morning at the latest.'

Set off? To where? Why?

Unlike Sonni, she didn't show any surprise at hearing my feelings – if that was what was happening.

I had no intention of abandoning my father and brothers. Once this stupid malady had resolved itself, I would do what had to be done: stand by my family, help make sense of my mother's murder. I only needed a little time.

'It will never pass, if you stay.'

Dainefin placed both hands on my shoulders.

'You have to trust me, Lyria.'

What is wrong with me?!

She knew I'd tried with all my might to scream, talk, sing silly songs even, just to reassure myself that my voice wasn't actually gone. And she knew that I'd failed, that I was always on the brink of ramming someone – anyone – with my emotions, that I had no idea how to control this.

The weight in my stomach became a little lighter. Dainefin understood.

'I know people who can help you recover. It is your only chance.'

Or else? Will I be like this forever?

'It will only get worse, Lyria. And then, there will be no way back.'

Not only did Dainefin absorb the torrents of thought

and emotion rolling off me without flinching, she interpreted them as if they were a language she knew.

Even though I found a little comfort in the fact that not all conversations would be as disastrous as the one with Sonni had been, there was nothing reassuring about Dainefin's alarm. I could tell she felt guilty for not noticing what had happened to me sooner. But she had been too busy holding my father together, while also taking care of practical Council matters.

My conviction that I'd soon get better on my own was growing more uncertain as her anxiety increased. I couldn't think of anything worse than being trapped in a world where I had no control over what I communicated to others.

'We have to go,' she went on. 'Myrain will support your father in my absence. The truth is, I have done as much as I can here.'

She had tried, at least. I hadn't lifted a finger.

I needed to stay. I would do more from now on, dedicate more time to my father. Bring him back to himself. But you could smell the excuse a mile away. I tried again to convince myself: If I didn't stay, who would care for Father? Myrain the Valiant, who was about as sensitive as a hunk of stale bread?

Dainefin must stay too. I trusted no one else to ease Father back into politics.

But Dainefin had picked up the gist of my internal debate, and had the perfect rebuttal to end it.

'I shall talk to Sonni and ask him to join the Council. I'm sure he can't wait. You trust Sonni, don't you, Lyria?'

Sonni taking responsibility for a king who wasn't acting as one . . . . That responsibility was meant for Anur's shoulders: he was the eldest and the heir to the throne.

What about Anur?

'He won't join the Council, if that's what you're asking. As far as I know he is also preparing to leave. He'll be spending some time with your aunt and uncle in Murihen.'

Anur doing a runner. What a surprise. He always disappeared at the first opportunity, and when he was with us he made sure we knew that he didn't like having us around. For a few years, the only person whose presence he would deign to suffer was Dainefin's, but that had been long ago. And once the rumours about her had started circulating . . .

'Lyria, listen, I don't care what Anur thinks. He'll recover from the shock, just as your father and Sonni will. Everyone is grieving in their own way, they just need time.'

All I needed was time too, then I would move on like everyone else. I didn't want to leave.

Anur is the one who leaves. Anur does what he likes. Sonni and I are loyal. We stick around.

But she had already told me that if I stayed, I would deteriorate.

'Things are different now, Lyria. To help your Father, the kingdom, yourself, you must go.'

A long string of questions was forming inside me, and I felt them spill out in one big tangle.

What is wrong with me? How can this get any worse? Have I somehow unlearnt how to speak?

Dainefin stooped a little to look into my eyes. Even when seated, the physical difference between us was striking. She was extremely tall and slender and I the complete opposite.

'Your mother's death is a wound inside of you. It will take a long time for it to heal. When you first felt the pain of it, you shut a door inside your heart, and behind it are trapped not only the terrible things you are experiencing now, but *all* of your emotions.'

I never shut anything!

The thought slipped through my fingers. Dainefin caught it in mid-air.

'I'm not saying you did it on purpose. This is an illness. It behaves as all illnesses do, with causes and symptoms beyond our control. You may even have more symptoms than you're aware of.

'Your voice is the channel you use to control what you want to communicate to others, and what you'd rather keep to yourself. Right now, you are communicating whether you want to or not. Anyone close enough will feel what you are feeling, without understanding why. Your feelings are escaping through a crack under that door in your heart.'

I shivered. To hear Dainefin spell it out made it real.

How far do they go?

'That depends,' Dainefin answered. 'Let's say that the radius of transmission varies according to the intensity of your emotions, and the sensitivity of the people around you. You will notice that some will be able to interpret your thoughts as if you were speaking them aloud. Others will only pick up vague feelings. Either way, you won't have the power to decide what to share and what to keep to yourself. But this is only the beginning,' she warned. 'The Empathic Aura manifests in other ways, too. You must rid yourself of it as soon as possible.'

Empathic Aura . . . . It had a name. That meant I wasn't the first person in the world to suffer from it.

'The illness has no official name,' Dainefin corrected me. 'Empathic Aura is what *I* call it. But it's more descriptive of the symptom than . . .' The Priestess caught herself and brought her explanation back on track. 'You are right to believe you're not the first person to have this illness. Nor would you be the first to succumb to it if we don't hurry. You have already begun the fight. Now, go and pack.'

Chapter 2

As I dug out my haversack, I thought about how easy it is to take one's circumstances for granted. It had been a long time since I had reflected on the fact that my brothers and I were the children of King Uriel, himself a direct descendant of Aur-Lee, the first king of Amarantha. We had done nothing to deserve any of it – it had been good fortune, pure and simple.

I lived in a castle, in the kingdom's capital, a city of a thousand churches and as many dialects. 'The sun doesn't set on Amarantha until a neighbour has knocked thrice on your door,' was the saying beyond the city walls. And it was true that Amaranthians needed no excuse to gather, as long as there was a meal and some wine to go around. Any celebration, from feast days to an ordinary Sunday, would see the cathedral square and the marketplace fill with stalls, performances, and families and friends strolling together along the main avenue.

Those less mobile, like the sick or elderly, were visited by neighbours, friends, and acquaintances, and would live off the feast leftovers for the rest of the week.

I would miss the city, even if I only used to watch it all from a distance. And even more than that, I would miss my every-day life, which was much more solitary and for the most part confined to the interior of my home, Amarantha castle.

The castle stood on a promontory in the south of the city. The granite of its walls and towers changed colour according to the weather and the time of day. When the sun rose and set, it took on a peach hue; at midday in summer, when the sun was high, it shone as if made of salt. But it was on cloudy days that the stone came to life in a gloomy play of shadows, menacing enough to repel anyone who approached with less than good intentions.

Four enormous towers rose within the castle walls, with smaller turrets on top, decorated with stone spheres. My bedroom was in one of those turrets, while the rest of my family had their bedrooms one floor below, in the larger towers. There were more rooms along the corridors that joined the towers: the Council Chamber, the Audience Chamber, the Dining Hall, and the Royal Library. The ground floor housed the kitchens and various service rooms, along with apartments for the three families that worked at the castle full-time, and others for the staff that came and went.

In the weeks following my mother's death, I kept out of sight of the domestic staff, who seemed to be suffering as much as my family. Serving women would be tearfully reciting prayers while hanging out washing or mopping the floors, and their husbands – the groom, the cook and the handyman – had stopped their usual banter and went about their work in silence, only speaking in whispers.

Those whispers, prayers and weeping came together in a background hum that irritated me, even though what I felt towards them wasn't resentment – it was guilt. And it was guilt that stopped me from showing my face to people I had known my whole life. I just couldn't. In the state I was in, I felt I would die of shame; even more so now that I was about to leave.

I didn't know where I was headed, and I can't say I had ever travelled much in my life. The yearning for travel, though, I knew that feeling well. I was an authority on mentally preparing for a journey, having fantasised about it for years. I used to imagine crises to attend to in border villages, the opening of a new mountain pass, an invitation to inaugurate a school or library. I had dreamt of being called to report to the Council, of being told that my presence was now indispensable. I would bow to my father to receive his blessing and then throw myself into the most exciting phase of my daydream: planning what I was going to take with me. But never had I considered leaving home because of something like this.

I'd always imagined Sonni travelling with me too. When we were little, my twin and I used to spend the whole day together, from breakfast to bedtime. We were taught by Dainefin until age twelve, when Sonni developed his incomprehensible passion for what I called 'kingdom stuff', and got it into his head to take his education into his own hands. Part of me had resented him, yet part of me understood. Most of me just envied him the effort he put into it. Dainefin left him to it; she knew he would study from dawn 'til dusk like one possessed, fascinated by the dynamics of the market, trade relations with Murihen, local elections . . . Sonni really cared about all that. But I didn't, not really.

The greater his enthusiasm, the more indifferent or even lazy I appeared. I did try to pay attention when Dainefin insisted that a certain topic would be instrumental to my education, but my brain retained little or nothing of what she taught me about Amarantha. Father wasn't pleased. He always reminded us that even if Anur was the heir to the throne, Sonni and I were also expected to take on political roles, because 'we must all play our part'. It was just that my part had never been defined, and I'd never cared to ask. Not that I was daunted by it, but it all felt so far off in the future that I preferred to turn my attention to different things, like music and reading.

I also gave my etiquette lessons a wide berth. The pompous behaviours endemic among the nobles at court disgusted me. My mother had come from country people and I knew she felt under pressure to match court manners, but I felt those manners marked them out as fools.

Even though our family's royal traditions were much more accommodating than they had been in the Old World – Aur-Lee had been no aristocrat and had always refused to act like one – my mother would not disappoint the people's expectations. Sometimes the pressure weighed heavily on her and she would lecture me for my 'ignoble pursuits'. Then Dainefin would remind her that she owed the people justice, not etiquette, and reassured her that, sooner or later, I too, like Sonni and Anur, would find my 'calling'.

I did study, I just wasn't as diligent as Sonni. He would work out his own schedule and attend Council meetings, while I needed the Priestess to turf me out of bed.

I was never bored with her though. She always said she didn't claim to teach, she just told stories. And that's exactly what she did. Stories from all over the Continent, stories from the Old World. I asked where she had learnt them, whose voices she was bringing to life. She replied that the typographer in Shamabat used to print books for the whole kingdom. The stories came from there.

Dainefin also knew when to stop telling stories. If she saw I was tired, or a bit down, she just let me be. Then I would take refuge in the library on rainy days, or by the sea when it was sunny.

My favourite little cove lay just below the promontory. That's where I would go and wait for the sun to set, even though it actually went down to the west, behind me. It would have been lovely to see the sunrise, but I never woke up in time.

The library and the sea held a very particular meaning for me. They were there for me to go and daydream. Digging my feet into the sand, or lying on my stomach by the fireplace, I dreamt of the journeys I would someday make, the people I would meet, the things I would take with me.

I always picked the same few objects. First, a shell bracelet Sonni had made me for our twelfth birthday: little periwinkles in all shades of white, pink and orange. He'd pierced them with an awl and joined them together with a cream-coloured cord that he must have pulled from the fringe of an armchair. *Since you like the sea*, he'd scribbled on the card that went with it. It was a simple bracelet and had been too big at the time.

I'd had loads of presents in my life. But none as good as that.

I had long since stopped wearing it for fear of losing it and kept it in my bedside drawer just as it was given to me, in a little drawstring bag still gritty with sand.

I reached into the drawer and started to put the bracelet into a pocket of my haversack. Then I changed my mind and put it on. It fitted perfectly now.

But the haversack was still empty.

It was an unusually cold May, so I picked some tunics and warm trousers and made a pile on my bed. A few light shirts, and some woollen underwear. I also added a small, soft leather bag, containing a stick of graphite and a sheaf of paper, in case I felt like writing, and a purse with my savings in it. Dainefin hadn't told me much but I guessed that she herself didn't know how long we'd be gone. I wondered how far from home we'd be going. Where were these people who could help me? In a nearby village, or days and days away, close to the border?

I was also worried about our mode of travel. As Anur never failed to point out, I was on the bulky side,

AMARANTHA

and a shallow hill was enough to leave me out of breath.

Anur . . . . Now *he* was a force of nature. He began every day with an uphill run – from the beach all the way up to the ridge rising behind the castle – then he'd swim all morning, whatever the weather. Sonni and I were built more or less alike – comfortably soft – while Anur was an entirely different species. Every line in his body had been drawn without hesitation, like those sketches of Old-World sculptures. Even his complexion was much darker, with no sign of the freckles sprinkled all over mine and Sonni's faces. According to my father, he was all Uncle Hervin – Father's twin – as a young man, while Aunt Rehena said that Anur and our cousin Ambar had been cast from the same mould.

I briefly wondered whether Ambar would have grown up to be as arrogant and vain. From what little I could remember of my cousin, Ambar had a big head but also a good heart. The only real memory I had of him was a game of marbles that he'd let me win, just to make me happy. Anur would sooner have swallowed the marbles one by one.

I had no gifts from Anur, and I wasn't sure I would want to take anything to remind me of him. I did love him deep down, but it was a complicated love. We spent most of the time sulking at each other.

I stopped thinking about Anur and stuffed the pile of clothes into the haversack, filling it almost completely. There wasn't much room left for personal effects. In a flash, I realised I couldn't leave without something of my mother's. I looked around and my gaze met her smiling face that lit up the family portrait. It was a lean face, with sharp cheekbones, like Anur's, which made her appear sterner than she was, but she had a wide mouth and big white teeth that changed her appearance entirely when she smiled. Mother looked delicate standing next to Father, but though she was small and thin, she had strong arms and wide hips. If only I could take the portrait with me . . . I loved it so much that I had asked Father for permission to have it moved from the Council Chamber to my bedroom.

It was a good likeness. Natural. Mother seated in her armchair, Sonni leaning his head on her thigh, Anur peeking out behind her, sulking for who knew what reason. My father holding me on his hip like a trophy. I couldn't remember the day we had posed, I'd been too young. But my mother told me that the painter only had us pose for a few minutes, just long enough for a pencil sketch, then continued by himself. I liked the thought that he had painted from memory. A memory on canvas.

But the painting was too large to take with me; I needed something else.

I ran down the stairs, hoping I wouldn't bump into my father in the royal bedchamber. His clothes were all over the floor, the bed unmade, various pieces of furniture out of their proper places. I knew that Dainefin would come in soon, unseen, and clear up the mess. The task was beneath her – there were plenty of servants to do it – but I knew it was her way of making herself useful, fixing whatever she could fix.

The only thing Father didn't dare touch was Mother's impeccable dressing table. The mirror looked as if it had been polished that very morning, and there was not a speck of dust on the mint-coloured glass table top. Her few jewels were kept in the drawers that, as a little girl, I had often pulled out and emptied all over the bed. Mother never got annoyed, she would only laugh in delight as I paraded around in her necklaces, so heavy for such a small child.

Lined up beneath the huge mirror were a dozen scent bottles of all shapes and sizes. My mother wasn't one for powder and paint. She had battled against vanity her entire life, which couldn't have been easy at court, where she was adored and venerated. Scent, however, was like underwear to her: it was unthinkable to go without.

I took my time opening and sniffing each bottle. The scents I recognised were in empty or half-empty bottles, the ones she wore most. Each of those scents held a memory of her.

Lemon and lily of the valley, a souvenir from a village in the south that she had once visited while Father and Dainefin were there on Council business. It had been given to her by some villagers she had made friends with – she could befriend anyone.

Orange blossom and lemongrass brought back the summer Mother took me and Sonni to Murihen to spend time with Aunt and Uncle just after Ambar had disappeared. It had been strange to be in Murihen without him there.

I lifted a green, blue and violet vial. It was hard to tell the notes of the fragrance apart from each other, but it was fresh. It had been Mother's favourite scent and on her it recalled almond blossom, with a zesty note in the background. I remembered that she'd worn it the day of Ambar's funeral – when the family had buried an empty coffin – to give herself strength, she'd said. This was the one.

The bottle was nearly empty, so I resolved never to wear it. I didn't want to associate new memories with that scent. It was my mother's, and hers alone. I would only open the bottle to breathe it in and remember her.

I wrapped the bottle in a handkerchief and left my parents' room before my father caught me rifling through Mother's things. I went back to my bedroom and made space for the scent bottle in my overflowing haversack.

Only one more thing was missing.

My feet knew the way, and almost as soon as I'd decided to go, I had passed the threshold of Aur-Lee's Royal Library.

I hurried over to the clavichord taking pride of place in the room, and leafed through the few books I had left on the music stand. I could take the anthology of traditional Old-World songs that I had started to learn. I knew how to sight-read, and with time I would have learnt them all .... But how would I sing them now? I opened the anthology to a random page and recognised the melody. I knew it. It was within me. I felt my whole body stiffen with the intensity of an attempt that, like the ones before it, was bound to fail. There was no way. My voice would not come out.

I left the anthology on the instrument and then moved to the shelves to look for the perfect book. In my daydreams it had always been easy to pick which one to take. For a journey to the south, I'd pick a collection of poems dedicated to the Mediterranean – a sea of the Old World that I had read about in some book or other – about the whitewashed houses of hill villages, the breeze carrying sand from the sea. The scent of bay leaves and oregano shrubs on the edge of the roads . . .

For a trip to the border villages, I would take an epic poem to read at night; the kind of adventure more suited to Myrain the Valiant, commander of my father's guard.

For a retreat in the mountains . . . a love story. As heart-wrenching as possible, thank you very much.

But now that I actually had to make that choice, the night before my departure, I didn't dare pick up any of the books in front of me. What if I chose the wrong book? A novel's attractive cover might, for example, be concealing a pile of rubbish. Perhaps it would be best to take one of my favourite books and leave it at that. Dainefin – the library's official custodian – had given me permission to keep them all on the same shelf. Unlike her, I loved to read the same book over and over. I devoured them in long sessions by the fire or under the covers, and easily forgot secondary characters and plots. For me, reading a book again was like reading it for the first time. Dainefin, on the other hand, would take days and days to finish a book, but then every character, every line, every landscape, would remain forever impressed on her exceptional memory.

I spent an eternity contemplating those walls lined with books brought from the Old World by my ancestor

Aur-Lee. And then I gave up. I had one last look at my shelf of favourites, but didn't feel drawn to this collection of stories or that novel. None of those books, which I had read enough times to make myself sick, seemed appropriate for my first proper journey; nor for such a sombre time of my life. And looking back on it now, my mother's death was only the first dance at that ball.

Before I walked out of the library, I wanted to say goodbye to my clavichord. I didn't like to improvise, but what I wanted to play was not to be found in any of the scores at my disposal. I wanted something sad and bare, free of the tragic flourishes typical of Old-World composers, who could not express a state of mind as simple as sorrow without staining page upon page with ink.

Simple chords for the left hand, a few notes and recurring phrases for the right. The result was a neat progression, almost banal in its predictability, but satisfyingly circular. On the fourth repetition I held back the closure, and returned to the initial chord and position.

A slow, unexpected clapping brought me back to reality. My father had walked in without making a sound, and listened to my playing. I stood up abruptly, even though I hadn't done anything wrong. Nor did he give the impression of having been disturbed. Quite the opposite. His lips were attempting a smile.

'It's been a long time since I last heard you play.'

It's been a long time since I felt like it.

'Good tune. Is it yours?'

If he had asked, 'Did you write that?' I would have been furious. I would have felt like a child, showing a drawing to a parent, who can't think of anything better

to say than, 'Did you make this?' Instead, Father chose
to ask whether it was mine. And it was. It belonged to
me. It had been born inside me, conceived for an audience of one: me. But how could I resent my father for
listening in secret, when I'd done nothing but avoid him
for three weeks?

I nodded in reply.

He approached me, cautiously, as if, of the two of
us, I was the one ready to explode at any moment.

'I spoke to Dainefin,' he said, sitting down in one
of the armchairs by the fire.

Well, then you'll know more than I do.

He didn't appear to understand me as Dainefin
had, but he shifted as he sensed my frustration.

'I'm not sure I understood,' he continued. 'She
says you can't speak any more?'

I wished he would leave off the pauses. He knew I
couldn't answer. I gave a small nod.

'That . . . instead of words, you communicate with
your . . . emotions.'

Another nod.

'That's the part I find confusing.'

He was telling *me*.

'Your mother, perhaps, would have understood
this better.'

If my mother had been around, none of this would
be happening. And yet, in that moment, I abandoned
myself to the irrational thought of my mother trying to
make sense of my illness.

She wouldn't have understood it. She was too

strong a woman. She had been raised by an even stronger woman, my Granny Maya, who had been a midwife. It was my maternal grandmother who had delivered my father and Uncle Hervin, and my mother had spent her childhood helping Granny bring the city's children into the world. She never flinched at the sight of blood, and was used to being left on her own for weeks on end while Father was away on kingdom business. Strength, trust, and goodness made up her character. But when confronted with vulnerability and emotion, my mother was at a loss.

'Did I ... did I say something wrong?' Father asked.

I shook my head.

'Now I understand what Dainefin meant. I can almost hear your thoughts. Well, I ... can feel them.'

As Dainefin had explained, some would be able to understand me word for word, while others would only perceive my emotions. Father seemed to belong to the second category, and while I wasn't surprised, its confirmation chilled me.

He wasn't insensitive. In a way, he was probably more sensitive than Mother had been, but one of his limitations was to turn all that sensitivity inwards. Mother had been able to take care of others even when she didn't fully comprehend their feelings.

I felt my father's disquiet. He was perplexed and didn't know what to say. I felt guilty for all the thoughts that had just whirled through my mind. As caring and open-minded as I thought I was, I now had to admit how often I judged others. Now it was all out in the open.

He indicated the leather satchel he carried over his shoulder, and rummaged through it.

'I wanted to say goodbye before you left,' he said, 'and give you this.' He pulled a book from the satchel and handed it to me.

I turned it around in my hands, savouring the anticipation. I could feel the dust coating my fingertips, and I was dying to peek under the faded red leather of the cover to find out its contents.

'I've had that for so long and I've never read it,' he said, almost apologetically.

My father did not read, not in the way Dainefin and I did. He had lived the same path as Anur, of having to take responsibility for an entire kingdom. It wasn't hard to picture him behind a pile of books, learning the laws of Amarantha by heart, but I had never seen a novel or a collection of poems in his hand.

'It was a gift from your grandfather on the day he left the kingdom to me and Hervin,' he said.

I examined the book, which seemed older and more precious with every glance.

'I've kept it in a drawer my whole life. I picked it up recently and thought of giving it to Anur on the day of his coronation,' he continued. 'But I don't know what he'd do with it.'

He'd use it to prop up a table leg.

My father's face softened. 'Then I thought it may be best to give it to you and Sonni for your next birthday. But now you're leaving . . .'

I opened the volume to the first page, raising a puff

of dust that went straight to my throat.

There was only one line at the bottom of the page.

A name.

Aur-Lee.

Even under normal circumstances, I would have been speechless. Like my mother, Father was not one for grand gestures. He was loved by all for his sense of justice, rather than his gifts to family and friends.

'We've never been good in this family at taking an interest in where we come from,' he said. 'You're the only one who's never stopped asking questions. This should take you back to the beginning.'

I had heard the story of Aur-Lee many times; there was no one in Amarantha who didn't know it. Before becoming the founder and King of Amarantha, he had been a seminarian in the Old World. As he'd waited to take his vows, the abbot who mentored him recognised his intelligence and encouraged him to pursue his studies, which was how Aur-Lee came to spend his youth reading the classics, sciences and arts. But he soon discovered his real passion: navigation. He became so taken with the new theories on the shape of the world that he left monastic life behind and travelled far and wide across the Old World, striking up friendships with other academics and taking part in the debate that mystified scholars of the time: What could be found beyond the Great Sea?

I could not believe that I was holding in my hands the personal journal of Amarantha's founder. I resisted the temptation to immediately study the ornate handwriting – Father was waiting expectantly. I closed the journal, but did not put it down.

Thank you, it's perfect.

Inside, I was beaming; it really was the perfect gift. But my face felt frozen in its mask of grief. Nevertheless, Father understood that his gesture had been appreciated.

'Dainefin says she can't tell me where she's taking you, and it's pointless arguing with her. I'm sure she knows what she's doing. Trust her, Lyria, and please, be careful.'

So not even the King was privy to our destination. I could already hear the tirades of the Council members if they ever found out. They loved any excuse to remind Father that Dainefin took too many liberties.

'You're going to be fine, my dear,' he said.

I wished I felt the same.

'Dainefin will never leave your side. Nor will the Valiant.'

Wasn't he supposed to stay to keep an eye on you?

I hoped that my father had not picked up my last thought. At least not word for word.

'Dainefin insisted that Myrain should stay, but he will not hear of it. For once in my life I agree with him.'

That must have been a blow for the Priestess: to find herself in disagreement with the King *and* with the King's Valiant, the only Council member who always sided with her.

So Myrain would be coming along. He would be of little help with the Empathic Aura, but no one would harm a hair on our heads.

'Sonni was not happy at the thought of you and Dainefin setting off on your own, either.'

Typical Sonni. The Hero Syndrome that had taken hold of my twin over the past few years would not allow him to leave two damsels to their fate, embarking on a journey to an unknown destination . . . while his Responsible-Son Syndrome kept him bound to the court, where he could compensate for the Priestess's absence and the King's malfunctioning judgement.

Father's gaze rested on the clavichord keyboard, and I took advantage of the moment to study him one last time. His face was marked by unfamiliar lines, a map unfolded over skin that a few months before had seemed decades younger. His eyes were dimmed, the blue tending to grey, the edges of the irises blurred like those of an old man. He no longer shaved, and his beard made him look like those kings I had read about in Old-World books. But he was so different from them. He did not wear rippling mantles, nor did he parade around all day with a crown on his head. The only thing distinguishing Father from anybody else was his presence. Whenever he walked into a room, all conversation would dwindle with an air of expectancy, of nervous, solemn excitement. He was the King, and he didn't need a sceptre or a crown to remind anyone of that.

'I'm sorry that you're going through all this,' he concluded, heaving himself out of the chair and onto his feet. This once-powerful man had carried Sonni and me throughout our childhood, and we had weighed as much as two full wine-skins when we were born! I wondered now if the dull, tired gentleman in front of me still had the power to suspend the lives of others with his mere presence.

Before leaving the library, my father bent down and kissed my forehead.

'I hope this journey with Dainefin will bring you back to what you were before.'

What I was before . . .

Chapter 3

'I'm famished. If we don't start right now, my Foundation Meal will be nothing but bread,' Sonni declared, stuffing another piece into his mouth.

Dainefin moved the bread basket out of my brother's reach.

'I'm starving too,' I chimed in, my comment emphasised by a well-timed stomach gurgle.

It was a family tradition to gather together for a meal on the Friday just before the official opening of the Foundation Feast. An unofficial tradition was that this meal was never ready on time.

The Foundation Feast lasted three days, from Friday evening to the Monday morning of the first weekend in April. The festivities were initiated by sumptuous fireworks, and a musical parade along the city's main boulevard. Saturday was reserved for the extensive games and competitions between the Sixths – the six

44

districts of the capital – which I rarely went to see (partly because they began at daybreak, but also because they bored me to death). The winning Sixth, announced in the afternoon, would then host the Sunday feast on their streets, even though some food would also be brought by families from the other districts, along with fruit, vegetables and flowers. An afternoon of music and dancing would be followed by a recital of the speech Aur-Lee had made at his coronation, and that would bring the Feast to a close.

From the dawn of our kingdom, the throne had been passed down to the king's first-born son in his nineteenth year, but always after a Council vote. Consuls had the power to block the legitimate heir from the throne and propose a new candidate instead. That had never happened though, and for one hundred and seventy-five years Amarantha had been, in practice, a hereditary monarchy just like those of the Old World.

But that was where the similarities with the Old World ended. Aur-Lee had made a point of ruling with utmost restraint, and charging the Council with ensuring that his heirs, too, would avoid falling into the bad habits of the Old World. On official occasions, for example, wasting food was absolutely forbidden – a practice that my mother had no trouble continuing, since she'd been raised by Granny Maya. Queen Levith of Amarantha was as serious about helping out in the kitchens, laundry room or vegetable garden as she was about attending any official engagement. She could have easily avoided household tasks, but taking care of the home was one of the pillars of her values, there was no argument about it. And the only person who ever

E.R. TRAINA

had reason to argue was me, because my mother expected of her daughter what she expected of her-self. But when it came to domestic affairs, I was a lost cause.

True to form, Mother had spent the morning before the Foundation Meal in the kitchens on the ground floor.

'I don't understand why every year we have to sit down two hours before the food is ready,' said Sonni. 'We know the kitchens are always running late.'

'You could show some appreciation, you two,' Dainefin intervened. 'Your mother has been up since seven, while you have been out of bed less than half an hour. If you'd offered to help, we may have the roast on our plates by now.'

'Oh yes, so Lyria could poison every last one of us,' quipped Sonni.

I pricked his hand with my fork. In retaliation, he mimed slicing off a chunk of my forearm with the blunt side of the knife and putting it in his mouth.

'If you're done being childish . . .' Anur drawled from the opposite end of the table.

'"If you're done being childish . . ."' Sonni mocked him. 'Don't pretend you're not starving too.'

'This may come as a shock,' Anur replied, 'but the world has other things to think about apart from filling your stomachs.'

'Like your coronation?' The words just slipped out.

The alarmed look on Sonni's face told me it would have been better to keep my mouth shut. There were still many months to go until Anur's coronation – his birthday was in December – but as soon as the subject was raised, there would be talk of nothing else for hours. No one was in the mood to spend the Foundation Meal discussing, for the umpteenth time, what Anur would wear, what speeches he would make, or what he would decree once he was king.

My comment had caught both Dainefin's and Father's attention; we all waited for Anur's reaction.

'Speaking of my coronation, Father . . .' he said, turning his back to us, 'there's something I've been thinking about for a while.'

'Tell me,' said Father.

'Since Uncle Hervin no longer has an heir . . .'

As Anur paused, I glanced at Father and Dainefin to see how they would react. While Dainefin appeared interested, Father looked worried, or perhaps unsure of how best to keep the peace – especially considering Anur's famously short temper.

'Maybe,' Anur continued, 'we could begin thinking about uniting the kingdom again. Imagine how beautiful it would be if—'

'A bold idea,' Father interrupted. 'But you forget I have two sons. And I doubt Rehena or the citizens of Murihen would—'

'I'm sure that Aunt would agree with me,' said Anur. 'If it brought peace to the continent.'

I'd never seen him so animated, I was almost sorry to witness Father's cold response.

It had never occurred to me that Sonni may reign

over Murihen; I had assumed that their Council would elect another king.

Amarantha had been born as one kingdom. Then, during the reign of Grandfather Rugier, who had died before I was born, there had been a long war between the province of Murihen and the rest of the kingdom. When my grandmother had given birth to twin sons during the war, Grandfather Rugier promised he would divide the kingdom when they turned nineteen. His promise had quelled the fighting, and under the rule of King Hervin, Father's brother, Murihen seemed to be at peace – with Amarantha and with itself.

The only unrest was in the border villages, but that had nothing to do with the partition of the kingdom. Anur knew that. Though he was haughty, he could not be accused of naïveté or ignorance.

Neither Father nor Dainefin were quick enough to respond, and the conversation was interrupted by Mother bursting into the Dining Hall.

'I hope I didn't keep you waiting too long,' she said, holding a gigantic tray of roast boar. Father rushed over to take it from her hands, and she cleared a space on the table.

'We decided to only make one main course this year, so you'll have some room left for dessert,' she said, serving slices of meat first to Father first and then to Dainefin. 'You can help yourselves,' she told me, Sonni and Anur as she took her seat.

Anur filled his plate, not needing to be told twice.

'Just as well he wasn't hungry,' I whispered to Sonni.

'Better this way, at least it will shut him up,' Sonni replied.

'What's all this whispering? If you're not hungry, I can take it back,' Mother said, but from the glint in her eye I could tell she was teasing.

I didn't love eating meat, but the smell of the sauce had already made me scramble for the bread basket to prepare two morsels, torn in half and ready to be dunked, for the not very polite, but obligatory ritual of 'mopping up'. Out of respect to the cook, I also put a forkful of roast in my mouth. It tasted of herbs and honey and – like every dish my mother had a hand in making – it was a masterpiece.

'What were you talking about when I came in?' she asked once we'd all filled our plates. Anur had inherited her blunt and impulsive nature. But while those traits seemed to be part of her personality, he put them on with a flourish.

He puffed up, preparing to answer Mother's question, but Dainefin was quicker.

'We were discussing Anur's coronation, but I suggest we begin our meal with Uriel's speech,' she said, pretending not to notice that our plates were already half empty.

Father nodded, smiling at the Priestess. Mother squeezed his hand as he stood.

'People of Amarantha,' he intoned, wielding his fork like a sceptre. Dainefin and I burst out laughing, while my mother gave him one of those looks that said, *'remind me why I married you?'*

Anur wasn't listening, but simply waiting for the

best moment to steal the scene.

'Dear all,' Father composed himself, 'this could be the last Foundation Meal that it befalls upon me to open with a speech ...'

'Boo!' I heckled, thinking that Sonni would join in. Instead, he was quivering on the edge of his seat, rigid as a marionette, waiting for Father to continue.

'. . . luckily, I dare say, because I doubt I am the best speech-writer at this table,' he added, looking at Dainefin who humbly lowered her gaze. Mother was nodding enthusiastically.

'I would like to wish us all another happy year, and remind each one of my children that Aur-Lee's courage and greatness runs through your veins. Life will sometimes force us to make very difficult decisions, but if Aur-Lee has taught us anything, it is that we have the capacity to face every difficulty, every failure with courage.'

'Together,' Dainefin added.

'Together,' he repeated.

It was a very deep speech, far deeper than I expected from Father.

'May the feasting begin,' Mother concluded.

And it was Mother who resumed the conversation a few mouthfuls later.

'A friend of yours came by to see you today,' she told Anur. 'From Murihen.'

Anur appeared annoyed and surprised at the same time. Sonni and I were surprised too, and even Dainefin raised an eyebrow. While Anur had a posse that followed him around the city, I couldn't remember a single time he had invited anyone to the castle. And since when did he have friends in Murihen?

'Really, a friend from Murihen?' asked Dainefin.

'It must be someone from court,' Anur answered vaguely. 'I met a few people last time I was over there.'

'Interesting man,' Mother continued. 'I came across him in the vegetable garden. We had a little chat and he asked about Denhole and your grandmother . . .'

'He asked about Granny?' I had never heard anyone ask after Granny Maya when she was alive, and it seemed very strange to me that someone would now that she was gone.

'He did,' Mother confirmed. 'To be honest, I almost welled up. He brought back memories . . . it was lovely to talk to a normal person.'

My mother never used the word 'subject', and neither did Father. He would say 'citizens of the kingdom' or 'citizens of the capital', while she always talked about 'normal people'.

'You should have invited him to eat with us, Levith,' said Father.

'I did,' Mother answered. She seemed a little disappointed. 'But I got the impression he was in a hurry. Anur, he said to tell you he's leaving tonight, but he'll wait for you on the beach at sunset.'

'How romantic!' Sonni's comment was pitched for my ears only, but my laughter drew Anur's attention.

'I haven't seen many of your friends around recently,' he sneered.

That was low. I bit my tongue, not wanting to make a scene.

'Did he not give his name?' Dainefin asked.

'I don't think he did,' my mother answered. 'Or perhaps I forgot . . .'

'Don't worry,' said Anur, with the fake smile I knew so well. 'I think I know who it is. I'll meet him this evening if I can fit him in. If not, whatever he has to say will have to wait for another time.'

Our parents may have fallen for the way he brushed the whole thing off, but Sonni and I didn't. We knew that no matter what, at sunset, Anur would meet the fellow from Murihen on the beach.

Once again, Sonni sank into a preoccupied silence. It occurred to me that he looked like someone who had more problems than solutions.

'Everything all right?' I nudged him.

'Yes,' he said, blinking and coming back to the present, 'I was thinking about something else.'

The conversation, in the meantime, had circled back to Anur's coronation.

'Haven't you picked a date yet?' Mother was asking Father and Dainefin.

'Not yet, there is just so much to take into account,' Father replied.

'We're not in a hurry,' Dainefin added.

'Speak for yourself,' said Anur.

Sonni and I wouldn't have dreamt of addressing the Priestess that way. But she had only ever been our tutor, not Anur's, and he was always disrespecting her.

'Anur!' Mother warned him, in the tone she used when we were heading for trouble. He didn't talk back. Dainefin pretended not to have heard.

'Uriel has not made a single mistake,' she said, 'At least not since I've lived here, That is what has granted him a peaceful reign.'

Anur was visibly unhappy with what she was driving at.

'But over the last few years,' she went on, 'avoiding mistakes has been harder and harder. There have been warning signs . . .'

'Those riots in the border villages,' Sonni butted in, his curiosity sparked, as it always was by the first mention of 'kingdom stuff'.

'Yes,' said Father. 'Trouble that has been dragging on for years.'

'There's more to it than that,' Dainefin said pointedly. 'But we certainly don't want to ruin this lovely meal with—'

'Typical,' Anur snapped. 'You cast the first stone, then you run and hide.'

'Anur!' Mother exclaimed again. 'How dare you?'

But his gaze remained locked on the Priestess, hoping to provoke a reaction.

'We mustn't rush into anything,' said Father, 'that's all. My every decision needs to be approved by the Council, and they're awaiting a report from the border. Once we're given the go-ahead, we shall proceed with a date and all the rest. But you take too much for granted, son. This is no way to behave.'

Anur was livid.

I turned to Sonni, expecting to share the satisfaction of having witnessed Father shut up our brother. But Sonni was growing paler by the minute.

'Potatoes?' Mother asked. Sonni shook his head, smiling weakly at the generous portion she nonetheless spooned onto his plate.

'We have plenty to think about before the coronation, too,' said Mother, winking at me.

Like how to avoid it, I thought.

Since the topic seemed to have disturbed more than one person at the table, I tried to lighten the conversation.

'Yes, I have nothing to wear,' I said.

It was true, not a single dress could be found in my collection of tunics and trousers. As a little girl, I had insisted on trying on a pair of Sonni's trousers, and I hadn't worn a skirt since. Mother used to say that I was the only girl in the kingdom to wear trousers, and I would answer that I was also the only one who could say she was the King's daughter. Of all the royal privileges I could have exploited, Mother agreed that I hadn't picked the worst.

'You will. I'm making you a dress,' she said.

I hoped against hope that it wouldn't be white. Or pink. Or baby blue. Or cream. Or basically any colour that would make me look like a puffball, or a cupcake.

'Maybe you could try it on after lunch! I've almost finished it. Best try it on a full stomach, that way it'll be large enough to fit the whole coronation banquet.'

It wasn't said with malice, but her comment stung. I always felt self-conscious about my body around her – Mother stayed slim no matter what she ate. I wasn't sure I would feel like stuffing myself with cake at Anur's coronation anyway. Instead I imagined Sonni and me taking off once the big moment was over, hiding out at the beach.

We ate in silence after that until we were all full to bursting. Even though my stomach protested at the thought of more food, I perked up when Father asked:

'What's for sweet?'

'Baked apples and custard,' Mother answered. 'Shall I have it served?'

As usual, she didn't wait for a reply before sweeping off to the kitchens. I turned to Sonni.

'What is the matter with you?' I hissed.

'I don't know, I'm a bit worried,' he said quietly. Across the table, I could almost see Anur's ears twitching. 'About those riots at the border,' he hedged. I could tell there was more, but he wouldn't say.

In the meantime, Mother had returned with the dish of baked apples, followed by a kitchen maid carrying a tray with custard and hot drinks. While my mother served the apples, filling the cored centres with custard and topping them with cinnamon, the maid poured the infusion. Not a familiar face. *She must be new,* I thought. When she handed Anur the first glass, he sniffed it and made a face.

'It's a herbal digestive,' Mother explained. 'I gave instructions to follow your recipe, Dainefin, but I'm afraid a little mead may have slipped in.'

'That's not a problem, Levith,' the Priestess smiled.

'A little mead never killed anyone,' Father agreed, winking at Mother.

The maid poured me a glass too, and I held it in my hands for a long time, breathing in the aromas of mint, liquorice, and anise rising from the warm liquid. Dainefin had been teaching me to recognise aromatic herbs by their scents, but I hadn't reached her level yet. She didn't just know how to tell one from the other, but she could also measure them out into countless combinations that could cure almost any illness.

I looked around the table as I inhaled my infusion, and felt a twinge of melancholy. Was this really the last Foundation Meal over which my father would preside? Perhaps that had been the thought tormenting Sonni earlier.

We raised our glasses and toasted Amarantha's new year.

An hour later I was standing in my mother's room in my undergarments, about to try on my new dress.

It was emerald green.

'It's beautiful.'

I wasn't just saying that. It was darker than my favourite shade – a sort of grass green – but it was the perfect compromise between a dress I would have designed and one appropriate for the occasion.

I looked at myself in the mirror. The sleeves were fitted to the arms and puffed at the shoulders. The bodice ended just above the hip, where it opened into a wide, flowing skirt. It felt perfect all over my body, and I absolutely loved it. It emphasised my top curves while minimising the ones at the bottom, making me look completely different from what I was used to seeing in the mirror every morning.

Mother was examining the material inch by inch for anything that needed taking in, but the sleeves fitted well and it wouldn't matter if the hem of the skirt brushed the floor. Standing behind me, she bent over a little and placed a hand on my lower back.

'Ready?' she asked.

'For what?'

I felt the bodice tighten, though not quite enough to take my breath away. It made me look amazing.

I admired my reflection, finally able to imagine myself in a hall full of ladies who would have spent a whole year preparing for the coronation, without feeling like—

The laces slackened. In the mirror, I saw my mother crumple and fall.

'Mother?' I crouched down next to her. She was struggling to breathe, her forehead damp with sweat.

'What's wrong?' I asked. 'Shall I call for help?'

She could only manage a single word.

'Dainefin . . .'

Chapter 4

I looked at the emerald green dress hanging in the wardrobe and considered taking it with me. But the haversack was crammed full, and I didn't think I would have an occasion to wear it. It still looked brand new, even though I hadn't taken it off for a whole week after what had happened to Mother.

She'd spent that week semi-conscious in bed, with Dainefin watching over her. The Priestess tried every possible concoction on her, but none brought any sign of improvement.

The herbal artistry that had once earned her the nickname 'Priestess' was no match for whatever poison was in my mother's system. Most of Dainefin's mixtures were rejected by Mother's body within seconds of her swallowing them.

None of us slept that week. Father and Sonni were no longer themselves. Even Anur, who was vainer than all the women in the castle put together, walked around in odd socks and shirts done up askew.

Every conversation began with: 'How is . . . ?'

The same. No change. As before. The door to my parents' room never closed, there was a steady flow of people in and out.

On the seventh day, I found it shut, with Father standing in the corridor, staring at the handle. My brothers arrived then, and we joined him in his vigil.

When Dainefin stepped out of the room, we knew what had happened even before she took a deep breath and said, 'She did not wake. The Queen went peacefully in her sleep.'

Her eyes had never looked larger, nor her skin paler.

Father threw the door open, running to Mother's bedside. Sonni and I made to follow, but Dainefin held up a hand.

'Give him a moment.'

We watched from the doorway. Mother looked unnatural. Pale, even though she always kept her tan year-round; so still, when she'd moved animatedly her entire life.

The Priestess nodded and retired, leaving us to our grief. I would not see her again for days.

Sonni hugged me as I sobbed.

Tell me it's not true, I said.

But no sound came from my mouth.

I pulled my clothes out of the haversack, folding them more neatly, trying to fit in more, but it was pointless. It would have to do.

It was late, but I didn't feel like going to bed, so I decided to wash the dress Mother had made me. I took it from its hanger and folded it with care. A few stitches had popped, nothing I couldn't fix. They would certainly pop again if I fixed them myself, but it was a risk I was prepared to take rather than ask anyone for help.

I went down to the laundry room with the dress under my arm.

One of the servants stopped me to ask if I wanted her to wash it for me. She would have had it laundered and pressed by morning if I needed it, but I shook my head. Not wanting to be rude, I patted her shoulder in passing to thank her. She looked puzzled and hurried away. I realised that I couldn't think of her name. My mother would have known. She knew every single person who worked at the castle by their first and last names and their relatives too. She would stop and ask, 'How is your husband, has he recovered from that fever?' or 'Congratulations on the new arrival, what will you call him?' Unlike Father, who had been raised as royalty, she addressed everyone as her equal.

The laundry room was empty. I rolled up my sleeves and filled a basin with water. The washing powders were in the cupboard, along with five or six bars of soap, all different sizes. I had no idea which to use. I looked through the whole collection and picked a powder that smelt like clothes my mother had just laundered. I dropped a handful of it into the basin and lowered in the dress, keeping my fingers crossed that the dye wouldn't run. Not quite knowing what to do, I began to knead the dress with both hands. I decided

I would leave it to soak for a little while, squeeze out the suds, then immerse it again.

After repeating the process a few times, I pulled out the dress and prepared to hang it up.

'It will go stiff if you don't rinse it first.'

Sonni didn't wait for me to acknowledge him, he just came over and filled another basin with water. He helped me move the dress without flooding the floor. The water in the first basin was cloudy, but at least it wasn't green. Sonni rinsed out the dress with an economy of movement that made me think he knew what he was doing.

Who'd have thought.

'Mother taught me to wash the mud off my trousers,' he explained. 'So she wouldn't have to do it herself every blessed day.'

I heard my mother's voice intoning, '*every blessed day*,' one of her favourite expressions.

We hung the dress on the washing line. I was looking round for clothes pegs when I noticed a basket full of dirty clothes, ours for the most part. I pointed it out to my brother.

'You want to wash those too?' he asked.

I nodded. I really didn't feel like going to bed.

'We might as well,' he said. 'It'll be less work for someone else. Shouldn't you be sleeping, though? Myrain told me you're setting off at dawn.'

I shrugged.

My brother seemed at ease as he juggled lye and dirty clothes, and I could have sworn that he too was happy not be tossing and turning sleeplessly in bed. He found a mud-encrusted pair of his own trousers and beat them on the washing board with a hunk of maize-coloured soap. Just as well there had been no need for all that exercise with my dress, which had been stained with sweat but otherwise immaculate.

I rummaged around in the basket for a tunic to wear the next day, then realised it would never dry in time. Instead, I pulled out a burgundy shirt belonging to Anur and held it up for Sonni to see.

'Give it here,' he said with an evil grin. 'Let me bleach it for him.'

'Sonni!' I heard Mother's warning tone clearly in my head, but my own voice was more silent than ever.

'He's left, you know,' Sonni said as he sprinkled a dangerously white powder all over the burgundy shirt. 'Didn't even have the decency to say goodbye to Father.'

Nor to me, I thought. Then again, I'd been avoiding Anur for weeks. Guess we were even.

'He never came looking for me either, obviously. And just as well, I would have given him a thrashing to remember.'

I was finding it hard to picture my half-pint twin brother thrashing Anur. But he seemed perfectly serious.

'What was he thinking, leaving like that? It's like he tries his hardest to be a rat-bag.'

I wondered if Sonni thought the same of me – I too was about to leave. My eyes filled with tears, guilt and shame radiating out of me.

'No, no, no,' he said quickly. 'I didn't mean that. You need to leave. If Dainefin thinks it will make you better, then there's no doubt . . . is there?'

No, no doubt. Dainefin was always right. Dainefin always fixed everything. Dainefin had a solution for every problem. She had only ever failed once. For a second, I allowed the circulating whispers about her to enter my mind, where they reverberated insistently.

It was very late and I was exhausted, and now in the bad mood that possessed me every time my brother Anur was mentioned. But I couldn't entertain the possibility that those whispers were true.

She's treacherous.

Not to be trusted.

You can't be sure about anyone any more.

'Don't think like that,' Sonni said, feeling my thoughts. 'Father trusts her and so do I. We've known her our whole life, Ly. She would never hurt Mother. Never. No way,' Sonni said firmly as he rinsed out Anur's shirt and hung it up, admiring his handiwork.

The shirt was now fuchsia pink with large rose-coloured patches, while the basin disturbingly looked full of blood. My brother was less morbid. 'Looks like wine, doesn't it?'

I nodded hesitantly.

'How about we make him a pink pair of breeches? Two pairs, even.' He paused. 'I'll take your silence as a yes.'

He was bent over, searching the pile of washing for Anur's undergarments, when he stopped and looked up at my face.

'I'm sorry, I didn't mean to imply . . .'

I wasn't offended. I knew Sonni like I knew myself, and vice versa. With me, he could put his foot in his mouth – something Sonni did more often than most – and not need to apologise.

I took a deep breath and placed my hand on his shoulder, as I had earlier with the servant who had offered to wash the dress for me. Maybe if I focussed I could . . .

Sonni looked at my hand on his shoulder, then at me, and burst out laughing.

I thought laughter had been banned from our lives while we mourned. But that wasn't the case. It was possible to laugh. Maybe even allowed? Who knew. For now, I shook with laughter alongside him.

It had been a ridiculous gesture after all. Sonni imitated me a couple of times, putting on a solemn, pompous expression as he placed a hand on my shoulder.

Eventually, the laughter dried up, but our tears didn't.

We couldn't look each other in the eye any more. It was unbearable.

There were still a few garments in the basket, so I pushed my sleeves up and started copying what Sonni had done earlier. I washed the clothes, he rinsed and hung them up.

The shells of my bracelet tinkled mutely through the sloshing of the water.

When every tunic, shirt and pair of trousers was

hanging from the washing line, my brother and I stood, contemplating the results of our joint effort. What had taken us nearly two hours, our mother could have done by herself in a quarter of the time.

'You'll be back as you were,' said Sonni.

It was his turn to place a hand on my shoulder. Dainefin's warning lay in the pit of my stomach, and in that corner of the mind where premonitions lurk.

You'll be back as you were.

It was a statement, not a question.

Chapter 5

I had no idea where we were headed, but we were travelling inland on horseback, towards Hatablar Forest. We were surrounded by endless expanses of amaranth, the plant after which Aur-Lee had named the capital, and eventually the kingdom. The branches of the small shrubs were green and devoid of buds. It was early in the year for flowers: amaranth blossomed between early and late summer, when the red of the petals intensified and bunches of dark berries began to appear on its branches.

I had gazed at those expanses of amaranth every morning and night as I opened and closed the curtains in my room, but I had rarely had occasion to travel across them. I paused, turning in the saddle to look for my window among all the others blinking down from the castle.

The standards of the royal house were still adorned with black velvet ribbons, and the central design – three square topsails on a green field – was partly obscured by them. Sonni had told me that the Sixths were all still flying black streamers alongside their own flags, and candles still burned on people's windowsills even though the city's official mourning period – the three days following the funeral – was long over.

I had only taken a quick glance at the castle, but had to urge Yodne into a trot to catch up with my two escorts. I wasn't bad on horseback, but that was mainly thanks to my horse; Yodne practically rode herself with very little input from me. It had taken me over a year to bring myself to mount her. At first, I had just visited her in the stables. I liked to feed her a few plums or apples, and stroke her muzzle, gazing into her dark inquisitive eyes. Yodne, like Sonni's horse, Cesa, had been well-trained before I'd even met her. And when I'd finally decided to start riding, I discovered that it wasn't as difficult as I'd imagined it to be. She wasn't fast like the bolt of copper lightning that was Cesa, but that suited me just fine. I was more than a little frightened of speed, which was why this trip was going to be unpleasant.

I nudged Yodne closer to Myrain and Dainefin to listen in on their conversation.

'Four days to Hatablar, if the weather holds up,' the Valiant was saying. 'Maybe five if it rains.'

'And through Hatablar to Styr?' Dainefin asked.

'At least a week. The horses won't be able to navigate the forest, so we'll have to travel on foot.'

I pictured the map of the kingdom that hung on the Council Chamber wall. I did wonder why we were going through Hatablar instead of riding via Shamabat, which sounded to me like the quickest and most obvious idea. But something prevented me from asking Dainefin – Shamabat was her home village so she must have had a good reason for wanting to avoid it. In any case, Hatablar sounded like a nightmare. Walking for a week? I wrinkled my nose.

'Your Highness, how many miles can you do in a day?' shouted the Valiant, flashing the smile that had broken many a young heart.

Three or four, if you really want to see me collapse.

His laugh made me blush. Had he felt my answer or was he just pleased with himself for putting me on the spot? Whichever it was, I wished the ground would open up and swallow me.

'There's nothing to worry about,' said Dainefin. 'In less than four days we'll be at Denhole and there will be plenty of time to rest and prepare for the next leg of the journey.'

I had only been to Denhole once before. My mother's family came from there and Granny Maya had taken me when I was little. Of that whole trip, I remembered nothing but the marzipan sweets I had brought back for Sonni. We'd scoffed them all in secret, and spent a hellish night trying to digest them.

In those first three days of the journey to Denhole, we rode hard and Dainefin and Myrain barely spoke. During the day, it was hard to hear over the sound of the horses' hooves and the rushing of the wind, and in the evening when we stopped at an inn or tavern, both Dainefin and Myrain were careful not to be heard by the other guests.

On the fourth evening, we finally got the chance for a little chat over a pot roast at the inn at Saint Josef's crossroad.

'We'll have to stop at Denhole for a few days longer than planned,' said the Valiant. 'We don't want to be in the forest when this storm hits.'

He was right. The sky had been darkening since late afternoon, with swollen black clouds massing on the horizon we were riding towards.

'I'd rather lose a few days in some godforsaken village,' he continued, 'than risk getting stuck waist-deep in mud in the middle of a cursed forest.'

I too had heard the rumours that Hatablar Forest was cursed, but knowing what Dainefin thought of them, I anticipated her reaction.

'Don't talk nonsense, Roy,' she reproached him. She was the only person, other than his mother and sister, who called the Valiant by his first name. 'Hatablar is just a forest like any other.'

Myrain decided not to argue. 'The problem is, I don't want to advertise the fact that the Princess is on a little holiday in Denhole. We don't want to draw the attention of the King's enemies.'

I wasn't aware of Father having any enemies, but then, I didn't know much about what was going on in the border villages; perhaps I'd been naïve to believe that their strife wouldn't reach me.

'Everyone with power has enemies,' said Dainefin. 'If anyone asks, we'll just say we're passing through on the way to visit a sick aunt near the border.'

I looked at Dainefin. She had never revealed her

exact age, but from what she'd told me about her life, she must have been in her forties. Myrain was at least ten years younger, but with the scruffy beard ageing his face beside the Priestess's perfectly smooth skin, they made a plausible couple. The real sticking point would be me, the mute, pale, overweight daughter. No one would believe I'd been produced by those two demigods. Dainefin's complexion was the colour of chestnut honey, and Myrain had a soldier's body: hewn by exercise and bronzed by the sun. Not to mention that they both had dark eyes, while mine were unquestionably blue. Our credibility as a family didn't hold water.

'We won't say you're mute,' said Dainefin, glossing over the absence of physical likeness. 'A bad case of laryngitis is as good an excuse as any other.'

No one said anything for a while. Then the Valiant came out with the question that had been tormenting me for the past three days.

'What awaits the Princess in Styr?'

'I'm not taking her to Styr,' was the Priestess's reply. 'That's just where you will turn back, Roy, and the two of us will go on alone.'

Knowing Myrain, an answer like that was an invitation to argue, presented on a silver platter. The Valiant carried on chewing his mouthful of roast, washing it down with wine, but the temperature in the air seemed to drop a degree or two.

I began to suspect that very private conversations were happening between the two of them in my absence.

'I won't let you go alone,' he finally said, without

raising his eyes from his glass.

'We shall see,' said Dainefin.

The friction between them could have set two faraway villages on fire. I had always thought that the Valiant and the Priestess got on fine. Could it be that Myrain doubted her too? I saw myself standing with Dainefin near the edge of a sheer cliff over the ocean, and my stomach dropped. What was wrong with me? How could I even doubt her? Sonni had been so sure.

I pretended to stifle a yawn and ducked out, hoping the Empathic Aura hadn't had time to slap all my worries in their faces.

It was late when I heard Dainefin open the bedroom door. The Valiant must have kept her up, trying to change her mind. Their discussions only ended when one of them had had enough and gave up. As far as I was concerned, our arrival at Styr was still far in the future. It was everything before then that worried me. The people of Denhole were my mother's people. What would they think if they found out that the princess was gallivanting around the continent instead of mourning as was proper?

It would probably be best if I never set foot outside the inn until it was time to leave for Hatablar.

But then I thought once more of my trip with Granny Maya. I remembered next to nothing. Did I want to waste the chance to walk the streets where my grandmother and mother had played as children? Miss the sounds and smells of a place that was not Amarantha?

No. Since I was on this journey, I would do it properly. If I returned with no tales to tell, Sonni would never forgive me. And neither would I.

The next afternoon, Denhole came into view over the crest of a hill. The ridges and hollows around the village were different from the seaside landscape I was used to. It was surrounded by fields the colour of burnt gold, dappled with the dark green of the shrubs that grew wild here and there. Long groves of olive and orange trees lined the path to the village.

I slowed down for a closer look at the olive trees, which did not grow anywhere near the capital. The gnarled trunks and branches put me in mind of the wrinkled skin of the elderly; their roots seemed to sink down to the centre of the earth. The sky had darkened, and their leaves reflected the silvery light penetrating through banks of low, threatening clouds.

'Shamabat too was surrounded by olive groves,' said Dainefin. She answered my question faster than I could think it: 'I haven't been back there since before you were born.'

You should.

How could anyone be so far from their place of birth for so long? Did she not miss her childhood friends, the people she grew up with?

'I do miss those olive trees, but there seem to be plenty here,' she said as she quickened our horses' pace.

The Valiant had already started down a path branching off the main road. The narrow lane led to a redbrick inn partly grown over with vines, before meandering through the surrounding fields.

'This may look small, but it will be packed,' said Myrain. 'Not many stay the night, but scores of people will stop for a meal. Mind who you trust, Your Highness.'

He had leave to call me Lyria, as everyone else did, but his formal manner didn't irritate me. As a military man, he was a firm believer in rank.

He helped me dismount, and I stroked Yodne's neck to thank her for her toil. She deserved a little rest, after four and a half days of hard riding. She seemed happy though. She loved long hacks and I hadn't taken her out myself for the best part of the season.

'She's a beauty, your Yodne,' said Myrain as he bundled his horse's reins with hers. He took Dainefin's reins in his other hand and headed to the stable.

'What will you do this evening?' Dainefin asked me as we turned to enter the inn.

I shrugged. Aur-Lee's journal lay unread at the bottom of my haversack and I was dying to make a start on it, but something kept me from showing it to the Priestess.

'Don't worry, I understand how hard it must be to keep anything to yourself, with the Empathic Aura always in action,' she said. 'I don't need to know everything. Just take heed of Myrain's words. Let's try to be as inconspicuous as possible.'

The inn's common room had the feel of a servant's mess: two long tables crossed the oblong room, with a counter on one side for customers to place their orders of food and drink. Of the many lanterns mounted on the walls, only four were still burning, and several extinguished oil lamps sat on the tables. Finding an empty tavern at mealtime really was unusual, and I noticed that the Valiant too was perplexed as he came in and joined us at the deserted counter. We waited there until a young woman came through a door that wafted the steam and scents of a kitchen into the room. She spotted us out of the corner of her eye and came to greet us.

By her exhausted look and the dirty rags hanging from her apron, I guessed we'd just missed the evening rush. I saw her features rearrange from irritated to intrigued when she spotted Myrain. She tightened her ponytail and tucked away a few unruly strands of hair, then beckoned us to follow her to one of the tables.

'This is the last Thursday we close early for the mourning period,' she explained as she ran a cloth over an already spotless surface. 'You're lucky we haven't had that many customers today, there's a bit of food left.'

She lit two clay oil lamps, and laid the table with plates and cups of colourful glazed pottery: maiolica, as it was known in this part of the continent. My plate was illustrated with a peach surrounded by a motif of green and red leaves and five bunches of lemons.

I looked up and realised that Dainefin had ordered for me; the maid was nowhere to be seen. Fifteen minutes later, she came back out of the kitchen with two loaded trays, which she put down on the counter.

Myrain hurried over to help her, and they exchanged a few words that I couldn't hear.

He brought the trays over to the table as he carried on chatting with the maid. Myrain took one whole tray for himself, and put the other in front of me and Dainefin. There was more than enough on it – a veal casserole and stew of vegetables and potatoes – while Myrain's was piled high with wild boar ribs, polenta, stewed vegetables and three focaccias.

I took advantage of his distraction to steal one focaccia and a generous spoonful of polenta. I dunked the fragrant bread into the stew; it was so rich and smelled so delicious I couldn't resist.

The maid lingered briefly. 'Can I get you anything else?' She turned to me. 'I could ask the cook to mix an infusion for your throat. Your uncle told me you've lost your voice.'

I shot Myrain a withering look. What happened to being inconspicuous?

Dainefin answered for me.

'You're very kind but she's fine, thank you.'

The girl turned to Myrain. 'If you need anything else, you know where to find me,' she said with a blush.

In her room, covered in rose petals and surrounded by a battalion of candles, I thought loudly at Myrain.

The Valiant of course didn't hear me, he was too focussed on the boar rib he was gnawing on.

I couldn't be sure if there was something between Dainefin and Myrain. My suspicions changed by the day. When they bickered like an old married couple, I had no doubt that they had already planned their future life together. At other times though, I couldn't make sense of the silences between them. Right now, if I were in Dainefin's place, I would not have deigned to grant him another word for the entire evening.

Dainefin however paid the maid's flirtation no mind. 'So, what shall we do?'

'We'll stay here until we can be sure it won't rain for at least two days,' he answered. 'Only the first section of the forest is tricky. Once we're through that, waiting out any more rain for a day or two shouldn't be a problem. Though I'm hoping for clear skies after this storm passes.'

I groaned inwardly. No, thank you. It was still unclear to me how Myrain thought he could drag me across the forest on foot, with a haversack on my back, when even the short trek from the castle down to the beach and back had me clutching my sides, lungs on fire.

'In the meantime,' he said, turning to me, 'you can do what you like. Perhaps a stroll around Denhole tomorrow, to stretch your legs?'

From what I'd seen on the way, it would take no longer than half a morning to walk from one end of the village to the other. I was curious, though. I wanted to do what my grandmother had done when she was my age. Pick oregano from the roadside, drink from the stream . . . I wanted to meet the children of those she'd once played with, see in them a trace of shared kinship. My grandmother's face was the face my mother would have had if she'd lived longer. Perhaps we still had relatives here.

That night, I drifted off to sleep imagining a family who had never known me.

The dirt track leading to the village sloped slightly upwards, but it wasn't insurmountable. I didn't see anyone, no farmers, no children at play or women heading to the well for water. Perhaps they had been put off by the menacingly overcast sky, or it was simply too early. For all my efforts to enjoy the moment, this deserted village had lost its appeal.

But the stillness couldn't last forever: sooner or later, the village would rouse itself, and the ghostly silence now reigning over it would melt away along with the morning mist. I only needed to be patient. Until then, I should savour the anticipation, and observe this sleeping creature in the moments before it woke.

Following one lane after another, I eventually found myself in a small square bordered by cloistered walks. From there I reached the high street, lined with orange trees in full bloom. I walked back up it in the hope of glimpsing a sign of life, but all the shutters were closed and no sound could be heard from any of the houses.

At the end of the avenue was a hill with a small church atop it. I remembered visiting a nunnery all those years ago with my grandmother: the Convent of Saint Josef. But that had been outside the village proper, not right in the centre. By its appearance, this church had been here since the day a bored explorer had left the capital and founded the village. The main entrance was closed, so I went around the church intending to walk down the opposite hillside. Instead, my curiosity was piqued by a tiny door at the back of the building. There was no keyhole, knob or handle. It was just a board positioned in the doorway, perhaps a stand-in for something more dignified. I looked around, then pulled my sleeves over my hands to avoid splinters, and moved the board aside. Without much effort I was able to shift it far enough to squeeze through the gap.

I found myself between two lines of wooden seats arranged in a semi-circle. In front of me was a pipe organ, braced against the back of the altar as if propping it up. I was in the church choir.

The candles weren't lit, but the light filtering in through the small glazed windows was just enough for me to see by. The dark odour of wood, dust and incense was almost stifling, so I shifted the board a few more inches to let in a little fresh air.

The pipe organ was, unsurprisingly, the first thing to attract my attention. Compared to the organ standing over the choir of Amarantha Cathedral, it looked like a toy. Still, the carvings decorating the three sides of the instrument's casing were the work of an artist, and matched the figured choir seats. It saddened me to see that the keyboards were covered by a layer of dust.

I took a step towards the instrument, but was distracted by the faint scent of fresh flowers. I followed it, and peered from behind the altar: every row of seats had been adorned with orange blossoms, and huge silver drapes hung from the columns between the naves. The church was empty, but a special Mass would soon be celebrated here – perhaps a wedding or a baptism.

I returned to my inspection of the organ, running my fingers over the wood in search of the secret compartment I knew would be there. I found it below the keyboards. Enshrined within was a stack of handwritten scores. I picked up a few, afraid they'd crumble in my hands. I recognised some psalms and songs, and tried to air-play a hymn I had never come across before. The temptation to give voice to a real organ, even one as small as this, after practising on a clavichord my whole life was irresistible. If I was quick, maybe no one would notice. I looked around for the bellows and pumped as much air as I could into the windchest.

Then I sat down and tried the middle C. What a voice this toy had! Forgetting I was trespassing, I formed the rest of the chord with my right hand, playing the root in one of the lowest octaves with my left. The intensity of the sound caught me by surprise, but I didn't lift my fingers off the keys. I closed my eyes to listen, opening myself up to the sound that enveloped me, traversing the air as the wood vibrated beneath me. I stretched my dangling feet, and added the pedals.

When I finally withdrew my hands and feet from the instrument, the church walls gave me back the chord I had played, full and booming.

I shivered then with the feeling that the world would not have been the same without that chord. I began to search my musical memory, playing everything that came to mind: traditional Old-World songs, lullabies, pieces I had practised for months before I'd even been able to tack them together without wobbles.

I stopped playing and let the sound fade to silence.

'I don't know who you are, but to me, you are a gift from Heaven.'

From the doorway to the sacristy, a priest was watching me in astonishment. 'What is your name? Where did you come from? How did you get in?'

Of his three questions, it was only in my power to reply to the last. I turned and pointed at the gap in the makeshift door I had squeezed through.

'That should have been replaced ages ago. But it worked out better this way, didn't it?' he said with a dazzling smile.

The priest's good humour was contagious. He was a chubby little man who appeared to be that indeterminate age typical of priests – anywhere between fifty and eighty. His nose and cheeks were flushed with the chill of morning, and he was slightly out of breath.

Unable to reply I merely nodded, dropping my gaze. My fingertips were black with dust. I rubbed them clean on my trousers.

'I didn't mean to frighten you, I was just . . . . No one has played here since . . . . Where are you from? Have I asked you that already? . . . Today of all days! . . . The last time I heard . . .'

It seemed that the priest couldn't make up his mind on what he should say first. He quivered with sincere emotion and frenzied gestures accompanied his rambling, breathless speech.

I wondered where that agitated little man found so much energy at this ungodly time of day.

'Did you know you almost moved me to tears?' he said. 'You're a real talent!'

I pointed at my throat.

'You have a sore throat?'

I nodded.

'It will pass, it will pass,' he said light-heartedly, and continued: 'You are a gift from Heaven, did I already say that? I don't know how you got here but this cannot be a coincidence. Would you like to play at Mass today?'

My heart soared. At the keyboard I was at ease, and playing would allow me to think of nothing but music. No Empathic Aura, no Dainefin, no tramping through the forest to the fjords of Styr.

I nodded enthusiastically.

The priest wiped at a tear.

I knew old people cried at the drop of a hat, but I still felt that was a bit much. I liked the priest, but I felt a little uneasy just then.

'You must excuse me, but it's not every day that…'

I never found out what didn't happen every day. The priest dried his tears on the sleeve of his cassock, and sniffed. He must have really missed the sound of that organ.

'It's nearly time, I'll help you find the score.'

He emptied the music compartment of its contents and settled into a choir seat, leafing through the yellowing pages of old choral scores and loose sheets, After a minute he found what he was looking for.

He handed me a booklet whose cover only bore one word: *REQUIEM*.

I scanned the sung Mass. It didn't seem beyond my capabilities: it would be complicated, but not impossible. Still, I was losing my nerve.

Now that I knew this was a funeral, all my courage was fleeing out that little back door. Slipping up at a wedding would be one thing, quite another at a funeral. In an atmosphere of mourning, a wrong note would sound like an insult to the memory of the deceased.

I heard the front doors opening to the people of Denhole.

I shook my head, handing the booklet back to the priest, praying with all my might that he wouldn't make me do this.

'Please, little stranger, I am begging you. Play for her . . .'

Who am I playing for?

I didn't even know who the people of Denhole were preparing to mourn. Besides, except for that one time before we left the castle, I had not played since Mother's funeral. A wound had opened in my soul, and I already felt guilty for how much I'd enjoyed playing just now. It was selfish of me to be happy only one month on from Mother's death.

One month, exactly.

'. . . Play for the Queen.'

It was then I understood that Mass was being held for her. An intercession for the little girl from Denhole who had become Queen of Amarantha.

Levith, I mouthed. The priest nodded.

'Please,' he implored. 'Play.'

I nodded. I would play for my mother, not for the faceless people of Denhole. I wished the priest would leave me on my own with the Requiem. The Empathic Aura must have done its job because he disappeared off into the sacristy.

'*In nomine patris et filii et spiritus sancti . . .*' I heard him intone.

I placed my hands on the keyboards and did not lift them again for the best part of an hour.

I played laments, psalms, invocations. The Requiem's progressions were unpredictable. Whoever had composed it must have been trying to show off. I tried to simplify the trickiest passages and the elaborate phrasings, which sounded so forcibly tragic. The composer had written twenty pages' worth of eulogy on the wrong premise: that grief is complicated.

Grief is simple. It may seem hard to understand from the outside looking in, but when you lose someone you love, there is nothing simpler than grief.

Just as I had that thought, the Requiem changed. I wasn't even sure it was still the same work; there were half a dozen pages, penned in a different colour at the end of the score, entitled *Chara Chairei*.

The words meant nothing to me. The piece built on the eulogy but it had obviously been composed by a different hand, a different ear. Stripped of the first part's pseudo-classical embellishments, it bewitched the listener into following the composer on a journey: a journey that ended in exultation for a new soul entering the kingdom of heaven. I abandoned myself to it and did not change a single note, because each one was essential, perfect just where it had been placed. The final progression leaped from octave to octave to the last five chords, the five steps bringing the listener face to face with Saint Peter himself.

I owed a huge debt to whoever had written the *Chara Chairei*. Not only was it the most beautiful thing I had ever heard, I'd had the privilege of playing it at the Mass of Intercession held for my mother's death.

My fingers lifted from the keys. I absorbed the echo of the last chord as it rose from the church, touching the heart of each worshipper. For a second after the sound dissolved into the air, no one so much as breathed.

Then the crowded church exploded into applause, an expression of sincere joy that took my breath away. There couldn't have been a single empty seat in the church; the entire village must have been in attendance.

I thought about why those people had risen from their beds so early. Maybe because attending this Mass was the right thing to do. Or maybe, because to some of these people, Levith wasn't only the Queen of Amarantha but also a niece, a distant cousin: their own blood. Again, I thought of the children who had once played in the lanes with my mother and grandmother, who would have bid them goodbye when they left for the capital. Were any of them here today, weeping for their childhood friend? Were any of them with Mother, witnessing a village in mourning from above?

The applause continued for some minutes, but grief still hung in the air. I accepted the condolences of the village and I grieved with them. Only now, it wasn't so devastating, unbearable or thankless. On the contrary, this closure exposed within it a secret gift, a savage, inexplicable feeling that rose like a bubble inside me.

'The Queen!' a voice cried out.

'The Queen!' the crowd replied. The scraping of seats being pushed back mingled with the din of the applause.

'Queen Levith! King Uriel!'

It was too much for me. Before my Empathic Aura flooded the congregation with my grief, I gathered my things and fled the way I had entered, through the tiny door.

Once outside, I gulped in a lungful of air as if I had narrowly escaped drowning. I ran back down the high street, barely able to see through the tears streaming down my face.

Rain fell insistently, but what else could be falling from the sky on a day like this?

Chapter 6

I shut myself in my room and spent the rest of the morning in bed. I awoke later with a sore throat and a grumbling stomach. There was no sign of Dainefin or Myrain, so I took that to mean I was free to do as I pleased. I slung on my small leather bag, and went down to the dining room.

I was welcomed by the smell of freshly-baked bread and the chitchat of customers gathered at the counter. The floor was covered by a thin layer of flour, which rose as people hurried across it, clutching their loaves of bread.

A loud rumble from my stomach conquered my reluctance to join the queue of strangers. I let about a dozen shouting people go in front of me, before the baker realised I'd been waiting for quite a while. She turned to me, and said gently, 'You must be that handsome man's niece. My daughter wouldn't stop talking about him last night. What can I get you?'

It wasn't Myrain's fault that all women fell at his

feet, but it annoyed me nonetheless. I hadn't anticipated needing to communicate with strangers without Dainefin or Myrain there to speak for me. I remembered the paper and graphite in my bag. It suddenly dawned on me that if I was ever caught without writing materials on my person, I would be lost.

I leaned on the counter to write down my order.

'I'm sorry,' said the baker, 'I can't read. I can do my sums all right, but letters . . . . My daughter can read, though,' she added, raising her voice to include the five or six people queuing with me, 'I sent her to school, you know.'

I pointed at a flat loaf, then at the tables behind me, muddling through with gestures.

'Go and sit down, I'll bring it over. Look, that's my daughter, Reya, over there. Why don't you sit with her?'

I didn't feel like it, but it felt rude to sit elsewhere now. I approached the young woman whom I recognised as the maid from the night before and raised my hand in greeting.

'Hi! I like your trousers,' she said. 'Is that the fashion in the capital?'

I nodded.

'Hear that, Ma?' Reya shouted to her mother. 'It's the fashion in the capital!'

'That's as may be,' the baker replied, 'but not in my house!'

'Pig head,' Reya muttered.

'Look who's talking,' her mother shot back.

Reya turned to me. 'How's it going, then?'

I shrugged, and felt my face compose itself into an expression I had seen thousands of times on my grand-mother's, roughly translating to: *'Well, what can I say, I'm getting by.'*

She burst out laughing, and stretched her feet to push out the stool in front of her so I could sit. I felt a bit bad for judging her the previous evening. We must have been more or less the same age, but the dark circles under her eyes made her look older. Her eyes themselves were large and black, her hair the same colour. She wore it braided down one side, the braid falling all the way to her elbow leaning on the edge of the table. I noticed her empty plate and my stomach rumbled again.

'Your stomach talks more than you do,' she laughed. 'You got a name?'

She'd caught me by surprise, and that made her curious.

'Come on, it can't be worse than Reya. If it's any consolation, I have a friend called *Dill.*'

Maya, I scribbled on a piece of paper, to stop her imagination from running away with her.

'Aha, that's why you wouldn't tell me . . . . Half the girls in this village are called Maya. I thought it was only a common name in Denhole.'

Reya's mother carried a steaming board to the table. The flat bread had been cut in half and seasoned with olive oil, salt, pepper and oregano. I hadn't had bread and oil like this since my grandmother had died. After the first mouthful I had to look away from Reya, to hide the tears filling my eyes.

Outside, the weather was an invitation to stay indoors, wrapped in a blanket with a hot drink.

'This drizzle is getting me down . . . . This time last year we could swim in the stream. I'm meeting a couple of friends tomorrow, maybe we'll go if it clears up by then,' Reya went on. 'You should come with us, if you're still around.'

I nodded weakly. I would have loved to . . . but I wasn't about to let anyone I'd just met see me out of my clothes, not for all the gold in the world.

I was still calculating the effort it would cost me to go out with her and meet new people – *girls* even – when Reya's enthusiasm got ahead of my reply.

'That's all set, then. I've got a few errands to run now, but want to meet in the square in about an hour?'

Before I could respond, Reya was out the door, leaving me by myself at the table, to nibble on the rest of my bread and oil. When I was done, I felt around in my purse for a few coins to leave by the empty chopping board. I only had gold bezants, even one of which would be excessive for a hunk of bread and a drizzle of olive oil. I left it anyway.

I spotted a trace of blue in the sky, so I decided a short walk would be good for stretching my legs after spending half the day in bed.

The path that branched out from the lane to the village continued past the inn, winding among the olive groves and lush vegetation. I ventured along, hoping I wouldn't run into a bad-tempered farmer, careful not to tread on any plants and resisting the temptation to pluck a juicy-looking peach. I followed the path until

I could no longer tell it from the space between one row of plants and the next. I found myself on the bank of a stream, in view of a mill that must have been where the inn got its flour. The building itself was an ancient-looking, tumbledown stone cottage. For an instant, I thought I saw someone behind the second-floor window. I was startled by a voice behind me.

'Would you be so kind as to . . .'

An elderly woman was struggling up the riverbank with two buckets full of water. She was in black from head to toe, with a few strands of white hair escaping a black shawl that covered her shoulders and reached down to her ankles. Her silvery hair emphasised the bronze tone of her almost wrinkle-free skin. I hurried over to help and relieved her of the buckets, carrying them with much less ease than she had.

'This way.'

She led me into the millstone room, and motioned me to put the buckets down in a corner.

'I'll get him to decant them tomorrow.'

I didn't know who she was referring to. I imagined the mill didn't run itself: there must be someone else helping her take care of it.

'What's your name? I haven't seen you round here before.' She sounded suspicious.

My cheeks must have flushed the colour of amaranth at the peak of summer. This old woman somehow made me feel small.

'Can't you talk?'

I shook my head.

'Then do me a favour and go,' she spat. 'I have no time for *your kind*.'

By the time I reached the square at the end of the high street, I was out of breath and my trousers were muddy halfway up my calves. I couldn't say that I had run all the way exactly, but I had pushed my body to its limit to get away from the old woman as quickly as I could.

I didn't see Reya yet, so I sat down on one of the benches in the square, trying to let off steam: rage had turned my Empathic Aura into a nocked arrow. I curled up, hiding my head between my knees, under my arms. My elbows dug into my thighs and it was beginning to hurt, but as uncomfortable as that position was, it seemed to soothe me. Cutting out the world starved the Empathic Aura of stimuli and targets; forced to turn on itself, it gradually started to fizzle out.

Reya's voice brought me back to reality, making me lose control all over again.

'Hey. You all right?'

She was already on the third hair style I had seen on her: a low bun that, to be honest, didn't suit her much. It gave her an old-fashioned look.

It was futile to nod that I was all right with the Empathic Aura stating the opposite.

'You look like you need some proper girl talk, Maya. Let's go to Ott's and you can tell me what's wrong.'

I nodded, reaching into my pocket for a handkerchief to wipe the tears and snot off my face.

E.R. TRAINA

I let Reya's chatter wash over me and the little walk did me good. When we arrived at the tavern, which was conveniently situated in a narrow lane behind the church, I was ready for a normal conversation – so to speak.

Half a glass of orzata was enough to calm me down and give me time to put what had just happened in writing, in the most concise and least pathetic way possible.

I filled half a page and passed it over. Reya picked it up and I watched her eyes as she read.

'Ah,' she said at the end, 'I see you've had to pleasure of meeting Old Bedevilled.' And then, upon seeing my confused expression, 'She got her name when all sorts of bad things happened to the miller family in the same year. First her daughter got pregnant at our age – not married, of course – and then she died giving birth, and then it became clear the baby wasn't right. Deaf as a post.'

And the father? I wrote.

'He never stepped up,' Reya answered. 'You can imagine the rumours doing the rounds about the millers, for people to start calling them "Bedevilled". The old man who lives up by the Passion is deaf too. That's his uncle, the miller boy's I mean.'

'You talking about Noalim?' The serving girl had come over to refill our glasses. 'My mother says they're all trash and it's best to steer clear of them. That miller boy is as much of a lowlife as his mother and his grandmother.'

'Well, that low-life you're talking about mills the

flour my Ma uses to make bread with. The bread you eat every day. And he's been doing that since he was six years old,' Reya retorted. 'When you were playing with your dolls, he was heaving sacks of flour to the inn and back.'

'I didn't know you had a crush on him,' the serving girl said with a sniff, stalking off.

'Load of rubbish,' Reya rolled her eyes. Then, changing the subject, she said to me, 'You should see how Old Bedevilled treats him. She only lets him out to do the deliveries and go to church. Were you there this morning, by the way? For the Intercession? I heard it was beautiful. I couldn't go.' Reya sounded a little disappointed. 'Did anyone find out who was playing?'

I couldn't risk the Empathic Aura betraying my unease at the conversation turning to the morning's Mass. I grabbed the piece of paper and asked Reya why she hadn't been able to go.

'Oh, the usual,' she answered. 'I was up cleaning the hall 'til four this morning. I'm trying to save up to move to the capital. I'd love to open my own bakery, or a tavern. Meet new people every day.' She looked at me, wide eyed. 'Go on, tell me what the city is like.'

Was it pride I felt just then? I was the centre of attention, with a girl my age who wanted to chat with me. No one was forcing her. I wished Anur could see me at that moment. I envied his confidence, the ease with which he related to the shoals of boys and girls who orbited round him.

The best, most beautiful things about home ... my only difficulty was knowing where to start. I picked up the graphite and filled both sides of a new sheet of paper.

I told her about the sun rising over the promontory, the colour of the sea on rainy days. The sea salt that you could smell as far as the gates, the copper hue of the city walls in the evenings. I told her about the market square, open once a month to traders from all over the kingdom who called out their wares in all their different dialects, a raucous symphony of voices and smells.

I wrote down everything that I could think of about the days of the Foundation Feast. Every doorway decorated with garlands of amaranth leaves and berries; music playing at every corner; the marching band that woke you early in the morning, but it still made you so happy that you would run to your window to watch it pass.

You should go, Reya. Amarantha is the most beautiful city in the world.

Or it was for me, at least. Since it *was* my world.

Chapter 7

That evening, at dinner, I received a rare scolding from Myrain.

'Didn't we decide it would be best not to attract attention? Keep a low profile?' he hissed at me. 'What were you thinking, playing the organ at church at seven in the morning? And paying for bread with a gold bezant?'

Dainefin was watching him apprehensively, but she remained neutral. If she too had thought I'd been foolish, she would have let me know; instead, she quietly waited for the Valiant to be done with his lecture.

He was red in the face, his chest visibly rising and falling with each breath. 'Don't you know how quickly rumours spread in a place like this?'

I could imagine. The scene he was making now had an audience of about ten, all set to unleash the gossip the minute they stepped out of the inn.

'And as if that weren't bad enough, you spent

another bezant on two glasses of cheap orzata!'

I had been hoping that last incident wouldn't reach his ears, but he seemed to have a good source.

Who told you about that?

'More than one person,' Dainefin sighed.

'Everyone knows about it, Your Highness,' Myrain's voice dropped even lower. 'The whole town is talking about the mute girl doling out gold left, right and centre. Wait until they find out it was you playing the organ this morning, then they'll put two and two together and be all over us.'

The villagers?

'The Separatists. Roy thinks they may be behind your mother's murder,' Dainefin explained. 'Either a whole cell, or some fanatic who's lost his mind. Just in case he's right, we think it's best to avoid attracting attention.'

But then why on earth hadn't Myrain stayed in Amarantha, where he was most needed?

'You're not leaving the inn tomorrow,' he said.

'Roy . . .' the Priestess began, but the sentence died on her lips.

I tamped down hard on my emotions.

Very well.

I rose from the table and went to my room, looking as calm as I could manage. Once the door was shut behind me I threw myself on the bed, cursing Myrain and Dainefin. Reya had invited me to go with her and her friends to the river the next day, and I really wanted to go. It made me feel like someone was interested in *me*, not just in the princess. I had no intention of letting them down just because Myrain had ordered me to stay put. The message had been received: I would just have to be more careful.

A noise caught my attention, taking me straight back to Amarantha and my bedroom in the castle where, on windy days, blackthorn branches would tap on the windowpanes. It was a noise I found relaxing during the day, and terrifying at night. I could see no branches just outside this window and wondered if I'd imagined it.

Something struck the glass a second time.

I rose and went over. And saw a young man preparing to throw a third pebble at my window. He smiled and gestured for me to come down. I held up my hand for him to wait, grabbed my bag, and ran down the stairs.

I slipped behind the counter, looking out for Myrain and Dainefin in the dining hall. He had his back to me, but he was alone. I looked around for Dainefin, and suddenly found myself facing her.

'Where are you going, Lyria?' she whispered, pointing at my bag. She sounded weary, but not angry. She took me to one side, moving me away from the doorway.

A friend came looking for me.

Dainefin nodded distractedly. 'Roy's not all wrong,' she cautioned. 'You've been a little . . .'

Careless. I know.

I wasn't angry with Myrain because he'd been unfair towards me. It was the exact opposite: I was hurt because he'd been right.

97

Please let me go. I need to talk to people my age.

'People your age . . .'

She seemed surprised, but didn't comment. She had always been the one I had turned to, sometimes in tears, when the tension I felt between the different sides of my personality pulled me in opposite directions. I yearned for a group of friends like Anur's: People I could spend time and have fun with . . . . But I was too shy to talk to anyone my age because I didn't feel like I fitted in. And not just because I was the princess. Sonni had always been my best friend, but he wasn't enough anymore. Now I wanted to prove to myself that I had been wrong before. Maybe I *could* fit in.

Dainefin didn't take much persuading. Out of curiosity, perhaps, she asked, 'How was it? Spending time with Reya?'

Strange. We're so different . . . . She reminds me of . . . of Mother. Maybe it's the way she speaks or the things she talks about . . .

'You need to find out who you are,' said Dainefin.

I thought she was dismissing me. But she wasn't done.

'. . . But for goodness' sake, be more careful.'

The chatter of the inn faded away as I shut the door behind me. The evening chill caught me unprepared; perhaps I should have worn another layer over my knitted tunic. Even though the sun had set two hours ago, the sky wasn't completely dark yet.

The approach to the inn was lit by two large torches mounted by the entrance, and there, waiting for me in the torchlight, was a boy close to my age. From his thickly muscled arms and the flour in his hair, I pieced together that he was Old Bedevilled's grandson, the deaf miller I'd heard so much about.

He met me with a gush of frenetic gestures that evidently meant something to him. My spirits fell.

I don't understand.

I saw the Empathic Aura slam into him. He paused, studying me; then he made more of those hand gestures, slowly indicating me, himself, his mouth and his head.

I'm sorry, I don't know how to do that.

By his expression I could tell he had made out every word in my thought. He stepped back; perhaps he was changing his mind about being near me.

Please don't go. Can you write?

He nodded. I pulled the graphite stick and some paper out of my bag, and handed them to him.

Are you Princess Lyria? he wrote.

Yes.

Before I could stop it, the answer slipped through the crack under the 'door', as Dainefin had called it that day in the library.

The boy took my shoulders and moved me closer to the light. He carefully studied my face, then wrote: *You look just the same as when you were little. I recognised you at the mill.*

It hadn't been my imagination. I really had seen someone in that window, but I didn't remember meeting that boy before. Maybe he'd seen me the last time I'd been here with Granny Maya.

The young miller began to write frantically.

How do you do that?

You mean, the way I communicate with you?

He nodded.

It was a good question. Until now, only Dainefin and Sonni had understood word for word what was going through my mind. Everyone else seemed to receive waves of emotion from the Empathic Aura. I couldn't control who understood what, but Dainefin had been right: the more empathetic the receiver, the more clearly they seemed to be able to decode my emotions into a string of words or thoughts.

I don't know how to explain. It's an illness. I don't do it deliberately.

I want to learn.

No, you don't. You wouldn't get to decide what you say or don't say. Everything is laid out for anyone to see.

The boy thought about that, but didn't seem completely convinced.

I'm Cam.

Hello, Cam.

Are you here to get better? How long are you staying?

Partly. And I don't know. We're just passing through. We have to get to the fjords of Styr.

He was intrigued. He motioned me to follow him, and even though the thought of walking away from the inn into that dense, dark tangle of vegetation should have terrified me, I realised I trusted Cam as much as Sonni. Cam obviously knew where he was going, but my fear of the dark, of animals that might attack at any moment, extinguished my meagre sense of direction. Suddenly, I couldn't see him any more. I could only hear his movements, his muffled steps on the soft ground, but I couldn't tell which direction they were coming from. I froze.

Sensing that I was no longer beside him, Cam backtracked a few steps. He grabbed my hand to lead me better.

No boy had ever taken me by the hand. No girl either, in fact. The unwieldy weight of my royal position had always raised an invisible barrier between me and my peers.

We emerged into the open. I noticed that the moon had risen, a waxing moon that was a day or two from full. The mill was lit by its reflections on the water flowing under the great wooden wheel, now stopped for the night.

Cam took me up the stone steps that led to a landing at the top of the wheel. When we reached it, he pointed to a window just above us, then held up his hand to indicate I should wait outside. I sat down on the cold stone, the night breeze raising goose bumps on my arms.

The view from the top of the mill was breathtaking. The moon shone brightly enough to dim the stars and glow off the pale stone of the houses in the village. It seemed almost like daylight. My eyes followed the course of the stream from the hillside where it appeared, down to the valley where tomorrow – whatever Myrain said – I would meet the village girls.

Cam climbed out of the window carrying an oil lamp and a few rolls of canvas. He unrolled them one by one and I knew he sensed my shock as I looked down at them.

Hatablar Forest. The fjords of Styr. Amarantha castle.

Thanks in part to the light of the lamp, every detail of his paintings appeared to leap from the parchment. My eyes were drawn to my home. Flowering blackthorn peeking over the top of the wall. The cliff looking over the beach, the rock streaked with pink. Sea foam collecting in the sandy hollows at the foot of the promontory.

These are amazing.

When I tried to return them, Cam took back the paintings of Hatablar and Styr, but gestured for me to keep the one of the castle.

Thank you. I had been gone less than a week, but I was already homesick.

I'm sorry you're ill.

It wouldn't be so bad if my guardians told me a little more. All I know for now is that we're headed to Styr, but I don't know why. Can you think of anything there?

There's nothing at Styr. Just a bunch of houses. But the views are incredible.

I looked again at the paintings lying on the step where Cam was sitting, hugging his knees. The fjords had something savage about them, they weren't the green cliffs I had imagined. Their rock faces appeared naked in comparison with the cliffs of the capital, which were lush with grass and amaranth all the way to the edge. The rocks of this headland were dark and cold, braced to repel the waves. I could almost hear the sea crashing furiously on the crags.

You must have travelled loads.

A corner of his mouth curled upwards, forming a dimple on his cheek. I took in his features, from the flushed cheeks to the shimmering green of his eyes, as changeable as late summer leaves. Nothing in his face recalled Old Bedevilled's strong features; his was a very soft, Nordic face, like my father's. Even Cam's hair was much lighter than everyone else's in Denhole.

Once, maybe.

It was strange to communicate in complete silence. I liked it, though. With one faculty out of action, the others seemed to live a second life.

Will you teach me to talk with your hands like you do?

We started with my name. Cam taught me the alphabet, and then my name, letter by letter. Then he showed me his, followed by his 'name sign', explaining that his uncle had encouraged him to find a sign that represented him, a symbol of his identity. Cam brought his thumb and index finger together as if holding a pastel, then he rubbed a few times on an imaginary surface, and finished off the gesture by opening out his finger and thumb to form the letter C.

After that, I learned signs for the things around me: 'mill', 'stream', 'village', 'inn'. A few verbs, and I was ready for my first sentences, which I repeated without too much difficulty.

Cam's language was very satisfying to learn, and Cam alternated between patience with my mistakes and excitement at my successes. He seemed determined for me to learn everything in one night.

Every time he introduced a word I didn't know, he would sign it alphabetically or scribble it on a piece of paper. I followed him gladly. The more words I learnt, the better I was able to make myself understood without using the Empathic Aura.

Cam made a sign I didn't know yet, then he pointed at me and signed 'Mother'.

I signed my lack of understanding. 'What does . . .' I repeated the sign he'd made, 'mean?'

'D-o y-o-u m-i-s-s h-e-r?'

I do.

'I miss Granddad,' he signed.

He picked up the graphite and wrote about Old Bedevilled's husband, who had been gone some years, having died of old age. His granddad had taken him on trips all over the continent since he was a small child, selling their wheat flour and buying types of grain that didn't grow around Denhole.

The inn used to be the most important bakery in the region, he wrote. *It's just an inn now.*

'But I bought bread there this morning,' I signed.

They bake bread for the village, but it's not the same, he wrote.

A few years after his granddad's death, Reya's

father had taken over the bakery. The inn had changed; Reya's father was a good worker, but he lacked passion, according to Cam. He didn't travel, he was happy with local flours and local customers.

There was no animosity as he told me about this, only a little disappointment.

'My granddad, he put his heart into it,' Cam signed.

You should travel like he did. Bring those flours back to Denhole.

'My uncle keeps telling me that.'

He repeated the sign for 'uncle' and also spelt it letter by letter. Then he showed me his uncle's name, Noalim, and his name sign: the index finger of the left hand pointing at one eye then the other.

My fingers were beginning to stiffen from all the exercise, but I refused to give in to tiredness. I couldn't make myself stop. It was like one of those days at the clavichord, when I would play for hours until my body was begging for mercy.

Nor did Cam give the impression that he wanted to turn in, so I asked him to tell me more about his uncle.

Granddad's brother, he wrote. *He used to help at the bakery and travel with Granddad. We invented this sign language together when I was little.*

'Is he deaf, too?'

Between the words I had already learned, the ones I was able to guess, and those that Cam signed letter by letter, he explained that his uncle hadn't been born deaf, but at sixteen he had fallen ill and spent a month in bed, suffering from a high fever and convulsions. He'd defied everyone's expectations and recovered, but had lost his hearing in both ears. As a young man, he'd learnt to read lips, and never had problems speaking, but he'd lost his sight as he aged, and became isolated from the rest of the world.

That was how he and Cam had saved each other, inventing a hand-sign language that set them both free.

'Set free' had been Cam's chosen expression and it struck a chord in me. I wanted to keep listening to everything he had to tell me about his past.

I understood that his uncle had taught him to paint as well as read and write, and that the two of them used to spend most of what they earned at the mill to buy paints, canvasses, and ceramics from the towns they visited.

The mention of ceramics reminded me of something.

'Were the inn's plates painted by your uncle?'

'Most of them, yes,' signed Cam, explaining that there had been a time when that kind of illustrated ceramic had been in great demand.

Noalim used to make a little money on the side by selling his maiolica to the bakery's patrons, but his biggest market had been the capital. There, he'd also been able to sell a few paintings on canvas. One day, news of his talent reached one of the Consuls, who told the king himself.

My family portrait . . .

'Your mother loved it.'

I wished I could remember sitting for it, but I had been too young. Cam was either a couple of years older than me or had a sharper memory.

Again, he motioned for me to wait and disappeared through his window. I was hoping he had a sketch or a drawing, maybe even a copy of the painting, but when he came back outside, Cam was carrying nothing of the sort. Instead, he showed me a box made of dark wood and engraved with the D'Aur-Lee coat of arms: the three square-rigged masts of the ship that Aur-Lee had sailed to the continent.

Cam opened the box to show me a collection of oil pastels in every colour of the rainbow.

Your mother's present to my uncle when the painting was done, he wrote. *He gave it to me when he saw I liked drawing.*

Most of the pastels were used up by half or three quarters. The colours were easily discernible in the glow of the lamp and moonlight. The emerald green and ultramarine blue ones were mere stumps, barely longer than the tip of my thumb.

Cam pointed at the green. 'Your brother's eyes,' he signed. Then the blue. 'Yours.'

He grabbed a new piece of paper then thought for a moment before beginning to write.

For my uncle, colours contain sounds and sounds colours. This, he stopped writing to pick up the ultramarine and rub it lightly on the paper, *he says it's a C note, but only if the other colours are cold and together they make a minor chord. And this,* he stained the paper emerald green this time, *with yellow sounds like D major.*

He's a musician as well, your uncle?

'The best.'

Noalim started playing as a child, Cam told me, many years before the fever that nearly killed him. Losing his hearing didn't stop him from playing; in fact, that was when he realised that sounds and colours bled together.

Inevitably, the Empathic Aura decided to ask the question as soon as it popped into my mind.

But you can't hear . . . . How can you enjoy music?

If I'd had any control, I would have kept such an insensitive question to myself. Yet he didn't seem offended at all.

He opened his arms and vibrated his hands. Then he signed 'm-u-s-i-c'.

You feel the vibrations?

He nodded.

I thought about that for a moment before my mind returned to Cam's uncle, who seemed to have enough artistic talent for a whole village. Out of curiosity, I asked Cam about the sign for 'talent'.

He clenched his fists, stacked them one on top of the other, and made the twisting motion used to pull the cork from a bottle.

Same as work, he wrote.

We carried on signing, me asking him for different signs and him talking about his travels, my family, and Amarantha, until dawn began to lighten the sky.

My eyes felt gritty from staying awake all night. My

hair was as messy as it ever got, and my trousers still muddy, but none of that concerned me in the slightest.

All my attention was focussed on Cam. I knew instinctively – had known since I'd first met him – that I could trust him. He wouldn't tell anyone who I was. I had spent an entire night with a stranger, someone I had nothing in common with.

No, that wasn't true. We did have something in common: we were both different. He had been different since birth, while I had carried my unwieldy legacy. But Sonni had helped bear that weight. I had always felt different and then a new difference had descended on me. Now I wasn't just different from others, but also from my former self.

I was a version of myself deprived of the freedom of choice. I couldn't choose what to say and what not to say. And I couldn't seem to think of anything other than the Empathic Aura.

Only twice had I managed to feel free: playing *Chara Chairei* and that night with Cam.

I had been able to pick the words I wanted to use, like picking out cherries at the market, one by one, a sign or letter at a time. I had tricked the Empathic Aura into silence. It was a game at which I had to cheat to feel free.

I suddenly remembered that Cam had been at the church yesterday morning and heard me play.

The Empathic Aura awoke. I saw the look of shock in his eyes as he was hit by the full force of my emotions. He now knew I'd been the organist at my mother's Intercession. He grabbed the few scraps of paper and frantically began to scribble.

I have to take you somewhere.

Now?

No, later. Tonight at vespers. Meet you in the church choir.

I nodded. I would be happy to follow him wherever he wanted to go. My stay at Denhole could end at any moment and I wanted to seize every opportunity to spend time with him.

We watched the sun rise beyond a hilltop, shining bright and free from the pink shades of dawn. Cam gave me a sad look, and told me that any minute now his grandmother would wake, expecting him to be working already. I followed him back down the steps and watched him open the water wheel's sluice gate with the ease of someone who had repeated the same actions day in and day out, year after year.

He turned, and suddenly we were standing very close. Cam needed only a hint of movement from me and he did the rest. He wrapped his muscular arms, all dusty with flour, around me and I laid my head on his chest, listening to his heartbeat.

Only when I pulled away from him did the exhaustion of that sleepless night finally roll over me. I still don't know how I made it back to the inn without falling asleep halfway there in the inviting shade of an olive tree.

My last conscious thought as I fell into bed was that I owed Cam a debt of gratitude. I had to find a way to get him out of here, one way or another.

Chapter 8

Reya was wearing a white linen camisole that made her complexion appear even darker. She was sitting at a table in the back of the inn, her forehead nestled in the bend of her elbow and her hair slightly damp. I wasn't sure if she was awake, and I didn't know how to attract her attention without startling her.

'So, what happened to you this morning then?'

Her overly indifferent tone made it clear she was upset. I sat down in the chair next to her and scribbled a few sentences about my meeting with Cam while she sat up and fixed her hair. I was careful about what to write and what to leave out, keeping a few details for myself.

'I'm surprised he spent time with you,' she commented after reading. 'He never does that with anyone. He has a temper you know. Mind you, I'd have a bad temper myself if I were my gran's prisoner. He must really like you,' she added.

Are you upset? I wrote, dreading her answer.

'No, we're fine,' she replied. When she smiled, she

surprised me like a fine day in the middle of a rainy autumn. During her brief sulk, I had forgotten how lovely and contagious her smile could be.

'I'm just a bit dozy with all the sun I caught this morning. You know, down at the river.'

I'm sorry I didn't make it, I wrote.

'It's all right. I had to put up with Fran and Dill though – they wouldn't stop talking about you.'

That was more worrying than flattering. I hadn't even met them and they were talking about me?

'You should have seen them . . . . They turned up in their old man's work trousers, held up I don't know how. "Heard it's the latest fashion from the capital." What a show. As if I hadn't been the one to tell them that yesterday. They'd never admit it, but they're dreaming of seeing the capital too, one day.'

You should take them with you, I wrote.

'Yes,' she said, a little wary. 'Maybe.'

When are you thinking of moving there?

Reya shrugged, her eyes fixed on somewhere far away in her mind's eye. Then she gathered her knees up on her chair and started telling me the ins and outs of everything she and the girls had discussed: who had split up with whom, who'd been cheating, who was no longer speaking to whom and why.

Reya reeled off name after name, reporting everyone's private business as acquired from the chitchat that circulated at the inn. Obviously, I didn't know any of the people she was gossiping about, but it was a relief to see her cheerful again. I was happy she wasn't still upset with me for standing her up. Deep down though I wasn't completely at ease. I hadn't forgotten that moment of cold distance between us.

'So, what about your guardians? Are they a couple?'

I shrugged.

'Be a shame if they weren't,' she replied. 'Where have they got to today?'

Again, I had no idea. I assumed they must be checking the weather conditions over Hatablar Forest and would soon spring up from nowhere to tell me we were setting off. I kept forgetting about our quest only to suddenly remember it again. I knew Denhole was only a stopover, but I was beginning to feel at home here. The thought of having to leave the village at short notice was making me re-evaluate every minute. I mustn't waste any time.

Reya looked out the open front door at the midday sun and sighed. 'I have to go back to work. What a pain.'

I nodded and waved as she hurried off.

Once she'd gone, I thought about what to do with my day before my next meeting with Cam, who at that moment was probably tending to the mill under his grandmother's watchful eye.

I hadn't seen Myrain all morning, so I considered going back to the tavern for a glass of orzata, or to the church for a chat – so to speak – with the priest. But in truth, the sun called to me, so I decided to wander down to the river on my own, to find a patch of grass and maybe a place to take a dip.

When I returned to the inn, Reya's mother cursed when she saw the mud I'd dragged in with me. But she fired up the oven again in the middle of the afternoon just so I could dry out. Once her mother-henning was done, she left me in Reya's care, ordering her to make me a hot drink.

Reya burst into raucous laughter when she saw me, perched on a high stool so I could be as close to the fire as possible. I must have been blue from head to toe.

'If you were looking for a way to make your throat worse, you found it,' she teased, passing me a cup of spiced wine. 'You know what, I forgot to tell you about the fireworks earlier.'

She told me that the feast of Saint Josef, the patron saint of the village, would be celebrated the following week, and the villagers were preparing to gather in procession that night. It would have been unkind of me to point out that I saw fireworks on three consecutive evenings every year during the Foundation Feast. For all I knew, the people of Denhole looked forward to their patron's feast all year long.

'We usually have fireworks at the end of the week, but the priest has decided to have them early this year because of the bad weather. I can't go. I'm working all hours as usual, but you can't miss them,' she added. 'If you're feeling up to it, that is.'

The warmth of the oven had dried my hair and put the colour back in my cheeks, but my undergarments were still unpleasantly damp – even alone I'd been too self-conscious to swim naked.

'They're holding vespers just before the fireworks. Then the procession will start from the church, and . . .'

She was still talking, but I'd stopped listening, because Reya had just reminded me of my date with Cam in the church choir.

Without even meaning to, I signed a question about what time it was.

Reya blinked. 'It must be around half past eight? Vespers start at nine.'

I jumped off the stool and gave her a hug to thank her, then hurried up to my room to get changed. She followed me to the top of the stairs and asked:

'Are you going to see him tonight?'

She was twisting a corner of her apron around her fingers.

I nodded a yes, knowing the Empathic Aura was already tattling on the butterflies in my stomach.

'Have fun then,' Reya said.

Before heading to the village, I decided I should check in with Dainefin. With all the time she must have spent taking my side against the Valiant, it would be unfair not to let her know where I was going.

I found her lying down in her room, a hand over her eyes. I crouched next to her.

What's the matter? Where's Myrain?

'Headache,' she answered, sitting up. 'And he's away for the night. Are you going out again?'

I nodded. **Going to church.**

'With the boy from the mill?'

Yes.

'Should I be worried?'

Dainefin was not consulting me on matters of the heart. She was asking me if I was going to behave irresponsibly. I shook my head and promised I would be back just after the fireworks.

Is there anything I can do for you before I go, Dainefin?

She shook her head. 'No, darling, thank you.'

As I walked to the church, my mind was clouded with guilt. It was my fault that Dainefin and the Valiant were always arguing. But how could making friends with people my own age hurt? It wasn't like I was telling them who I really was or drawing attention to myself. Besides, Dainefin had told me to find out who I was.

And that's exactly what I was trying to do.

Chapter 9

The priest found me seated at the organ, air-playing *Chara Chairei*, still on the stand from the day before.

'You can play, if you wish.'

He saw me hesitate, and reassured me. 'I won't make you play at vespers as well, don't worry. This village has already had its miracle.'

'Miracle' seemed a big word, especially coming from a priest.

'You can't imagine how many people have asked me to reveal the identity of our mysterious organist. But I think mysteries are best when they aren't shouted from the rooftops.' He sat down in one of the choir seats. 'Go ahead.'

I played *Chara Chairei* again. I wasn't interested in the rest of Requiem, I wanted to get to the end, to elation.

As I played, I had the feeling the priest was no longer by himself. Cam was there, I could feel his presence. He wasn't displacing air by signing, or fidgeting, or even breathing. He was there, but he didn't exist. None of us did.

We had all become a part of the church, and as one we witnessed the miracle – the real miracle – of the *Chara Chairei*.

After the last chord, Cam and the priest applauded. I gave a little bow, but as I straightened up I felt dizzy and flopped sideways next to the organ. The priest hurried over to pull me up, and laid a hand on my forehead.

'My child, you're burning up!'

Cam asked what had happened.

Using a mix of sign language and the Empathic Aura I explained my clever decision to bathe in the stream without towels or a change of clothes.

'Good God,' murmured the priest. 'I didn't realise you could sign too! Tell me, do you also speak the language of angels? Where have you been hiding her, Cam?' I noticed the priest was using Cam's sign language with his hands as he spoke aloud.

Cam shrugged and smiled at me.

'You, young lady, should be in bed with a cup of milk and a spoonful of hata honey. I have some somewhere. Wait here, I won't be a moment,' said the priest, heading to the sacristy.

When he reappeared, he was holding a jar full of a clear, sky-blue liquid.

'I inherited this from an aunt who used to live near Hatablar Forest. She was a little . . . eccentric, shall we say.'

Blue honey was new to me. I instinctively found it unnatural, but all it took to change my mind was a suspicious sniff at the open jar: it had the fresh aroma of peppermint and eucalyptus, along with a reassuring, sweetish note of honey.

'Have you ever visited Hatablar Forest? Wonderful place,' said the priest with a dreamy look in his eyes.

He replaced the lid on the jar. I thought it would take far more than honey to cure *all* my ailments, but I didn't want to tell the Priest that.

'You can keep that if you wish. I have another jar open that I think will last me the rest of my life,' said the priest. 'Cam, take her home. I have to go and officiate.' He turned back to me with a wink: 'You are dispensed from attending, given the state you're in. I'll pray in your place.'

Cam felt my forehead. I closed my eyes, taking advantage of his hand supporting my head. I hadn't realised how heavy my head felt until Cam took his hand away to pull a notebook and a stick of charcoal from his haversack.

Sure you don't want to go back to the inn?

I could hardly breathe through my congested nose, and my face felt like it was on fire. My forehead and the nape of my neck were filmed with sweat and the slightest draft set me to shivering. My eyes were watering for no reason.

I'm sure.

Cam couldn't argue. The Empathic Aura had decided for both of us.

At the top of the hill beyond the church was a large wooden crucifix stood over a drinking trough. 'T-h-e P-a-s-s-i-o-n,' signed Cam. We walked past it and climbed a different hill, taking a path through an olive grove.

After a few minutes, we reached an open space lit by a band of stars that split the sky right over our heads. An abandoned hut stood in the middle. Cam covered my eyes and took a few steps around me, turning me in the direction we had just come from. Then he took his hands away.

Below us, a river of light was winding through the darkened village. Hundreds of lanterns moved in a line along the lanes. Hands were clapping out the six-eight rhythm of a distant melody.

The music was as bittersweet as Denhole, as nostalgic as an ancient, faded fresco. I wished Cam could hear it too.

Can you feel the music?

He shook his head.

I took his hand and placed it on my back, between my shoulder blades. Then with my right hand I began to tap out the rhythmic framework of the piece on my breastbone. Doom-dah-dah, doom-dah-dah, doom-dah-dah, doom-doom-doom, doom-dah-dah, doom-dah-dah, doom-dah-dah, doom-doom-doom, doom-dah-dah ...

He began beating out the rhythm with his feet,

marching on the spot. He was smiling, and I wondered if my heart would continue to beat in six eighths for the rest of the evening.

Even after the music ended, I couldn't stop watching the illuminated procession. I had never seen anything like it. I followed the lanterns with enchanted eyes until Cam tugged at my sleeve, pointing at the small house behind us.

He motioned for me to wait, and opened the door with great care. The house looked like it was about to fall to pieces.

I heard him bump into furniture and open drawers. He struck a match and lit a couple of candles, which revealed a small, dusty room.

The figure of an old man in a rocking chair gave me the fright of my life.

'Noalim,' Cam signed, smiling. 'My uncle.'

Noalim was braiding ears of wheat together, staring intently ahead. His eyes didn't follow us.

Cam bent over to kiss his cheek, and his uncle responded with a smacking triple cheek kiss, just like the ones Granny Maya used to plant on me when I was little.

'He can hardly see any more. Only shadows and bright lights,' Cam explained.

Cam's uncle was skin and bones, but I could see the muscles of his arm leap under that dark, wrinkled skin as he ran the straw through his fingers.

Cam beckoned me closer.

I approached Noalim a little apprehensively.

Sensing my presence, he dropped his work into a basket by the chair and extended both hands in front of him, palms up. I looked questioningly at Cam.

Cam knelt down and began to sign on his uncle's hands. Noalim followed his nephew's fingers with the same imperceptible movements with which he had been braiding the wheat.

My name is Lyria, the Empathic Aura announced.

No, I wanted to tell him properly. I traced the letters of my name on Noalim's hand.

'Doll,' he said in a rich, resounding voice, like that of a bronze church bell.

A blush compounded the heat of my fever. Cam's uncle was gripping my hand, as if something terrible would happen if he ever let go.

Cam attracted his uncle's attention by gently shaking his shoulder and Noalim let go. I watched the frenetic dance of their fingers with fascination. I only made out a few of the signs that Cam was making on his uncle's palm: 'princess', 'Levith', 'organ'.

Tears filled Noalim's distant eyes. He signed to Cam for a while; I understood next to nothing. Every now and then he would stop and sign a name letter by letter, and he had to do that three times for me to understand that he was talking about my grandmother. Once he and Cam were done catching up, he turned to me.

'Your grandmother, when we were children she lived next door to me,' he said, his hands signing along. 'We used to play together, a band of little rascals, we were . . . None of the others are still with us, rest their souls. And then one day, Maya said she was going to work at the castle, and I never saw her again.'

Noalim spoke clearly, though his accent was much stronger than any I'd heard over the last few days. It actually sounded more like the way my grandmother had spoken, the sentences turned back to front.

'I never forgot her though. I wrote *Chara Chairei* for her when I heard she'd passed. To honour her joyful spirit,' he said.

I crouched down next to Noalim, and tried signing on his hand the way Cam had. It took me almost a minute to spell four words.

'Y-o-u w-r-o-t-e t-h-a-t p-i-e-c-e?'

On the last letter, Noalim squeezed my fingers with both hands and shook them, as if in congratulation.

'Yes. She liked orange blossoms,' he said with a smile. 'I wrote her a song in those colours: white, green, yellow and orange.'

He stood and shuffled over to a dark shadow in the corner. At first, I thought it was an armchair, but as Cam brought the candle over, I realised it was a harp with a stool behind it. Noalim sat and began to play. He started with *Chara Chairei* then continued on with all sorts of melodies, not a spare note in any of them. Behind each of his compositions, behind every phrase, whether joyful or anguished, was the story of a man or woman he had met in his lifetime. I wondered if I too would have my own melody one day.

The crack of a shot shook the floorboards.

The fireworks!

Cam signed quickly in Noalim's palm and helped

him up. I moved closer to Noalim, and after a little hesitation I signed 'thank you'.

'Doll,' was his response once more.

I hugged him, as I would have hugged my grandfather – if I'd had the chance to know either of mine. Noalim patted the nape of my neck gently, as if I really were a porcelain doll.

Cam held his uncle's arm and together we stepped out to watch the fireworks. Noalim smiled ecstatically at every flash of light. Only then did I realise that his eyes were two different colours, one blue, one green. Cam's favourite colours. I remembered Noalim's name-sign.

Cam . . . what's my name-sign?

He looked at me. Then he formed the letter 'L' with one hand and a 'D' with the other, and vibrated both hands.

'You're the music,' he signed after that, and turned his eyes back to the sky.

After the fireworks, I remember next to nothing. Cam somehow took me back to the inn, while I shuddered with fever. I'm sure the Empathic Aura was pulsing as strong as my pounding heart. The joy of meeting Noalim. Fear of having to leave Denhole at any moment. The anguish I felt at the thought of never being rid of the Empathic Aura. The huge black hole of my immediate future. Poor Cam. If I'd been myself, I would have died of shame, but at the time, I could barely stand upright.

I dragged myself to my room, and allowed Cam to help me out of my shoes and under the covers, still in my sweaty clothes. I heard the door open and close and felt sad that I had lacked the strength to even wave goodbye before he left.

I thought I'd pass out right away, but suddenly a blade of pain, cold and heavy, was splitting my head in two. I opened my eyes, but the light of the candle made them burn as though I was staring into the sun. I squeezed my eyes shut as hot tears made their way from the corners of my eyes down to the pillow, collecting in minuscule puddles below my ears. Every muscle in my body was begging for mercy, moments of infernal heat alternated with chilly shivers, and my skin was a sweaty carpet of goose bumps.

Then, sudden relief.

My eyes flew open again. Cam was holding a wet cloth to my forehead. He had found the jar of hata honey that I'd been given by the priest and held it to my lips, pouring in a few drops at a time. For a moment I felt as if I were back in the stream, immersed up to my neck in icy water. The honey expanded my lungs, letting in some fresh air. Cam tucked the blanket tightly around me.

'Sleep,' he signed.

So I slept.

Chapter 10

The gap left by the family portrait has been filled by a tapestry depicting the castle and the capital, with the opposite wall almost completely taken up by an enormous map of the kingdom. There are no other decorations, and no furniture other than a round table surrounded by ten chairs. Seven of those chairs are habitually occupied by the King, the Valiant, and the five Consuls. Anur only joins when the occasion requires it.

If Mother were alive, the tall casement windows leading into the palace yard would be open, and the table at the centre of the Council Chamber would be polished and gleaming.

Today, its top is thick with dust. But even the room's staleness is nothing compared to that of six men convening for hours, day in, day out, with no one to remind them to let in a little fresh air every now and then. Sonni rises and opens the windows, before returning to the table.

This is his first time standing in for Father. When the King is detained, he is usually represented by Dainefin; if she is not available, the Council meeting is postponed. The Priestess's absence will be felt, and Sonni prays that the Consuls won't get bogged down in one of their endless circular arguments today.

'We must send our best men to head them off,' Rila is saying.

'No,' Sayd replies, 'we're not sure that they're on the offensive. Shall we risk war based on a piece of gossip?'

'I agree. Nothing we've heard so far rings true with King Hervin's character,' says Lumio. 'When has he ever given sign of wanting to expand? It's all foolishness.'

'Or worse still,' says Catam, 'rumours circulated by the Separatists.'

'That's true, it could all be part of a Separatist plot to lower the capital's defences. What if they intend to attack?' Lumio points out.

'No one is suggesting we lower our guard,' says Rila. 'We'll begin recruiting as soon as possible. But someone must be sent to Murihen, to dispose of the patrol coming our way.'

'*Presumed* patrol,' says Sayd.

Sayd and Lumio may be sceptical to a fault, but at least they do stem Rila's impatience – he's all set to order a preemptive strike. Just as well Myrain has not yet returned to lead the armies out.

Sonni props his elbow up on the table with one hand over his mouth, and drums erratically on the wood with the other. 'I could go to Murihen,' he says, 'and see for myself.'

The Consuls fall silent.

'Or we could send someone else we trust,' he continues. 'In any case, Father would never respond to an attack he wasn't certain of. He wouldn't run the risk of sparking war over a misunderstanding. We must clarify the issue with Uncle Hervin directly.'

'With respect, Your Highness, your father is not here,' says Rila, 'And while the King is in the state he's in . . .'

'I'd like to see how you would cope if you were in his place, Rila,' Sonni bites back, feeling rage surge through him.

'I did not mean—'

'I know,' Sonni cuts him short. 'You meant that he is not here. But I am, and I will do as he would.'

Rila's about to say more, but he holds back. He is the Consul Dainefin gets on least well with, and Sonni has to make an effort to avoid letting that colour his opinion of the man.

Lumio clears his throat. 'Your Highness, Catam and I think that the Separatists must be involved.'

Sonni slumps against the back of the chair, arms folded across his chest. 'What are their numbers now?'

'About fifty,' answers Lumio.

'That doesn't seem quite so many,' says Sayd.

'Don't be naïve – their ideas spread like fire in a hayloft,' says Rila gravely. 'First, they refused to pay their taxes, then they accosted travelling merchants.

And now we have news of violence: fields have been torched, goods stolen, herds of cattle decimated.'

'Yes, I've seen the reports,' Sonni replies. 'Even if I wish it weren't true, it does seem plausible the Separatists are involved. We should prepare to defend the capital, just in case.'

'Are we recruiting then?' asks Catam.

Sonni sighs. He's beginning to wish he hadn't taken part in this morning's meeting. 'I think we must. In the meantime, we shall verify whether these rumours are true or false. May I remind you that Anur is currently in Murihen. If we can contact him, he'll be able to bring us up to date on the situation there.'

'How do we know he is not on their side?' asks Sayd.

'I didn't make myself clear,' Sonni answers calmly. 'There will be no sides until we are certain about what's happening. We will trust my brother.'

'If we are in Anur's hands, we might as well consider ourselves subjects of Murihen.'

'I may not have my father's authority, Rila,' Sonni says, 'but that does not give you free rein to slander a royal prince. You have been warned.'

Rila falls silent.

Sonni wonders whether he's gone too far, but a firm hand is needed with those who, like Rila, are prone to overstepping boundaries.

'Your father . . . ?' Lumio falters.

'Is the same,' Sonni says curtly. 'For now, we must let him be. Any news of my sister?'

'None,' says Catam.

'I want Myrain back here as soon as possible.'

I remember waking up. It was still night, and I'd had a very strange dream. I had never dreamt of the Consuls, nor had I ever understood Sonni's mind like that in my dreams. It had been so vivid, as if I'd really been there, but it was difficult to remember....I tried to grasp the details before they slipped through my fingers, but they were already melting away. Someone was in danger. Sonni was in the Council Room, without my father. The Separatists. Maybe if I went back to sleep—

There was a sharp knock on the door.

'Get up, Lyria, we're leaving soon.'

Dainefin's voice snapped me wide awake. I sat up in bed, gathering all the information that my brain was trying to process.

I was fine. My clothes were drenched with sweat, but the fever was gone. I felt refreshed, and I had no aches and pains. It was as if all my senses had been amplified. Was it just my imagination, or could I see perfectly? My nose wasn't blocked, and my throat didn't feel inflamed – it wasn't even a little bit sore. I remembered taking hata honey the previous night and feeling immediate relief just before falling asleep. The damp cloth that Cam had held to my forehead was in my lap, and I stretched over to put it on the bedside table. I glanced down as I did and saw Cam on the floor. He was fast asleep next to my bed, on the bare floorboards, with no pillows or covers, not making the slightest noise.

I wanted to wake him. I wanted to tell him how stupid he'd been to watch over me all night, lying on the floor like that. I wanted to thank him for holding that wet cloth to my forehead – repeatedly, judging by the puddles around the half-full bucket. I wanted to tell him I was going to take him away from Denhole, that he could live at the castle with me and my family.

Instead, I let him sleep.

I touched the tip of my graphite to paper, forcing myself to write one thing only. Because no matter how much I wrote, it would never be enough.

Don't think this is goodbye.

Everything else I wanted to say I saved for the next time we would see each other.

It took all my self-control not to put a pillow under his head or a blanket over him. I didn't want to wake him. I wished I could kiss his forehead and sign on the palm of his hand that I wouldn't stop thinking and caring about him for a single day of my life.

I dressed in a hurry, then I shoved my things into the haversack, heaved it onto one shoulder and slipped out without looking back.

Dainefin was waiting in the corridor. One look was enough for her to understand that something was wrong. She opened her arms and I took refuge in her familiar embrace.

When I stepped back, I saw she wasn't having a good day either. For once, her face was like that of a normal person – I even spotted the hint of a line on her forehead.

Everything all right?

'Yes, but Myrain is more stubborn than a mule. I don't know when I last dealt with a man who can give as good as he gets.'

I snorted. My father, who undoubtedly inspired awe and respect in the other Council members, was well known to cave to Dainefin's will.

'I can't tell if he likes to argue with me for the sake of it, or ...'

The frustration dangling from the unspoken end of that sentence was very familiar to me – I had felt that way so many times after a row with Anur – but on Dainefin's lips it sounded wrong.

She composed herself and changed the subject.

'He's saddling the horses. We'll ride to the edge of Hatablar today and stay with two of his friends. From there, we'll proceed on foot.'

What will happen to Yodne?

'We'll leave the horses with Roy's friends for now, then he'll take her to Amarantha on his ride back.' Dainefin sighed. 'I've told him he doesn't need to accompany us all the way to Styr, but he won't hear of us travelling alone. I don't like this compromise, but it will allow us to get him out from under our feet once we've reached the fjords. If Myrain really wants to go all the way through the forest and back, that's his problem.'

How long until we leave?

'Half an hour.'

I had to find Reya. There was something I needed to tell her.

I ran down to the kitchen, but she wasn't there. Her parents didn't know where she was: her father was fuming because she hadn't shown up to help with the second batch of the morning, and her mother told me she had already looked for her in her room and the surrounding fields, with no luck.

'She must have stayed up all night with her friends after the fireworks. This generation,' she grumbled as she spread peach jam on a slice of bread for my breakfast. 'And look at you, all bright and bushy-tailed after the fright you gave me yesterday,' she said, handing me the bread, still dusty with flour.

She brushed a speck off my tunic and added, 'You may be a girl of few words, but I like you. Come back and see us, all right? Off you go now, your uncle's waiting in the stables.'

The mystery of Reya's disappearance was soon solved. I found her deep in conversation with the Valiant, but she wasn't alone. She had two girls with her – I assumed they were the infamous Fran and Dill – and all three looked like they hadn't yet been to bed.

'Look who's here, Your High—' For once it was Myrain who risked a false move. He bit his tongue and glanced furtively at the girls, who didn't react.

I gave an exaggerated curtsey, prompting a more

raucous laugh than usual from Reya, and giggles from her friends.

'Reya's come to say goodbye,' said one girl.

'I think that's obvious enough,' Reya quipped.

'I'm Dill, by the way. And this is my sister, Fran.'

'We wanted to give you a few things for the journey,' said Fran.

Reya pointed at the saddlebags on Myrain's horse.

'Thanks to your friends we won't need to worry about provisions for at least three days,' said Myrain, loosening the cord on one of the bags. It was full to the brim with peaches, strawberries, vegetables, dried meat and bread.

'Thank you,' I signed, without thinking.

Fran and Dill exchanged a perplexed look.

'You're welcome,' said Reya.

'It's almost time, young lady,' said Myrain. 'Say your goodbyes while I have a bite to eat and find Miss Thorn-In-The-Side.'

He winked at Reya as he spoke, then left the stable.

'Trousers are going to be the fashion of the summer,' said Fran, proudly showing off her father's work pants. The excess material was gathered in an almost elegant knot at her waist.

Dill nodded enthusiastically. Then the sisters waved and headed back to the village to be reunited with their beds, tripping occasionally over the too-long hems of their trousers.

Once we were alone, Reya's eyes scanned me from head to toe.

'I'd imagined you taller and prettier, Your Highness. And certainly not mute,' she said. 'My friends and I, when we were little, we used to play at being you. We'd pull each other's hair because we all wanted to be Princess Lyria. No one wanted to be the baker's daughter, or the bricklayer's. We wanted to be princesses.'

Reya knew. Was it her intuition, or had Myrain's slip spilled the beans? I wondered where this was going. Was I supposed to feel flattered? Embarrassed?

'Then we grew up, and we started to behave like all the grown-ups in this village,' she continued. 'Gossiping about everything and everyone. If there's one thing that keeps this dump going, it's other people's business. We wouldn't get out of bed in the morning without it.'

The scandal of spending one coin too many . . . the gossip . . . . Not that I had a right to judge, but even my short stay here had made it pretty clear to me how things worked in Denhole.

'We'd say all sorts about you. We thought we had the measure of Princess Lyria,' Reya carried on. 'But we were wrong. *I* was wrong. I have no idea what it's like to be you. How it feels to lose a parent, or be forced to leave my home. I judged you before I knew you, and I got you really wrong. I understood that when I saw you learning to sign for Cam. No one else in this village has ever bothered.' She dropped her gaze. 'I hope you can forgive me.'

She paused expectantly, and I realised she was ready to promise anything in return for my forgiveness.

I pulled out the graphite and a piece of paper, and wrote:

Don't make the same mistake with Cam.

'I won't,' she said, and she seemed sincere.

But there was something else she had to ask me, I could sense it in the air.

'Is there . . . ? Between the two of you . . . ?'

No.

That's what I had wanted to tell her. I still wasn't sure what I felt for Cam. He had found a place in my heart as my first true friend. Something more, perhaps. But Reya had been added to that list, too; I couldn't choose one over the other.

Myrain and Dainefin arrived, bringing our good-byes to an end.

Reya hugged me. 'Come back soon,' she said.

For a brief moment, I thought of how beautiful Cam and Reya's children would be, if they ever had any. The thought crossed my mind without a hint of jealousy. I was ready to let go of an unexpressed feeling, an ellipsis inside a parenthesis I had just closed. I was ready to leave Denhole behind.

Chapter 11

Myrain's friends lived a day's ride away, at the very edge of Hatablar Forest. The Valiant told me that he and Gaudrot had trained together, but then his friend had fallen in love and married, and moved away to live at the back end of nowhere – though Myrain had used a less delicate expression. For a social animal like Myrain, that must have been impossible to understand. As far as he was concerned, a man didn't go off and live in the woods for love alone. And not just any woods, either.

Hatablar stood at the heart of the kingdom, but most avoided it at all costs. Travellers favoured other routes to the capital, the coast, or Murihen. The forest had no beaten paths, and before setting out, travellers had to make sure they had provisions to last the whole journey, since no edible plants grew there. 'Hatablar gives nothing for nothing, and takes everything you have,' was the saying taught to Amaranthian children.

Myrain was fixated on Hatablar. He'd scared the life out of me at first, with his stories of spirits and curses and what-have-yous. But Dainefin said they were nothing but legends, exaggerations inevitably inspired by the peculiarity of the place. She didn't seem inclined to debate the topic as we travelled, and Myrain's stories were beginning to get on her nerves.

'And who do the spirits belong to?' she teased. 'Three royal travellers who lost their way while crossing the forest?'

'Yes, yes, very funny. They're ancestral spirits, Your Highness,' he said, turning to me. 'They've been around much longer than we have, and will still be here when we're food for the worms.'

Dainefin chuckled. 'You're quite impressionable, Roy, for such a big, hard man.'

I was about to jump on the bandwagon of her teasing, but to be truthful, a little bit of fear was swilling in the pit of my stomach. Spirits or no spirits, I didn't relish the thought of spending any longer than necessary in a forest inhabited by untold dangers.

Pushing our horses as hard as we could – they had had a good rest in Denhole – we reached the edge of the forest just before the sun went down.

Even from a distance the forest looked otherworldly. It was blue. Blue like my eyes, like the sea on a bright day. And like the sea, the forest shimmered in the sunlight because the immense trees lightened at the top, their cerulean leaves tending to silver towards their crowns.

Before venturing very far into the forest, we dismounted and walked around its edge for nearly an hour. Myrain navigated according to instructions he had memorised. He knew which stones to follow, which trees marked our turnings. We were only a few steps away from the forest boundary, but already the foliage was so thick that we walked in semi-darkness, even though the sun had not yet dipped below the horizon. All that blue, the shade, and the strong aroma hanging in the air, made me shiver.

'We're almost there,' Myrain said. 'Really, is this a place where you'd want to live? What sane person would ever think, "Yes, here, right here is going to be just fine. This is where I can spend the rest of my life. Far away from any form of civilisation, surrounded by leaves and insects."'

'First of all, there are no insects in this forest,' came a male voice that sounded amused, rather than annoyed. 'Second, if I may, I had my reasons for moving here, Roy.'

A man emerged from the trees, dragging a load of firewood on a handcart. That firewood was, inexplicably, a normal, plain brown colour.

'Look who's still alive,' cried Myrain, hugging his friend.

'Alive and kicking, thank you very much,' the man replied.

Myrain too noticed the colour of the load of wood and commented, 'Since when does hata wood turn brown when it's dry?'

'Oh, this isn't hata. It's illegal to—'

'I *know* it's illegal to cut the hatas,' snapped Myrain. 'But harvesting fallen hata wood is allowed, isn't it?'

'Good luck finding dry branches on the ground round here. Take it from me, these trees were planted by the devil himself, they'll resist any kind of weather. This is perfectly normal wood; I have to buy it from Denhole a couple of times a month. But I don't mind that too much, the village girls are taking a shine to me,' he said, winking at Dainefin.

It appeared that shamelessly flirting with any female in the vicinity was a custom among young men who joined the King's Guard. Not that Dainefin was just any female. But even so.

'See?' Myrain turned to the Priestess. 'This forest has nothing to recommend it.'

'Oh, it's not so bad,' said his friend. 'You get used to it all: the damp, the vicious cold, the spirits . . .' He smiled at me. 'How rude of me, I forgot to introduce myself . . . . Your Highness, you may call me Gaudrot.'

'She won't call you anything,' said Myrain. 'Poor thing has a bad case of laryngitis.'

I had not expected the Valiant to be so cautious around his friend. He and Gaudrot went back years. On the other hand, Myrain wasn't one to waste his breath on unnecessary words.

'We'll give you some hata honey then,' was Gaudrot's reply as he led us through the dark forest. Then, 'Here we are,' as a house came into view.

Gaudrot's cottage was situated in a large clearing, lit by a fragment of sky. It was a single-storey cabin built from ordinary wood and raised off the ground, the visible foundations perhaps a strategy to avoid losing heat. It looked like it had been constructed quite recently.

'My wife takes care of these,' said Gaudrot, pointing at a row of flowerpots under the front windows. 'Phinnean!' he called out as he opened the door.

Gaudrot's wife appeared in the doorway. They could not have been more different from each other. Gaudrot was a version of Myrain with red hair and beard, a smattering of freckles, and a solid, muscular build. Phinnean was a small, well-built woman, no taller than me, with bright little eyes and thick blonde hair down to her hips. She didn't seem happy to have guests and gave us a hurried welcome.

'Shut the door, quick, we don't have that much wood left,' she said as she let us in.

'I've brought the wood, woman,' Gaudrot replied, emphasising the word 'woman' and in so doing, raising more than one female eyebrow in the room.

'I'll warm the soup,' said Phinnean, walking over to the kitchen corner across the room. 'And you would do well to brief them, before they get themselves into lots of trouble.'

Phinnean's tone did not match her jolly-forest-gnome appearance.

'Yes, ma'am,' Gaudrot answered. 'Sit down, first of all. Here, close to the fire. The cold in this forest gets into your bones and never lets go.'

He pulled two wooden chairs near to the sofa in front of the fireplace for himself and his friend, leaving the sofa to the ladies. Myrain's chair, and the floor beneath it, creaked under the heft of his body.

The cabin was bigger than it looked from outside; it seemed to have at least two rooms, aside from the living room and tiny kitchen. On the kitchen side of the room, all sorts of utensils and earthenware crockery hung from a beam along the ceiling. There were no decorations on the walls, only vases of fresh flowers on the windowsills. From the living room window, I saw a vegetable patch, a water well, and a row of still-young sunflowers.

By the warmth of the fire, revived by the wood Gaudrot had brought, my mood lightened. Living here can't have been too bad. The enchanted silence of Hatablar was only broken by the whistling of the wind and the lively crackling in the hearth.

'The missus knows what she's talking about. Before you continue on your journey, it's my duty to warn you off at all costs.'

'Warn us off what?' Dainefin asked.

'Crossing Hatablar Forest,' Gaudrot answered, his expression serious.

'If it's about the spirits, I've already tried —' Myrain began.

'Oh, no, this is nothing to do with spirits,' Gaudrot interrupted. 'We're talking flesh and blood.'

Phinnean placed a big steaming pot on the table at the centre of the room, and served us soup in mis-matched bowls.

'Separatists,' she said, lowering her voice.

Even Dainefin seemed surprised. 'In Hatablar Forest? What are they doing here?'

'Nothing good,' Gaudrot replied. 'Roy . . . I have to tell you the truth. I didn't move to Hatablar just because

I fancied a change of scenery.'

The look on Phinnean's face told us that whatever Gaudrot was about to reveal had been the subject of many a domestic discussion.

'Well, I did at first,' Gaudrot corrected himself. 'Phinnean and I had had enough of the city, working like pack horses just to live in a hovel. Neither of us inherited a house, and you know how expensive the capital is. Without my soldier's pay it was even harder.'

'You could have moved to Denhole,' said Myrain. 'Or the countryside.'

'Yes,' replied Gaudrot. 'That was the plan at first. But then . . .'

'The forest was my idea,' Phinnean interjected. 'I was sick of people. I just wanted to enjoy nature and need nothing and no one. Here, we live off what we produce.'

'I knew that a few years away from the capital would do me good,' her husband continued. 'But I still wasn't convinced. I kept travelling back and forth to build the house, it took months . . .'

'. . . And months and months,' Phinnean said.

'Then one day I ran into Alibert, remember him?'

Myrain nodded.

'We used to be comrades, in the same battalion,' Gaudrot explained to Dainefin and me. 'He's sound, helped us a lot with the move, the house. Well, Alibert told me he'd heard from a pair of smugglers that Hatablar was infested with Separatists. You know what some villagers can be like . . . see no evil, hear no evil . . .

Alibert and I thought that an inside man would come in handy,' Gaudrot concluded.

Myrain gaped at him.

'But in the end, I never had the courage.'

Myrain leaned back in the chair, shaking his head. 'I can't believe you never told me. I am your superior.'

'I'm not a soldier any more. And I would have told you, really. But then the Queen . . . and I thought you must have plenty on your hands. The point is, when we finally moved here four weeks ago, I'd already changed my mind.'

'I told him that if he started playing spies, I would leave,' said Phinnean, almost proudly.

'But . . . you still moved here, even though you knew . . .' Myrain started gravely.

'I was quite fond of the idea by then,' said Phinnean. 'We'd been preparing for months, I wouldn't have walked away from this for anyone. Not even Separatists.'

'And anyway, it's well-known that Separatists aren't a threat to simple farmers like us. It's not like they're murderers and pillagers . . .'

'They do kill, though,' Myrain pointed out. 'Queen Levith . . .'

'Yes, yes, I've heard that theory too. But think about it, Roy, why haven't they claimed responsibility for the assassination? What good does it do their cause to kill the Queen? We're talking about people who until the other day had soil under their fingernails – they're farmers turned political.'

'Mind you, that doesn't mean they aren't capable of some other vile acts,' said Phinnean.

Gaudrot nodded. 'I feel better now you're here, Roy,' he said. 'I wanted to go back and warn our lot in the capital as soon as possible . . . but I can't leave Phinnean on her own. She . . . we . . . we're expecting a baby.'

He didn't even give Dainefin and Myrain the chance to congratulate them. 'You must tell the King immediately,' he went on. 'I think the Separatists may be preparing to storm the capital.'

The news made Myrain choke on his soup. Gaudrot thumped his back, making the Valiant cough up a piece of potato.

For some reason I couldn't quite put my finger on, none of what they were saying came as a surprise to me.

'Why would they do that?' Dainefin asked once Myrain had recovered. 'To assassinate King Uriel?'

'I don't think so,' said Gaudrot. 'I get the impression they may want to throw the cat amongst the pigeons, give the King and our side a good fright.'

'What makes you think that?' asked Myrain.

'They've been camped out here for months. What other reason could they have to leave their villages and come to Hatablar? They're playing for time, making plans,' replied Gaudrot. 'Think about it, Roy. There's no one around, they can do what they want without the wrong people getting wind of it.'

'People like you, Myrain,' added Phinnean. 'You must return to the capital and warn whoever needs to be warned. Don't try to cross the forest.'

'How many are there? This could be the perfect opportunity to gain the upper hand,' said Myrain, his face lighting up.

Dainefin exchanged a worried look with Phinnean.

Myrain directed his enthusiasm at Gaudrot. 'You and I could stop them before they even leave the forest. We could gain an advantage, gather the information we've been after for years. Who they are, how many strong, who and where their leaders are,' he said. 'They're serving us their own heads on a platter!'

Gaudrot shot a glance at his wife as he listened, and she shook her head. Her eyes said, *'don't even think about it.'*

'There are too many, Roy,' he said.

'What are their intentions?' Dainefin asked.

'I'm not sure,' Gaudrot replied. 'When I heard them speak I couldn't believe it. Some of them aren't from the border – they spoke in the Murihen dialect.'

'No!' Myrain exclaimed. 'That's a new one. Separatists from Murihen? What the hell is their aim? A new kingdom between Murihen and Amarantha?'

'I suppose then they wouldn't have to pay taxes to the state any more,' Gaudrot reflected.

'And . . .' the Valiant surmised, 'both Murihen and Amarantha would depend on them for the safe passage of goods.'

'Something's not quite right, though,' said Gaudrot. 'Who's recruiting them? Who do they answer to? Until a few years ago, all their attacks and provocations were little more than pranks. Now they're really starting to worry me . . .'

Dainefin remained strangely quiet. I was trying my hardest to put the pieces together. My mother's murder . . . . A nest of Separatists in the forest . . . . On the one hand, Gaudrot didn't think they were too great a threat, but on the other hand, they sounded like they were becoming more radical, and therefore more dangerous.

Myrain was struck by a sudden thought. 'We'll need you back in the capital,' he said, turning to Dainefin.

I didn't think of her as a military strategist, but the truth was, Dainefin could do anything. I knew Father would want her by his side if the city was attacked.

The details of my forgotten dream came back to me – that was why the news hadn't been a surprise!

There is something you need to know right now.

Dainefin picked up the message. She excused us and thanked Phinnean for supper, saying we'd be back to do the dishes in a moment. When I nodded, picking up my bowl to take it to the kitchen, Phinnean objected.

'I won't live to see the day when a princess does the dishes in my house.'

Having said that, she stood and showed us to the room where Dainefin and I would sleep that night.

'I hope it will be large enough for the two of you,' she said with a blush. The room was modest, but it was fine. Dainefin and I were to sleep in the couple's double bed.

'Lyria and I would be quite comfortable on the

floor,' said Dainefin. 'No need to give up your bed.'

Phinnean shook her head. 'I insist! Goodnight.'

I didn't mind the woman's curt manner; I was grateful to her for leaving us alone. I closed the door behind her and sat on the bed.

The emotion burst out of me. *I had this dream, last night... I was in Amarantha. I... Sonni was meeting with the Council members, but Father wasn't there. They were discussing a piece of news, it wasn't clear whether it was true or not, but anyway, some of them think that soldiers from Murihen are heading to Amarantha... with the worst possible intentions. They were debating whether or not the Separatists were involved too.*

Dainefin didn't interrupt as the story flooded out of me.

Dainefin, it wasn't a nightmare, it was true! It was like I was there. Like I was Sonni. I know it sounds strange, but somehow, I'm sure it actually happened.

'I believe you,' said Dainefin. 'This is grave news, and graver still to hear that you have already had a vision.'

You knew this would happen?

It would have been nice of her to let me know.

'You're going to have to trust me, for now,' she said, feeling my annoyance. 'I trust Myrain, but I can't tell you anything while he's still around. I don't know how he would react if he found out more than he needs to know.'

I don't get the impression that Myrain picks up all that much from my Empathic Aura.

'Before long, he'll start to hear your thoughts too,' she sighed. 'The stronger your thoughts, the clearer they become. Soon, you'll understand that you're not learning to control your condition, it's the Empathic Aura that is learning to control you.'

Can I at least know how I managed to be at the council meeting, when I'm hundreds of miles away from them?

'It isn't simply a question of distance,' said Dainefin. 'The most absurd thing about the Empathic Aura is that you have no way of knowing when the events in the visions took place. You had the vision last night, but that doesn't mean it was taking place right at that moment.'

Dainefin sat down next to me. 'Imagine that as we're talking right now, an invisible hand is recording every single word, gesture, movement and thought, writing over and over on the same page. That page is Time. Forget about the idea of time as a line running along. Past, present and future are all taking place at the same moment. Each one of our actions – and by "our", I mean humanity's – remains suspended forever, and not only in time. As incredible as it may seem, the Empathic Aura gives you access to anything that may happen, or has happened, anywhere.'

If what you're saying is true, then I can't be sure that the vision I had has already happened . . . By your reasoning, it could be a vision of the future.

Dainefin nodded, but I could see she wasn't happy with my eagerness.

'What I am about to tell you is, without doubt, the

149

most important thing you need to know. Soon, I promise, you will know everything about the Empathic Aura: why it is affecting you and how to overcome it. But none of that will be as important as this.'

She paused to make sure she had my attention, then went on, 'Do not lose your mind over these visions. They may not be as important as they seem.'

But . . . how . . . I had the vision yesterday, and now we're finding out about Hatablar being the Separatist headquarters . . . . How can my visions not be important?

Dainefin sighed, but she let me finish.

There has to be something we can do!

'See, this is what visions do – they make you feel as if the destiny of others is in your hands,' she said. 'And it isn't, Lyria. You must focus on your task of returning to your normal self. Please, do not get swept up in this. You are the most important thing right now.'

The Empathic Aura relayed my frustration. I could see no drawbacks in the chance to take a peek at the 'Page of Time', especially if it allowed me to protect my family. What if, at some point, I had a vision of my mother's murder? Dainefin was crazy if she thought I wouldn't take advantage of something like that.

And as for 'returning to my normal self', I didn't know where to begin. Crossing the kingdom on foot certainly wasn't helping.

Before Dainefin could say any more, we were interrupted by a knock.

'Are you two in bed already?' Myrain asked through the door.

'No,' answered Dainefin. 'We were just about to get changed.'

'Perfect. I just wanted to let you know that we're staying here an extra week. You get a few lie-ins, Princess.'

Dainefin stood up and opened the door.

'We'd agreed to leave at dawn.'

'With what Gaudrot's told us about Separatists lurking in the forest, we've got to take at least a few days to decide what to do.'

'But a whole week?!' The Priestess's voice had reached a volume I hadn't thought her capable of. She quickly composed herself. 'You don't have the slightest clue about—'

'No,' Myrain cut in, raising his voice in turn. 'I don't. But guess what? I'm not the one keeping my cards close to my chest and expecting the rest of the world to put up with it. I'm not the one—'

'Not here!' she hissed.

'All right, let's take it outside then,' he challenged. 'I'm used to it by now. I actually can't sleep if I haven't been treated like an idiot by you for at least a couple of hours.'

I saw on Dainefin's lips the beginning of a reply that was bound to put her on the back foot. But she had the presence of mind to check herself.

'We are not done,' she told me as she shut the door behind her.

I understood Myrain's anger. He was far from clueless. He was the King's Valiant, after all, and had shed blood to get to that position. He'd been of no rank or class when he'd joined up, but had worked hard to gain the respect of his peers, his superiors, and eventually even the King himself. He may have made mistakes over the course of his career – he was a notorious hothead – but had proven himself time and again.

I understood Dainefin less. No one knew with any certainty how she had come to be on the Council. No one remembered when she had started making decisions on behalf of the King. Presumably, she too had got there by herself. But how? Until that moment, I had never wondered. A schoolteacher from Shamabat, who was now simply a part of our family. I could not remember a single moment of my life when she hadn't been by my side.

I didn't know what to think anymore. Deep down I knew that she was acting in my best interest, even though I had no idea what was going through her head. I needed to know what she and the Valiant were deciding.

I left the room in my nightdress and quietly slipped out the front door to avoid waking Gaudrot and Phinnean, who were asleep on the sofa. Gritting my teeth against the cold, I followed the sound of a whispered shouting match taking place in the backyard, and hunched behind a thick hata trunk to eavesdrop.

'Levith was *murdered*,' Myrain was saying, 'and we still don't know why. If the Separatists hiding here are involved in even the most marginal way, we'd be idiots not to take advantage of that, not to gather as much information as possible.'

'We have no time to waste, Myrain. Lyria seems stable now, but her condition will worsen. The life of the King's daughter is at stake. I am sure you wouldn't want that on your conscience.'

'She doesn't seem that ill to me,' he shot back. 'All right, so she can't speak, she bombards you with her bad moods, so what? Once everyone's got used to that, it won't be strange any more. She'll learn to live with it, as with any illness.'

'Oh, so that's how Lyria should go on? Accepting that she can no longer speak, waiting for others to accept her? Do you actually hear yourself? Would you accept that fate if it were you? I really don't think so.'

Myrain tried to change tack. 'Even assuming that I decided to waste this opportunity and escort you to Styr, why would I ever lead the King's daughter through a forest teeming with Separatists? You think those thugs will bow to her and roll out the red carpet? Aren't they more likely to hold a knife to her throat, and use her to pull King Uriel's strings?'

Myrain's words were so blunt that they sent my anxiety spiralling up like a swarm of raging wasps. I hoped that Dainefin was out of the Empathic Aura's range.

'I have no intention of crossing the forest,' the Priestess said eventually.

Myrain was lost for words. Did Dainefin mean we were turning back? For an instant my heart was filled with joy at the prospect of spending more time in Denhole: I would see my friends again, convince them to move to the capital with me. But that thought lasted only an instant. After that, my heart sank as I realised that if I went home now, I'd never be rid of the Empathic Aura. I would never be the person I once was.

'We're going to change direction,' Dainefin continued.

'What?'

'And go through Shamabat.'

The forest was silent.

Dainefin rarely spoke of Shamabat. On the few occasions she did, it was clear that just the name of that village carried painful memories.

There was a long pause before the Valiant whispered, 'You would still lose three days getting there, and then who knows how many more in the diversion. We should return north. Retrace our steps to Denhole and head out to the coast from there. Circumvent the forest entirely.' Myrain's tone had softened.

Shamabat was on the coast, like Amarantha, but much further south. Going through Shamabat would mean stretching our journey to over twice its length.

'That would take too long,' said Dainefin. 'We have to get to . . . we have to shorten our journey in any way possible. One day's sustained marching will get us out of the forest and we'll have reached Shamabat by the next. It's better than sitting here for a week risking an attack, or walking directly into the midst of the Separatists.'

'If we're out of Hatablar by nightfall tomorrow . . .'

'Exactly.'

The conversation sounded like it was ending, so I slunk back to the bedroom before Dainefin caught me out of bed. I curled up under the covers to absorb as much heat as possible after the bone-chilling cold of the forest at night.

When the Priestess came into the room, I pretended to be asleep. I counted my breaths, forcing myself to think of nothing. A few minutes of that and I was ready to fall asleep for real, but something was wrong. Dainefin was still sitting on the edge of the bed. I peeked out from under the covers and saw her with her head in her hands.

Was Dainefin . . . crying?

Chapter 12

Myrain had evidently agreed to skirt the edge of Hatablar because at daybreak the next morning we made our goodbyes to Gaudrot and Phinnean. Gaudrot gave Myrain a map of the forest that he had drafted over the months he had explored it. He told us he could find his own way, but we wouldn't stand a chance out there without it.

I wasn't exactly jumping with joy at the thought of walking two days straight, but it didn't seem impossible.

We set out, stuffed with the fruit and cakes that Reya and the girls had given us for the journey, which we had shared with our hosts at breakfast. We still had enough provisions for two or three days, but Myrain had thought it better for us to be carrying less weight on our backs.

Even with the lightened load, I was not used to carrying such a heavy pack for so long, and my legs began to shake before the sun had even reached its peak. Thankfully, Hatablar Forest was all on level ground, but despite that I could feel my calves, hips, and the muscles in my back burning with the effort. The third time Myrain said, 'I'll carry that for you,' I gave up and let him.

I tried to stay focussed on anything other than my aching muscles and the immense effort of putting one foot in front of the other. I counted my steps, but that soon became as boring as it was pointless.

I resorted to playing *Chara Chairei* in my mind, followed by every other piece in my repertory. My fingers tapped out musical phrases on my hips and I tried to adjust the rhythm of my steps to the music, to the rustling of the wind through the trees, to the trilling of a bird in the distance.

I was trying to cheat my own fatigue. Every step cost me one more token of dignity, and I was fast approaching the moment I would have to implore Dainefin to stop for a break.

Gaudrot had told us we were hardly likely to stumble upon the Separatists on our day's march. He hadn't been able to locate their camp – Phinnean wouldn't let him go 'nosing around' – but he was convinced that it was in the very heart of the forest to the southwest and we would be safe travelling east.

Despite my body's exhaustion and the tense silence that reigned between the Valiant and the Priestess, walking through the forest brought me the same peace I found in the library or on the beach. All that blue, all those shadows, made Hatablar appear like a deserted underworld, a place suspended between our universe and some other.

I had learnt my maps, but every mention of Hatablar had offered only vague reference points. For the most part, the textbooks just advised people to stay away.

While I had never been inside a proper forest, I was well acquainted with the woods north of Amarantha, and I had heard people talk about those of the Serra del Lárr. Neither of those were blue. Green, yes. Light green, dark green, green with a hint of blue. Or depending on the season, red, yellow, orange . . . but who had ever seen a forest the colour of the sea?

Not only did hata trees endure any type of bad weather without losing a single branch, the forest was also supposedly indifferent to the seasonal cycle and the blue of the foliage never turned rusty. The trees would shed a few leaves every day, and every morning fresh buds would appear, ready to blossom over the course of the next.

The path we were following appeared natural rather than one beaten by human feet, and it was clear of any major obstacles. Our steps, muffled by the damp ground, were barely audible and there were no other plants to be seen. No shrub, flower or fern, only those massive hata trunks. A few birds, temporary visitors, fluttered high above our heads. As Gaudrot had said, there were no insects in Hatablar Forest. Nor, apparently, any other wild inhabitants. No squirrels, rabbits or deer. Nothing. Which meant no dangerous creatures to fear.

Or so we thought.

Around mid-afternoon, our path nearly crossed

that of two Separatists.

It was Myrain who noticed them first. At every bend, the Valiant would stalk ahead to ensure the path was clear.

This time, when he returned, he informed us that there were two Separatists coming, both young and seemingly unarmed.

'Are you sure they're Separatists?' said the Priestess. 'They may have nothing to do with—'

'Their accents are from Murihen, not from the border villages. But you heard Gaudrot, didn't you? They're in Murihen now too . . .'

Dainefin said nothing, even though she patently disapproved of the Valiant's habit of jumping to conclusions.

'Do you think they know Lyria is in the forest?' she finally asked.

He shrugged. 'They were too far away for me to hear what they were saying. As soon as I heard voices, I came back to warn you.'

'Which way are they headed?'

'Straight towards us. They'll catch us up if we turn back and we don't have time to argue about leaving the forest.' Myrain glanced at Gaudrot's map, and pointed out a path that exited the forest on a level with Shamabat. 'Our only option is to go around them this way. It means going a little further in, but they'll see us if we go any other way.'

Dainefin nodded and we hurried from the path before the Separatists found us.

After a few hours of walking in silence, Myrain said, 'We'll have to set up camp here for the night. This new path will take us at least another morning.'

I blushed – it was partly my fault we were running behind schedule.

'I don't see a problem with that,' said Dainefin. 'You and I will take it in turns to keep watch. Now, less talking, more walking. We have at least two hours before it's too dark to carry on.'

Under different circumstances, the prospect of walking for another two hours would have deflated my spirits completely: I would have collapsed to the ground and refused to move unless dragged by my ankles. But the knowledge that two Murihen crooks were prowling in the vicinity set my feet on fire. I wanted to put as much distance as possible between us.

'Nothing will happen to us while Myrain is here,' Dainefin whispered to me, sensing my fear.

I nodded, but matched my pace to Myrain's, who was walking far ahead of us.

When it became too dark to see further than a few steps away, we stopped in a small clearing by a brook. Myrain swept away a layer of leaf mulch and prepared the ground for a camp fire by digging a hole with his hands and putting down stones in a circle.

Dainefin sat to one side and brushed her hair, then braided it with all the calm and care in the world. Every now and then she glanced at the Valiant, who carried on building the fire without paying her any mind.

When the ground was ready, Myrain opened his haversack and pulled out three logs of perfectly normal firewood and plenty of kindling.

Dainefin didn't say anything. Once her hair was done, she sat behind me and brushed mine, which over the last few days had taken on a shape and texture that was hard to describe. I hoped that her animosity towards the Valiant would not be vented on my already mistreated locks, but she was gentle and patient. One by one, she unravelled all the tangles that had formed at the back of my head, and smoothed my hair with a sesame and dog-rose scented ointment.

Myrain had to work a long time to get the fire to take in that humid forest, as long as it took me and Dainefin to do our hair and spread our bedding.

After the fire was lit, he pulled a stick from the fire as a torch and grunted, 'Going for a walk.'

I felt guilty. After breaking his back to carry our firewood all day, and again to build the fire, he was scouting to make sure our camp was safe for me.

'He's walking off his temper,' said Dainefin. 'He's not really expecting to run into anyone.

He's not the only one who's been in a mood all day. I was so exhausted the thought just slipped out.

'I'm not angry at him.' She stroked my head and added, 'You nosy thing.'

You can talk to me, if you want. Why are you two always fighting? Is it because of me?

'No,' she answered. 'It's nothing to do with you. It's an old thing that rears its head every now and then.'

Whatever the problem is, it will be easier to solve if you talk about it.

I thought of the fights Sonni and I had as children and how bitter we'd been until Dainefin had forced us to talk to each other. The sense of calm and happiness we'd felt after we'd resolved our misunderstandings. I tried to push those feelings towards Dainefin.

'I'll go find him,' said Dainefin, stroking my hair again and adding gravely, 'Don't move. I'll be back in a moment.'

The Priestess took another burning stick from the fire and disappeared in the direction Myrain had taken a few moments earlier. I curled up on the bed she had prepared for me, seduced by the crackling of the fire. Warmth and fatigue soon combined to lull me to sleep, winning over my curiosity about whether they'd find a way to patch things up. The rustling of the wind through the trees and the crackling of the fire were so soothing ...

The whispering of two unknown voices jolted me awake. I was sitting up in an instant.

There was no mistaking it: the voices of two male strangers, coming from the opposite direction to where Dainefin and Myrain had gone. It must be the two Separatists the Valiant had spotted hours earlier. And they were heading straight for our camp! I listened without moving a muscle.

Myrain wouldn't have gone far, even as annoyed as he was, because that would have put us in danger. Dainefin must have caught up to him already. But I had no way of calling them back and no time to think of anything I could use to make a warning noise. Suddenly, I was on my feet and hiding behind a tree trunk. I concentrated on the scent of the hatas to slow my shallow breathing.

The two men cautiously approached the fire-lit clearing.

'See?' one of them whispered. 'What did I tell you? They must be off gathering more wood.'

They were perhaps a year or two older than me. The lad who had spoken was clean-shaven, with dark eyes and long brown hair tied at the nape of the neck. He was as tall as he was thin and angular, and the geometric precision of his features put me in mind of my brother Anur. His comrade was shorter and rounder with blond hair also tied back, but not as long. He was biting his cuticles, and seemed to be having difficulty finding the words for a reply.

'Isehar,' he finally said, 'let's go back. I don't want to think about what this lot will do to us if we're here when they return.'

'What are they going to do? They're Separatists, not cutthroats. They'll have nothing against us, as long as they don't get the impression we're connected to the royals,' Isehar replied, squatting down on Dainefin's bedding. 'And between you and me, there's hardly a risk of that.'

I recognised their accent by the high, drawling vowels: they could only be from Murihen, just as the Valiant had said.

Isehar started rifling through Myrain's saddlebag. The last remaining Denhole peaches were peeking out of the opening, and he threw one to his friend who just about caught it – awkwardly.

'Look at this, Fayrem,' he said, unfolding Gaudrot's map of Hatablar. 'I know people who'd pay a lot of money for a map like this.'

'Plenty of detail,' Fayrem mumbled through a mouthful of peach. 'But the proportions are wrong. All wrong.'

He bent over for a better look at the map, and lost his balance. If Isehar hadn't been quick enough to grab his thighs, he would have fallen right on top of him.

Isehar couldn't hold back a smile. '*All wrong*,' he aped him.

I released my breath. These two weren't Separatists. Something told me I was safe. Fayrem was still poring over the map, while Isehar was gazing distractedly into the flames.

The raised voices of Dainefin and Myrain reached me from the darkness. As I had imagined, they weren't far from the clearing, but by the volume of their argument it was clear that they were nowhere near any kind of compromise. Isehar and Fayrem had realised they were in danger of being discovered, and were whispering about which way to go. Apparently Isehar's bravado had worn off.

Still, they had guts to be in Hatablar by themselves

Amarantha

at that time of night. The rumours about the spirits haunting the forest were enough to keep most people out . . . but they'd known about the Separatists too, and they'd taken their chances anyway. They could have been thieves or smugglers, but something told me they were just trying to get to the end of each day with something in their stomachs.

I don't know what made me do what I did next, but I stepped out from behind my tree.

The boys' eyes widened, and I quickly raised my hands to show I wasn't hostile. Then I motioned them closer. They didn't move. As I opened the bag containing our provisions, I tried to project peace and friendship at them. Fayrem's shoulders relaxed slightly and Isehar stared at me for a moment, perhaps trying to interpret what he was feeling while also wondering what I could possibly be doing there on my own.

I handed them each a flat bread.

Wait.

I rummaged through my backpack until I fished out a couple of silver coins, which I offered to Isehar.

'No, no,' he hastened to say, shaking his head and waving his hands. 'No money. We were just hungry. Sorry.'

Having said that, he realised he was still holding on to Gaudrot's map and handed it to me, looking down in shame.

Keep it.

I pressed it back into his hands then pulled out my paper and graphite.

What are you doing here? I wrote, hoping one of them could read.

'We're from Murihen,' Isehar began, still staring at me as if trying to convince himself that I wasn't a hallucination. 'We're here on an errand, but we're leaving soon.'

Fayrem held open his haversack, showing me a three-quarters-full jar of hata honey.

Where did you get that?

'You know what this is?' asked Isehar. He seemed to be weighing up how wise it was to share certain information with a strange girl.

I nodded.

Hata honey.

'Yes. Even though it's not actually honey,' Fayrem corrected me. 'It's resin. I don't understand why people don't call things by their proper names . . .'

Hata honey wasn't honey . . . Well, how could it be, if there were no bees in Hatablar Forest? I felt a little embarrassed. I, too, was very particular about words. It wasn't my fault that no one had, until that point, spoken of 'hata honey' as resin, but I should have got there on my own. At the same time though, I doubted I would spend the rest of my life pointing that out to everyone else.

'So pernickety.' Isehar rolled his eyes.

Is it worth much? I wrote.

'On the black market it is,' he replied. 'But we're not smugglers, we're collecting it for a friend.'

'A friend, ha!' Fayrem barked.

'Keep your voice down!' Isehar scolded.

We all paused to make sure Dainefin and Myrain's raised voices were still far enough off.

What does your friend need it for?

Isehar and Fayrem each seemed to be waiting for the other to answer.

'We don't know,' Isehar whispered at last. 'Selling it, maybe.'

'Have you tried it?' Fayrem interrupted, pointing at the jar.

I nodded, thinking of the honey – or resin – I had in my possession, the gift from the priest in Denhole.

'It's amazing,' said Isehar. 'They say it can cure anything.'

'It's *dangerous*,' Fayrem corrected him, this time making the effort to keep his voice down. 'Otherwise everyone would know about it.'

Why don't more people know about it?

'Usually smugglers come into Hatablar for wood, which is worth way more. There's no need to venture in too deep for wood,' Isehar explained. 'But to fill a jar with this stuff . . . . You only find it on very few trees, and even scraping the bark of the whole tree will get you only a few drops. Pain in the –'

'And anyway,' Fayrem interrupted, 'if you have a lick of sense you're not going to start experimenting with substances that no one knows anything about.'

By the way Isehar pursed his lips, I could tell they didn't agree on that.

'This place is like a graveyard,' said Isehar. 'We'd

be better off not…messing around with things we don't really understand,' he concluded, pointing at the jar.

They bickered a little bit more about hata honey, but I didn't hear what they said because I had noticed Dainefin and Myrain's voices were calmer now and sounded nearer.

Isehar and Fayrem heard them too. They looked at each other, and got to their feet.

Good luck, I wrote, knowing that the Empathic Aura had already conveyed the message.

'You too,' they replied as one. Then they scarpered, and I bedded down so I could be found 'sleeping' by Dainefin and Myrain. I thought I would hear Dainefin getting in her bed at any moment, but I started to worry when the clearing got eerily quiet. I lifted my head and saw them standing opposite each other, only steps away from the tree that had hidden me earlier, lit by their respective torches. As I watched, Myrain stooped to kiss the Priestess.

Before I even thought of turning my face to avoid intruding on their intimacy, Dainefin broke away from the embrace. Her face was bathed in tears.

'I'm sorry,' I heard her whisper.

'For what?' the Valiant asked, without resentment.

'For everything,' she answered.

He wiped her tears with the back of his finger.

'I'm not giving up,' he said. 'But sometimes I feel as if I'm torturing you. So I won't try to change your mind again.'

'Thank you,' Dainefin murmured, her voice breaking.

'Don't make me wait for the rest of my life, though,' he added, with an uncharacteristic seriousness that made him even more handsome.

They each wrapped one arm around the other's waist, framed by their torches like lovers in the illustration at the end of a storybook. There should have been a caption telling the reader that they lived happily ever after . . . but there was no hint of happiness in their embrace.

'Why are you still awake?' Dainefin asked as she sat on her bedroll. 'You weren't worried about us, were you?'

I shook my head.

Those two men Myrain saw earlier . . . they were here.

Myrain's eyes bulged, then he looked to Dainefin for confirmation that he'd just felt my words in his head. I too was shocked he had 'heard' me. At Dainefin's unsurprised look and calm nod, he regained his composure.

'Did they hurt you?' he asked, drawing his sword. 'Which way did they go?'

I held up my hands to stop him.

They're not Separatists. They have nothing to do with them. In fact, they thought we were the Separatists! They're just out collecting hata honey.

'Drifters,' Myrain growled. 'But better that than . . . . Well. You two should get some sleep. I'll keep watch for a couple of hours.'

'Wake me up when you're ready to swap,' said Dainefin in a tired voice. I glanced at the Priestess one last time: her worried eyes were red from crying. Myrain was trying to avoid her gaze, but every now and then his eyes flitted apprehensively towards her. They were an odd couple, it had to be said. But I hoped that it would end well between the two of them, that they would realise all they had to do to *know* what the other felt was . . . to ask.

Chapter 13

My father is in the Seat of Audience, gazing out of the window and gently scratching his jaw.

Sonni stands next to him, waiting; every now and then he glances at the door. 'I don't think anyone's coming today,' he says, measuring his words carefully.

'Better this way,' Father sighs.

Suddenly, the door bursts open.

'King Uriel,' says Catam, striding into the Chamber. The rest of the Consuls watch from the doorway, along with a man I do not recognise. 'A messenger from Murihen has arrived.'

Catam waits for the King to meet his gaze. My father lets a few seconds go by, then beckons him closer with a grimace.

Catam whispers something in his ear.

'When?'

'About two weeks ago.'

Father slumps in the Seat and turns his head to one side, as he does when he's thinking.

'How is he now?' he asks eventually.

Catam motions to the messenger, and he comes forward. He is followed by the other Consuls, who have the decency to remain at the other end of the room. Father doesn't seem to appreciate their intrusion: the grimace of irritation tightens until his whole face puckers around it.

The messenger sits in front of him, on one of the chairs set out for those who come seeking audience.

'He is gravely ill, Your Majesty. He may not pull through.'

Father sighs. 'I would send Dainefin to him, but...'

The other Consuls have no need for him to finish that sentence. 'Our best physicians are already trying everything they can,' the messenger replies.

'I shall send mine too,' says Father. 'Is there anything else I can do?'

'We can but wait,' says the messenger, shaking his head. Then he adds, 'There is one other thing.'

Father steels himself for the worst. 'Rehena?'

'No, the Queen is well. She is a strong woman. She takes care of your brother day and night.' The messenger hesitates. 'It's...it's about your son, Prince Anur.'

'What has he done?' asks Sonni, intervening for the first time.

The messenger's eyes stay glued to my father. 'I have been sent to announce that your son has been proposed as Prince Regent by the Council.'

'Anur?' asks Sonni, astounded. 'In Murihen? Now?'

'Yes,' the messenger replies. 'But King Uriel's consent is required to formalise the resolution.'

The messenger unrolls the scroll signed by the members of Murihen Council, and my father gives it his full attention. He gasps when he reaches the end of the document. 'According to this, if Hervin should . . .'

'I'm afraid so, Your Majesty,' says the messenger. 'Prince Anur would be considered the legitimate heir of the throne of Murihen.'

The Consuls, who until that moment have been listening in silence at the other end of the room, stir at this news, and start muttering amongst themselves.

'Silence!' Father orders, rising to his feet. 'I need to think.' He takes the scroll and reads through the terms once more.

The Council members move closer to the Seat, ready to be consulted. For a few minutes, my father stands perfectly still, reading the scroll.

'Isn't this what you wanted?' Sonni asks cautiously. 'Anur in Murihen, like Dainefin suggested? And me . . .'

'Yes,' Father nods. 'But we wanted to give you at least another couple of years. You're so young, and Anur . . . . That's why we decided to postpone the coronation.'

'You are right, Your Majesty,' says Lumio, 'but given the circumstances . . .'

'It's a terrible idea,' Rila interjects.

Lumio, Catam and Sonni turn to him in bewilderment, but Father appears relieved that someone else sees it the same way he does.

Sayd lends his support. 'Rila is correct. We had our doubts back when Prince Anur was meant to be crowned King of Amarantha. As I've always said, sending him to Murihen will not solve the problem.'

'Quite the opposite,' Rila continues. 'He will merge the two kingdoms at the first opportunity and that will be the end. He won't simply antagonise the Separatists, but the subjects of Amarantha too.'

'If I may . . .' says the messenger in a small voice.

'No one asked your opinion,' hisses Rila.

Ignoring his adviser, Father gestures for the messenger to continue.

'Your son would not be the only ruler of Murihen.'

'Rehena would guide him,' says Father.

'She would, but,' the messenger fidgets as he pauses, 'the Murihen Council supports Prince Anur. And King Hervin trusts his Consuls as you trust your own.'

Father looks thoughtful but offers no reply. Finally, he says, 'Those in favour of allowing Prince Anur to rule over Murihen along with Queen Rehena and their Council?'

He raises his hand. A moment later, so do Catam and Lumio.

'Those against?'

Rila and Sayd declare themselves against it.

Father turns to Sonni. 'You are abstaining?'

'No,' Sonni replies. 'I just think Rila may have a point. If Anur becomes Prince Regent and heir to the

Murihen throne, what will happen in Amarantha?'

'You will inherit the throne, Your Highness,' says Lumio. 'As has already been decided.'

Father nods.

'So I will,' my brother continued, 'but what will happen if Anur decides he wants to merge the kingdoms back into one, once he is crowned? Does the Constitution say anything about that?'

'No,' answers Lumio. 'The Constitution certainly doesn't, nor do the Acts of Independence. When the kingdom was divided between your father and King Hervin, when they came of age, the possibility of merging again was not contemplated. It has always made sense for Murihen to be a separate kingdom. It's too far from the capital for Amarantha to rule it well.'

'Not to mention that the split benefited the economy of both kingdoms,' adds Sayd. 'If Prince Anur unified them again, it would lead to an economic – as well as a political – catastrophe.'

Father thinks for a moment.

'Let's make things plain,' he says eventually. He dips his pen into the inkwell and spends the next minute writing on the end of the scroll. 'The Kingdom of Amarantha supports Prince Anur's ascension to the Murihen throne, on the condition that Prince Anur abdicates his position as heir to Amarantha's throne. It must be clear that Murihen and Amarantha will remain two separate kingdoms. Just so there are no misunderstandings.'

He reads out his amendment and calls a second vote. The majority votes in favour.

I woke in the middle of the night. The dream vision
came back to me in fragments. Once again, I had witnessed a Council meeting. I remembered my father's
reaction to the news that Uncle Hervin was ... dying? It
wasn't clear, but if Anur had been appointed Prince
Regent .... I squeezed my eyes shut, trying hard to
remember. I forced myself not to brood over the dream,
as Dainefin had suggested. There was just one thing
that tormented me: When had the Council proposed
that Sonni replace Anur as heir to the throne? And why
hadn't Sonni told me about it? With everything that
happened after the Foundation Meal, he must have kept
it to himself to avoid compounding our worries. Or
perhaps he hadn't known yet.

Perhaps none of that had happened yet. Perhaps
the Council had only just decided that Anur was
unworthy of the crown – after all, he had abandoned the
capital at a delicate moment. Perhaps Sonni had only
just found out.

Dainefin had expressly told me that the visions
should not inform my actions. That there was no way of
knowing whether what I saw had happened, or was yet
to take place. But I couldn't help feeling guilty for not
being closer to Sonni, for not being more persistent
when I had asked what was on his mind ...

And why would Anur be in Murihen? He couldn't
wait to become King of Amarantha. I thought of all his

unbearable gloating, his scorn towards Sonni and me. But then a little voice in my head asked how I would feel knowing I had to inherit my father's throne. To feel the pressure of ruling as well as he had. To have to live up to the example he set.

Maybe that was why Anur was always so angry.

Dainefin stirred and I worried my Empathic Aura would wake her, so I wrapped myself tighter in my blanket and tried to calm my mind, succeeding in bundling my emotions into a tight knot.

Just as I was drifting back to sleep, an indistinct murmuring arose nearby. My eyes flew open but I didn't see anyone. I froze under my blanket, straining my ears. I could clearly hear the voices of a group of people, and the more convinced I became of their presence, the clearer those voices were.

I sat up, drawing my blanket around my shoulders. I couldn't make out a single word they were saying. Was the Murihen dialect so unintelligible? Or was this a border accent?

The voices were growing louder, and still I couldn't see anyone. Better this way, perhaps, because if I couldn't see them, they couldn't see me. Or so I told myself. The campfire had burned down to a glowing pile of embers that barely cast enough light for me to see Myrain, who sat keeping watch nearby.

The voices were so close . . . if I could just see the people they belonged to . . .

And finally, I put two and two together.

The spirits who inhabited the forest. An indefinable number of voices speaking one over the other, male indistinguishable from female. I didn't get the impression they were evil . . . just that there were a lot of them.

I became aware of two things:

The first was that I wasn't afraid.

The second was that Myrain obviously couldn't hear them. I smiled to myself as I pictured him fleeing the cursed forest. I sat still, listening. The spirits' language sounded familiar somehow, but instead of being reassuring, it filled me with melancholy. As if I had just found out that a dear childhood friend had been dead for some time.

All those voices, all that pain. I couldn't help but perceive a sense of disorder. I thought of my mother, of her passion for order and precision.

I remembered a conversation I'd had with her three years before, when I was beginning to study harmony and composition from the books in the royal library. She had noticed that I was disappearing after my lessons with Dainefin for far longer than usual, and had come looking for me.

She'd found me surrounded by open books and drawings of planets and various schemes that appeared mathematical, even though they'd all been made up by me, and as such devoid of any scientific foundation. Or rather, the foundation was there, all right – I'd dragged up the circle of fifths and several astronomical models – but all those different elements had been thrown in together willy-nilly, according to whatever theory I had most recently come across.

'What are you studying?' she asked.

'The harmony of spheres,' I answered in the tone of a monk who has just discovered proof of God's existence. With irrepressible enthusiasm, I proceeded to explain that there had been Old-World composers who believed that music could somehow exist in the universe independently from us.

'Maybe music simply exists, and we just discover it!' I said, almost immediately regretting my words. My mother was such a practical person, philosophical debates were really not her thing. I'd feared she would mock me for having my head in the clouds.

Instead, she was very attentive, taking a few seconds to consider what I had said. She eventually replied, 'Perhaps it does exist, and your task is to bring order to it.'

In her simplicity, my mother had brought order to my thoughts too, completing a picture that I had already been slowly putting together. The disposition of notes in a melody, the vertical relationship tying them together into a chord, the connections between chords or the degrees of a scale . . . . It was all about order . . .

My yearning for her was suddenly so strong that my stomach hurt. I realised just how different we'd been, but also how neither of us had ever tired of trying to understand the other, whatever it took.

The chaos inside of me wasn't that different from what was taking place around me. As I allowed the anguish of the Hatablar spirits to pass through me, I fed my own pain into it. The forest was animated by a chorus of asynchronous voices that were only in need of direction.

I focussed on the voices, discerning timbre and range, identifying different melodies. Unable to sing myself, I resorted to gestures, directing my choir as I had often imagined doing during a sung Mass in the cathedral. The voices followed me and, little by little, each one found its place in the ensemble.

A polyphony wrote itself in the air, and for the duration of the performance I felt the Empathic Aura loosen its grip, allowing me to enjoy the music I had discovered.

It wasn't mine, I had only brought some order to it.

I laid back down, but kept my eyes open, listening to the forest. When I saw the first glimmers of dawn filter through the trees, I realised Myrain and Dainefin were both asleep, unaware of the hymn of pain slowly fading into the air of Hatablar. The voices were sometimes louder, sometimes softer. They died down completely in the end, or perhaps the murmuring continued as I dozed off, I don't remember.

Chapter 14

Myrain was so relieved after the previous night's reconciliation that he nattered all morning, determined to make his mark on Dainefin's heart with banter and jokes. But she wasn't in the mood, and hardly responded. I made a special effort to give him a little attention by writing down a report of my night.

I couldn't tell whether it was my Empathic Aura becoming more sophisticated over time, or the Valiant simply learning to interpret my signals, but in any case, he was beginning to pick up a few more things. He was visibly emotional, and asked for every little detail of my encounter with the forest spirits.

When I asked Dainefin for her thoughts on the voices I'd heard, she gave a frosty reply.

'It was probably just a dream, Ly.'

That was unlike her. Myrain and I decided it was best not to pester her, so we let it slide.

I was sure I hadn't been dreaming, and I certainly wasn't losing my mind. It was of course possible that the

Empathic Aura had been playing nasty tricks on me as I slept, but I was still able to distinguish visions from real life. I knew what I had heard, and if Dainefin didn't believe me, that was her problem.

I'd only had the Empathic Aura for a short while, but that had been long enough to cast doubt over everything I had ever been certain of. I had accepted the Empathic Aura itself so easily, the visions, hata honey, spirits . . . . The truth was, I had exhausted my capacity for wonderment. I was becoming quite skilled at putting my mind to rest.

It was evening by the time we emerged from the forest and found an inn. Myrain announced that instead of going back to Gaudrot's, he would ride north to reach Amarantha as soon as possible.

Be honest now . . . you just don't want to go back into the forest because you're scared of ghosts.

Myrain ruffled my hair. 'No, Your Highness, I'm more scared of the living.'

What will happen to Yodne?

'I'll go back to Gaudrot's to collect her when things have calmed down a little. He'll take good care of her. For now, I'll just use one of the horses they have here.'

We parted the following day at dawn, me and Dainefin heading southeast to Shamabat, and the Valiant north to the capital. After Dainefin and I had stopped for breakfast and continued our march, I told her about my most recent vision. She remained silent.

Later that morning, Dainefin proposed a lesson, and even though I wasn't exactly in the mood, I took her up on it; I was hoping it would distract her from the thought of returning to Shamabat.

'What do you want to learn about today?'

Politics. Tell me about the Separatists.

Dainefin studied me with her piercing eyes and eventually nodded.

'Remember when you'd just turned nine, that summer when it wouldn't stop raining?'

Now she mentioned it, I did. It was the summer that I'd discovered the Royal Library, and since then not a week had gone by without me visiting at least three times. I'd forgotten why I'd begun to spend time there in the first place: it had been the incessant rain.

'Between that spring and the autumn of the following year,' Dainefin continued, 'the weather went crazy. We had torrential rain throughout spring, and storms in summer. There was no more rain in the autumn, but it was as cold as the dead of winter. For us in the capital, the rain eased off by the winter of the second year, but Murihen and the border villages were gripped by frost.'

The harvest . . .

'There was no harvest. The farmers only managed to salvage enough to survive. Both kingdoms had to live off their emergency stores, of salt as well as grain because the salterns of Murihen couldn't be operated, it was too damp.'

I had never seen a saltern. Dainefin told me there was one just north of Shamabat, but unfortunately it would be out of our way.

'Murihen was hit much harder than Amarantha. Your father started sending over wagon-loads of essential provisions, but frost and famine were still killing people in droves. That was why your father and uncle negotiated the transport of people across the border. These measures became known as "The Salterns Edict". Your father decided to give precedence to the poorest in Murihen, in and around the capital, over his own people in the border villages.'

I was starting to get a picture of what must have happened next, but I let Dainefin finish the story.

'For a few years, all of our efforts were focussed on limiting the consequences of those two disastrous years. Not only hunger and poverty, but also all the crime that followed, particularly along the border. Some families stopped paying taxes, or held back part of them as a sort of compensation for being discriminated against by your father during the famine.'

Discriminated against?

'Left for last. At the time, there was no alternative. In the border villages, families struggled. But in Murihen they starved.'

But why are they called 'Separatists'? What do they want to separate from?

'During the first few years people said they'd rather separate from Amarantha and become annexed to Murihen. Roy is thinking that now they may have moved beyond that idea and started to plan the creation of an independent territory, a strip of land running from the Serra del Lárr to the south coast. Then the only land border between Murihen and Amarantha would stretch along the mountains to the north. Where there are no viable commercial routes at present.'

I knew that the mountain passes north of the Serra del Lárr lay under snowfields that only melted in the summer months. I was no longer surprised that Sonni could be so fascinated by this topic. He loved puzzles as much as he loved making everyone happy; I just knew he must be straining to get to work and start helping Father in the negotiations. I wondered if Anur, too, would engage once he became Prince Regent. For a moment I hoped he would be happier in Murihen than he'd been in Amarantha, and that the Separatists would not resent him.

I don't understand how that would lead to—

'Neither do I.' With her interruption, Dainefin spared me from articulating the thought that my mother had been murdered over politics. 'Roy and I are beginning to think that the poison was not meant for her.'

A mistake?

She nodded. 'I'm sorry,' she said, as if it had been her fault. 'I am so very sorry, Lyria.'

I was horrified. A twist of fate? It was easier to bear the thought that my mother had been murdered for a reason. But for it to be a cruel mistake . . .

If not her, then who?

'I don't know,' she said. 'Your father, probably.'

I asked no more questions. We walked on in silence, and when we stopped for lunch, Dainefin didn't eat a single bite.

My thoughts were spinning so fast I was beginning

to feel sick. We didn't know who the poison was meant for, nor who had poured it or why. If even Dainefin didn't know what to say, what was I to make of it all?

I turned my attention back to music to try and placate the swirling vortex of thought and emotion in my mind, pushing back distractions with a violent 'no thanks' every time they threatened to intrude.

It was mid-afternoon when we had our first glimpse of the sea, but we didn't reach Shamabat until just before dinner time. By then, my mind had reviewed every single reason to put one foot in front of the other and played every tune I knew.

As we walked downhill, the scrub became more and more dense, and it was impossible to see through.

Where are the olive trees?

'On the other side of the village,' said Dainefin. 'You can't see them from here.'

Once we had passed the last conifer, we were faced with a fork in the path: one led to the village, the other to the shore.

The houses of Shamabat were aglow in the setting sun, as if the village were a little drop of amber set in the finger of sand that extended from the bay. The sun, preparing to slide beyond the hills behind the village, gilded the houses with its dying light. The sea was a lilac-coloured sheet pierced by a stretch of rocks and a handful of fishing boats.

'We can go round by the seaside, if you like,' said Dainefin, taking the path paved with wooden boards half-buried in sand.

Dainefin took off her sandals, and that seemed like a good idea to me. As the sand tickled my toes, I was transported back to the little cove below my home. The sand of Shamabat was much finer though, as pale as the crags that stood out at the far end of the bay. The crags, the sand, the houses on the hilltop: all white, apart from the dozen or so brightly painted cottages along the shore. Red, yellow, green. Pink, blue, orange.

Dainefin explained that those were the fishermen's cottages. 'The boats are painted the same colours,' she added, pointing at the ones currently on the beach.

I nosed around a boat painted lemon yellow. A fishing net hung over the side, the clay weights covered by a thin layer of sand and encrusted with limpets. A few shells were caught in the mesh, but when I reached out to loosen one, Dainefin warned me off.

'Don't touch. There are some crabby fishermen round these parts.'

I was intrigued by her absent-minded tone. Dainefin was standing in front of a long, sky-blue boat. She reached over, as if to touch a spot on the hull where the paint was peeling off. Her hand stopped in mid-air.

Suddenly, she started off again and I had to run to catch up.

Why are there no fishermen in the capital?

'Because of its position,' she replied. 'The city is raised above the sea. The strip of sand at the base of the promontory disappears under the high tide.

'At Shamabat, the range of the tide isn't as great, so the boats are safer.'

How long has it been since a ship last arrived in Amarantha?

She understood immediately that I was referring to the ships loaded with men and women from the Old World. During my afternoons in the library I had come across the immigration records, which documented every single traveller who had made landfall in the capital. I had scanned those lists over and over, imagining the stories of people I knew only by their names and cities of origin.

'Since Aur-Lee's fleet came over. In the beginning, he maintained the first ships. The idea was to use them to transport goods along the coast, but that turned out to be impractical so they were dismantled for wood.'

To make what?

'The seats in the cathedral, among other things,' Dainefin answered.

How do you know that?

'The bishop told me. You're not the only one who likes to ask lots of questions,' replied the Priestess.

Perhaps I should have left her alone and searched Aur-Lee's journal for the answers I needed, but it was so convenient having a living encyclopaedia at my disposal.

But if all the ships that landed here were dismantled . . . do you mean that not a single one ever went back?

'Back to the Old World?'
Yes.

'No, not one. Who would have wanted to do that?'

I had heard this story before, but I couldn't recall the details. I did remember the day Dainefin taught us about the foundation of Amarantha. Sonni had taken notes, while I had yawned.

'Aur-Lee stated very clearly that anyone wishing to return to the Old World would only have to ask, and he'd take charge of funding the whole enterprise. But no one ever came forward. Who would want to cross the oceans of half the world, only to turn around and go back to . . . well, whatever they'd fled from?'

She wasn't wrong. But I had known neither war nor hunger, and as far as I was concerned, I wouldn't have minded leaving again – perhaps forever – in search of answers.

'Your answers are closer than you think,' said Dainefin, anguish settling on her face once more.

I didn't know what had happened to her in Shamabat, or why it made her so sad. Perhaps she wanted to avoid seeing someone who'd hurt her. An old love or a broken friendship.

Come on, no one will recognise you. It's been seventeen years, so much must have changed.

I was used to change, I lived in the capital. I had no idea that in villages like Shamabat – or Denhole – time flowed to a different rhythm, passing down memories and grievances from generation to generation.

'I wish . . .'

We turned onto a lane between two rows of colourful houses, then emerged onto the high street. It was a market day, but the stall-holders were packing up for the night, loading carts and mules, washing the street down.

The first to notice us was a woman around sixty or so, who turned to her companion and whispered, loud enough for us to hear: 'What is *she* doing here?'

'She's back,' someone else murmured.

'The nerve.'

'Shame!'

'The bare-faced cheek of it.'

'Shame!' someone said a little louder.

That pillorying was what followed us the entire gauntlet of Shamabat's high street.

I no longer had any doubts about Dainefin's reasons for dreading her return. The entire village seemed to hate her. A woman putting leftover loaves into canvas sacks spat at Dainefin's feet when she saw her. The other market women followed suit.

Dainefin swerved to give the stalls the widest possible berth.

A woman carrying her shopping home put her bags down when she saw the Priestess. She stood staring, arms crossed over her chest, and if looks could kill hers would have done so in the most horrid possible way.

'Welcome to Shamabat,' said Dainefin wryly.

As if the villagers' rejection of Dainefin wasn't enough, I could sense that the Empathic Aura was driving them off and that I too was not welcome there.

We picked up our pace.

We walked along a couple of narrow lanes, then

down a long ramp whose steps led to the door of a dark green building. It stuck out like a sore thumb amongst all the white of the surrounding walls. A sign above the door read '*Typographer*'.

Dainefin opened the door without knocking and stepped inside.

'Master Lohm,' she called.

An old man turned towards us, his hands stained with ink. It took a second, but I knew he'd recognised Dainefin once he began to hop around her, laughing like a madman.

Dainefin let herself be hugged. The old man kissed her on both cheeks and ruffled her hair.

'I knew you'd be back!' he crowed.

'Did you? How, when I didn't know it myself?' Dainefin smiled.

'Call it a hunch . . . or just an old man's wishful thinking.'

His eyes filled with tears and he seemed about to burst from happiness at any moment. He was hunched over and thin as a rake, with a pointy chin and a few grey hairs clinging to the nape of his neck and above his ears. I looked around the windowless room, finding that piles of books were the only decoration.

They were everywhere. Brand new books. And paper! Rolls of it taller than me filled one corner, partly obstructing a passage to a semi-hidden box room. I wanted to go over for a better look but Dainefin was introducing me.

'– A dear friend from Amarantha,' she said.

'Thelonius Eugenius Lohm, at your service.'

'Those aren't his real given names,' Dainefin revealed in a stage whisper. 'He just likes to make up new ones every day.'

'All right, you may call me Lohm,' he obliged without a hint of resentment.

I extended my hand to shake his, but he grasped it and kissed it instead, with a bow. In my seventeen years as Princess of Amarantha, that had only happened to me once, and Uncle Hervin had done it as a joke. Lohm's back made an alarming noise as he straightened, but his smile never faltered.

'We're on our way towards Styr,' Dainefin explained. 'We need a bed for the night.'

'There's no need to ask,' he replied. 'Just let me clean myself up.'

Master Lohm disappeared into the box room. When he came out of it, he was holding a wet rag at least as filthy as the hands he was trying to clean.

'There we are, much better. Does anyone know you're here, child?' he asked Dainefin.

'Since we came by the market place,' she answered, 'I presume the rumours must be travelling to the four corners of the continent as we speak.'

'Oh. I am sorry, my dear,' said Lohm.

Even though I'd been able to keep the Empathic Aura in check so far, I couldn't pretend I hadn't noticed the terrible things the villagers had whispered as we passed them, not to mention the spitting.

In any case, Master Lohm's irrepressible happiness

compensated for our unfortunate parade. He pulled an old mattress out of a cupboard and laid it on the floor. Then he exhumed blankets and sheets that were more or less clean – though it looked like not even bedding was safe from the ink here – and let Dainefin help him make up the bed.

Dainefin's gaze rested on a portrait on the shelf of a small display cabinet. Lohm noticed. 'I can call him over, if you want,' he said.

'Not now, Master Lohm. He'll hear about it anyway. I'm sure he'll wash up . . .'

The portrait showed two men – probably brothers – who were almost identical, both dark-haired with green eyes. One of them had an unkempt beard and a darker complexion. I wondered which of the two Dainefin and Lohm were referring to.

Master Lohm told us to make ourselves at home, and went upstairs to start cooking dinner.

Is he the typographer you used to work for?

Dainefin nodded.

I thought he was dead.

The Priestess burst out laughing. 'Who, Master Lohm? He'll never die, that one, I'm telling you.'

She seemed to have cheered up, but the Empathic Aura didn't think twice about ruining that rare moment of peace.

Who was Master Lohm talking about?

'An old friend.'

Dainefin clammed up again, and began to walk around the room reading the spines of all the books. I would have done that myself, if I hadn't been distracted by the lovely smell of seafood stew drifting down from the kitchen.

Lohm peeked round a door at the top of the stairs, lilting: 'It's rea-dyyyy!'

Weird old man.

'Oh. Just wait 'til you know him better,' said Dainefin with a grin.

Master Lohm's kitchen comfortably held . . . half a person. Lohm himself, to be precise, who was so thin he could have fit in the gaps between the tiles. The table in the middle of the room was barely larger than a stool, while the four stools around it looked like they had been made for dolls, rather than human beings.

'Eat, eat, you're looking peaky,' he told me. 'Is Dainefin not feeding you? You'll never get over that sore throat if you don't eat. It is a bad sore throat you have, isn't it? You're showing all the signs. You don't speak, for one. Bad sign, that. And you're a bit off colour, as well. That's why you have to eat. Lohm's stew will have you back on your feet in no time.'

The smells of his cooking alone had helped me recover from the exhaustion of the journey, and the old man's good humour was rubbing off on me, making me even hungrier. I dipped my wooden spoon into the sauce. Drops of olive oil floated on the surface, along with a few parsley leaves and flakes of hot pepper. Master Lohm was a serious cook: by the second mouthful I was ready to dance on the table. There was a zesty hint of wine to the stew, and it was rich with breadcrumbs. Chopped tomatoes and chunks of toasted bread bobbed in every spoonful.

'Lohm!' shouted a voice from outside. 'Lohm, you old fool!'

Master Lohm sat upright on his stool. 'It appears we have a guest. Just as well there's enough for everyone.'

Dainefin smiled weakly.

'Where is she?' the stranger roared from downstairs.

'Up here,' Lohm shouted back. 'She came with a friend. Lovely girl. Of very few words. Zero words, in fact.'

I heard the newcomer thundering up the stairs three or four steps at a time, and I shifted closer to Dainefin, fearing that he wanted to harm her.

'You could have written!'

An enormous figure filled the doorway to the kitchen. But there was no trace of hostility on his face, which was cracking in a huge smile. He was the bearded brother from the portrait – albeit with a little extra weight on him.

'I didn't know I would be passing through, Móiras, or you would have been the first to know.'

Old Master Lohm cleared his throat.

'The second to know,' she corrected herself.

Móiras wrapped the Priestess in a big hug, and for a few seconds she disappeared entirely into his arms. Then he released her and kissed the top of her head, as if they'd known each other all their lives.

'The old fool kept saying you'd be back, but I

didn't want to get my hopes up. And now look!'

'We're only passing through, Móiras. We're headed to Styr.'

As if he were in his own home, Móiras served himself a few ladlefuls of stew, which he bolted down standing up, leaning back against the wall. The kitchen had already been at maximum capacity with the three of us and now that Móiras was in the room, it was bursting at the seams.

'Styr? How are you getting there?' he asked.

'On foot,' answered Dainefin.

'No way,' he said. 'I'll take you in the cart.'

'That would be a pointless trip for you!'

'Yes, but at least I'll get to spend time with you,' he replied in a brotherly way. 'We've missed you round here.'

She didn't answer, but Móiras seemed to understand what was going through her mind.

'Forget about those old biddies. Sooner or later they'll bite their tongues by accident and die of their own poison. You'll see. If they don't, I'll make sure they choke on a nice big fishbone.'

'How long will you stay, child?' asked Master Lohm.

'We were thinking of leaving tomorrow at first light.'

'No, we'll set off around nine,' Móiras decided. 'That'll give me time for my morning fishing. I'll take out the cart tonight so we can be more quicker after I get back.'

'Just quicker,' Dainefin corrected him. 'There's no

need to add the "more".'

'You what?'

'"So we can be quicker", not "more quicker".'

Móiras roared with laughter. Dainefin and Lohm joined in.

'I can't tell you how much we've missed you,' Móiras repeated. He licked the sauce from his bowl, and once he'd polished it properly, gave me a curious look.

'What about the kid, where did you find her?'

'In the capital. A pupil of mine.'

Master Lohm turned to her with glittering eyes. 'You're still teaching?'

'In a way,' she replied.

The old man murmured, 'Good for you, good for you. Since you went away . . .'

'No one comes to teach any more,' Móiras picked up where he'd left off. 'The only people who can read in the village are those who learned from you. And you could count us on your two hands and have fingers to spare.'

'But even they don't read any more,' said Lohm. 'Everything I print goes to the capital or the towns of the north, nobody wants books in this fish-eater's den.'

'Hey! I read,' Móiras protested. 'I may take my time, but I read. I'm not as fast as Ruthven was, but I still make the effort.'

Ruthven. It became immediately clear that I was the only one in the room to have no idea who he was. Old Lohm glanced at Dainefin in alarm, then at Móiras.

I looked to Dainefin and saw her fingernails

digging into her thighs, her dinner suddenly forgotten, her eyes wet. Since she never spoke of her past, I assumed she hadn't said or heard that name since moving to the capital seventeen years ago.

I watched her haul back the tears and smile weakly at Móiras. He didn't seem to notice, expanding on the topic while serving himself a second portion of stew.

'He could borrow any book he wanted from this old grouch,' he said. 'I have to go down on my knees and beg.'

'That's because it takes you two weeks to get through a book. You take it out on the boat and when you return it, the pages are warped and there's sand all over the cover,' Lohm shot back.

'You know what? The next one you're not getting back at all. I wish I'd kept the last one, I loved it.'

Móiras launched into a passionate argument in favour of the book he'd read, but the life had gone out of the Priestess. Master Lohm stood and cleared the table. I squeezed by Móiras to give him a hand with the washing up, but kept an eye on Dainefin. Móiras sat on Master Lohm's stool and Dainefin was nodding along to his enthusiastic chatter without seeming to take in a single word.

It took Móiras a while, but he did eventually notice that he no longer had an audience.

'Forgive me, it's just been so long since I last saw you . . .'

'It's not that. Sorry, I just need a little fresh air,' said Dainefin, stroking his shoulder as she got up to leave.

'Poor love,' said Old Lohm once she had left the

kitchen. 'It can't have been easy, coming back here. All those geese in the market must have put the wind up her.'

I remembered all the terrible things the village women had said to Dainefin, and hoped I would never see them again.

Móiras was studying me. 'Are you her only pupil?'

I nodded. In theory, Sonni was her pupil too, but he hadn't been to our lessons for months. He was passionate about politics but less interested in the subjects Dainefin taught me: languages, literature, Old-World history.

'You must be pretty special,' he said.

Old Lohm put his arm around me. 'Of course she's special. You should have seen the way she looked round my workshop . . . devouring the books with her eyes, she was,' he said, filling me with pride. Then he turned to me. 'Ruthven would have liked you. He too had that spark in his eye, but we were all a bit absent-minded and his spark went out too soon.'

'Has Dainefin told you anything about my brother?' Móiras asked, interrupting Lohm.

I shook my head, lowering my eyes. Dainefin never told me a thing about herself.

'She never let me in either, and I was going to be her brother-in-law.'

That detail caught me completely off-guard. Dainefin's past in Shamabat suddenly became more real. It wasn't a vague past made of childhood memories, but a whole other life. Before she'd arrived in Amarantha, Dainefin had been a bride-to-be.

'I'll take you out on the boat with me tomorrow, if you don't mind getting up early. I'm like a bear with a sore head first thing in the morning, but I promise I'll be on my best behaviour. Want to come?'

I nodded, remembering something my mother always used to say: *'We'll sleep when we're dead.'*

Chapter 15

Móiras woke me up with a whistle. I looked out through the open door and saw him in the street with Dainefin, both of them bursting with energy despite the grey light of dawn. He told me he'd wait for me on the beach, and I had to exert quite a bit of self-discipline to stop myself from going back to bed. I took my time getting dressed, and declined Master Lohm's offer of breakfast of bread and onions so I wouldn't be late meeting Móiras. And because, well, who ate bread and onions at five in the morning?

Móiras's boat had been pushed to the shoreline and he was standing next to it, waiting for me. Many of the fishermen were already on the water, but a few stragglers saw me walking across the beach and started heckling him.

'Who's that, your new girlfriend?'

'No, she's the one from the capital, in't she? Turned up with Miss Schoolteacher.'

'*That* schoolteacher? You thinking of throwing this one overboard to get your revenge, are you?'

It was all water off a duck's back. Móiras pushed his sky-blue boat into the water – the boat Dainefin had stopped by the previous evening – and motioned for me to follow.

'Ignore them, they're a pack of morons. They're like this every morning, because they have nothing else to do.'

He, on the other hand, brought something to read every day, he said. It must have been so annoying to be surrounded by people like that while trying to read. I was grateful there weren't ever many people in Aur-Lee's Royal Library, nor in the cove where I went to hide out with a book.

I followed Móiras into the shallows with my trousers rolled up to my knees, and was surprised by the temperature of the water. It was almost warm on my skin. The sea at Amarantha was too rough to hold on to any of the previous day's heat.

Móiras helped me on board and pushed the boat further into the water until it was up to his thighs, then he gracefully climbed in and sat down in front of me. He inserted his oars into the rowlocks and began to row with his back to the prow.

I was riveted by the sight of his arms flexing and stretching in synchrony with his body. I was impressed he wasn't gasping; he acted as if he weren't doing anything more complicated than peeling an apple. He didn't even need to turn and look where he was going, he was just keeping an eye on the fishermen who'd set sail after us, to make sure they didn't get too close.

'Me and Dainefin had a chat,' he said.

When?

Móiras looked surprised, but only a little. If he had spoken to Dainefin, she must have prepared him for the feeling of my Empathic Aura.

'Earlier, while you were sleeping.'

So you know about the Empathic Aura.

He nodded.

'I didn't know it was called that 'til today, but obviously it wasn't the first time that . . .'

What?

'Dainefin. She had it when she turned up in Shamabat out of nowhere. Didn't she . . . didn't she tell you?'

Turned up? Out of nowhere? Dainefin wasn't born here?

I skipped right over the fact that Dainefin had suffered from Empathic Aura – what Móiras had just told me unmade the picture I had created of her life in my head. A niggling little voice that I hadn't heard in over a month piped up: *She's not who you think she is.*

Móiras cast his nets and sat down again with a sigh. 'I wish I could say that she has changed since then . . . but she hasn't, not one jot.'

Where is Dainefin from? Why did she have the Empathic Aura? Why did she choose to come to Shamabat?

'I have no idea,' said Móiras. 'But I can tell you about her life after she moved here. That part, I know well.'

The nets had been cast; all we had to do now was wait for them to fill. The other fishermen were much closer to shore, while Móiras had opted to fish by the arc of rocks that opened out on one side of the cliff. We found ourselves some rocks to sit on and tied up the boat.

He pulled a few limpets off the surface and as he sucked them, I entertained myself by imagining a younger, thinner version of Móiras sitting on the same rock with a book, many years before.

'We weren't quite thirty yet, me and Ruthven, when Dainefin knocked on Lohm's door. I was out fishing that day, Ruthven was doing deliveries for the old man. He found her in Lohm's study, copying out a bunch of pages by hand. When he got home that night he just went on and on about her. You know what I mean? He was cooked. Like a fish. Smitten.

'Anyway, I was dying to meet her myself, so I went round to Lohm's for a coffee the next day. Ruthven was already there, sitting next to her while Old Lohm . . . well, he was teaching her to read and write.'

This was too much. Dainefin, unable to read and write? At the age of twenty, or twenty-five, or whatever age she'd been then?

'From then on, my brother, who had never before in his life expressed a wish to learn his letters, would only talk about two things: Dainefin and books. Bit by bit he got me into it too, and Old Lohm found himself teaching three fully grown adults what the children of today learn at six years old. Well, not all of them. Those in the capital, like. Children round here are more ignorant than these limpets,' he said, adding another shell to his little pile.

'I became quite fond of Dainefin, even if she was the strangest person I'd ever met. She never said a word, but she and Dainefin would "talk" for hours. It took me a while to understand her. It made me feel uncomfortable at first . . .'

To feel what she was feeling, while she was feeling it?

'That's right. But then I learnt to read her, that's what Ruthven used to call it. Like how I can with you, now.'

This was how Dainefin knew everything about the Empathic Aura. She'd experienced it herself. I felt stupid for not realising that sooner.

When did she start speaking again? What happened?

'Nothing,' said Móiras. 'Nothing happened. She just spoke. Ruthven told me that he took her out to the rocks, and declared his love. And she said . . . well, I don't know exactly what she said, but she answered out loud, that's the point.'

Great. All I need is a boyfriend then.

Móiras burst out laughing. 'Sorry, darling, I'm a bit too old for you.'

I rolled my eyes good-naturedly.

So Dainefin had been through it all herself, had she? But two things were still unclear:

What caused Dainefin's Empathic Aura? And why did she leave?

Had something happened to Ruthven?

'I don't know how she got ill or why she got better,'

Móiras continued, 'but when she started speaking again, she had the idea of setting up a school for the village children in the typography workshop. Lohm, as you can imagine, was in heaven. She and Ruthven were teaching together. Two years later he asked her to marry him. A few months after that, he died at sea.'

He paused to search for words. 'He just . . . he died at sea,' he repeated softly. 'There's some who think he killed himself. There's others even think it was Dainefin who did it.'

Dainefin? But why would she . . . ?

It was absurd.

'Don't ask me,' sighed Móiras. 'The sand-heads in this village, well, they never did like Dainefin. The women especially. For me, I don't believe either theory.'

You think someone else killed him?

'Oh no,' he hurried to clarify. 'I think it was an accident. Wouldn't be the first round here to take sick with sunstroke or be swept off by the sea while out fishing. Accidents happen. It's a fisherman's life, that's how it is.'

How could Móiras take his brother's death so casually? I wouldn't dream of thinking about my mother's death in terms of 'accidents happen', even if the poison hadn't been meant for her . . .

'Hey minnow, don't think I took it so philosophically at first. If it hadn't been for Old Lohm dragging me out of bed by my ear, I would have stayed shut up in my bedroom brooding over the how and why for months. I didn't want to see anyone. Not even Dainefin, who kept looking after me in spite of everything. She forced me to eat, came fishing with me . . . . She gave me books to read and then talked about them with me.'

But . . . wasn't she upset too?

'She was. And on top of everything, the village women were making her life hell. She was forced to close down the school, but she carried on helping Lohm with the books and work and all that – I think she had to keep busy. It looked like she was doing as well as she could be. Then, one day, four months after Ruthven's death, she packed her bags and left without a word to anyone. It was the third of December. The day she and Ruthven were going to get married.' He paused, deep in thought, then shook himself and said, 'And now, seventeen and a half years later, here she is again.'

For one day.

'Even less than that,' he said, with another sigh.

She'd gone from Shamabat to Amarantha, one tragedy to another. I could not banish from my mind the thought that something terrible must have happened to Dainefin before she washed up in Shamabat. What calamity had led her here in the first place?

'She's no good at personal questions, is our Dainefin. She never told us where she'd come from. I imagined she must have had a hard life. If you can't speak at that age . . .'

Now I thought of it, Dainefin had never shared a single childhood memory with me. I'd assumed that she must have spent her youth amongst the fishing boats of Shamabat.

'What's past is past,' said Móiras.

He said it weakly but without sarcasm. It sounded like a phrase he'd repeated so often it had lost all meaning.

He stood, throwing the limpet shells into the sea. Then he helped me get back on board without hurting myself, and hauled his net back in. It was almost empty.

'I have a feeling we came out a bit late,' he said.

I was mortified to have ruined his catch with my laziness.

'Don't worry about it. I wasn't planning on taking my wares to the market anyway, not after that scene yesterday. They can go and fry their brains in the same pans as their squid. I'll keep these to myself,' he concluded, pointing at the handful of fish he had pulled up.

Móiras rowed the boat back to shore, and we dragged it onto the sand.

'Hurry back to Lohm's and get your things ready. Dainefin wants to set off in an hour,' he said.

Less than an hour later I was all packed and trying to say goodbye to Old Lohm.

'Nooo, don't you go as well!' he howled. 'It's been so nice having you around. Would you like to take some fish stew to eat on the journey?'

I gave him to understand that I wasn't hungry. Just the thought of travelling by cart made my stomach roil, so I didn't want to push my luck.

'You give the impression of someone who could talk about books from dawn 'til dusk,' said Master Lohm. 'I'm so sorry to see you go.'

He gave me a hug, then disappeared into the box room at the back. 'I have something for you.' He returned and handed me a small package wrapped in brown paper.

Thank you.

'You're welcome,' he replied, pausing a moment as he tried to figure out if he'd really heard that, or just imagined it.

The package contained a notebook bound in blue leather, with thick, rough pages, and a reed pen with a graphite tip engraved with my initials. The 'L' and the 'D' were entwined in such a way that a three-quarter turn made them look like a treble clef.

'The engraving is Móiras's work. That's why it's not as neat as it could be . . .' Lohm pointed out.

'These aren't the hands of a goldsmith, but guess whose table they put fish on every day?' said Móiras, who was just coming in with Dainefin. He handed Lohm a bag of salt-fish and told us to hurry our good-byes.

'I want to get going before the streets start swarming with old biddies.'

Old Lohm hugged Dainefin, holding her tight.

'I will not die before you come and see me one last time.'

'You'll say the same next time I come and see you. And the time after that.'

'Good, we'll just see when the last time stops being the penultimate time.'

'There will always be a next time, Master *Thelonius Eugenius* Lohm.'

It took six days to reach Styr. During our journey, the Empathic Aura didn't make a big fuss over all the things Dainefin had kept from me, even though deep down I was smarting that she hadn't confided in me as I always had in her, even before I fell ill. Móiras's company during those days revived the Priestess's spirit and I gave them space to reconnect.

I tried reading Aur-Lee's journal, but immediately felt sick. Writing was no good either. No sooner was the tip of the graphite poised over the paper than my stomach protested.

I closed the notebook, telling myself that I didn't know what to write anyway. I paused to consider everything that had happened: my mother's death, Denhole, Hatablar, Shamabat and the rest of my journey, still unknown. Did I really feel like writing it all down? No, I couldn't see the point. Fixing the most painful moments of my life on paper would not help me overcome them. And writing down what I was unable to say out loud would only be one more excuse never to speak again.

Since there was nothing else to do, I listened to Móiras and Dainefin's conversation. They talked as if

Dainefin had never left Shamabat, chatting for hours on end about Lohm's books and his strange antics.

Móiras told her that a few years earlier Lohm had circulated a fake edict from my father obliging every citizen of the realm to learn to read – only to be thwarted by the fact that hardly anyone was able to read his placards.

Then there was the time Lohm had gone on hunger strike: he'd sat down in the middle of the market place and declared he would only start eating again when someone bought a copy of his history of Shamabat, a collection of interviews with local people. He lasted two days, until Móiras tempted him with a dish of peppery mussels steamed in white wine.

Móiras had enough tales to keep us entertained throughout the journey, but I could feel his carefree tone become more strained the closer we got to Styr. On the morning of the sixth day, the time came for the two of them to clear the air. A few hours more, and they would be saying goodbye for some time, if not forever.

They sat next to each other up front, while I perched on the back of the cart. Eavesdropping had become a habit by then. Maybe it was my way of trying to understand Dainefin through the things she said to others, since she never told me anything herself. I shifted, searching for a listening position that wouldn't bring on a bout of nausea.

'. . . And so, partly because I didn't want to walk out on the children, partly because of Council matters, I haven't left the capital since,' she was saying.

'You're on the Council?' said Móiras.

'I am. It was King Uriel who put the idea to me, once Lyria and Sonni had grown up a bit. It's been a godsend. At least I can make myself useful.'

'You, on the King's Council . . .'

Dainefin nodded, omitting that most decisions were first vetted by her, *then* by the King, and *then* by the Council. Móiras was having enough trouble believing her story.

'So you've been living at court all these years . . .'

'Yes.'

'With the royal family.'

'Yes.'

'And you took care of Prince Sonni and Princess Lyria – who is, at this moment, sat in the back of my cart.'

'Precisely.'

I wouldn't have known what to say either. To become tutor to the King's children was quite a leap from working at a village typographer's.

'To think that all these years, back and forth to the capital with Lohm's books . . . I never knew you were living there. I imagined you in a village somewhere, changing the lives of another bunch of their kids.'

'What about you?' Dainefin asked him.

As it turned out, Móiras too had a story to tell.

'I got married.'

Dainefin was about to congratulate him, but he went on, 'It's not . . . going that well. Kyriann is in love with someone else. She's started talking about children, but I . . . I don't want to be asking myself if they're mine, you know?'

She nodded. 'Is that the only reason you don't want children?' she asked after a brief silence.

In his shoes, I would have told her to back off and mind her own business. I hadn't fully understood how deep their friendship was until Móiras answered the question.

'No, it's not the only reason. I've never really loved her. And I've always known that.'

Why did he marry her, then? Dainefin didn't ask him that, which could only mean one thing: she already knew the answer.

'Your parents,' she said at last, to confirm. Or to include me, perhaps.

'That's right,' he replied. 'After Ruthven . . .'

Móiras had no need to finish that sentence, it was clear enough.

'You can't let them decide for you,' said Dainefin.

He shrugged. 'I just wanted to make them happy.'

'Do they know?' Dainefin asked.

'That Kyriann has another man? I don't know,' he answered. 'My mother might. But she's never asked me anything.'

Mothers don't need to ask questions, I thought. My own mother had always known more than she let on too.

Móiras's silence said he'd run out of things to say on the matter. Dainefin, who usually eviscerated a problem until she'd dredged up at least half a dozen possible solutions, was respectful of her friend's personal space and allowed him to change the subject.

He asked her about her duties as a Council member and Dainefin satisfied his every query. But when Móiras asked her about Anur's future coronation, I heard her hesitate. I realised that when I'd told her about my latest vision, I hadn't mentioned Sonni – I had only talked of Anur.

Did you know about the Council wanting to put Sonni on the throne? Instead of Anur?

'It was my idea,' she answered, turning to face me. 'I've been having second thoughts about Anur over the past few years, so at the end of March I called a Council vote on delaying the coronation. The idea was to propose that Anur reign over Murihen, instead of Amarantha. I thought he'd be happier there with your aunt and uncle, away from your father. And then Sonni would . . .' she trailed off, leaving the rest to be understood. 'The Council voted unanimously in favour, and your father discussed it with Sonni a few days before the Foundation Meal. Anur had no idea yet.'

Two things were suddenly clear. The first was Sonni's odd behaviour that day. The second was Father's ambiguous speech, which now made perfect sense. He'd been trying to tell Anur to stop taking everything for granted and behave more maturely over the coming months.

'Your father and I were planning on sitting Anur down after the Feast to explain,' Dainefin went on, 'but with what happened . . . everything was left up in the air. I imagine we'll be revisiting the topic as soon as Anur and I are both back in the capital, so we can all discuss it together.'

No, there would be no need for that. Because Uncle Hervin had decreed Anur the legitimate heir of Murihen, Father had accepted and Sonni was consequently on course to inherit the crown of Amarantha. Everybody should be happy. Right?

I wasn't sure how Sonni was getting on. From the vision I'd had, I sensed he'd accepted things for what they were. I was proud of him. I knew he'd make ten times the king Anur would have. He had not grown up hearing people tell him, 'Once you are King . . .' He'd grown up with, 'Once your *brother* is King.' And that made all the difference.

Dainefin didn't go on and Móiras didn't press further. I lay down on the pallet, cushioning my head on my arms, and watched the clouds. Nausea was superseded by boredom, but a good boredom, the kind that would at least allow me to rest. I counted the clouds above me, and some time between the seventeenth and the eighteenth, I dozed off.

'What will you do now?' was the first thing I heard Móiras say when I woke.

I was alone on the stationary cart. I sat up and saw Móiras and Dainefin sitting at the edge of a breathtaking cliff. I climbed down from the cart and started getting my bearings, leaving them time for their goodbyes. We must have passed the village of Styr while I was sleeping, but I knew I hadn't missed much. According to Cam, there was nothing worth seeing in the village; it was the view from the cliffs that would make the sickening ride in the cart worth it. The sharply indented coastline leading to Murihen didn't allow us to see far beyond the steep crags and ravines; yet if I turned back towards Shamabat, the cliffs gradually softened and the inlets widened, hugging sandy bays that looked more peaceful, more familiar.

I knew which direction I would have preferred to take. My eyes followed the uneven path that disappeared south into the jagged rocks. I wondered why Dainefin had brought me to the fjords . . .

'We're just stopping here for the night. We'll continue the journey tomorrow,' she answered, raising her voice against the roar of the sea.

That was all she said. Apparently not even Móiras was allowed to know where the next stage of our journey would take us. I would have to wait to find out where we were headed – most likely until the moment Dainefin stopped and traced a cross in the dirt, announcing, 'Here we are.'

'Be careful,' said Móiras. He turned to me, 'Be good.' He hugged Dainefin and said, 'Just remember it's never too late to come home.'

It was the sort of thing that Dainefin usually said. The tenderness of the man who, in a different life, would have been her brother-in-law, made the Priestess's face melt into a smile.

Móiras climbed back onto his cart, waved one last time and left.

'Just a little further.' I never knew if Dainefin was

talking to me at that moment, or to herself. Shortly after that she turned and marched off, and I followed her.

Just a little further.

Chapter 16

We trudged westward until late in the afternoon. A sharp breeze had risen, but at least the sky was still clear.

'We'll have to stop here for the night,' said Dainefin when we came across an abandoned hut. It was a square building with a ceiling as high as that of a barn and two doors on opposite sides. Three shallow steps elevated the building from the grass, and ivy climbed thickly around the doorframes. Most of the cheap glass panels set in the doors were broken.

Inside, it was no bigger than Uncle Noalim's hut – ten feet, wall to wall – and the furnishings were just as basic: a pallet and a small stone basin in the middle. It was hard to tell the ash filling the basin from the dust that covered the whole room; a salty, humid smell penetrated through the broken glass.

I shivered.

This place is straight out of a ghost story.

The hut seemed at once unreal, and the best thing

we could have come across: at least we wouldn't be sleeping under the stars.

'It's just for one night,' said Dainefin. 'After tomorrow you'll have a proper bedroom.'

In whose house? At the inn of which village? There was no way of knowing. But I was comforted by the thought that a real bed was waiting for me somewhere.

Dainefin lifted a floorboard from a corner of the room and broke it into pieces for burning. She instructed me to light a fire in the stone basin, then, saying that it made no sense to burn the whole hut to keep warm, she went out alone to search for firewood.

I lay down on the pallet. I wasn't tired in the slightest since I'd spent the afternoon napping on Móiras's cart. I was cold though. The weak flames of our fire quivered in the chilly, humid drafts that ran from one window to the other. Outside, the wind was howling, and that put me off sticking my nose out of the door even for a few seconds.

I was stuck inside, wide awake and full of energy.

Earlier, I'd thrown my haversack in a corner and now the red cover of Aur-Lee's journal and the blue one of Master Lohm's notebook were peeking out.

I picked up the journal.

13 August

East. Blue.
North, South. Still blue.
West. Blue.
All blue.

This ten-word opening on the first page was followed by pages of tiny, barely decipherable writing. I moved closer to the fire to see better.

Every day of the crossing, Aur-Lee had recorded his thoughts. There were sunny days and stormy days. Days when half the crew was close to mutiny, days when women would sing and children would chase each other on the deck. Not a single line even hinted at Aur-Lee losing faith in their reaching the New World. And if anyone knew about faith, it was Aur-Lee.

The young seminarian wrote about leaving the church after he discovered that his vocation lay beyond the confines of the altar. He wrote of war breaking out in the Old World, of finding a glimpse of hope in the theories that a continent existed beyond the Pillars of Hercules. Neither the Church nor his family approved of his mission to find it, but it had become more and more urgent as conflict worsened between the various kingdoms.

He'd invited those who had lost everything – their land, their friends and relatives – to set sail with him, offering hope in return, leaving each one free to believe that God was either on their side or turning a blind eye, thus absolving them from the sin of ambition.

After forty-six days at sea, God sent them a seagull. Twenty-one days after that, one hastily scrawled line . . .

4 October
Land.

I scanned pages and pages, becoming more intimate with my ancestor. Aur-Lee recorded every event of his life, from the small to the momentous. From his coronation to his first love.

Her name was Sari and he had no idea who she was before he met her in the New World. He didn't know her family – so many people had made the crossing with him, and so many more carried on disembarking over the following months – nor did he have a way of finding out, since Sari barely spoke his language.

She only said a few words at a time, and kept her past shrouded in mystery. Aur-Lee respected that, thinking that every person in his kingdom had the right to be whoever they chose, independent from their past and their family.

It was as if I were reading my father's diary. He too hadn't thought twice before marrying Mother, who was of humble birth. I felt a burst of admiration for the men in my family.

Aur-Lee first met Sari on the beach at the foot of the promontory, where he strolled every sunrise and sunset. She was sitting on a rock gazing out to sea.

While arriving in Amarantha had been a godsend, Aur-Lee knew that it was impossible to begin a new life without reckoning with one's past. Many New World citizens would stop to gaze out to sea, weeping when they thought no one could see them.

After their first meeting, pages of silent walks followed, until one day Aur-Lee went down on one knee and asked Sari to marry him.

I wiped a tear and carried on reading about the

most important love story of the kingdom. Dawns, sunsets, hands seeking each other, flowering black-thorn: all details that might have made me cringe in a novel, but were somehow made romantic by the fact they had been lived by a real person – someone I knew, someone I was related to.

He only had one doubt about their relationship, and it was their age difference. He thought Sari must be at least fifteen years younger, and every now and then Aur-Lee wondered whether that would be a problem.

Sari reassured him that age didn't matter. Where she was from, she said, people were obsessed with time. But she wanted to be different. She wanted to be free.

Every page was covered in writing, but the entries became further and further apart. From page to page, months passed, then years. After the wedding, two pages full of joy, then the journal paused for a whole year, until:

9 December
We are expecting a child.

This wasn't news to me, I was his descendant after all, but I felt his joy as he described Sari's pregnancy in detail, their fantasies about who their child would take after, the search for a name. I knew they would pick Manil, after the abbot who had been Aur-Lee's mentor at the monastery.

But as I read on, another lone entry, written in

large letters in the middle of the page, brought me up short.

5 June

It's a girl. Sari is certain of it.

That was impossible. I was sure they'd only had one child, a son, Manil, who would be the first of a long line of male heirs. I couldn't possibly be wrong. As a child, I'd been told time and time again that I was the first princess in the New World.

I wanted to skip ahead to when she was born, but Aur-Lee kept me riveted to every word, every new development. And I soon understood why I had never heard of his first-born daughter.

14 June

Sari says we cannot tell anyone about the pregnancy. That we must hide the baby girl as soon as she is born. I think she is going mad. What does she mean, hide the girl? She wants the baby to be raised at court, but not as our daughter. Not as the princess. Have her fostered by Feyal and Marahn. I told her I would not hear of it. I was not expecting a male heir at the first try. And there is nothing wrong with having a daughter. We shall love her all the same. Who cares if I never have a male heir? My daughter shall be my heir. She may have the kingdom, if she wants it.

223

But Sari wasn't concerned with the kingdom. After a few pages of arguments, Aur-Lee wrote about how he had backed Sari into a corner.

> I told her that I will never consider having my girl raised by foster parents, not without a valid reason. I don't think I am being unfair. It's my child. My family.

I felt an almost physical pain in the pit of my stomach. I was as concerned for the child as Aur-Lee was.

> But Sari says that the girl carries her family's blood too . . . and that is what we should worry about. It is as if she has thrown a pail of ice water over me. I worry. Will the girl be healthy?

I took a deep breath and mentally prepared myself to read the rest of the story.

> She says the child will not be ill, she will only be different, and that by the time I can see that, it will be too late. Sari begs me to trust her, but how can I?

The following pages were full of Aur-Lee's turmoiled thoughts on the meaning of the word 'different'. If the child turned out like Sari, he could see why she would appear 'different'. Sari was beautiful, like no other woman. She was intelligent, more so than anyone else he had ever known. And then there were her unique features: honey-coloured skin, hair a thousand shades of amber, the unusual slant of her eyes . . .

That was when I realised that I was seeing a familiar face in my mind's eye. Someone I'd had by my side my whole life.

I quickly scanned the journal in search of more about the baby girl.

31 July

Sari asked if she can choose the name. I told her that it will make no difference, since she has made her decision. What need have I for a name that I am never to utter? She says she will call her Dainefin. I do not mind. It is everything else that I mind. Even if Marahn and Feyal agree, I . . .

Again, I skipped ahead.

8 August

She is here. I went to see Sari. 'This is Dainefin,' she told me. And I, like a fool, burst into tears. I held my daughter. She is the most beautiful thing in the world. The sweetest, most delightful, most important thing. I told Sari she could not take her from me. I would give the kingdom away before my own child. I became angry. I raised my voice and the baby woke and began to cry. I clutched that little bundle to my chest and Sari began to sob.

This was not how I had imagined the day I became a father. Nor the first sounds my daughter would hear.

Only a few pages before, he had been the happiest man in the world. Now, as I read on, helpless, the love Aur-Lee had once felt for Sari turned to hate.

I wept. I wept because I didn't know how the story would end. Because I didn't understand. What had happened to Aur-Lee's daughter? Was she as 'different' as Sari had feared? And most of all, was it just a coincidence that Dainefin bore the same name as her? It was an unusual name. Of course, it may have simply fallen out of fashion over the years, but I couldn't remember ever seeing it in my history books. Was Dainefin related to the royal family? But then, why hide it?

I kept reading, hoping I'd find answers to all my questions.

Sari eventually convinced Aur-Lee to give up his child by promising him that on her twelfth birthday, Dainefin would be told the truth. Aur-Lee agreed, and so became complicit in a lie, or as Sari called it, an unspoken truth. In her mind, since her pregnancy had never been announced to the kingdom, this wasn't a lie. Other than the King and Queen, only two other people knew the truth: Dainefin's adoptive parents.

Dainefin grew up in the castle, loved by all. Aur-Lee saw her every day but did not allow himself near her. He learned to keep his distance, telling himself that Dainefin was a child like any other. He might have been able to believe it, if she hadn't been the spitting image of his wife.

Aur-Lee's frustration overwhelmed me. I stopped reading to catch my breath, tears rolling down my cheeks. I lifted my eyes from the journal and found Dainefin standing in the doorway, staring at me in horror.

'What's happened?' she gasped through the waves of unbridled emotion that flooded from my unguarded heart. She dropped the bundle of firewood she'd collected and ran over to me, her eyes scanning me for injury.

You tell me.

I placed the journal in her hands.

'What's this?'

Aur-Lee's journal. Father gave it to me just before we left. I don't know why I didn't read it sooner, I feel so stupid. If I had . . .

Dainefin paid no attention to the barrage of my Empathic Aura: she was turning the journal in her hands, as if touching it confirmed its existence.

She lingered on the first page.

Explain to me why your name turns up in Aur-Lee's journal.

I grabbed the book, turning to the entry for the 8th of August and shoved it back at the Priestess. She stared at the page where her name appeared for the first time. Then she went back a few pages, to the moment Sari announced her pregnancy to Aur-Lee. She sat down next to me without taking her eyes off the page.

'I can tell you the rest of the story myself,' she said, quietly. 'I was meaning to tell you in any case, before we reach Cloch.'

I had to hold back from asking where Cloch was and if it was our final destination.

Dainefin closed the journal and handed it back to me.

'When I turned twelve, my parents – well, the people I thought of as my parents – told me I had been adopted. You can imagine my shock. My mother looked me straight in the eye and told me I was the daughter of the King and Queen of Amarantha.'

You're . . . Aur-Lee's daughter? The Dainefin in the journal?

She nodded.

That wasn't possible. The time gap was immense – it was a chasm more than a gap. This girl had been born over two centuries before me. How many generations separated us? My mind churned, listing Aur-Lee's every descendant until my father . . . . Nine. Nine generations. Dainefin was my great-great-great-great-great-great-great-great-aunt.

That's impossible! You can't—

'It's hard to explain, I know. For now, let me tell you what happened.'

I nodded numbly.

'My parents told me the King and Queen wanted to speak to me. I had seen them plenty of times before, I lived in the castle after all, because my mother – my foster mother – was a serving maid in the kitchens. I used to play in the castle corridors with my foster brother. The King and Queen always had a smile for me, but it had never occurred to me that behind their kindness . . .' Dainefin shook her head. 'Anyway, that day I was called to the royal chambers, and my mother – my birth mother – told me the whole truth.'

Was Aur-Lee there too?

I felt sorry for him. From what I had read, he was always the last to know anything. A little like me. If Dainefin hadn't found me in tears with the journal in my hands, would she have told me the whole story?

'Yes, he was there,' said Dainefin. 'He was . . . well, he was in pieces.' She was picking her words carefully, as if she were searching the furthest corners of her memory for them. 'He held me for a long time, and that was when I accepted that it was all true.'

Dainefin sighed and continued her tale. 'Sari was colder. More composed. She bade me to sit and asked me a question: "Do you feel at ease?" I answered that I did not understand. Did she mean at that moment, or in the castle, or in general? "In general," she said, "with other girls your age." No. Children my age avoided me. I told her that I was only at ease with my brother, the son my parents had had before taking me in.'

A completely different version of the Priestess'
childhood was unfolding before my eyes. The story I
had believed my whole life – that of a girl who'd grown
up in Shamabat – had been wiped clean and rewritten
so many times in just a few short weeks. Dainefin and
her foster brother, running around the castle corridors.
Dainefin taking refuge in the library, amongst the same
shelves where I too had found sanctuary.

What did Sari say?

'She asked if I had ever wished I were somewhere
else. I answered that I had, quite often. Then she asked
"Would you like to go?"'

'I was beginning to feel uncomfortable and
scared,' she continued. 'Aur-Lee noticed and cut Sari
off. He told me that now I knew the truth, I could
remain in the castle as their daughter if I wished.'

Did Sari agree?

'She didn't say anything. They left the decision to
me: we could reveal the truth to the citizens of Amarantha and I could join the royal household as the long-
lost princess, or . . . I could choose to keep things as they
were. I loved my foster parents, I didn't blame them for
keeping the secret all that time.

'From that moment on, I should have been the
happiest girl in the kingdom. I had just discovered that
I was the King and Queen's daughter. I had two sets of
parents who loved me and lavished me with attention,
as well as a brother, and another on the way – the Queen
was pregnant again. Still, I couldn't stop thinking about
what Sari had said. Why was I not comfortable around
children my age? Why did I feel like I was *different*?'

230

I had asked myself those very questions. And, more than once, I had opened up to the Priestess about them. Whenever I longed for friends, whenever I felt that everyone else seemed to know who they were and how they fitted into the world, whenever I felt particularly misaligned – like a painting always slightly askew on the wall.

'Some days I felt so carefree,' Dainefin went on. 'I would leap out of bed to explore the castle, help my mother, play with Reydn ...'

Reydn?

'My foster brother,' she explained. 'We were inseparable, like you and Sonni. But then there were days when everything was dark. It was as if ... I was unable to be happy. I would isolate myself and cry, hiding away, wondering why I felt so different.'

Different ...

'Yes. I can't think of a better way of putting it. Not special. Not strange. Different.'

So what did you decide?

'I decided I'd had enough. As terrifying as it was, I went looking for Sari and confronted her. I was ready to know what she had intended to tell me the day she had summoned me, before she had allowed Aur-Lee to dissuade her.'

Our fire had dwindled to a flickering flame, and Dainefin left me on tenterhooks for a few moments while she fed it fresh firewood.

'What Sari told me then is what I was intending to tell you tonight. I would have just skipped the boring part about my childhood.'

If *that* was boring, I wondered what was in store for me.

'When . . . when Aur-Lee first reached the New World, he believed he'd found virgin land. Swathes of amaranth stretched over half the continent. The other half, from the rocky landscapes of the Serra del Lárr to Hatablar Forest, were pristine. There was no trace of anyone, either living or long dead. But Sari told me that the New World had once had another name, and a whole civilisation had put down roots and flourished here. As far as I know, Aur-Lee died without ever knowing any of that.'

What happened to that civilisation?

'Hundreds of years earlier, there'd been a great war. An epidemic wiped out its survivors.'

How could an entire civilisation be wiped out, leaving no evidence behind, nothing to bear witness to the fact they had ever existed?

'Most of their villages were in the north, in the valleys around Lake Hoírh,' Dainefin explained. 'If we dug deep enough, perhaps, something would turn up. But Aur-Lee never thought of doing so. He took for it granted that the continent was uninhabited.'

But there must have been someone left?

I had read too many books not to be ready for a dramatic turn of events. Dainefin nodded and smiled.

'More than just "someone". A whole community of people, who fled during the war and left their homeland.'

Like Aur-Lee.

'Yes,' said Dainefin, 'I suppose so. I never thought of it like that. They didn't venture as far as he did though.'

Where did they go?

'An island off the south coast.'

But there are no islands—

'There is one,' Dainefin interrupted me mid-thought. 'The Isle of Cloch.'

I've never seen it on any maps.

'That's because no one from Amarantha has ever found it. It's just west of where we are now.'

It must be miles away . . .

'It isn't that far, but you can't see it from the coast. It's a trick of the light on the horizon, an optical illusion. You will see for yourself very soon. That's where we're headed.'

I had carefully avoided the most important question, but I wasn't able to hold back any more.

Why? Why didn't you tell me all this sooner? Why are you telling me now?

'Cloch is where you belong. It's where your people are,' said Dainefin. 'Like me. Like my mother.'

My people?

'The Maír. They're called Maír.'

Chapter 17

My mind churned with unanswered questions. Had that been where Dainefin was before she showed up in Shamabat? Why did she look like she was barely fifty years old, when she was actually over a hundred? And why hadn't she been able to read or write when she'd first met Old Lohm? I wanted all the answers now, but Dainefin wouldn't say any more. I knew that if Dainefin didn't want to speak, I wouldn't be able to get another word out of her. I slept little and badly that night, tormented by curiosity.

The following morning, Dainefin interrupted my fitful dozing to announce it was time to go. Not far from the shack where we'd spent the night was a cliff that dropped over a small empty bay. The ocean was smooth and blue as far as the eye could see. I followed Dainefin down a natural path that wove amongst rocks, shrubs and creepers along the least precipitous side of the cliff, landing on a half-moon sliver of beach made up of shingle and shell fragments. Once on firm ground, I took a deep breath. I looked up at the cliff face and gave thanks for not realising sooner how high up we'd been.

Dainefin stepped into a recess in the rock, stooping to avoid banging her head. She was bent even lower when she re-emerged, dragging behind her a row boat half the size of Móiras's, the wood a resplendent blue.

That's...

'Hata wood, yes,' Dainefin confirmed. 'It was my mother's idea. So it would last forever.'

So that means it's been here since...

'Since I came back, yes.'

The boat showed no sign of decay. There weren't even any barnacles or moss on its hull. I ran my fingers over the wood; it was cool and smooth and smelt of the forest.

The idea of a hata being chopped to pieces was somehow obscene. A superstitious thought gripped me. If Hatablar was the underworld, this boat belonged to Charon, helmsman to Hades himself.

Isn't this a bit... small?

'It's not as far as you think, I promise. Look.' Dainefin pointed at the horizon. 'That is Cloch.'

Even knowing where to look, I could barely see the mass of rocky spurs. I understood what she meant when she said Cloch didn't look like an island. The harder I tried to make out the shape of an island in that rock formation, the more blurred and flickering it appeared.

It's as if the rocks are moving.

'It's just an illusion,' Dainefin said, tying up the hem of her skirt to push the boat into the water.

We climbed aboard, sitting side by side, our backs

to the prow, and did our best to heave forwards with one oar each. She knew what she was doing – as usual – and I copied her, trying to mimic Móiras parting the water with an economy of broad movements. Even with our combined efforts we were unable to maintain his pace and were forced to stop every few minutes to catch our breath.

I held my haversack firmly between my knees so it wouldn't get wet, but the sleeve on my rowing arm was soaked from the splashes each stroke of my oar raised. Salt water got into my eyes and I tried to ignore it, but the longer we rowed, the more it burned. My head was still exploding with questions, and my physical exhaustion left me too tired to repress the Empathic Aura.

So, when Sari told you the truth about the Maír ...
'She suggested I go and spend some time with them.'
And Aur-Lee?
Dainefin didn't answer, so I tried a different tack.
Tell me about the Maír.
'It means "survivors".'
What are they like?
'Different.'

Different? Like you and me? I wanted Dainefin to tell me everything about them, to tell me everything that had happened to her as a young girl. My unease was beginning to turn into hope. I would soon be free of the Empathic Aura. I could feel it. I would meet the last of the civilisation that had inhabited Amarantha before Aur-Lee arrived. I would get better, return home and tell Sonni and Father all about my travels.

How long are we staying on Cloch?

'*You*,' she said pointedly, 'will stay until you feel ready to return.'

Just like that, my enthusiasm fizzled out.

You mean you're abandoning me?

I stopped rowing and turned to her, waiting for an answer.

'It wouldn't make sense for me to stay with you. This is something you need to do by yourself.'

You couldn't have told me that before?

'Would you still have come?'

I don't know. But neither do you! You could have asked.

'I couldn't risk it, Lyria,' the Priestess answered.

That's right. You tell me what to do and I just go along with it. All right, thanks for keeping me company this far. I'll write.

I stared hard at my white knuckles gripping the oar. Dainefin began rowing again, ferrying me to the other side just like my own personal Charon.

'Please don't be like that,' said Dainefin with a long-suffering sigh. 'I promise you that Cloch will change your life.'

I think I've seen enough change.

'I know you have,' she said more gently. 'And I know it hasn't been easy. But things will start to get better now. You're going to love the island.'

If you liked it so much, why did you leave?

Dainefin paused. She had that look on her face that said she was trying to decide between slipping me a half-truth or skipping the question altogether.

She went for the half-truth.

'I needed a change of scenery.'

Dainefin really had to stop speaking like a sphinx. One minute she was telling me that Cloch was heaven on earth, the next she was dodging my questions. Had there been anywhere she'd been truly happy?

Where will you go? Shamabat?

Dainefin allowed herself a small smile. 'I wish I could. I'm going back to the capital. The kingdom needs me.'

I thought of all the ways in which Dainefin had wronged me. All the chances she'd had to tell me the truth. All the times I had let her in by confiding my fears to her, yet she'd never let *me* in. I wanted her to acknowledge it all. I wanted her to apologise.

The Empathic Aura left no room for doubt. Dainefin must have been very aware of my demanding feelings, yet she didn't address them directly.

'Nearly there,' she said instead.

I turned and saw it. Up close, the outline of the island was a neat line curving along the horizon. It appeared thickly wooded except for a volcano visible at its centre.

Our boat eased into the shallows. I sank my foot into the crystalline water, stirring the rose-coloured sand. The foreshore was scattered with white shells and tiny coral pebbles. Dainefin passed me my haversack and I set it down on the beach as I looked around.

I expected to see the contour of the mainland back where we'd come from, but even with a clear sky, I couldn't see anything other than a few trembling dark shapes on the horizon.

What are we doing with the boat?

'I'm going straight back.'

Did Dainefin really mean to abandon me? Here? Now?

How am I supposed to find the Maír?

Dainefin took my waist and turned me so I was facing the forest. The sun was high in the sky, right above my head.

'Go south.'

Just go south?

'Straight on, you can't go wrong. Through the forest, and in a couple of hours you'll be at the Maír village.'

I can't do this alone!

My breath hitched, my knees gave way. I shook with sobs. For a moment I felt like I was outside my own body, like I couldn't control it. I felt like I might throw up. Or faint. Dainefin's grip tightened on my hips to hold me up.

'Lyria, please. Please don't make me,' she whispered.

She was really leaving me here. I couldn't believe it. I jerked free, backing away from her.

You really are something else. The things you hid from me. You didn't say anything about Cloch and the

*Maír 'til the very last minute, and now that I finally know
something, you're off? Tell me, why did you wait so long?
Were you so afraid of Myrain finding out you're old
enough to be his great-grandmother? Oh wait. You'll just
do what you did to me my whole life and lie to him.*

Dainefin's eyes flashed, then softened. A single
tear escaped her self-control, and that was enough to
make me wish I had never been born.

I took a deep breath and tried to put myself in her
shoes. Dainefin, who had walked through Shamabat
without batting an eyelid, had just begged me not to
make her step foot on Cloch. What had happened to her
here?

Even so, I was still angry. I grabbed my haversack,
heaving it on so furiously that I nearly lost my balance.
At least my rage had given my legs back their full
strength; they were now firmly planted on the scorching
hot sand.

Fine. Go.

My heart was thumping. I was about to say
goodbye to the one person who knew me better than
anyone else, even Sonni. I could barely look at her.

'Don't worry,' she said. 'When you arrive, you'll be
able to communicate with the Empathic Aura. Ask for
Kolymba.'

Kolymba?

'That's right. He'll teach you the Maír language.'

I want you to teach me.

'I know. But you'll be in good hands. Kolymba is
the most capable person I have ever met.'

I was clutching the ties of my haversack at my hips, but I stood rooted to the spot.

Will he heal me?

'No,' she answered. 'I'm afraid no one can. He will help, but you have to find your own Reason to get better.'

Like you did in Shamabat?

Dainefin nodded, betraying no sign of surprise that I knew.

But I have no one. I don't have a Ruthven. My mother is dead. My family . . . . How do I . . . ?

'You'll find a way,' she replied. 'You'll find your own Reason.'

She hugged me. Only when I decided to hug her back and lay my head on her chest, did I realise that she really was leaving. I panicked.

How will I get back?

'You know the way now. You're free to come back whenever you want. Kolymba will help you.'

She pushed the boat into the water and prepared to set off. She had her back to me, but I saw her wipe away a tear with the back of her hand.

Dainefin, wait!

There were so many things I wanted to say to her, but instead I asked:

How old are you? I just needed to hear her say it.

She turned to face me with a strained smile. 'I've lost count.' Then, more seriously, 'They're a bit obsessive about time on this island. Try not to pick that up.'

As I watched the boat shrink into the distance, I thought of the journey ahead of her. She was alone, on foot. I might have been worried if it were anyone else, but I knew Dainefin would get home safely.

I turned to face the forest. It didn't appear to be dense, and vast segments of clear sky lit the way ahead of me. I decided it wouldn't be hard to reach the other side: it was a beautiful day, my legs weren't tired, and I was actually beginning to feel excited again. Only two more hours and I would know the truth. I walked briskly, rationing my water because the sun was beating down mercilessly through the trees. I kept looking around for landmarks but saw nothing more than ferns, of all sizes and shades of green, and vast trees with biscuit-coloured trunks that stood incredibly high, topped by thick, dark canopies. I recognised the song of thrushes, while other birds of various colours flitted about from branch to branch. A rustle of leaves drew my eye to a tiny vole scampering around the roots of a tree. The sounds of that forest, so alive, made me feel welcome.

In less than two hours, I would no longer go to bed every night with more questions than the day before, I thought as I walked. Only an hour and a half now. Only—

Suddenly, everything went black. I was being wrenched about, I was gasping for air. Someone had pulled a hood over my head.

I thrashed my arms, fighting strong arms that were trying to hold me still. I managed to scratch someone before they took my wrists and someone else bound them together behind my back. I kicked out, but the harder I fought, the more painful their hold on me became and the louder they shouted.

Perhaps Dainefin hadn't told the islanders to expect my arrival. Perhaps the Maír were frightened of intruders.

I am Maír, I am Maír!

I heard both men's voices suddenly fall quiet, as if to check whether I was speaking. The Empathic Aura must have caught them by surprise. They spoke to each other in a language I didn't recognise.

As I listened, I realised it didn't resemble any of the Old-World languages I knew were related to Amaranth and the Murihen dialect. There were some striking consonant clusters that were just not possible in Amaranth, and the vowels had varied tones and lengths. The rough sing-song of this language roused in me a sense of bitter estrangement, a hopeless certainty that I would never, ever learn to understand it.

A rough hand between my shoulder blades pushed me forward and I began walking.

My sense of direction had been muddled by the hood, but at some point I realised we were on a different path now: it didn't feel as well-trodden and I was constantly tripping over small shrubs and protruding roots.

Who are you? Where are we going?

Something told me my Empathic Aura was being ignored, but I tried again anyway.

I come from the mainland, I am here to be healed. Please don't hurt me!

What would Dainefin do in my place? She'd make a speech, that was what she would do. She could convince the most ferocious Separatist with her impeccable logic. But I wasn't her, nor was I able to utter a sound. And even if I could have, I didn't know a single word of their language.

No. I did know one word.

KOLYMBA!

They understood me, no doubt about it. They fell silent and stopped so suddenly I stumbled.

Kolymba! I want to speak to Kolymba!

The two exchanged a few words and pulled off my hood.

I blinked in the bright light and squinted at my captors.

They looked to be around forty years old and both had Dainefin's dark complexion. They were wearing identical maroon robes, long and sleeveless with a wide neckline and unusual headdresses – one was a dome shape, like an onion, the other looked more like a cucumber.

The one with the domed headdress had a white sash tied around his waist. He was tall, with wavy hair and a thick beard and moustache. He turned to me, speaking a string of unintelligible words. All I understood was 'Kolymba', which he said twice, in bass tones so strong I could feel the vibrations.

I do not speak your language.

The man in the tall headdress became agitated. His bushy eyebrows were drawn together over mean, dull eyes, and I understood I had annoyed them. The timbre of his voice was sharp and petulant – it reminded me of a mosquito. I would have bet on him being the second-in-command, the more chaotic and consequently less dominant personality of the two.

They tried to pull the hood over my head again, but I dodged it in every way I could. I was a princess! I was the great King Uriel's daughter! My heart twisted at the thought of my father seeing me like this.

Just then, they jerked me harder, waving the hood at me again and that was the last straw. I was aware of the Empathic Aura trying to shout my outrage at them, but I didn't want them to have the satisfaction, so I forced it down.

From the outside, I must have looked like I was about to explode. Inside, I was roaring. I had never felt so determined, so capable of concentrating the frustration brought on by the Empathic Aura and crushing it, along with all other emotion, only allowing to the surface a cool strength that said, '*You have no idea who you're dealing with.*'

In truth, I had no idea myself. Was the person resisting those bullies without betraying a single emotion really me? I felt strong, worthy of the title 'Princess' in a way that had nothing to do with my lineage.

The two would not let go of my arms, but they loosened their grip as they began another animated discussion. At least they'd stopped trying to put the hood over my head.

I took advantage of their distraction to gather as much information as I could about my surroundings. We seemed to have been following a single path up until then and, if I managed to escape, there was no way I could get lost. The main path, the wider one I had been taken from, would be easy enough to find.

They hauled me off again and after a further two hours' tramping through the forest, we arrived at the edge of a settlement. Even without following Dainefin's directions, it looked like I may have reached where I wanted to go.

I hadn't really thought about how many people lived on the island, but I certainly hadn't imagined such a small village. There were fewer than twenty dwellings, grouped together in a hollow at the foot of a low hill, beyond which I could see a wheat field, a vineyard and some grazing land.

As we approached, I desperately tried to find a sympathetic ally, but there was no one around. I spotted a few figures working in the fields, but they were too far away for me to attract their attention.

I was dragged through the lanes of the settlement. Some dwellings were simple dry-stone buildings, homes of one or two rooms. Others were humbler still, wooden huts with thatched roofs of straw or pine needles, and creepers along their walls.

We passed a large two-storey house, built mostly of stone. White Sash said something to Cucumber and went inside. Cucumber pulled me along and stopped in front of the next house.

This was barely more than a hut, held up by

wooden beams and screened in at the sides with reeds. The two windows at the front were mismatched.

He shouted 'Kolymba!' at the top of his voice.

The door opened and a Maír man appeared in the doorway. He was incredibly tall and powerfully built, with long dark hair. His faded robe was streaked with every shade between wine-red and peach.

My escort addressed him arrogantly, but this man, Kolymba, remained unfazed. He spoke a few words, then let us in. He pulled out a chair from the table in the centre of the room, and invited me to sit down.

In a corner on the floor, earthenware pitchers were arranged by size. Other than the low table and chairs, the only furniture was a four-cupboard sideboard with two drawers beneath each door.

Cucumber pounced on the piece of furniture I was admiring, and began to rifle through the drawers until he found some rope, which he used to tie my legs to the chair. I wanted to laugh. Had these people *seen* me? If I'd run away, I would have needed to stop at the door to catch my breath. But Cucumber was doing his best to make me uncomfortable, and he was succeeding.

He muttered something to Kolymba before stalking out and slamming the door.

It was just me and Kolymba now.

The first thing he did was untie the rope.

Thank you.

Not at all.

I nearly fell out of my chair. I'd never been on the receiving end of the Empathic Aura before. It felt like having mislaid something important – unpleasant, frustrating, temporary, yet at the same time, enduring – just sitting there, in the pit of my stomach.

For a moment I forgot that I was in a stranger's home and I loosened my grip on my own Empathic Aura. Kolymba sat down in front of me. He waited for me to recover. My throat tightened at the realisation that someone else was going through what I was.

Are you a friend or an enemy?

I am a friend amongst enemies.

This certainly wasn't the welcome I'd been expecting after what Dainefin had told me.

Why are the Maír my enemies?

Because you've ended up in the wrong village, Lyria.

You know who I am?

So Dainefin had been able to warn someone I was coming after all!

I saw your arrival in a vision a long time ago. It took me many years to understand who you were.

You mean, Dainefin didn't tell you? Wait . . . you have visions too?

Yes.

And the Empathic Aura.

Kolymba nodded.

But I heard you speak only a few minutes ago.

I can speak, but that does not mean I am well. The Empathic Aura reduces you to half a person. Some things . . . some things, I cannot say out loud. I am unable to translate them into words. I have to fall back on the

Empathic Aura for them. We are the language we speak. If you can only say half of what you feel, you are condemned to live that way too. By halves.

We are the language we speak. It made sense. Still, I had never considered that before.

Kolymba reached for my haversack, which Cucumber had thrown on the ground.

May I?

I nodded.

He went through my things respectfully, pulling out Aur-Lee's journal, my blue notebook, the jar of hata honey and the purse containing my few coins. He paused to look at the honey, but didn't waste any time. He hid the jar and both journals in one of the drawers of the huge sideboard. He seemed undecided about the purse.

I'll have to let them find this. Or they'll become suspicious.

Was he protecting my belongings? Perhaps that meant he was on my side. He did seem to be wise, as Dainefin had said. I kept my resentment towards the Priestess in check by convincing myself that even if she hadn't left me on the island by myself, we still would have found ourselves in trouble.

The door flew open and my two abductors came in, barking orders at Kolymba. I heard one of the men say the name 'Dainefin', and I started.

Is Dainefin here? I aimed my question very carefully and quietly at Kolymba.

You are Dainefin. It's a Maír word. It means 'leader's daughter'. They know you are important where you come from.

I let the meaning of Dainefin's name sink in. Sari had decided for her from the beginning – from before she was even out of her mother's belly. Dainefin was Maír.

But what about me? Wasn't I supposed to feel at home here, welcomed by my second family? Wasn't Cloch going to 'change my life'?

They're not all like this, Kolymba communicated to me. *Only Mana Pun and Sama Kas.*

Which is which?

Mana Pun is the one with the white sash. He's the head of the village. Mana means 'chief'. Sama Kas is his right-hand man.

And what does Kolymba mean?

Again, his emotions went straight to my stomach. Regret, nostalgia, guilt.

Teacher.

Once they were done with their tirade, Mana Pun and Sama Kas left, grabbing my haversack and slamming the door behind them. Kolymba rolled his eyes. I too had trouble understanding why they couldn't just shut the door like normal people.

What did they say?

That I must keep you here. That I can't let you escape.

Why?

Kolymba seemed like a good person, but I was on the island to get rid of the Empathic Aura, not to be held prisoner.

You will not have to stay long. Only until Mana Pun receives his payment.

Suddenly, I felt like I'd misjudged Kolymba. A scenario formed in my mind: Kolymba has a vision about my arrival and tells the other two. They decide to kidnap me, and ransom me back to my father. Father pays. Poor, naïve Lyria is free. Rescued like a good little Princess. I grimaced.

But weren't visions timeless? How could they have known exactly when I would reach the island? And how would they ransom me if they couldn't speak Amaranth? No, too many things didn't add up.

Who's paying Mana Pun? And why?

I don't know, he admitted. *But I do know that when you're free, you'll be able to go to the other Maír. Until then, I will not allow anyone to harm you.*

There are two villages, then?

In a way. The village you were headed to is the original Maír community. They are known as The Faithful – 'Pamau'. This is the Rebels' den – 'Tángaor'.

'Ama-Tángaor,' he continued aloud, pointing out the window.

So that was the name of this village.

Dainefin said I was supposed to find you. I don't mean to be rude, but you don't seem the ideal person to teach me how to overcome the Empathic Aura . . .

Kolymba smiled.

No, I am not. But I can teach you Maír. It will at least come in handy once you leave here. You wouldn't be the first Dainefin I teach our language to.

Did he mean he'd taught the Maír leaders' children or did he know my Dainefin?

I looked at him suspiciously. How old was he? The question of Maír people and their age was becoming more and more confusing. Were they immortal? Would I too look like a twenty-year-old at forty, like a forty-year-old at one hundred?

I shall answer all questions I have the answers to. But only once you have started learning our language.

I'll never be able to speak it.

How do you know? Try. Give yourself time.

Something inside me shifted. This whole journey, I had done nothing but bide my time, waiting to find out where we were going, waiting for a chance to escape. Now I clung to Kolymba's words. I wanted to *do* something.

For once, I was grateful that the Empathic Aura existed. There was no way for it to lie to me. It was comforting to be near someone who would always tell me the truth, whether he wanted to or not.

Do we have an agreement?

I nodded. It didn't seem like the worst of deals. I was stuck on an island, in a village full of hostile people, with nothing else to do. I might as well learn their language while I figured out how to escape.

Chapter 18

Her small escort includes a carpenter, a blacksmith and a couple of labourers. Dainefin knows them all – some only by sight, while others are friends of her foster parents, though people with whom she's never personally interacted.

It is strange for Dainefin to have a retinue. This is not how she'd imagined leaving the city. The Queen's presence, which should be a comfort to her, intimidates her instead. She'd hoped that she and Sari would come to know each other better on the journey, but they both seem hesitant to invade the other's space.

Only three days have gone by and already her initial enthusiasm is fading. Why did she agree to this? Why did she leave the castle – her home – behind?

She had been so upset when her foster parents had told her that Reydn didn't have the heart to say goodbye, and even more so when she discovered that he'd always known she wasn't his real sister, and had kept it from her all this time.

They arrive at an inn on the edge of a village. Hatablar Forest is visible, a dark blue shape on the horizon, and her anxiety grows the closer they get. Later, Sari knocks on the door of their shared room, announcing Dainefin has visitors.

'Marahn and Feyal ... your ... parents ... are downstairs.'

Her mother and father must have set off shortly after they did and caught up with them.

Dainefin flings herself out of bed, throws on a tunic and jacket, and follows Sari into the dining hall. There are two bubbles of warmth radiating from the fireplaces at opposite ends of the room. Reydn and their parents are sitting at a table near one of them.

Dainefin flies into her mother's arms. Her father kisses the top of her head. Both are trying to hide their sadness behind big smiles, but her mother's eyes are red. Reydn is waiting with his arms folded on the edge of the table, head tilted to one side. Not only does he appear tamer than usual, he's almost in a good mood. His dark eyes, usually buried under a frown, are wide and bright, for once matching his chubby cheeks and childlike features.

'We're not here to talk you into coming back,' says her father.

'Reydn gave us a whole speech,' says their mother, eyes brimming with pride.

'He wants to go with you,' their father adds.

Dainefin sees surprise and worry cloud Sari's eyes, but the Queen allows them to continue.

'We've come to appeal to you, Your Majesty,' their

mother directs this at the Queen. 'Surely this would be a good experience for both our children.'

It is clear that the adults need to speak amongst themselves and Dainefin wants to talk to Reydn, so the two cross the long dining hall to the opposite fireplace. At first they sit in silence, trying to overhear Sari's long speech, though she's speaking too softly.

'How did you convince them to bring you?' Dainefin asks at last.

'Good manners, then bad manners, then good manners.'

'Meaning?'

'I thought they'd let me come if I made them feel guilty for letting the Queen take you away —'

'Reydn!'

'— but that didn't work. So I told them that if they didn't take me of their own free will, I would find a way to go by myself. They couldn't lock me up in my room forever.'

'Poor Mother and Father . . .' says Dainefin, shaking her head.

'*Then*,' he continues, pretending not to hear, 'when that didn't work, I said I wanted to go with you to remind you of who you are so that, one day, you would come home to them.'

'Reydn . . .' she says gently.

He interrupts her again. 'You're the Princess! You could claim the throne. And if you want, I could be your consul. Always by your side.'

Reydn has let his imagination run wild, as he

always does, dreaming of living in the castle as a prince rather than a servant.

'Reydn,' she says, her tone sharp now. 'How silly. I don't want to claim a thing.'

'You can be such a little girl,' he shoots back in a long-suffering tone.

Few things hurt her as much as being called a little girl by Reydn, who is nearly fourteen. He is only a year and a half older than she is, but unlike Dainefin, who still feels like the bony, formless thing she's always been, Reydn has grown all at once, and his voice has dropped an octave. Only his face, with its smooth skin and plump cheeks, has yet to catch up with the rest of his body.

'You're the first-born, it's your right.'

'I don't want to be Queen!' she protests, but a small part of her can't help imagining what it would be like to have the attention and reverence of so many people . . .

'If I were you,' says Reydn, 'I would spare everyone this waste of time and do it straight away.'

'Do what straight away?'

'Talk to Aur-Lee. Tell everyone who you are.'

'*I* don't even know who I am!' Admitting this out loud, to Reydn of all people, catches her by surprise. Her eyes fill with tears. It's not like her to cry, and Reydn knows it. He softens.

'If you need to go on this journey to get your head round it all,' he says, 'then go. But I'm coming with you.'

Dainefin feels a swoop of sisterly affection. No one loves her as much as Reydn.

'Are you sure?' she asks. 'Won't you miss home?'

'It's not forever, is it?'

'No, of course it isn't,' Dainefin says, feeling a bit lighter.

Kolymba's house only had two rooms, a day room and a night room, but he created a private space for me by raising a wooden partition in the middle of his bedroom. Three strides would take me straight across my 'bedroom', but I had everything I needed. A real bed, built by Kolymba – it was a plain woollen mattress on a wooden frame, but it felt like a cloud compared to the surfaces I'd slept on over the past few weeks – a chest and a desk, made of the same copper-veined wood as the furniture in the other room. Inside the chest were seven identical white cotton robes.

Kolyma had been apologetic when he'd given them to me.

I'm a terrible tailor . . . I'm much better with wood.

Every morning, for at least three hours, Kolymba would pace to and fro between my bedroom and the day room, teaching me grammar and useful vocabulary. For the first few days, I felt as if I were back in Dainefin's Latin lessons in Aur-Lee's Royal Library.

I realised how easy it was to learn Maír through the empathic connection linking me to Kolymba. I didn't need to ask him to repeat anything – each rule and pattern of the language became immediately clear to me.

That's not the Empathic Aura, he explained when I pointed that out to him. **You have Maír in your blood.**

I found that hard to believe. Nothing in me was reminiscent of Dainefin or Sari. I was small and light-skinned, I carried a little extra weight and I had blue eyes. How did he explain that?

You are Maír in your heart and mind.

And my brothers, Sonni and Anur? My father, my uncle, my grandfather?

Kolymba thought about it.

There have never been mixed marriages amongst the Maír before. Your family is the exception.

Sari had sent Dainefin to Cloch, but not her son. I had assumed that she wanted to send Manil too, but that Aur-Lee hadn't allowed it. Maír blood ran through the veins of all Aur-Lee's descendants, not just the women. But why me and not Sonni or Anur? Our Maír identity belonged to all three of us.

You are very wise, as was Dainefin. But only you have the Empathic Aura, so only you have sought us out.

Kolymba was confirming what I already knew, deep down: the Empathic Aura was Maír.

So all Maír become ill? Why? What causes it?

It's not exactly an illness, but it can cause torment to those with unprepared minds. The Maír have been carrying it inside us for centuries, perhaps always. We don't all get it, but each one of us runs the risk of suffering from it over the course of our lives; some for a period, others 'til the end.

Can you die from it?

**Only very few people have. Their hearts weren't
strong enough, or in the end they refused to eat. They let
themselves go because they felt life wasn't worthwhile
any longer.**

Kolymba wasn't trying to bring me down, he just
wanted to make sure I understood the risk of allowing
the Empathic Aura to take over. I hadn't forgotten. I was
particularly aware that in the moments when homesick-
ness, grief and uncertainty filled me to the brim, I also
had to contend with the embarrassment of having to
share them with a Maír man, who, though he didn't look
it, was much older than me.

Kolymba was never caught off balance. He encouraged me to hold on to my enthusiasm, to keep learning
something new every day – beyond Maír syntax and the
seventeen meanings of the word *hari* (water, river, rain,
sea, brook, lake, sap, mirror, dew, to weep, to drink, to
flow, wet, damp, liquid, transparent, blessing).

Within one week I was running out of the paper
I'd brought from Amarantha. My blue notebook was
reserved for writing out my notes in fair copy. In the
meantime, though, I was dying to practise the language
aloud.

'Don't rush yourself,' Kolymba would say.

I became aware of how much I preferred the sound
of his voice to his Empathic Aura. True, by communicating through emotion, Kolymba and I had built an
indestructible bond – comparable to the one Sonni and
I had developed over seventeen years together. But
Kolymba's voice was as deep and harmonious as the

lowest octave of a wooden xylophone, and immersing myself in its music was infinitely preferable to the unsettling shiver his Empathic Aura sent through me.

When I'd first heard it spoken, Maír struck me as rough and impossible to learn. But I was prejudiced by Mana Pun and Sama Kas's use of it. When spoken by Kolymba, the language *shone*, even in its complexities.

Amaranth and Maír differed in the same way as tonal and modal music. My ears were used to Old-World tonal music, just as they were used to the Amaranth language. Yet Maír was more like modes, which have many more types of scales, resulting in strange, unfamiliar melodies. It was difficult in its difference from every other language I knew, but gained substance the more I heard it, becoming easier to appreciate.

Amaranth and tonal music, I realised, were only two little islands in an ocean of languages and types of music: some older, some more difficult, but all of equal worth.

After our morning lesson, Kolymba would go out to gather berries, herbs and fruit, then spend the afternoon at his woodwork, while I was free to do as I pleased.

I began to make myself useful around the house. There was always a job to do, and even though I wasn't exactly having fun, we created a sort of harmony in Kolymba's house, which – after a month of continuous upheaval, encounters, and revelations – was an absurd thing to happen now that I was essentially a prisoner.

I started visiting Kolymba in his workshop to take him his afternoon herbal infusion. The workshop was a corner of the backyard, enclosed by a dry-stone wall and containing a work bench, a high stool, and his carpenter's and engraver's tools.

Kolymba and wood were an extension of each other. It wasn't just that he embodied the spirit of a tree with his solid physique, the shade of his skin, the timbre of his voice. Mostly, it was because his hands carved wood as if they had asked it for permission and come to an arrangement. He could give shape to any object – kitchen utensils, gardening tools, small toys – which he then gave to other Tángaor households as gifts.

When he wasn't building, he was engraving small wooden tablets with words, phrases, Maír proverbs, or the ancient runes I was still unable to make out. Some were circular, with the writing laid out in a ring shape. Others were square with a single word or rune in the centre. All were made with exquisite attention to detail and the letters were so vivid they only lacked the power of speech.

What are those for?

'Remembering,' he answered. **When something is important, I write it down. When it's very important, I carve it into wood.**

He often took out those tablets during our lessons, encouraging me to run my fingertips over the engravings while he read aloud. I discovered that following the shape of the letters on the wooden tablets impressed their sound and meaning more strongly upon my memory. I had never experimented with such a tactile way of learning: it reminded me of Noalim's way of 'reading' words off his hands.

Kolymba's lessons were the most interesting part of my day. And soon, everything else lost its appeal.

Last time they'd visited, Mana Pun and Sama Kas had been clear: Kolymba would pay dearly if they turned up at the house and didn't find me there. Considering how well he was treating me, I didn't wish to put Kolymba in danger, but when they didn't show up after the first week, I began to feel less worried and more restless.

What's happened to those two?

They often go to Ama-Pamau at this time of year. They always come back on the same day.

Even though their return was approaching, Kolymba understood that I was champing at the bit for fresh air. I needed a release from being shut up in a cabin all day long in the sweltering heat. He offered me an exercise window – two hours before sunset, when the temperature dropped enough for me not to burn or get heat stroke – as long as he always knew where I was.

I discovered a beautiful vista: a grassy terrace overlooking the sea at the top of a small promontory that was less than a fifteen-minute walk away, and we agreed I would spend my outdoor time there. Every day I passed the same few Tángaor and nodded a greeting. But I quickly learnt that the Maír were private people. If I didn't offer any information freely, they wouldn't pry. It was at once a liberating and lonely feeling. On my walks, between climbing the hilltop above Ama-Tángaor and descending again towards my terrace, I would turn my gaze inland. I was searching for a sign, some indication of how far I was from Ama-Pamau, the

Faithful's village. But I could only see the forest and the volcano at the centre of the island.

Once I reached my spot, I would sit and gaze out to the open ocean. The view was so wide that I could almost make out the curve of the horizon. It was the same horizon about which I had fantasised many a time from my bedroom window, wondering which civilisations still inhabited the Old World and whether they would ever make contact.

I brought Aur-Lee's journal as a reminder that, one day, I would again gaze at the ocean from my home. I would have a new awareness then of who I was, where I'd come from, what would become of me and my family.

I had long since reached the end of his story and the very last line had brought tears to my eyes:

...my greatest regret...my lost baby girl.

It was as Dainefin had said: Aur-Lee had died without ever knowing anything of the Maír.

I looked back on the vision I'd had the first night I'd spent at Kolymba's house, just after I was kidnapped. Why didn't Dainefin tell me that her foster brother Reydn had come with her to Cloch? Did he stay here too? For how long? Or had she convinced him to turn back at the last minute?

I wish I too had a loved one here on Cloch. I imagined how different my imprisonment would be if I had

Sonni by my side. I wanted to ask Kolymba if he knew more about Reydn, but the thought of digging up another trauma from Dainefin's past was distressing. I still hadn't uncovered what had brought on her Empathic Aura, but I had a hunch that something unspeakable must have happened to the boy she'd believed to be her brother.

Chapter 19

In spite of their threats, Sama Kas and Mana Pun never came to check if I was still there. I hadn't forgotten they existed, but I'd stopped creeping around as if expecting an ambush at any moment. Along with the peaceful isolation, their absence also seemed to have an effect on my Empathic Aura and I had a few days of rest from the visions.

Unfortunately, that peace from the Maír leaders only lasted just over four weeks. Shortly before I set out on my daily walk, in the hours before sunset, Sama Kas and Mana Pun made an appearance.

They rattled off orders to Kolymba, of which I understood little. I gathered that we were to follow them to Mana Pun's house where someone was waiting for us.

His house was built of stone and much bigger than Kolymba's. Unlike most of the other houses in Ama-Tángaor, any vines had been removed and it had a tiled roof.

As I stepped into the room, I found myself faced with the two people I was least expecting to see: Isehar and Fayrem, the young men I'd met in Hatablar Forest.

They were sitting at the table, their arms and legs tied to their chairs. Fayrem had dark circles under his eyes, dirty hair and scratches on his face. Isehar's long hair was braided down his back and he was even thinner than I remembered. His dark eyes widened as I entered.

'Sit, Lyria,' Mana Pun said in Maír.

'*Princess* Lyria?' Isehar whispered when he heard my name.

Fayrem turned to him, gaping.

I nodded as I sat. By the look of it, they were as surprised to see me as I was them.

Mana Pun and Sama Kas tied me to the chair, then Mana Pun turned to Kolymba. He was waving a letter in his face and appeared to be accusing him of deceiving them. 'Dainefin' and 'mistake,' were all I could make out.

Kolymba read the letter. When he was done, he gave it back to Mana Pun.

'I didn't know,' he said dryly. Pointing at me, he said it was me he'd seen in a vision, not Dainefin.

It appeared the two Tángaor chiefs had captured the wrong Dainefin. Kolymba had said they knew I was an important person, a *dainefin*, a 'leader's daughter'. Since I was the one who'd turned up on the island, they'd assumed I was that *dainefin*.

'What are they saying?' Fayrem whispered to me.

Sama Kas turned to Mana Pun and Kolymba. 'Well, how do we fix this if we can't speak to them?'

Let me interpret, I blurted out.

Kolymba gave me a thoughtful look. ***With the Empathic Aura?***

Yes.

That night in the forest, I had decided to communicate with Isehar and Fayrem in writing because I hadn't known who they were or how they would react to the Empathic Aura. Now I knew I could trust them, it just made sense to keep a private channel between us, one that only Kolymba could moderate.

Kolymba turned to the others and explained my proposal. I could translate what Isehar and Fayrem said, and communicate it to Kolymba through the Empathic Aura; he in turn would translate it into Maír for Mana Pun and Sama Kas.

Mana Pun didn't reply immediately. He re-read the letter in his hand and scoffed. Sama Kas didn't seem to object to my suggestion, but said nothing and waited for his boss's reaction. Mana Pun read the letter once more and finally agreed.

Only then did I realise the complexity of the task I had volunteered myself for. What if I lost control of the Empathic Aura? What if I needed to lie, but couldn't? Would Kolymba lie for me? How much could Mana Pun and Sama Kas feel?

Then I remembered the moment I'd been kidnapped, how I had managed to suppress the Empathic Aura. Perhaps I could moderate it, even if I couldn't completely control it.

Kolymba placed an encouraging hand on my forearm and I quickly explained what was happening to the boys.

'Reydn instructed us to deliver a letter,' Isehar began.

Reydn? Dainefin's Reydn?

Even if I didn't know anything about him, I couldn't believe this was just a coincidence.

'What?' he said. I shook my head and motioned for him to continue. 'Reydn sent us into Hatablar Forest to gather some hata honey. It was supposed to be his payment for their service.' He nodded towards the Maír men.

Kolymba felt me process the information, which he translated for Mana Pun and Sama Kas.

What service?

'Keeping the Priestess away from Amarantha,' said Isehar.

'But we didn't know that at the time,' Fayrem hurried to clarify. 'Not until we met Reydn at Styr later. That's when he told us the deal had changed and we'd be delivering a different message instead.'

'He'd found out that she hadn't stayed on the island,' Isehar explained.

I couldn't help myself. *Where is she now?*

'The capital,' he answered.

I wanted to lie. With all my might I wanted to say that no one knew where Dainefin was, but all I could do was to stifle the Empathic Aura a little.

Kolymba covered for me: 'They don't know where

Dainefin is,' he lied.

'Now the conditions for payment have changed,' Isehar continued, jerking his head at the letter.

Changed how?

'We don't know. We don't understand the language.'

Kolymba translated for the two Maír, who started talking between themselves, excluding him. He took advantage of that to communicate with me.

Reydn wants them to hold you for another month. Then they'll be paid. I don't think they'll agree. They don't trust him and they feel disrespected.

What's going to happen to me?

At the centre of my thoughts lay the fear that Mana Pun may decide to get rid of me. I tiptoed around it, hoping that my fear wouldn't start seeping out; I couldn't let my emotions draw my kidnappers' attention. I felt the palms of my hands grow clammy with sweat.

I had an idea, but I needed to cool down before I could communicate it to Kolymba. I visualised a gust of wind sweeping my emotions away, an icy wind that wouldn't let any part of me flare up. Alone, in the midst of all that ice, was my idea. I aimed it and let it go.

If it's hata honey they want, I can pay my own ransom.

I felt Kolymba's heart skip. Now he was the one struggling to contain his emotions.

No. They wouldn't let you go if they thought they could use you to get more. Nothing's ever enough for them.

Mana Pun interrupted this brief exchange, visibly irritated. He spoke to Isehar and Fayrem, and Kolymba translated for us.

He says go back to Reydn, and tell him they never want to hear from him again. They're rejecting his offer.

I still wondered what that would mean for me, but I passed the message along. I fought to hold on to my nerve.

Isehar and Fayrem gave a small nod to show they understood.

Mana Pun ordered them be released. When Kolymba moved closer to help them free of the ropes, I felt his Empathic Aura, as light as a sigh, whisper a complicit invitation.

Stick around.

I relayed the message to the two young men.

'You can count on it,' Isehar replied.

'We had no idea—' Fayrem began apologetically, but then Sama Kas forced them up and out the front door, slamming it behind them.

The three Maír men stepped into the corner and started arguing in hushed voices. Every now and then, Mana would raise his voice, gesturing at me.

What's going on?

Mana Pun wants to take you into the forest tonight, so you can lead them to the Ata Mahari, Kolymba told me.

The Ata Mahari?

The River of Time.

But I don't know where that is. I don't even know what it is.

270

Yes, but they believe that you do.

Why?

'Tonight,' interrupted Mana Pun, untying my hands and throwing the door open.

When I didn't immediately move to leave, he lunged at me as though to throw me out. Kolymba shielded me with his huge frame. At that moment I knew, that whatever he'd done in the past, Kolymba deserved a chance at redemption.

The sky was still blue, but the clouds were taking on a pink tinge, and the evening breeze had picked up. It was the time I usually took my daily exercise, but it was obvious that I wouldn't be going to my terrace that evening. I realised that I may never return to it – so many things might happen before morning came that it was hard to imagine myself alive, let alone free.

Kolymba made me a herbal infusion to calm my nerves. I took it as his way of apologising for his lack of foresight, and for not finding a way to help me escape during the month I had spent on Cloch.

The infusion had a delicate taste and smelt of a flowering meadow, even though it left a vague bitterness in the mouth, like pine nuts. By the second sip, the tension knitting my forehead had melted away.

I should have realised their plan for you sooner.

But if you'd helped me escape, Mana Pun and Sama Kas would have taken it out on you.

I have nothing to lose.

What if they'd killed you?

Kolymba moved away to pour me more of the infusion. I could sense his frustration. He was tired, unhappy. He wanted nothing more than to reach the end of his story.

He handed me the steaming cup and sat down in front of me.

I am a coward. I've been saying for years that it's time for me to go, but the truth is, I'm afraid of death.

'Everyone here is,' he added aloud.

I was on the verge of understanding something important, but one fundamental detail was still missing.

Because . . . of the River of Time?

Yes. It's the reason why the Maír never left Cloch. At first, we were like exiles. Our ancestors couldn't return home for fear of the epidemic that was killing everyone who had stayed behind. Then one day, many years later, one of them had a vision. A spring at the heart of the island, an underground river gifting health and longevity to those who bathed in it.

Kolymba paused to let me absorb this. I had a strange disease that made my emotions public knowledge, I'd seen Hatablar, blue honey, heard spirits. But now we were in fairy tale territory. An enchanted river? Seriously?

He resumed his tale. *The man who had the vision was called Yan. He was the fifth Mana Maír on Cloch. He was faced with a difficult decision. I still wonder whether he made the right choice.*

I was riveted by the story and every sip of infusion was freeing me from negative thought, making room in

272

my mind for my teacher's tale.

Mana Yan waited years before revealing the exist-ence of the River of Time to the community. When he made up his mind, he said that the Ata Mahari was a gift, which we had received so we could live until we were able to return home.

To Amarantha?

Kolymba nodded and smiled.

Even if it wasn't called that, back then.

Then he went on.

Mana Yan maintained that he alone was able to calculate exactly when and where the river would surface on the island. But only those who demonstrated they were worthy of the Ata Mahari would be allowed to undergo the Time Ritual. To that effect, Mana Yan instituted a training program, at the end of which only those who had achieved certain results would be able to bathe in the river and, one day, return home.

I imagine that didn't make the people who failed happy.

Kolymba nodded.

Those who'd been excluded began to call them-selves 'Rebels', because they did not recognise Mana Yan's authority. Mana Pun and Sama Kas were their leaders.

Rebels and Separatists, two different titles for the same thing.

How did they carry out the ritual then?

Reydn helped them.

Reydn. Him again.

He was the one stoking discontent. The one who promised the Rebels that he would work out the exact day for the ritual, and find the spring. But something didn't go according to plan.

What?

Mana Yan had lied. There was no way to work out where the Ata Mahari would be. Nor when. The Ata Mahari may surface any day of the year. It's the river itself that chooses who is worthy of finding it . . . and who is not.

But Mana Pun and Sama Kas were still alive . . .

So how did they manage to find it?

Reydn discovered that some of the people – not all – who had undergone the ritual could locate the Ata Mahari again. So he approached the weakest of us who were on the Path, the only one who had not taken sides during the clash between the Rebels and Faithful. And he talked me into it.

Kolymba's guilt hit me with such intensity that I nearly threw up. He was leaning his forehead on his fingertips, his elbows on the table. He wanted me to judge him, to blame him.

He wanted to pay for what he had done.

But I couldn't judge him.

The more I heard about this Reydn, the more he reminded me of Anur, treating others as if he were entitled to everything. If Reydn was anything like Anur, it would have been impossible to say no to him. Men like Anur were aware of their own charm and knew how to manipulate people – and how to take advantage of them.

Mana Pun, Sama Kas and Reydn followed me into

the forest. I guided them through the ritual. They were the first and the only ones I led.

What about the other Rebels?

After that first time, I was no longer able to find the Ata Mahari. Mana Pun, Sama Kas and Reydn could never find it again either.

Of all the things that tormented him, that must have been the worst.

Since I betrayed my people, the Ata Mahari ... if I look for it, it will not let itself be found. It's as if ... as if it knows.

That was why Mana Pun and Sama Kas needed me. They wanted me to find it so they could keep the promise Reydn had made to all those people.

There is actually no one left of that first generation of Rebels, those who left Ama-Pamau with us. They all died of old age. The younger generation doesn't believe that Mana Pun and Sama Kas will ever succeed. Some Tángaor have been talking about elections. Others want to mend relations with the Pamau. That's why this means so much to Mana Pun and Sama Kas: they believe that if they could only reveal the location of the Ata Mahari ...

It struck me as improbable that the Ata Mahari would show itself to me, since I'd barely been on the island a month. But even if it did, I would do everything within my power to keep it a secret – even with the Emphatic Aura.

We won't let them find it.

'No, we won't,' said Kolymba. 'I'll make sure you escape tonight.'

Chapter 20

The plan was for me and Kolymba to slip away from Mana Pun and Sama Kas in the forest.

Twenty minutes later, the haversack Kolymba had given me was packed and I heard Fayrem's voice from behind the curtain divider.

Kolymba had let him and Isehar into the house. When I came out, Kolymba took my pack and handed it to them.

What are you doing? I demanded.

I want your friends to go ahead of us. If Mana Pun and Sama Kas see you with that on your back...

I see. Wait one moment.

I held out my hand and Isehar handed the haversack back. I took out my small bag, which I filled with the things I cared about most: my papers, the notebook, and the journal.

Fayrem, meanwhile, was watching Kolymba trace the path they needed to take on a map, repeating it back to him.

I rummaged even deeper in the haversack for my mother's scent bottle, which I retrieved from a tangle of clothes that had swallowed it up, and finally passed the haversack back to Isehar.

They'll be here soon, Kolymba warned.

Where is your bag?

'I don't need anything,' he answered in Maír.

He had me tell Fayrem how to get to Ama-Pamau: past the hill and along the coast. It was just over an hour away. We, on the other hand, would have to find our bearings in the forest. I hoped he was better at navigating than I was.

He handed a sealed letter to Fayrem to give to the Pamau when they arrived.

Isehar bid me good luck, and Fayrem gave me an encouraging smile. Kolymba made them repeat the directions to Ama-Pamau one last time, and then I watched them sneak away, across the now deserted fields. I hoped they'd reach the village before darkness obscured their path.

The moon was already high in the sky when Mana Pun and Sama Kas knocked on the door. There was no wind and the humidity was unbearable.

The forest was alive with the calls of nocturnal creatures. A pair of bats flew over our heads, dancing through the branches of the great *káori*. I startled at a distant bark and imagined that some otherworldly creature would leap out at us.

It's only a fox, Kolymba reassured me.

He and I walked slightly ahead of the others. Every now and then I would pretend to stop and think, closing my eyes and assuming a mystical expression. The two Tángaor were lapping it up until Mana Pun realised that we had been going in circles.

'We've already been this way, I recognise this clearing,' he grunted.

'All clearings look the same on this island, Mana Pun,' said Kolymba.

'I think I'll walk with her now,' he said, pulling Kolymba back and taking his place at my side.

I'd been feeling more in control of my Empathic Aura lately, but that night there were just too many emotions swirling inside of me, and I was nervous they would break through. If Mana Pun came too close, I wouldn't be able to keep anything from him for long.

Kolymba must have seen my fear because he immediately came to my aid.

When Kolymba spoke, it was like curling up in a blanket and watching the snow fall outside the window. But that night I learned that when Kolymba sang, the Earth stopped spinning.

'*Ata Mahari, hari mana,*
Ata Mahari, kodhna chmera noi.
Ata Mahari, hari mana,
Ata Mahari, kodhna chmera noi.

Mbissoi kadhmir an doi, mbissoi kadhmir an doi,
Ata Mahari, ata mana,
Ata Mahari, ata mana.

Mbissoi kadhmir an doi, mbissoi kadhmir an doi,
Ata Mahari, ata mana,
Ata Mahari, ata mana.'

I stopped, transfixed by his song. My Empathic Aura filled with the sacred chant and amplified it. I could feel the words inside me, and every fibre of my body longed to join him in song.

His voice reverberated in the air. The ground echoed its vibrations, but no one else seemed to notice it humming beneath our feet. And then I understood.

Kolymba's song had opened a crossing. The Ata Mahari was calling to me – and me alone.

I had to decide, and quickly. Follow the pull of the Ata Mahari and find the spring, possibly leading Mana Pun and Sama Kas directly to it, or resist its plea and get as far away from it as possible.

I wanted to resist, but it was calling me. It was calling me. I became inescapably aware that the Ata Mahari would not forgive my refusal. I had to follow it, find it, and listen to it whisper the answers to life's most important mysteries.

The River of Time became more insistent with every verse Kolymba sang, until taking a single step in the opposite direction would have cost me all the energy I had. Just standing still was making me sweat and struggle to breathe. I could no longer feel my arms and legs. I had to give in, let its current pull me along.

But I was spared when Kolymba's song suddenly broke off.

As my mind cleared, I realised we were surrounded.

A crowd of unfamiliar, white-clad Maír had emerged from the trees and positioned themselves around us in the clearing. Isehar and Fayrem were among them. I waved at them as if in a trance, receiving waves in return.

Two Maír picked up the chant where Kolymba had left off. Their voices were louder and more solemn.

> *'Ata Mahari, hari mana,*
> *Ata Mahari, kodhna chmera noi.*
> *Ata Mahari, hari mana,*
> *Ata Mahari, kodhna chmera noi.'*

Mana Pun and Sama Kas turned and fled. None of the Maír moved to stop them. The two singers softened their chant and fixed their eyes on Kolymba.

> *'Mbissoi kadhmir an doi, mbissoi kadhmir an doi,*
> *Ata Mahari, ata mana,*
> *Ata Mahari, ata mana'*

Kolymba had taken a few steps back towards the darkness that had swallowed Mana Pun and Sama Kas.

Come, I held out my hand. *Come with me.*
He hesitated.

> '*Mbissoi kadhmir an doi, mbissoi kadhmir an doi,*
> *Ata Mahari, ata mana,*
> *Ata Mahari, ata mana.*'

As the singing drew to a close, I realised the Maír had moved in, leaving Kolymba no way out.

'Our village needs another teacher,' one of them said. He stood out with his elderly appearance. He had a grey moustache and whiskery sideburns, a braid the same colour fell to the middle of his back.

'Sama Tar,' said Kolymba, extending a trembling hand.

'*Mana* Tar,' one of the Maír corrected him with a smile.

Kolymba respectfully lowered his head.

Mana Tar grasped Kolymba's hand. 'Brother.'

'I don't understand.'

'Come back with us,' said Mana Tar.

Kolymba went down on his knees.

Mana Tar said something I didn't understand. I looked around and saw that the Maír were nodding approvingly. Fayrem and Isehar were silent, looking questioningly at Kolymba.

Another Maír approached. 'You will need a new name.'

Kolymba's enormous body shook with sobs.

'You will be Kolymba *Kathún*,' said Mana Tar.

Forgiven.

It was the last communication I ever had from Kolymba's Empathic Aura.

'I am forgiven,' he repeated, turning to me, his eyelashes beaded with tears. Suddenly, his eyes widened as he realised his Empathic Aura was gone.

All those years, the only thing Kolymba had never tried was to forgive himself. A few moments earlier, he had been ready for his life to end. Now he was a new person.

I crouched down next to him and leaned into his shoulder. He was still trembling.

I squeezed his arm. **Come on.**

A few Maír came over to help him up. Each looked purposefully into Kolymba's eyes, and I saw the memories of broken friendships being pushed aside to clear the way for new beginnings.

The others turned to me and bowed. 'Welcome, Dainefin.'

The Maír filed out of the forest in a silent procession, respectful of the holiness of what had just taken place.

Kolymba walked beside me, freed from the Empathic Aura that had weighed on him for most of his life. He held me close, his arm like a wing wrapped round my shoulders. Even without the Empathic Aura, we were bound together for life.

He bent his head towards mine, squeezing me even tighter and whispering, 'Thank you. You have given me back my life.'

We emerged from the forest in the grey light before dawn. After at least a quarter of an hour walking across cultivated fields, we reached the Pamau village. It lay in a valley – an ancient crater perhaps – not far from the island's southern coast.

I had expected something the size of Ama-Tángaor, but this was a town, home to more than two thousand families.

Ama-Pamau was still asleep, and the procession shrunk as it went on, each Maír returning to their hearth as we passed their home.

Mana Tar took me, Kolymba, Isehar and Fayrem to a house where we could stay the night. I had so many questions for Fayrem and Isehar about the ins and outs of their story, all the missing parts, their roles – and Reydn's – in all this, but I was falling asleep on my feet. So, even though I was excited to chat with them, I allowed the Pamau elder to lead me upstairs and down a hallway to my new room.

I awoke some hours later with the warm mid-day sun on my face. My stomach growled loudly, so I rose and pulled on some clean clothes. The house wasn't large and it was easy to follow the smell of simmering stew and fresh-baked bread to find the kitchen. A note written in Kolymba's hand next to the stove said he had

gone out but that we should make ourselves at home –
in fact, this house *was* his old home, which Mana Tar
had tended all these years. I didn't see any signs of life
from the boys' room, so I helped myself to the food. Just
as I was going back for seconds, Isehar and Fayrem
shuffled in. Fayrem's eyes were still glazed with sleep
and had deep black smudges below them just like mine.
Isehar, on the other hand, looked ready to hike to the
Serra del Lárr.

I got out two more bowls and filled them with
steaming stew. As I set the bowls down on the table
before the boys, my curiosity took over. I wanted to know
everything about them, where they had grown up, what
they did in Murihen. But first of all, I needed to settle
one unanswered question.

Who's Reydn?

'The most manipulative person on the face of the
Earth,' was Isehar's reply.

And what's he got to do with you two?

It turned out, Isehar and Fayrem were brothers. It was
hard to believe, but then again, I was the last person
who could say that. Sonni and I looked completely different to Anur.

'We're not proper brothers,' Isehar clarified,
adding, 'but we might as well be, really. I was adopted
by Fayrem's family when I was thirteen. I don't
remember anything before then.'

You don't remember anything that happened before you were thirteen?

'I fell off a horse,' he shrugged.

Isehar was one of those people who couldn't be still for more than two seconds. As he spoke, his leg bounced and he had a habit of fiddling with whatever was within reach of his fingertips – the cuff of his shirtsleeve, a breadcrumb, the back of his other hand.

'It was when everyone was moving to Amarantha because of the famine in Murihen,' said Fayrem. 'Hundreds of people were leaving every day; his family couldn't be found.'

I remembered those two years of famine from Dainefin's lesson. They had plunged both kingdoms into hardship, destroying Murihen's economy and filling Amarantha with more mouths than she could feed. When Dainefin spoke of it years later, I looked at it like any history lesson; I had been too young to understand the personal sacrifices everyone must have made during the emergency relocations.

I thought of Isehar's parents, imagined them retracing their journey, desperately searching for him everywhere. I felt my conscience twinge at the privilege I'd taken for granted my whole life.

'No one ever came looking for me.' Isehar wasn't bitter or self-pitying, but was simply stating a fact. 'Reydn found me and gave me to Fayrem's family. I didn't see him for a while after that, but he turned up again a couple of years ago, suggested I do a little job for him every now and then. He said I owed him and I figured it'd help my adopted family make ends meet.'

'It's not easy making a living in Murihen,' said Fayrem in his brother's defence. 'Without the money Isehar brings home from Reydn ...'

Reydn must be quite the businessman.

'I've never been clear about what he does,' answered Isehar. 'These past few months, he's been buzzing around the Murihen Council. I have a feeling he's going to run in the next election. Lately, he's been seen with your older brother a lot.'

It was a surprise, but not hard to believe. Reydn sounded just like the sort of person that Anur would hang around with.

Does he ask you to run errands for my Uncle Hervin?

'Ah come on, like I've ever been anywhere near court,' said Isehar. 'Reydn wouldn't ask someone like me to work for the royals. Can you imagine?'

I was suddenly filled with pride for my father. In Amarantha's court, we made no distinction between the wealthy and the poor. Whoever showed talent or willingness to work hard would be appreciated, and rewarded accordingly.

'He'd send me on errands here and there, to get things for him,' Isehar continued. 'Then one day he asked me to go into Hatablar to gather honey. I'd never been that far from home and my sense of direction is pathetic, so I talked Fayrem into coming along.'

'We didn't know what the resin was for,' said Fayrem. 'That is, until Reydn met us at the border a few days ago and told us it was to pay off a debt. He was very cagey about it. That was when we knew we'd got ourselves in big trouble. But he never said you were here. Just Dainefin. We thought we would drop it off and bring her back.'

'Ly, we didn't mean for you to get hurt,' Isehar said.

The way he said my name, using my family nick-name, gave me a strange feeling in the pit of my stomach. As if I'd known Isehar my whole life.

You two are the reason nothing's happened to me. Thank you for helping me escape.

'We couldn't leave you there, Your Highness.' Fayrem blushed as he spoke, slightly emphasising my title and glancing at his brother.

What happened after you left Ama-Tángaor? How did you know where we were?

'Finding the town wasn't a problem,' Isehar answered, looking to Fayrem for confirmation, who nodded. 'But the people . . . . All the houses were empty. Almost all of them. We knocked on a woman's door and gave her the letter. She took us to a field where some sort of ceremony was going on . . .'

'It was the summer solstice,' said Fayrem.

'You know everything,' Isehar was impressed. 'Anyway, the woman showed the letter around, and then some of them started asking us questions, which of course we couldn't understand. We tried all sorts of ways to explain ourselves, but nothing was working.'

Isehar stopped to think for a few seconds.

'Then we must have said something that caught their attention,' he continued. 'They got all agitated, started gesturing at us to lead us back to where we'd come from.'

What did you say?

'Dunno,' he shrugged. 'We said so many things—'

'Dainefin,' Fayrem interrupted. 'They got agitated when we said "Dainefin".'

I tried to put myself in the Pamaus' shoes. Hearing the Priestess's name, so suddenly, from two strangers who didn't speak Maír, must have been like finding themselves face to face with a spirit. Then it crossed my mind that perhaps they were disappointed to see me instead of Dainefin.

'You mustn't think that, Your Highness,' Fayrem whispered so quietly I almost didn't hear him. 'You should have seen the way Mana Tar was looking at you.'

It was my turn to blush. I hadn't realised anyone could feel my Empathic Aura at this volume. I took a tighter hold on it.

Perhaps the Maír had been waiting for me, after all. That thought relieved me of a weight I had been carrying ever since my arrival on Cloch, that the Faithful wouldn't know I was here, or who I was, that they'd have no interest whatsoever in helping me rid myself of the Empathic Aura.

What will you do now?

'We'll go back home,' said Fayrem.

'And keep an eye on Reydn,' said Isehar. 'I have a feeling he's up to something big.'

I wish there were something I could do to help.

'There is,' said Fayrem. 'Stay here and get better.

If Reydn stirs up trouble, Amarantha is going to need you to be strong and healthy.'

'My brother's right,' said Isehar. 'Your family has already lost too many, what with . . .'

Alarm flooded through me.

Has something happened?

Isehar and Fayrem exchanged a look that told me each brother was hoping to let the other be the bearer of bad news.

'Your uncle . . .' Fayrem began.

He didn't need to finish the sentence.

My thoughts flew to my aunt and father. Aunt Rehena and I didn't understand each other all that well, and I was sorry to admit that I had always preferred my uncle's company to hers. She hovered and tried to control everything. My mother once told me that Rehena hadn't always been that way. It was only after she'd lost Ambar that my aunt had started trying to force the world into submission. But there are things beyond anyone's control. And now she'd lost the rest of her family.

And so had Father. My mother, my uncle, Anur in Murihen, and me beyond reach, at the other end of the continent. At least Sonni was still by his side.

'Murihen is in turmoil,' said Isehar, 'and some dangerous ideas are floating around. The Separatists are making the most of it – they're multiplying like cockroaches.'

'The rumour is that they're preparing to declare war on Amarantha,' said Fayrem.

So many things were changing. My mother was dead – murdered. My uncle had fallen ill and succumbed mere months later. Reydn was in Murihen and so was Anur . . . . What shape did war take, in my imagination? That of something from the past, locked inside a dusty box in an attic.

It had been fifty years since the end of Amarantha's last – and only – war. But war remained a school subject for me, something I never imagined I would face in my lifetime.

Perhaps my uncle and father would have argued one day, but their brotherhood had kept the beast at bay. It hadn't killed it, though. And now my uncle was dead and one half of the truce was gone with him.

'Your father is an extraordinary man,' Isehar said, sensing my growing apprehension. 'He'll try to keep it from coming to that.'

What will happen to your family if war breaks out?

'We'll find a way to survive,' Isehar said with a shrug.

I liked them. I was intrigued by Isehar's confidence and admired Fayrem's humility. They were young, but they didn't let anything scare them. They reminded me of . . .

The Valiant! Don't go back to Murihen. Go to Amarantha and find the Valiant, Myrain.

'Why?' asked Fayrem.

Ask him to give you a job. God knows how much he needs men like you at the moment.

'The two of us? Under King Uriel's command?'

Isehar said with a half-smile. 'We're the sons of Murihen peasants, Lyria. We know nothing about—'

It's not like that in Amarantha. Just trust me ...

I ran upstairs and grabbed one of my last few sheets of paper. My letter to the Valiant and my father wrote itself. I asked Myrain to take the two brothers under his protection. My message to my father was short: there were only three things I wanted to tell him.

I miss you. I love you. I'll be back soon.

I folded the paper and wrote on the back *Virtue and Knowledge*, Aur-Lee's motto, proof that the letter was in my own hand, then returned to the kitchen.

'We don't know how to thank you,' Fayrem said as he took the letter and slipped it into his pocket.

My thanks to you.

After that, we ate heartily while Isehar and Fayrem told me about all their adventures and misadventures; the hare-brained plans to take a little extra money home, the oddest people they'd met on the road. I told them about my journey, about Cam and Reya, the parish priest of Denhole and Uncle Noalim; about Gaudrot and the forest spirits, Old Lohm and Móiras.

And I told them about Sonni, who I missed so much. I confessed I was afraid to return to Amarantha to find him changed; more grown up than me. A proper adult.

'I've heard a lot about your brother,' said Isehar, serious again. 'Great things are expected of him ... I can't imagine what it must be like to inherit King Uriel's crown. All those expectations, all those eyes on him ...'

'Tell the truth,' said Fayrem, 'at times like this you have to be grateful we're peasants.'

'Let's see . . . I *really* can't imagine how things could have gone better for me,' his brother teased.

Fayrem jabbed him with his elbow. Isehar cuffed him round the back of the head.

The whole conversation went on like this, joking and serious in turns; we confided in each other and regretted not having more time together. When it was time for them to go, I walked the two brothers to the path that led to the north-facing shore and wished them luck.

Be careful.

'Don't worry, Lyria,' said Isehar, winking at me. 'Our lives are pretty boring.'

Chapter 21

'Ata Mahari, hari mana,
Ata Mahari, kodhna chmera noi.
Ata Mahari, hari mana,
Ata Mahari, kodhna chmera noi.

Mbissoi kadhmir an doi, mbissoi kadhmir an doi,
Ata Mahari, ata mana,
Ata Mahari, ata mana.'

River of Time, ancient spring, River of Time, receive our lives.
We sing our immense joy, River of Time, of ancient things.

At the end of the chant, Dainefin quickens her step to catch up with Kolymba, asking him a question that's been weighing on her mind.

'What was there before time?' he repeats. 'It is interesting that you should ask me this question just now. My theory is that before time, there were Luminous Thoughts. That which comes before us, and remains of us at the end of our lives.' Kolymba pats her shoulder. 'But no one can be sure.'

'Dainefin, back in line,' the Mana says. Her eyes widen but she sees that he's smiling.

Dainefin stands to one side, waiting for the three boys they're with to overtake her. She looks around, just to be certain Reydn isn't there. They have been walking for the best part of an hour, pausing continuously to intone the Maír chant. She didn't see him at the meeting place, nor in line among the Elders and the Chosen. Again, she walks ahead of her fellow students, this time to catch up with the Mana.

'Mana Yan, what about Reydn?'

'You really don't want to stay in line tonight, do you?' Mana Yan shakes his head in exasperation. 'Kolymba, Sama, begin the next chant for me. I'm walking ahead with Dainefin.'

He takes her hand and leads her deep into the forest. In his other hand, he holds a small torch that he shifts around with quick, precise movements. Dainefin can only see a few paces ahead, while Mana Yan walks as if in daylight. She copies his movements: stepping over shrubs, walking on stones, stooping under the broken branches blocking their way.

Neither of them speaks and Dainefin doesn't let go of the Mana's hand until he finally comes to a halt.

They have reached a clearing large enough to hold perhaps five people with their arms outstretched. She looks up and sees the stars, the crescent moon. Then, another light source catches her attention. It looks like the sun reflected off the hand mirror of a teasing child, but weaker. Dainefin steps closer to the source of quivering light. A tiny gush of water is bubbling up between two rocks, sinking into the soil beneath.

'Ata Mahari,' says the Mana.

Dainefin inspects the surrounding ground, but there's no trace of a stream. Not so much as a trickle.

'Where's the rest?' she asks.

'Who knows,' he replies. 'According to legend, the river springs from the rock and moves underground, where it roars along until it flows into the sea. We have never found access to the underground river.'

Dainefin had imagined the ritual taking place on the banks of a moon-kissed brook, not something so small.

Mana Yan sits on the grass in the centre of the clearing. Dainefin has never seen him be so informal. She too sits on the ground.

Soon, her fellow students will join them, and they will undergo the Ritual. She's been waiting for this day for the last three years, picturing this very moment. But now she's wondering if it wouldn't be better to walk away. What's wrong with her? Dainefin fixes her gaze on the spring, finally realising how beautiful it is. She feels the sudden urge to cup her hands and drink from it, bathe her face, her feet.

Then she thinks of Reydn, of what he'll say to her tomorrow. Will he find her different? Will she be different? More grown up, more mature, more *Maír*?

Dainefin feels her heartbeat quicken. How long will it take the others to reach them? How much time is left? Enough for her to pull out?

It is all so *holy*. She sneaks a look at the Mana, and sees him gazing straight ahead, as if his eyes were on the spring, but his mind somewhere else entirely.

Dainefin tips a tiny stone out of her shoe. She can't hold back her question any longer.

'Why hasn't Reydn been Chosen? He's been working so hard.'

'It is true,' replies the Mana, with no sign of irritation. 'He is a hard worker. He has learnt the language and the runes, never missed a day's meditation. He has drunk the *inu-dhearma*. He has studied all of our traditions. He knows what it is to be Maír.'

Dainefin's raises her eyebrows. 'But . . . ?'

'But he is not one of us. He is not Maír. He does not want to be Maír. The bond between the two of you was not born on this island. When you decided to walk the Path three years ago, you both promised to forget your pasts. But not a day has gone by without Reydn thinking of the life he renounced. A life where there was only you and him.'

There can be no future for Dainefin and Reydn on Cloch. The day she set foot in the Maír village, Dainefin was reborn. She is home. Reydn has been living beside her happiness, unable even to brush against it.

'I assure you I have tried to accept him,' the Mana continues. 'Reydn's constancy and commitment have never before been seen in any of the Chosen. Perhaps because none of them have ever needed to work as hard as him. Not even you. Some things are natural to those of Maír blood. While for Reydn, this has been an uphill struggle . . .'

'He is trying, though,' says Dainefin.

'I doubt he will ever make it. Reydn will never have a Luminous Thought until he can distance his feelings for you. They are too heavy a burden for him. Reydn meditates and suffers, instead of filling himself with light and joy.'

Light and joy. They had once had plenty of that – in Amarantha. But on Cloch, everything is complicated. Why hadn't she stopped him from coming with her?

'I am so sorry,' she says.

'My child, it is not your fault.'

'Are you going to send him away?'

'No,' he reassures her. 'Of course not. On the contrary, I'll encourage him to try again. But for now, he needs to find a way to accept your decisions. Once he fully understands them, he will be ready to start over. Who knows, he may even achieve a Luminous Thought. If he does, and he is happy to stay with us, he will have the chance to abandon himself to the Ata Mahari.'

Dainefin wishes the weight oppressing her would lift. This is supposed to be the most important night of her life. She should be centred, but she feels at odds with herself.

'You may still change your mind, if you wish,' the Mana adds.

'About what?'

'About your feelings for him. Your feelings for each other are like the Ata Mahari – perhaps what I see bubbling up on the surface belies a river roaring underneath.'

'But what if I end up like him? Incapable of . . . of . . .'

'Of having Luminous Thoughts?' the Mana suggests. 'Is that what worries you?'

Dainefin drops her gaze.

'There are many paths to happiness,' Mana Yan points out. 'Some find it in communion with the whole universe. Some find it in their love for another person, here on earth. Some of us do not have a choice. When I carried out the ritual, I was alone. Now, I am surrounded by Chosen, and couldn't be happier. The path I've taken is the one of Luminous Life. You've had Luminous Thoughts, have you not?'

Dainefin nods.

'One morning, I woke up and that feeling has never left me,' he says.

'But,' she asks, 'is there room for love in such a life?'

The Mana smiles. 'I am loved by the community and I love it in return. That sustains me. But you are not obliged to follow the same path.'

Dainefin and Reydn. Cloch or Amarantha? He would only be truly happy in Amarantha. She is home here. They can never find happiness together. Amarantha is but a fading memory to her, the people she once loved a distant thought.

'Mana Yan, I love Reydn. We grew up as siblings. But once I reached Cloch . . . Mana, this is my home. You, the Elders, my friends, you are my family now.'

Mana Yan closes his eyes and begins to sing. A choir of distant voices joins him in song.

'Ata Mahari, hari mana,
Ata Mahari, kodhna chmera noi.
Mbissoi kadhmir an doi, mbissoi kadhmir an doi,
Ata Mahari, ata mana,
Ata Mahari, ata mana.'

Chapter 22

A roll of thunder woke me. It was mid-afternoon and I lay in my new bed listening to the rain drum on the roof of Kolymba's house. From where I lay, I could see the ruins of a building from my window. I hoped Isehar and Fayrem had made it to the fjords of Styr before the rain hit.

The events of the previous twenty-four hours – the forest, the white-clad Maír forgiving Kolymba, the time spent with my friends from Murihen – had taken on the powdery consistency of a dream. To top it all off, the Empathic Aura had shown me another vision, the first one set on Cloch. I picked through my thoughts, trying to bring some order to them and fill in the gaps. When I decided I couldn't do it on my own, I took a deep breath and got out of bed.

The room was vast and bare. My haversack lay in a corner next to a chair upon which Kolymba had placed a basin of water, a sponge and a cake of soap. I appreciated that he hadn't woken me. I shed the filthy clothes I'd been wearing since the day before, and dipped the sponge into the still-lukewarm water. The soap smelt of bay leaves, and that alone made me feel stronger, ready to face what I knew would be a difficult conversation.

I pulled one of the white gowns Kolymba had made for me from my haversack, and slipped it on. I walked down the stairs, allowing my aching muscles to wake slowly, enjoying the breezy feeling of the skirt around my legs.

Kolymba Kathún was kneeling on the stone floor. He was pounding unfamiliar-looking berries in a mortar. Mana Tar was seated at the wooden table, shredding leaves. The room smelt of damp undergrowth and an apothecary's shop; it reminded me of the room in the castle where Dainefin made her herbal mixtures.

Kolymba and Mana Tar paused their activities as soon as I came in. Mana Tar lit up . . . until I came close enough for my emotional state to wash over him. My uncle's death, the Separatists, war, Reydn; fear of what lay in store for Isehar and Fayrem, for my father, for me. Oh, and what the latest vision the Empathic Aura had shown me, which could have been caused by a whole host of things: being kidnapped, resisting the Ata Mahari, Dainefin's reason for never telling me about the Maír, her relationship with her foster brother.

I felt a little uneasy around Mana Tar, perhaps because he appeared so august. The age spots on his skin – a little lighter than Kolymba's – the wrinkles around his eyes and creases on the backs of his hands made him look to be over seventy years old. I wondered how old he really was. Two hundred? More?

The grooves around his mouth deepened and I glimpsed a smile behind his big moustache. The Mana stood up and came over to embrace me.

'*Eistehara-le*,' he said. It meant either 'I listen' or 'I hear'; Maír didn't differentiate between the two.

I told them about my vision.

'It's time you know the rest of the story,' said Kolymba.

He didn't apologise for not telling me sooner; nor did I expect him to. I had waited so long to ask about Reydn because I hadn't felt ready yet.

What happened after Dainefin received the Ritual and Reydn didn't?

'He talked me into leading him to the Ata Mahari with Kas and Pun, to show them the Ritual,' said Kolymba.

But ... how? Why did you do it?

How could such a conscientious man have betrayed his people? I realised that my questions must be rubbing salt into his wounds .... But I'd trusted him.

'I really believed that Reydn deserved a chance, that Mana Yan was wrong about him,' he said. 'I *wanted* to believe it. I cared for Dainefin, and I thought that if Reydn didn't complete the Ritual and their paths diverged forever, it would destroy her.

'The irony was that rather than stave off the conflict between them, my decision brought it to a head. But that's not all. After the Ritual ...'

Kolymba slowed, measuring words that were difficult to say aloud. Mana Tar came to his aid.

'Reydn set Mana Yan's house on fire,' he said gravely. 'And Mana Yan choked to death on the smoke.'

I froze in horror.

'Those ruins outside . . . . They are what remains of Mana Yan's house,' Kolymba continued.

Did Reydn mean to kill him? Or was it an accident?

'We do not know.'

Mana Tar seemed about to add something, but changed his mind.

'Dainefin and I fell ill a few weeks apart,' Kolymba went on. 'She couldn't forgive Reydn for what he'd done. And I could not forgive myself.'

Mana Tar laid a hand on his shoulder. 'Stop tormenting yourself.'

The Mana was right. Kolymba had been forgiven and given a clean slate. He had lived with the Empathic Aura much longer than Dainefin, and it was only fair that he put an end to that terrible part of his life.

I missed Dainefin. I remembered how we'd parted – how bad I'd made her feel about leaving me on Cloch. I wanted to run back to tell her what I'd always assumed she already knew: that I loved her like a second mother. And now that mine was gone, it felt even more wrong to be here, surrounded by these Maír men, discussing Dainefin's personal life.

'I didn't even like Reydn,' Kolymba added with a frown. 'But Dainefin cared for him, and I cared for her. I thought it would make her happy.'

'What happened, happened,' the Mana said, attempting to put an end to the conversation. 'Dainefin was admitted to the Ritual, and Reydn was not. Reydn talked Kolymba into baptising him, Kas and Pun. Then he set the Mana's house on fire, and ran away.'

'And I ran, too,' Kolymba continued. 'I couldn't bear to stay here, knowing that Mana Yan's death . . . . The shame was too great.'

'Dainefin left a few days later without a word to anyone,' added the Mana, answering the question I'd been about to ask. 'She was so angry, I thought she'd gone looking for Reydn, to have it out with him. But when she never came back, I imagined that she must have followed in her mother's steps and left the island for good.'

Kolymba listened to the Mana's version of the story as if he didn't know the ending. As if he'd hoped that Dainefin had recovered from the Empathic Aura *before* she'd left the island.

'Dainefin never visited Ama-Tángaor,' Kolymba said. 'It didn't even exist then. We were simple rebels, living in the forest, waiting for Reydn to guide us. But Reydn had already got what he wanted, he had received the Ritual. He didn't care about the other Tángaor; he had no intention of leading a new community. He built himself a boat and abandoned us.'

How could Dainefin have loved someone like that?

'They grew up together,' said Kolymba.

'But Cloch changed them,' said Mana Tar.

And have you seen Dainefin since she left?

They both shook their heads.

And Reydn?

304

'I only found out yesterday that he'd met with Mana Pun some months ago,' answered Kolymba. 'I didn't know where he was or what he was up to until then. I didn't realise he still bore such a strong hatred for Dainefin or that—'

Or that what?

Did he mean . . . ? If Dainefin was right – if my mother really hadn't been the target – then did that mean the intended victim of the poison had been . . .

I took a deep breath and gathered my thoughts. I stood up and walked to the window, to gaze at the sulking sky and the puddles on the cobbled street outside. At least the rain had stopped.

Why the visions? What am I supposed to do with them? Should I go back and warn Dainefin? She said I couldn't trust them.

'Everyone interprets them in their own way,' was Mana Tar's reply. 'Some believe that what they see is only one option of many. Others believe it will undoubtedly come to pass. But we cannot advise you to leave.'

Why not?

'We want you to stay,' answered Kolymba. 'So you can heal. But not only that . . .'

'Before you came to speak to us, we too had something to discuss with you,' said Mana Tar.

I imagined speaking the same words Mana Tar had used with me earlier: *eistehara-le*, I listen / I hear.

'Before you arrived,' Kolymba began, 'I dreamt of your arrival.'

I know.

'For a long time, I wondered who you were. Then I began to see Dainefin too, and I understood you two were connected in some way. When Mana Pun and Sama Kas told me to hold you prisoner, I did so because I believed protecting you was my penance for the damage I had caused. I never imagined that you would guide *me* home.'

'And for this,' the Mana took over, 'we shall always be grateful. However, there is something else. Since Kolymba told me about your visions this morning, I've become more and more certain that you must be here to put an end to our exile. To bring us home.'

To Amarantha?

They both nodded.

I can tell you how—

Mana Tar shook his head. 'It's not the journey we're worried about,' he explained, 'but our Pamau brothers and sisters. They no longer believe in Lyr.'

Lyr?

'Lyr is the continent you call Amarantha,' said Kolymba.

I was ashamed to admit that I didn't even know the origin of my own name, and had never been curious about it. Given my mother's scant imagination, I had assumed that Father must have chosen it, but I now suspected that the only person at court who would have known its meaning may have had a hand in it.

'You have just arrived in Ama-Pamau,' said Kolymba. 'Give us a chance, get to know us. Find out who you are.'

'Then you can decide whether you'll help us return,' Mana Tar added.

Earlier, he'd said that everyone interpreted visions in their own way and acted accordingly. I realised he hadn't been speaking in general terms, but drawing on a conversation that must have begun before I woke. Kolymba had dreamt of my arrival, and Mana Tar had chosen to believe that I was some sort of messiah.

What should I do? Go back and warn Dainefin that Reydn may be plotting against her? But I had only just arrived in Ama-Pamau. I was here to heal, yet the prospect seemed weeks or even months away. What would happen to Dainefin, and to my family, in that time?

'The decision is yours to make,' Kolymba reassured me. 'I will build you a boat. As soon as you want to leave, you just have to say so.'

If I stayed, I had to be sure I focussed on healing, not on assuaging my curiosity. Because curiosity, without a doubt, was my driving force just then. I thought back to the call of the Ata Mahari, to the vision I'd had after. What were those Luminous Thoughts that Dainefin had been talking about? What was the Maír's history? I was dying to know more, but at the same time I needed to get better, I needed someone to set me on the right path to getting rid of the Empathic Aura once and for all.

If Kolymba and Mana Tar really could help me, I would help them. It was the least I could do to repay Kolymba for his protection and friendship.

I'm going to need a lot of help.

Mana Tar's shoulders relaxed. He and Kolymba

placed both hands on their chests, as the Maír do.

Wait before you thank me.

What I wanted most was for them to tell me everything anew. About the Maír, and how they'd ended up on Cloch. About the Empathic Aura and the Ata Mahari. How people here recovered from my affliction.

Mana Tar granted my wish.

'Come. I'll take you to the Kymirama.'

Kymirion. Ama. Book and house.

It was so strange to imagine a library on the Isle of Cloch. Ama-Tángaor had given me the impression that the Maír were a simple civilisation. The Tángaor lived in simple dwellings of stone and wood, too basic for even the poorest back home. The only exception had been Mana Pun's house – a show of power, perhaps, but still nothing compared to the houses of merchants and physicians in the city of Amarantha.

But Ama-Pamau had nothing in common with Ama-Tángaor. A city planner's dream, it radiated out from the central square along avenues traced like the spokes of a wheel and crossed by concentric lanes. The avenues were wide enough that five or six people could walk shoulder to shoulder; gutters ran down both sides and manholes indicated the presence of underground sewers.

Mana Tar didn't take me directly to the library. Instead, he zigzagged through the lanes, pointing out only slightly larger than those in Ama-Tángaor, but better built. The building blocks, the Mana explained, had been levelled and bound together with lime and sand; the sloping roofs supported by wooden beams and thatched with layers of clay and straw. Every dwelling had its own internal patio. Mana's contained a single lemon tree, while Kolymba's was overrun with wild creepers. Through the windows of some of the houses I glimpsed dainty gardens adorned by potted plants, climbing strawberries, cherry trees and wisteria.

The shops were the same design as the houses, but with open entrances. Curtains of ropes braided with flowers or shells separated them from the street. People greeted me with smiles from their shop doorways, some bowing their heads, others inviting me in.

The baker, a barefoot woman with long braids, gave me a roll so soft it melted in my mouth. The potter let me into the back of the shop to admire his creations, as did the glazier and the weavers – a couple who wove the white material everyone's tunics were made of.

Not a single person asked where I was from, even though my skin was several shades lighter than their own and my eyes stood out like cornflowers in a field of amaranth.

I was enjoying the tour, but I was also growing impatient to arrive at the Kymirama. I wanted to read Maír books, learn who wrote them, what they were about, how many there were.

And most of all: what they said about the Empathic Aura.

Mana Tar took us to a piazza at the end of the main

street. It was divided into eight grassy segments delin-
eated by gravel paths converging around a well. A few
villagers were chatting away in an orderly queue as they
waited their turn, holding jugs identical to the ones the
potter had just shown me.

Of the eight sides of the square, seven were
bordered by spacious porticoes, built in a pale, slightly
pink stone. The remaining side of the square was taken
up by the largest building in the whole city.

The monumental entrance to the circular building
was framed by two enormous trapezoidal stone blocks.
They were slightly darker than the stone of the surrounding buildings, giving the place a serious, solemn
appearance.

Is that a temple?

'In a way,' the Mana replied. 'It's the Kymirama.'

Mana Tar smiled contentedly while I stepped back
to view the building in its entirety. I went nearly as far
back as the well before I could see it all at once.

I noticed the writing on the lintel: *Kymirios kymimanna.*

What does this say? I know Kymirios *is literature.
But* kymimanna*? Isn't that 'book covers'?*

'You're right, it does mean "book cover", but we
also use the word to say "to embrace" or "to protect".
It's a metaphor.'

Literature embraces and protects ... what?

'Everything,' he answered. 'Everything worth
remembering.'

The Maír language surprised me every day. The

grammar wasn't straightforward – the exceptions out-weighed the rules – but then I came across wonderful words that existed on the edge of the untranslatable, with layers and layers of meaning.

The interior of the Kymirama was an amphitheatre of books. Hundreds of steps surrounded a small central space, each step covered in shelves of books upon books upon books. I slipped through the spaces that had been left clear for people to move up and down the steps and I began to inspect the volumes. Even Anur would have been impressed, and he didn't even like books.

Every step corresponded to a different genre. The lowest housed cookery books, manuals on vegetable growing and care of the home. On the next, I came across architecture and engineering, scientific tracts and papers I would have avoided like the plague in Aur-Lee's Royal Library. Prose and poetry were on the highest and therefore longest steps: tales and legends, fables, epic poems, illustrated children's books. Some were lettered with ancient runes, others in contemporary writing.

Mana Tar climbed up behind me and looked through the titles. He handed me a leather-bound tome – the only one with no writing on the spine. The first page bore one word: *Maír*.

'This is the most precious book here,' he said. 'It embraces and protects our entire history.'

I carefully leafed through it. It was all hand-lettered. I had not considered that the Maír didn't have typography. The amount of manual labour behind all these books was shocking.

I skimmed the titles: Legends, Chronicles, The Exodus, The Discovery of the Ata Mahari.

'This was written by Mana Yan. He worked on it until shortly before his death. May I?' I passed the book to him and he flicked through it until he found what he was looking for: a picture of a flower resembling a lily, but with smaller and more numerous petals in an unusual colour. An intense blue – a shade I knew well.

'This is a *lyr*. It has the same name as the continent,' said the Mana.

I've never seen this flower before.

'It's a mythical flower. It is said to have disappeared from the continent at the time the Lyrién were at war with one another.'

The Lyrién?

'We haven't always been called Maír. Maír means —'

Survivors. Dainefin had told me that.

The Mana nodded. 'Those who survived. Mana Suppur, the first Mana of Cloch, chose this name when we reached the island. He wanted to make a fresh start.'

I studied the illustration of the mythical flower. Again, my thoughts turned to Dainefin, to all the things she had kept to herself all those years, when she could have shared them with me. I thought of how different our lessons would have been if she'd taught me about the Maír instead of Latin or Old-World mythology. I missed her so much.

I heard the library door being laboriously pushed open. A little girl's face peeped through the crack. She seemed surprised by our presence, and unsure of what to do next.

'Syleanh. Come, come,' the Mana encouraged her.

The girl ran over to have her head stroked by him. She was tiny and had a round, smooth face with small ears sticking out slightly from her braided amber hair.

'This is Lyria, our Maír sister from a faraway land,' he said.

I bent down to greet her.

'Lyria is special, like you,' the Mana told her.

The girl's eyes lit up.

Does Syleanh have the Empathic Aura?

'No,' he replied, 'but she does not speak.'

Because she can't?

'Not quite,' he said. 'Let's say that she prefers not to. She compensates by reading a great deal, though. She's here every day.'

Syleanh ran off and climbed up a couple of steps. She picked a book, sat down cross-legged on the floor and started looking through it.

How is she with other children?

'Syleanh is very reserved. But other children do nothing to exclude her, if that is what you mean,' he answered.

I wondered if Syleanh had once been able to speak, but had suffered a traumatic experience like me. What could bring a child to *choose* not to speak?

Every now and then the girl gave me a shy look, a mixture of curiosity and impatience. I was familiar with that impatience – the urge to be alone in a room full of books. I respected that. I returned the Maír history book to its shelf and opened the door to leave, looking back at Syleanh one last time. I gave her half a wave, and the girl responded by raising a hand towards me. She must have decided she liked me.

The book Mana Tar had recommended spoke of every single aspect of Maír life, the Empathic Aura included. It was, he said, the only book where the illness was mentioned, so if I wanted to overcome it, I should start there.

I had assured the Mana that I could manage by myself, so I returned to the Kymirama alone the next day and immersed myself in reading.

I sat on one of the lower steps with the enormous book in my lap, scanning page after page until I got to the chapter on the Empathic Aura. Even if I hadn't known the language at all, I would have had no problem finding it. The chapter was illustrated by an image of a young Maír man surrounded by indistinct entities emerging from his back. They were drawn in grey and pale blue, wraith-like, each representing a different emotion. One spirit was weeping with its head down, one holding its temples, another appeared dejected. There were about twenty of them, massed behind the man, his emotions turning inside out. Only one did not seem to represent any emotion, and it was the most terrifying. It was clinging to the man's back, holding him tight, one hand on his heart, the other covering his mouth.

That's what the Empathic Aura was. A nightmare. A weight that could not be shaken off. What a promising first page.

I was finding some passages hard to interpret, partly because of the gaps in my vocabulary and partly because of Mana Yan's elevated tone. I had heard from Kolymba that Mana Yan had experienced visions his entire life. After generations of Maír living on Cloch, the Lyrién were the stuff of legend, rather than memory. Mana Yan was the first to dream of the ancestors and tell the community how their exile had come to pass.

I skimmed the descriptions of how the Empathic Aura manifested – I had experienced most of it myself already, after all – and looked for anything on visions.

> *Time, a page written over and over again. The Empathic Aura is the key that unlocks the door to any point on that page, any point in History. Beware, you who believe you can command your own visions, summon or reject them. Each vision is a gift, and each of us has the privilege of choice.*

Up until then, the shreds I'd been able to interpret from my visions were few, incomplete and fragmented. I knew they were connected to my experiences, but I couldn't find the logic that connected them . . . . If there even was one.

It was like being confined to a prison, where the only news from the outside world reached me in stained, nearly illegible letters.

I skipped a few more paragraphs until I found the point where Mana Yan began to tell his own experience. Curiously, he wrote in the third person.

> THE SURVIVORS LANDED ON CLOCH. IN THE BEGINNING, THEY MOVED ALONG THE COAST FACING LYR. THEY SETTLED AT THE FOOT OF THE VOLCANO, IN A VALLEY IN THE SOUTH OF THE ISLAND FROM WHICH THE MAINLAND COULD NO LONGER BE SEEN. THE VISIONS BEGAN WHEN THE FIRST STONE OF THE VILLAGE WAS LAID. THE MANA DREAMED OF A RIVER. FOR MONTHS, HE CHASED THE RIVER. HE FOUND IT, AND UNDERSTOOD IT WOULD GIVE THEM THE GIFT OF TIME, THE TIME THAT LYR NEEDED TO HEAL.

Mana Yan had dreamt of the Ata Mahari: the only hope for the Maír to remember and return home one day. Compared to his, my visions were child's play.

I hoped that Mana Yan would expand on the topic of recovery. He did speak of the famous 'Reason' – which had healed Dainefin and Kolymba – but not of how to find it.

> *ONCE A REASON IS FOUND, THE EMPATHIC AURA NO LONGER HAS CAUSE TO EXIST, THE VISIONS VANISH AND WORD RETURNS. THE MANA*

> *UNDERSTOOD THAT HIS REASON WAS LEAD-*
> *ING HIM ON A LIFELONG PATH, THAT THE WOUNDS*
> *OF THE MAÍR MAY BE HEALED.*

After I finished the chapter on the Empathic Aura, I was leafing through the book, skipping whole pages, when the illustration of a tree caught my eye. Not just any tree: a hata. Unlike the hatas I had seen, this was a sapling, with a slender trunk and silvery blue leaves.

The Maír transcription of the tree's name surprised me. If read out loud, it would have sounded just like it did in Amaranth.

I read on about the hatas.

> *THE DAY WILL COME, THE MANA SAW IN*
> *ONE OF HIS VISIONS, THAT LYR WILL AGAIN BE A*
> *FERTILE LAND, A HOME. ON THE BATTLEFIELDS*
> *MANY TREES WILL RISE, A FOREST THAT WILL BE*
> *CALLED HATABLAR. THE HATA WILL FEED AND...*

Here he used a verb I hadn't encountered before. Since it had the same root as 'clean' and 'pure', I imagined it to mean something like 'they will clean', or 'cleanse'.

> *...CLEANSE THE LAND OF THE BLOOD THAT WAS*
> *SHED. THEY WILL WEEP COMPASSIONATE TEARS FOR*

THE SACRIFICE OF ALL THOSE LYRIÉN LIVES, AND THEY
WILL DRAW THE SPIRITS OF THOSE STILL WANDERING
IN SEARCH OF THEIR LOVED ONES, WHO SHALL
INHABIT THE FOREST UNTIL THEIR MAINT-URI RETURN.

The 'compassionate tears' had to be hata honey.
That was so poetic and heart-breaking.

Towards the end of the sentence, there was
another word – *maint-uri* – that I didn't recognise, but I
guessed it must mean 'offspring' or 'bloodline'. Hatablar Forest wept until the Maír returned.

I remembered those voices. I had listened, and
even directed their song, without ever wondering where
all that pain had sprung from.

I suddenly felt I was being watched, and realised
that Syleanh had snuck into the Kymirama. She was
waiting in the hallway. When our eyes met, she made to
open the huge front door and slip away.

Wait!

I didn't think the Empathic Aura had such a wide
range; I must have wished so hard for the girl to stay,
that she'd felt it. I motioned her closer.

Curious about what I was reading, she came over
to peep at the volume lying open in my lap.

I pointed at the page about Hatablar Forest and,
without thinking, I signed the word 'trees'. The sign came
naturally, even though I hadn't used Cam's language in
so long. Amused by my gesture, she copied it.

Trees. Well done. Then I signed 'crying'. *Tears.*

318

I leafed through the book, stopping at a picture of a river, 'river', and then 'moon', 'flowers'.

Syleanh repeated my signs two or three times, and even integrated some of them into elaborate choreographies. She was playing with the language the way children do, placing no importance on rules and meaning.

How long had it been since I had played with anyone?

When we were little, Sonni and I used to play all the time; but at a certain point, we stopped. We stopped chasing each other and playing hide and seek. Then, we stopped swimming and having snowball fights. Finally, our coded messages during Dainefin's lessons came to an end because Sonni stopped coming. Sometimes we joked or teased at the dinner table, or on the way back from the cathedral after Mass, always out of Anur's sight because we hated it so much when he called us little brats.

I'd forgotten how important it was not to take myself too seriously, and I was prepared to bet that my brother had forgotten it too.

Syleanh tugged on my sleeve. She wanted to show me what she'd learned. She was repeating the motions with breathless enthusiasm, as if seeking her teacher's approval in class. Well, she deserved it. She was learning quickly and putting her whole body into it – to the point that she was beginning to look flushed.

I looked around for a book that was more suitable for a child her age. I pulled out a couple of illustrated books, picking a collection of short fables, rather than fairy tales, just like the ones Mother used to read to me when I was little, before kissing me goodnight.

There was once a little bird . . .

I made the sign for 'past' and that for 'bird'. I didn't know how to sign more than three quarters of the text. But I decided it didn't matter. It would be more fun to make it up together.

Syleanh responded well to the Empathic Aura – she didn't care how it worked, she simply accepted that I communicated that way.

I, for my part, was trying to push it down, trying to rely on signs, pictures, and fragments of text.

If Uncle Noalim had used books to teach Cam to read, then I would need to use my hands, rather than the Empathic Aura, to teach Syleanh to sign.

I don't know how to say this word. I pointed to the well. *How shall we sign it?*

Syleanh paused to think. Then she enacted bending over to draw up a bucket from a well. I repeated the movement and she nodded approvingly.

All right, from now on that will be the sign for 'water well'. How about 'path'?

Syleanh made an undulating motion with her hand.

That could be the sign for 'snake'. What if . . .

I repeated what she'd done, adding the sign for 'trees'. She clapped her hands ecstatically, uttering a few joyful noises.

Shall we keep going?

Once we had got through the first story, we went over it again at least three times, becoming more and more skilled at signing from memory. I continued by asking, 'What's your name?' After repeating the alphabet a couple of times, I showed her the vibrating shape of my initials. Syleanh seemed confused, and I tried to explain that the vibration meant 'music'. That was a tricky one, because I was unable to sing, and she only smiled uncomprehendingly when I mimicked playing a keyboard in the air. In the end, I beat out a rhythm in four time; Syleanh understood then, and did a little dance.

She asked me what her name-sign was.

As I thought about it, my eye fell on the book of fables I was still holding.

I made the sign for 'little bird' – the thumb and index and middle fingers opening and closing like a beak – and used it to trace a long 'v' shape over my mouth, the sign for 'smile' I had learned from Cam.

Then I asked her, 'How old are you?' and showed her first ten fingers, then seven, pointing at myself. I turned the question to her, and with no hesitation, Syleanh showed me eight fingers.

I kept showing her other questions, and taught her to sign 'thank you', 'sorry', and 'I love you'. What a lonely world it must be for a child who can't say 'thank you' or 'I love you', I thought.

Syleanh then pointed at the Maír history book, and went back to the page I'd been reading about Hatablar. She gave me to understand that she knew everything about the Lyr legends. So I told her about how I'd had to cross Hatablar to reach the Isle of Cloch, about my encounter with the spirits, and what Isehar and Fayrem had been ordered to do in the forest.

Syleanh watched me sign, piecing the rest of the tale together with the Empathic Aura, just like Cam had done a few weeks before – though it felt like a century had passed since then. She was gaping at me, as if every word I told her was simply too incredible to be true. It was hard for her to phrase questions with the few signs she'd learned, so I tried to tell her everything.

I told her about my family, and what it was like to live in Amarantha. I meant to spare her the part about my mother dying and my father losing his mind, but as usual the Empathic Aura did its own thing.

The Maír child was filled with sadness; she made the sign for crying.

Yes, I cried a lot. But I've met loads of people who helped me, and are helping me still.

I told her about Cam, but not in the way I'd told Isehar and Fayrem about Cam. I told her about every moment I'd spent with him, everything we'd told each other.

Syleanh made the sign for question and the sign for 'love'.

Do I love him? As if I've known him all my life.

Again, she signed a question, followed by 'deaf' and 'love'. It took me a while to understand.

Do I love him even though he's deaf?

The girl shook her head.

Would I still love him if he weren't deaf?

She nodded.

While I wouldn't have hesitated to answer the first

question, Syleanh wrong-footed me with the second. It was a very deep question, coming from a child less than half my age. I thought of the people I'd met since leaving Amarantha. Would they still have cared about me if I'd been able to speak? And if they hadn't known I was the princess?

Cam, after all, cared about me even though I wasn't actually mute.

Of course I would, I nodded with conviction. Cam was Cam and that's what I loved about him.

A cold damp draught was filtering through the cracks around the door. Night was about to fall.

Run along now, before your folks get worried about you.

It was time for me to leave too. As I crossed Ama-Pamau, I greeted the Maír I met along the way. Some were on their way back from the fields, some were carrying baskets of fruit, or sacks of potatoes, others had children in their arms or by the hand.

They're all here, I told the spirits of Hatablar, *they just don't know you're waiting for them.*

Over the next couple of days, I returned to the Kymi-rama with Syleanh to continue our reading. She was becoming faster at signing, and got excited about the simplest things. When she learned the signs for 'Mother' and 'Father', she was so happy that she improvised one of her little dances. She was a different child from the one I'd met a few days before.

I enjoyed being around her and teaching her sign language, but every now and then I wondered whether I was procrastinating. The Empathic Aura gave no sign of being on its way out; nor did it seem to be getting worse. It was the same as always. It was a part of me. Which was the thing that frightened me most.

Kolymba had learned to live with the Empathic Aura – so much so that when he did begin to speak again, it had still lingered. Years passed before he was able to rid himself of it completely. Even then, it hadn't been his own doing, but rather the forgiveness of the Pamau community. It was the same for Dainefin. If Ruthven had not declared his love, she might still have been a prisoner to the Empathic Aura. How could it be my fault then that nothing was changing for me?

And then there was the other issue . . . I didn't know how to start convincing the Maír to return to the mainland, so I simply avoided thinking about it.

I began to feel guilty for doing nothing but reading Maír legends in the library. I might as well pack up and go back home. I needed clear instructions. Perhaps the Mana would help. I needed to act.

After my library morning with Syleanh, I headed to the Mana's house, hoping that a chat with him would help me decide what to do.

Outside his house, I found a man and woman arguing with him. The Mana was trying to pacify them, but they both seemed beside themselves with anger. As soon as they caught sight of me, I felt like the blade of an axe was suspended over my neck.

They were speaking fast – often over the Mana's

attempts to calm them down. I only just managed to understand the gist of their exchange: they were both furious with me for the stories of my travels I'd been telling Syleanh. I gathered they were her parents.

'Syleanh wants to leave the island!' said her mother.

'All those stories about Lyr—' her father started.

'She'll end up like Sari,' the woman interrupted. 'Somewhere at the bottom of the ocean.'

'Lyr does not exist!' said the father. Then he turned to me, trying to soften his tone. 'Listen, we're happy Syleanh is finding a way to . . . to express herself. But we don't want you filling her head with tall tales about Lyr.'

The Mana shrugged at me, as if in apology.

'Please, you seem such a good girl,' Syleanh's father said to me.

I'm sorry . . .

I did feel sorry for Syleanh, but not because of the things I'd told her. I was sorry for her that her parents did not believe a single word of what I'd told her.

. . . but Lyr does exist. You're the ones who are wrong.

I wasn't sure if Syleanh's parents had heard my thoughts word by word, so I raised my hands slightly to show them I had no intention of making a scene, then moved closer.

If they didn't understand me – if they didn't *want* to – I would show them what they were refusing to see.

I pointed to my eyes. I had not met a single Maír

whose eye were blue. Hazel or green, yes – though rare – but no Maír had blue eyes.

Nor did they have pale skin, but at the moment I wanted them to focus on my eyes, hoping that perhaps in all that blue they would spot a glimmer of honesty, that they could be convinced, just by looking at me, I wasn't lying.

Can't you see? I was not born here, I come from somewhere else.

Syleanh's father seemed to think about it, but his wife tugged his arm and they turned their backs on us without so much as bidding the Mana goodbye.

As soon as we were alone, I rounded on him.

Why didn't you try to convince them? I am living proof that Lyr exists! You couldn't have helped me?

'You're right,' he sighed. 'But we've been trying for so long . . .'

There's an entire civilisation over the strait of Styr. An entire civilisation! How can anyone not even believe Amarantha exists?

Mana Tar opened his front door.

'Come inside. I knew we'd have to talk about this sooner or later, we might as well do it over a hot drink.'

This Maír obsession with drinking infusions whenever there was something serious to discuss was starting to get on my nerves.

Mana tinkered about with his crockery, then offered me a herbal infusion. 'This will calm you down.'

What had Dainefin seen in the Maír? True, I had enjoyed learning the language and reading about their history. Kolymba and Mana Tar had been kind to me, but the rest acted as if I had always lived there. Not one of them had bothered to ask me where I came from or why I didn't speak Maír. How could they not question it? How could they be so blind?

'Here in our village, everyone has the right to start afresh. They are all assuming you came from Ama-Tángaor, wishing to change your life.'

But I'm so different . . .

'In appearance, perhaps. But as you have been told more than once, you are one of us. It only takes a moment in your company to realise that.'

What was it that made me Maír? I so wanted to know, but I never got a straight answer when I asked.

Why haven't you told everyone the truth? Why aren't you telling people I'm from Amarantha?

'Because the majority would think me mad. The Maír of this island believe there is nothing but rocks on the other side of the strait, nothing worth building boats for. That's what Douk and Teira – Syleanh's parents – think. They have never believed Lyr really existed.'

But they know about Sari.

'I'm guessing you don't know much about her past,' said the Mana. 'Everyone here knows her story, but over time it has become a sort of legend, a fable with a moral. Sari had a vision when she was still very young. She dreamt of your people's arrival on Lyr. She talked to Mana Yan about it, and he helped convinced her parents to let her leave. But she never returned. Those who do not believe in Lyr think she died at sea. That is the story that has been passed on.'

Sari did die – but of old age. After living her whole life by Aur-Lee's side, without ever telling him about the Maír.

'I can't explain her decisions,' he replied bitterly. 'Perhaps she realised that we really were too different.'

I don't understand you people. I really am trying, but I don't understand you at all.

'We are a community of old people, Lyria. We look young, but inside we are grey and wrinkled.' He sounded weary. 'The old don't like change. It makes us feel insecure. We always do the same things. And we demand that our children behave the same as us, regardless of the incredible events that have taken place between one generation and the next.'

Sari never went through the Time Ritual, did she?

'No,' answered the Mana. 'She said there was no need. She said she was going to take us all back home.'

Chapter 23

'Reydn, I've asked you to stop,' says Dainefin, scrunching up the scrap of paper. Reydn snatches the bunch of flowers from her other hand, turns his back on her and marches off.

'Wait, it's not that,' she call out, running after him. 'Reydn!'

He drops the flowers. She stoops to pick them up.

'They're beautiful. They are. It's just the note.'

Dainefin sits on the edge of the well. The sunlight casts a sheen of sweat on her legs.

Reydn forces himself not to look at them, pretending to check that there's no one around.

'I don't want you to write to me in Amaranth,' says Dainefin. 'I'm trying my hardest to forget. Drinking *inudhearma* isn't going to do much, if . . .'

His stomach turns at the mention of the slop they're supposed to drink to make themselves forget. It's having no effect on him, in any case.

'I'm working so hard. And you don't even have to try,' he interrupts her.

It's the first time he's thrown that in her face. All he wants is to see the merest sign of insecurity, but Dainefin isn't easy to break.

'That's not true,' she says calmly.

'Isn't it? Tell me then, who drew up endless lists of words and transcriptions to learn Maír, for nearly two years?'

'I used to make word lists too, you know!'

'Yes, but you were speaking Maír after the first week!' he shoots back. 'Two years, Dainefin. Who do you think I did that for?'

'It's not my fault,' she says. 'You knew it would be difficult, you still decided to come along. And then you decided to stay.'

'Well then, try to remember that sometimes.'

Dainefin doesn't say a word. There's no need. Reydn knows what's going through her mind: how to wrong-foot him with some high-minded speech about loyalty. He's heard plenty of those. He wants Dainefin to be honest for once. Does she mean to stay on Cloch forever? Or will she return home with him? She has a kingdom awaiting her, a life together with him. Why won't she make up her mind and be done with it?

Dainefin stands and hugs him.

'I do remember,' she whispers in his ear. 'And I appreciate it so much, I swear I do. You've always been so loyal .... Listen, there's something I need to say, but you have to promise you won't get upset.'

Reydn wriggles out of the embrace and waits with his arms folded across his chest. She's made her decision then. She will stay on Cloch. Then again, what was he expecting? She's taken this Path so seriously that she really doesn't remember home any more. Yet he still can't believe that she is turning down the life of privilege she's been offered, as if this life – *on Cloch* – were far superior. Not to mention how arrogant it is of her to assume that Reydn will always be by her side, while all the plans he made for her are going up in smoke.

'Something's been tormenting me these past few days,' she says. 'I've been trying to remember, but I really can't.'

Reydn snorts. 'What can't you remember?'

Dainefin opens her mouth but takes a few seconds to speak. As if she's rehearsed her speech, but can't think of the opening line just now.

'Did I ask you to come here with me? When Aur-Lee and Sari told me about . . . well, about all this.'

Reydn gives her a look full of contempt. She hasn't decided a thing. She just wants to unburden her conscience. He won't let her.

'I thought we weren't supposed to discuss the past.'

He's expecting his sarcasm to provoke the customary whining, but Dainefin rises above it.

'Reydn, please. I keep replaying that scene. After they told me, I ran to you. I remember that. You were the first person I wanted to tell. Answer me, Reydn. Or I'll never stop wondering. Did you offer to come with me, or did I ask you to? I keep breaking my vow to the Path, just to remember.'

'You want to know something?' he says.

She nods.

'I've never achieved a Luminous Thought.'

'You've never told me that before,' Dainefin replies.

'You've never asked. How many times has it happened to you since we started meditating? You got one a day just last week. I know that, because every time it happens, you come and tell me. Has it ever crossed your mind to ask me how my meditation is going?'

Dainefin lowers her eyes.

Reydn wonders if she may have taken for granted that he was on her level, but he knows it isn't that. It has simply never occurred to her to ask. Reydn is there as her escort. It's all been very lovely, him being accepted into the community and attempting the Path too. But Dainefin has only ever wondered if she would make it. What does she care if Reydn doesn't keep up with her? He's just her lapdog.

'You know what I do while you lot are filled with your pure thoughts?'

Reydn is remembering that night now. The night Dainefin found out she was Maír. He didn't think twice about talking his parents into letting him go with her. He's been cursing that moment ever since, praying to God for the strength to leave this hellish island, this scrap of land where he is a prisoner because of her. Would Kolymba build him a boat without Dainefin knowing? He knows Kolymba would be happy to be rid of him – he's besotted with Dainefin. For all Reydn cares, those two can get married, have children and live here together forever after. Reydn can return to Amarantha and start from scratch. Or maybe he'll go to Murihen, where he won't be hounded by memories of growing up with Dainefin.

'I revise Maír grammar, that's what I do,' he spits out.

He snatches the flowers from her hands and throws them into the well.

For four days, Kolymba rose at daybreak to walk across the island and build the boat that would take me back to the continent.

As Dainefin had said all that time ago, the trip from Ama-Pamau to the shore facing the fjords of Styr took two hours on foot. There was another shore closer to Ama-Pamau, about half an hour away, but if I'd set sail from there, I would have to row all the way along the coast and around the headland before starting towards home. Kolymba assured me that it would take much less time to cut through on land, even if that meant him walking to the far shore and back every day.

We were eating together on the fifth day when he announced that the boat was ready.

What will you call her?

'What will I call whom?'

The boat.

I had to explain that where I came from, it was traditional to name and baptise every boat. I told him that the ship on which Aur-Lee had set sail from the Old World was named *Virtue and Knowledge*.

'Virtue and Knowledge? A little arrogant, don't you think?' he commented, measuring out the words as he did the tiny bites of bread he savoured with an almost maddening frugality.

It's a quote . . . oh, nevermind.

I too had always found Aur-Lee's motto a little 'too much', but now that I knew him, I could forgive him that vanity. I often read his journal and thought of him as a close friend, someone who had let me in on his every secret.

Come on, you can think of something. Didn't you tell me that when something is important you write it down, and if it's very important, you carve it onto a piece of wood?

Kolymba chuckled at my stubbornness, but I knew he was taking my request seriously.

I left him alone to think and went for a stroll through the town, saying hello to passers-by and exploring. I'd already visited the nearest beach, but I didn't feel like being alone like I had in Amarantha or Ama-Tángaor. I preferred being around the Maír, not to force my friendship on anyone but because I enjoyed seeing how they passed their time, the structure of their everyday life. Sometimes I tried telling them about Amarantha, but their pitying looks always made me stop. Not far from the northern outskirts of town, nearest the volcano, I discovered two working mines, both opencast. There must have been dozens like them in the kingdom, but I had never seen one.

On the way back from the mines, I stopped in a place the Pamau called *ama-cóir – cóir* meaning 'rest'. At first glance, it looked like nothing more than a fallow field: levelled ground with a few grassy spots grown over with poppies, dandelions and forget-me-nots. Nothing indicated the presence of burial mounds other than small stone markers, common rocks smaller than my fist, with no writing on them. The Maír didn't honour the dead the way we did – by placing flowers on their coffins and reciting prayers – but they did gather at the *ama-cóir* twice a year, on the solstices.

It was a shame that I'd just missed the summer solstice, but I wouldn't have traded it for the memory of the Pamau forgiving Kolymba and welcoming me into their community.

I also dropped into the library looking for Syleanh, but I didn't find her. She hadn't set foot in the Kymirama since her parents had come to speak to the Mana, and the place had lost some of its appeal without her. I took the history book with me when I left. Syleanh was the soul of the Kymirama, just as I liked to think of myself as the soul of Aur-Lee's library, and using the library when she wasn't there didn't feel right.

When I got to Kolymba's house I found Mana Tar was already there. I had asked Kolymba to invite him over for dinner, so we could spend a little time together. The truth was, there were things I wanted to ask him about my visions of Dainefin and Reydn that I didn't feel I could ask Kolymba – not after seeing how close he'd been to Dainefin.

I could not have asked for better company. Spending my life next to Dainefin had taught me to appreciate being with those older than me, and my stay on Cloch made me realise that the age of those Maír who had undergone the Time Ritual didn't matter. It was only a number.

Kolymba roasted some fish, which he seasoned with berries, while I set the table and discussed my latest vision with the Mana.

I had dreamt of Reydn and Dainefin before, but this latest vision had allowed me to observe them interacting from a different point of view. As if I'd been in Reydn's shoes, seeing his version of events.

I must have seen something that took place before Dainefin underwent the ritual because they were both younger than me.

Even so, I had trouble deciding what I felt towards Reydn. He doubtlessly had feelings for Dainefin, but their ambiguity left me perplexed. His jealousy was so ambivalent, so complex, that even after the vision of him, I still couldn't make head nor tail of it.

Was he in love with her? Or did he just love her? Was he jealous of Cloch, of the Maír? Was he jealous that she had Luminous Thoughts and royal blood that she took for granted, while he had to pull himself up out of the mud? Dainefin's heart had belonged to Cloch, and she had been chasing the Luminous Life. I still only barely understood what that was, so I decided I'd start there.

So, if I've got this right, not all Pamau undergo the Ritual.

'Correct,' the Mana confirmed. 'It is a personal choice that begins with the Path.'

What exactly is the Path?

'The Path is what we call the training where one learns various things,' he explained. 'Those who are Chosen take it upon themselves to turn their knowledge to serving the community. Some work with wood, or teach children . . .'

Mana Tar smiled broadly at Kòlymba, who barely raised his embarrassed gaze from the *piyeda* he was making: maize flat breads, topped with stewed fish and vegetables.

'. . . and some,' Mana Tar continued, 'hone their knowledge of herbs and their properties, like myself and Dainefin.'

Dainefin's talent wasn't innate, I realised: someone had taught her that art and she had never stopped practising it.

'And then there is meditation,' he concluded. 'The Chosen practise it at the very beginning and end of each day. They learn to nip new thoughts and worries in the bud, and to keep memories at bay. Memories are the hardest thing to manage, so we use *inu-dhearma* to help with that.'

I'd heard about that infusion in visions. Now I understood why Dainefin didn't remember how to read or write her mother tongue when she'd first arrived in Shamabat. She had chosen to forget her life before Cloch.

But why is forgetting so important? Does it have something to do with Luminous Thoughts? Are they

different to normal thoughts? What are they?

'Instants of knowledge,' Mana Tar said without hesitation.

Knowledge of what?

'Of everything.'

I still don't understand.

'Lyria, when you walk, do you ever think about your legs walking for you?'

I shook my head.

'And when you pick up an object,' Kolymba continued as he laid the table, 'do you ever say to yourself, "My hand is closing around this object"?'

I don't think so.

I was getting the feeling that the word Mana Tar had used, *yuvidestra*, may not exactly mean 'knowledge'.

I knew that *yuvid* meant 'mind' and 'to know', but the suffix *-estra* threw me off. Didn't it mean 'present'? Both in the sense of 'now' and 'in the same place'. Perhaps *yuvidestra* meant . . .

Awareness. Moments of awareness?

Kolymba nodded and smiled.

'What does the book say about that?' asked Mana Tar.

I placed the book on the table and flipped to the chapter dedicated to Luminous Life. I waited for Kolymba to sit, then showed him which section to read aloud.

'"Luminous Thoughts are what precedes Time and Man,"' he read. '"They are what will remain once Time has run its course and Man has reached his end."'

He read more after that as we ate, but my fluency in Maír didn't allow me to understand the intricacies of long philosophical discussions. I did, however, learn one thing: Luminous Thoughts were the foundation of the Maír's belief system. Even though they had no overt religion, the Chosen followed a philosophical principle. They sought a universal awareness that they could only reach once they'd renounced their past and learned to live in the present, dedicating their lives to the community.

Dainefin had obviously reached that state. I didn't know anyone else who had such a strong sense of her place in the world or who dedicated so much of her life to others. It had never occurred to me she hadn't always been that way. I now knew that before the Path – before Cloch – Dainefin had been a troubled, vulnerable girl; the girl Reydn had fallen in love with. And because of his love for her, Reydn had never been able to achieve Luminous Thoughts.

I too would have trouble renouncing my past. How do you forget the people you love? Why would you want to erase yourself? That abstraction was not for me. The more I imagined living outside normal life, the more I remembered every little thing that made me human.

'It is not yourself that you need to erase,' explained the Mana. 'It is all the rest. The noise.'

Ah well, *that* sounded easier.

With my brain in constant turmoil from the Empathic Aura, it would be more like drowning out the sound of a drunken marching band. I kept re-experiencing everything that had happened since my

339

mother's death. Even while talking to Mana Tar and Kolymba, my brain was seething with concern about what may be happening in Amarantha while I wasn't there.

If only I could extinguish the Empathic Aura the way it had extinguished my voice, like blowing out a candle . . .

Kolymba must have followed the direction my thoughts had taken, because he said: 'It used to help me.'

What did?

'Meditation. With the Empathic Aura. It made me feel better, and kept me centred.'

'But you knew what you were doing,' said Mana Tar taking another bite of fish. He didn't speak with malice, just stated a fact.

He was right. Kolymba had practised meditating long before he fell ill. My understanding was that Luminous Thoughts didn't simply drop into people's heads. One needed to adopt a lifestyle dedicated to meditation and service.

Not that I found the prospect of a Luminous Life unappealing. On the contrary. I had often observed the Mana going about his daily tasks, his face not manifesting the slightest sign of worry, anger or concern.

I had seen him disappointed, that was true, in those villagers who did not believe in a return of the Maír to the continent. But it was only a temporary disappointment because deep down, Mana Tar had not lost hope, and was only waiting for someone to come to his aid. But what would be the point of me embarking on the Path when I knew I wanted to go home?

The thought that *I* was supposed to be that someone who led the Maír back to Lyr was worrying. How could I convince the Maír to return home? Mana Tar, Kolymba and Dainefin were wrong. I wasn't Maír. And if I was, I had more in common with Sari and Dainefin – who had left the island and never returned.

'If you want to try,' Kolymba suggested, 'I am at your disposal.'

It took me a moment to realise we were still talking about meditation.

I spotted a shadow of doubt on Mana Tar's face, before he quickly hid it. 'As am I. There is nothing you cannot learn.'

I had no time to feel proud at his words, because just then we heard a desperate cry from outside the house.

It was Douk, Syleanh's father, shouting that his daughter was gone.

We rushed to the door to find Syleanh's parents just outside. A wheezing Douk repeated that Syleanh was gone. She had left the house early that morning and not returned. No one in the village had seen her since the previous day.

He thought she'd been abducted by the Tángaor, and was insisting that Mana Tar and Kolymba Kathún go there and speak to them. Mana Tar tried to convince him that the Tángaor would have no reason to abduct an eight-year-old child – Syleanh had not yet been to the Ata Mahari.

The Mana's reassurances had no visible effect on

Syleanh's mother, who sobbed even harder.

'I scolded her yesterday because . . . because she kept writing that she w-wants to go back to Lyr, where there are d-deaf people who bake bread and forests full of M-Maír.'

She glared at me as if she expected an apology – which I did not offer.

Lyr really does exist – and so does my friend Cam, who is deaf and works as a miller, and Hatablar Forest—

The Empathic Aura only made matters worse, muddying the waters with a gush of thoughts that Teira was unable to make out.

'Have you tried the Kymirama?' Mana Tar asked.

Syleanh's father nodded. 'We thought she'd gone there to meet with her,' he said, jerking his head at me. 'But she wasn't there. We tried this afternoon, and again a little while ago. We've been over the whole town, the mines, the *ama-cóir*. She is not in Ama-Pamau.'

I felt a boulder plummet straight into my conscience. Fervently hoping I was wrong, I moved closer to Kolymba.

I think I know where she is.

We found her on the north beach, where Kolymba had left the boat he'd made. We crossed the shore, Douk and Kolymba running ahead. Mana Tar had stayed behind to comb the forest, calling Syleanh's name.

Syleanh!' Douk yelled, running to her little body.

'She must have tried to leave,' he said, kneeling on the sand next to her.

The boat was beached on the foreshore. It was full of water and one side of the hull had been ripped apart.

'The rocks . . .' said Kolymba, glancing at a rock formation I hadn't noticed before. It jutted out of the water to the west: half of an arch surrounded by a handful of solitary rocks. The arch seemed to draw the waves to it, like lightning to a rod. Syleanh must have been caught in a current, lost control of the boat, and then been swallowed by the rocks.

I stood frozen, staring at Syleanh's body. So small. Scrapes all over her forearms, her hands, her ankles. Her head was tilted to one side, and sand-encrusted hair had fallen across her face. I had to resist the urge to brush it aside. She looked like she was sleeping. I crouched down next to her and touched her face, her chest.

She's freezing, but still breathing. We have to cover her.

Kolymba took off his tunic and wrapped it around her. Douk did the same, then picked her up. It was then I saw a large gash at her hairline, still bleeding. Her tunic was bloodied down her back.

Douk adjusted his tunic to staunch the bleeding and ran back towards the town, clutching his daughter tight.

It was late in the evening when we arrived, out of breath and shivering.

Teira had been waiting at home in case Syleanh returned. I ran to fetch her back to Kolymba's house. When she saw the state of her child, she doubled over and retched.

Douk lay the little one down by the fire, which Kolymba was feeding with logs while Mana Tar tinkered with his herbs. He pounded together a few leaves and berries and held the concoction under Syleanh's nose.

She regained consciousness for a few moments, coughing hard. Then she held out her hand to me, and signed the word 'trees'. Then 'weep'. She started to shiver and fell back into unconsciousness.

Trees. Weep. Trees weep?

Trees weep!

I flew up to my room, grabbed my haversack and turned it over on the bed. I found the jar of hata honey and ran back to the fireside. Syleanh looked like she was fading. The wound on her forehead had stopped bleeding – perhaps she had no more blood to lose, I thought. The ground seemed unsteady beneath my feet.

I rushed to my friend's side and dropped just a little honey on Syleanh's lips. The colour instantly returned to them. Kolymba handed me a spoon and I used it to feed her. She coughed so long and hard that she brought up blood, but she came back to us. I made her swallow another couple of spoonfuls for good measure.

Douk and Teira were weeping with joy. They smothered their daughter with hugs and kisses.

I stepped closer to Kolymba. He hugged me tight, rubbing my back.

'She's fine,' he murmured.

But if we hadn't found her in time . . .

'She's fine,' he repeated.

Mana Tar handed me a cup full of some kind of infusion. If the moment hadn't been so emotional, I would have burst out laughing. The Maír and their blessed infusions.

I took a sip, and felt calmer.

'What did you give her?' Douk asked me. 'Is she going to be all right?'

I nodded, showing him the bottle and letting him smell it.

Syleanh had fully regained consciousness. Moaning, she tugged at her father's arm for him to help her sit up.

'Book, old, room, Kymirama,' she said. 'Cam, night, hata. Priest.' And then: 'Hata. Book. Take.'

Her voice was barely louder than a squeak. I looked at the Mana, terrified. What had I done?

Did I . . . break her?

He shook his head. 'That's the way she speaks,' he explained. 'Which is why she never does. She has trouble connecting words together.'

Syleanh called me insistently. 'Lyria, Lyria. Lyria. Book, Maír, take. Take. Read.'

I obeyed. I tried to banish from my mind the image of Syleanh lifeless on the beach, sand in her hair, dress soaking wet, her skin so pale. And her voice, the feeble little voice I had just heard for the first time.

I took the Maír history book that I had borrowed

from the Kymirama off the table – still full of our dinner things – and went back to the others, fighting back tears. I opened the book to the page about Hatablar Forest and showed Douk.

He read the section about hata honey, the mighty resin that had cured me of my fever overnight in Denhole. Syleanh had remembered. She remembered every single thing I told her.

Douk was eyeing the jar of blue honey with suspicion. He read that passage about four or five times over, finally deciding to taste the tip of the spoon. His eyes opened wide in amazement.

She'll get better soon, you'll see.

I didn't care if he ever believed that Lyr existed. Yes, part of me was still hopeful, but deep in my heart, I just wanted everything to go back to how it was before, with Syleanh playing, reading, and dreaming like all children her age.

'She'll have to stay in bed for a while yet,' Kolymba said, feeling her forehead. 'And you,' he added, turning to me, 'will have to wait a little longer before you go home, I'm afraid.'

Syleanh reacted instantly, her little body shaking with wheezing breaths.

'Home. Lyr. Back. Boat, broken. Lyria, Lyria. Lyria. Sorry. Back?'

I knelt by her and lay my hand on hers.

I'm not going anywhere for now.

Chapter 24

A tall, sharp-faced man approaches a little boy who is playing peacefully in the castle yard.

It's market day: busy, noisy. The man doesn't lure the boy away, he simply grabs him and walks off with him under his arm. Ambar kicks and screams and bites, but the stranger just holds him tighter.

All his attempts to escape are in vain. Ambar is now the bad man's prisoner.

Every day, the bad man wakes him and asks: 'Who are you?'

Every day, Ambar answers: 'Prince Ambar D'Aur-Lee.' And every day, the bad man gives him something to drink, an infusion so bitter it's difficult to swallow. Ambar spends the rest of the day by himself in a poorly lit room. He scratches at the wall to pass the time, crying off and on. He screams and calls for help, but no one ever answers. Then, one day, things change.

Ambar is taller, less childlike. He has grown strong and clever. He has stopped trying to think of ways to escape and accepted his captivity. It hasn't been easy, but if this is his life now, he isn't going to waste it. Every day, he makes an effort to remember who he is and where he comes from, the things he used to do in the castle when he was little. But every day one more detail escapes him, and his memories become a little more blurred.

He is a captive prince.

He is a captive prince.

He is a captive prince.

He is a captive . . .

He is . . .

'What is your name?' the stranger asks him.

'I don't remember,' the boy replies. He tries as hard as he can, but he has no memories. Only a headache.

'Do you remember me?'

The boy shakes his head.

'I found you yesterday afternoon, in the woods. You fell off a horse,' says the tall, thin gentleman.

The boy touches his head and finds a wound healing on his temple.

'You can call me Reydn,' says the gentleman. 'I'm sorry, you can't stay here, but I've found a family who can take you in.'

The nice gentleman opens the door, and the boy feels his eyes smart in the sunlight.

'You're still a little dazed from your fall,' says Reydn.

They leave the city walls of Murihen behind them, and stop at a house in the countryside.

Two adults are waiting at the door. They seem

kind. With them is a boy his age.

'These are your new parents,' says Reydn.

The woman bends down to hug him. That feels so good.

When she straightens up, she points to her son and says, 'this is your new brother, his name is Fayrem.'

His new father smiles at him, adding: 'Welcome home, Isehar.'

Wake up, Lyria, wake up, I told myself, but I always slipped back to sleep at the last moment. I watched, as if suspended in mid-air, the fleeting image of my Aunt Rehena weeping over Ambar's white coffin. Churchbells toll, cracking open the box of grief I'd unconsciously locked many years before.

Sunlight filtered through the window, but still I couldn't wake. I was aware of a bitter, metallic taste, like myrtle berries in my mouth, but at the same time I felt parched, as if filled with salt and flour. *Wake up, wake up,* I kept saying to myself, but then I saw Ambar on the beach, playing with marbles and diving into the waves.

'Lyria.'

The voice felt like a bowl of warm porridge in my stomach.

'Lyria, it's me. Everything is all right.'

Kolymba was sitting on the edge of my bed, but I was unable to cross into the real world.

'Lyria, wake up.'

His louder, firmer tone tugged me out of the muddy torpor.

I came back to my senses. My tongue and lips were dry, and I was still thirsty, but not as much as before. I heard the sound of Kolymba's breathing over the ringing in my ears. I felt his hands grasping mine, his heartbeat hammering through my wrists alongside my own.

I sat up, and at last wakefulness stripped away my vision.

Without so much as looking at Kolymba, I sank my forehead into his chest and burst into tears.

Isehar . . . he's my cousin Ambar . . . we thought he was dead . . . Reydn . . . Reydn!

Kolymba let me cry for a while, then whispered in my ear.

'Clear your mind, Lyria,' he said. 'Let it all go.'

At that moment, the Empathic Aura felt like a boon, and I convinced myself that it was.

I imagined that each tear was a thought, and with my forehead still planted on Kolymba's chest, I stopped sobbing, letting the tears run down my cheeks quietly, each one a tormenting thought trapped in a bubble for me to look at it better.

Isehar was my cousin. What was I supposed to do with that information? Was he in danger? Why had Reydn kidnapped him only to give him away?

Instead of demanding answers to my questions, I let them slide down my cheeks, to soak into my night-gown and Kolymba's robe.

'Good,' he encouraged me.

Only when my panic had ebbed did I feel that the earthquake was over – but not all of me was still standing.

Syleanh ...

'She's fine,' he reassured me. 'She's resting downstairs, just where you left her last night.'

Kolymba squeezed my hand. He had never let go.

'What happened yesterday really upset you.'

I wanted to reassure him that I was ready to see Syleanh, but I was still haunted by the vision I'd just had.

'Get dressed. We'll go and meditate before you visit her.'

I nodded and he left me on my own.

As I got up, I noticed my head felt heavy. I took my time washing my face, rinsing away that weight as well as my sleepiness. I drank deeply from the small water jug by the window. The bitterness of Reydn's *inudhearma* lingered in my mouth. He had deprived my cousin of both his past and future.

I had felt Ambar's fear, his confusion, his frustration as his memories gradually dimmed, slipping through his fingers, as intangible as smoke. I had witnessed his transformation from Ambar, Prince of Murihen, to Isehar, farm-boy, taken in by a family that had so little he had to depend on Reydn's errands just to make ends meet.

I pulled off my nightgown, had a quick wash and put on my white robe from the day before. At the bottom of the stairs I heard the hushed tones of Syleanh's parents, and realised Kolymba was right: I wasn't ready to see her yet.

He was waiting for me in the garden, in the shade of a mulberry tree. He handed me a cup of cold infusion.

Inu-dhearma?

He shook his head. 'I wouldn't dare.'

For a moment, I was tempted to forget everything. My mother's death. Who I was. The Empathic Aura. I stifled the thought before Kolymba sensed it.

I sipped my drink, a simple mint infusion.

What should I do?

'Sit down, and clear your mind.'

I began by sitting down. I regretted agreeing to this already. I thought of the nuns in convents kneeling with their hands joined together, soundlessly mouthing prayers for hours on end. The very words 'meditation' and 'contemplation' made my joints ache.

Kolymba didn't seem to notice my hesitance. His face was expressionless, as if he'd already transcended to a different spiritual plane.

'Take a deep breath in.'

I obeyed, and involuntarily closed my eyes.

'Wait before closing your eyes,' he instructed me gently. 'Look around. Gather what you can. Now breathe out.'

I saw the white mulberry that had already dropped its fruit and was opening above us like a great fortress of leaves; Kolymba's house, with its thatched roof and rose-coloured stone; the fluff from late-shedding poplar trees drifting through the air; the perfectly clear sky, a sign of the sweltering afternoon to come. When I did close my eyes, the vivid blue remained impressed on the inside of my eyelids.

'Again.'

I could smell the mint tea and the leaves above me.

Kolymba didn't say anything more. I continued breathing deeply, picturing the things around me: the mulberry tree, the house, the sky, the cup.

'Shall we go?' he asked after a couple of minutes.

I opened my eyes.

Already?

He nodded. 'Don't you feel better?'

I did. For two short, peaceful minutes I had not had a single thought. A few seconds longer, and a long litany of distractions may have intruded – I might have wondered whether I was doing it right, or thought of the nuns, or Amarantha, or Isehar, Reydn, Dainefin, Sonni . . .

Kolymba was already on his feet.

Don't you usually spend hours meditating?

'I do now, yes,' he said, helping me up. 'But I got there bit by bit. For now, start with what makes you feel well.'

The thought of facing Douk and Teira was certainly not making me feel well. Their child had nearly died and it felt like my fault.

Kolymba gave me an encouraging wave, and I followed him into the house.

Douk and Teira sat at the table, helping Mana Tar sort through a bundle of herbs and flowers. Even though they both bore the signs of a sleepless night, their fingers were as quick as butterflies as they placed each leaf, flower and berry in their respective piles.

They didn't say anything when I came in, but they watched me carefully as I crouched down next to Syleanh. Strangely, there was nothing angry about the tension in the room. It simply felt like they were waiting for something.

Mana Tar prepared a poultice of pulped roots and the leaves of a plant I didn't recognise, wrapped it in wet muslin and placed it over the wound on the child's forehead. The other wounds had already been cleaned, and Syleanh was wearing a fresh robe, one made of wool rather than cotton.

All that separated my friend from the floor was a woollen blanket, folded in two. The fire blazed bright and warm.

I could feel Teira's eyes on me as I looked around for the jar of hata honey. It had been placed on a shelf with the earthenware crockery. I picked up the jar and smeared a few drops on the wounds. The most superficial of them closed right before our eyes. The resin disappeared into the cut, leaving a thin but strong protective film behind. In a few days it would be as if the rocks and the splintered wreck of the boat had never lacerated her skin.

When are you taking her home?

Mana Tar repeated my question out loud for Syleanh's parents.

'We were hoping she could stay here with you,' said Teira.

'Until she's recovered,' Douk added, seeking confirmation from Kolymba.

'Of course,' said Kolymba.

Well then, we'll have to make her more comfortable than this.

I didn't wait for Kolymba or Mana Tar to translate; I went straight up to my room and took the bed apart, folding the blanket and cotton sheets and piling them, and the pillow, on top of the chair. I rolled up the woollen mattress. It was thin and light enough for me to carry downstairs by myself. I unrolled it next to Syleanh.

As I went back for the bedclothes, I heard Syleanh's mother ask Kolymba, 'But where is *she* going to sleep?'

'She'll manage,' he answered.

I couldn't make out Teira's reply, but I did hear the word '*dainefin*'. Whether she was comparing me to the Priestess, or wondering whether I really was a 'leader's daughter' where I came from, I couldn't tell.

I watched over Syleanh for ten days.

She slept soundly until the third day, and on the

fifth I asked her if she wanted go home to her parents. Syleanh begged to stay with me a little longer.

She would sometimes need four or five hours of sleep to recover from five minutes of wakefulness, but it was lovely being together for those five minutes. It would have been worth it just for the smile that flashed across her face whenever she woke and saw I hadn't left her.

Her mother visited every day and had got used to my presence. She would ask how I was, treating me like an equal. I was no longer the girl from Ama-Tángaor who filled her daughter's head with lies.

The Mana dropped in every day too, and Kolymba kept us all well-fed.

Kolymba, what am I going to do? I asked him once, when Syleanh was asleep.

'I cannot force you to stay if you do not wish to,' he answered, placing a bowl of soup on the floor, and perching on the edge of Syleanh's bed.

I'm scared of leaving. I'm scared of going back home.

'You mustn't stay out of fear,' he replied.

That was rich, coming from a Maír. I knew I needed to go home, but I didn't know what I would do once I was there. Nor did I want to leave Syleanh before she was recovered.

I felt responsible for what had happened to her, but I was also proud of her. She'd had the courage to try what generations of Maír never had – she'd decided to find Lyr and go beyond their horizon.

I had to stay, for her.

When Syleanh was awake, we would read books that I borrowed from the Kymirama, or the Maír history book that I never left out of my sight.

I told Syleanh about my vision of Isehar's past, trying to censor my strongest emotions. She was a sensitive, intelligent listener but I had to keep in mind that she was a child, and one who had recently survived a traumatic event. She didn't need me burdening her with my Empathic Aura.

If I felt the need to reflect, I did it while she was asleep. I often went back to the big book, in an attempt to understand the role the visions were playing in my own story. Mana Yan spoke of visions as gifts and responsibilities; Dainefin had warned me off them, and took them as a sign that the illness was getting worse.

I saw the visions more like windows into the lives of people who, for better or worse, moved in the same little corner of the page of Time where, since my mother's death, my life now took place. There were those who, like me, had only just arrived here now, and others, like Reydn and Dainefin, who'd been here since long before I even knew what the Maír or Cloch were.

I hoped that sooner or later the fragments I saw would come together to reveal the bigger picture. Until then, I would simply accept them as they came, though I remained determined to rid myself of the Empathic Aura.

With Kolymba's help I learned to meditate. I had no aim other than to be at peace for a handful of minutes at a time. I didn't feel different in any way and

I wasn't doing it for spiritual reasons. It was just nice that for ten, fifteen minutes – even an hour – I didn't have to think about anything but Kolymba's voice instructing me to clear my mind. Not only from memories and concerns but also the machinations upon which the human mind is compelled to ruminate – all those 'if only's .

I sensed there was an order to all things, felt aware of everything around me: Syleanh's breathing, her small chest rising and falling; the floor beneath my crossed legs; the scent of green anise coming off Kolymba's hands; the warm draft and voices coming through the window . . . I was equally aware of what was inside me: my small aches and pains, my worries.

But though I was aware of all that, I was also empty and free.

I understood why Mana Yan had believed Luminous Thoughts predated the beginning of Time – it was impossible to gauge how much time went by during my meditation.

All that is to say, I wasn't looking for the Luminous Thought. It simply happened.

Considering what Mana Tar and Kolymba had told me about them, it was absurd for me to achieve one. I didn't have the training, practice or experience that were required.

'That doesn't matter,' said Kolymba, when I told him about it. 'There is no need for one to seek a Luminous Thought. It comes to you. When you chose to remain by Syleanh's side, you chose the present. You forgot the past, you stopped worrying about your future.'

Kolymba . . . do Luminous Thoughts really keep the Empathic Aura at bay? Is this what I have to do to heal?

'I don't know if they'll help you get well,' he answered in a measured tone, as if he didn't want to encourage false hopes.

Perhaps I should consider starting on the Path . . . the River of Time, maybe—

'No, Lyria,' Kolymba interrupted me. 'The Ata Mahari only gives you more years to live, to chase what the Maír have been seeking since time immemorial.'

The Luminous Life?

Kolymba shook his head. 'The Luminous Life is not the right choice for everyone.' He stood up, murmuring, 'I'm sure it's still here, somewhere . . .' as he shuffled out of the room.

I heard him opening and closing cupboards and drawers, and then the pump in the garden as he ran some water.

When he came back into the room, he was drying a square tablet with a cloth. It looked incredibly old and it bore four short lines. I ran my finger over them as Kolymba read them out loud.

'E mana yendor,
u-kóinei gira.
Kóinei leheno,
koinéi amatha.'

The ancients used to say: there are only two ways. The wrong way and the right way.

It didn't sound like much of a proverb to me. Nor did it seem to answer the question about what the Maír had been looking for since forever.

'*Koinéi amatha*,' Kolymba repeated.

The right way.

He moved my index finger to the penultimate syllable.

'*Koinéi ama*-tha,' he said, one more time, changing the stress on the last word.

I thought about it.

The way back home?

He nodded, smiling. 'There are only two ways. The wrong way and the way back home.'

I didn't need to bathe in the Ata Mahari. I was already going home. The River of Time was a gift to the Maír so they could live until it was possible for them to return home.

But how was I to convince them that time was now? Perhaps Dainefin wouldn't have had trouble talking the Maír into returning, she had lived with them and undertaken the Path.

But I wasn't her. Cloch had been Dainefin's home, but it couldn't be mine. Maybe that was the key. Maybe Dainefin couldn't guide them home because Amarantha had never really been her home. I smiled. For the first time, I didn't envy the Priestess – after all, the world didn't need another Dainefin.

Isehar approaches the Priestess. He's taller than she is, but he's making an effort to stoop so their eyes can be on a level. Dainefin seems to appreciate the respect.

'I wasn't sure earlier, but now I have no doubt,' she says. 'I am certain I have met you before, when you were much, much younger.'

'Before . . . the accident? Do you know where I'm from?'

Dainefin does not answer. She steps closer and sweeps a hand over his forehead to move his hair aside. He has a scar on his left temple. She rubs it with the tip of her thumb. Isehar briefly closes his eyes.

'Is this . . . ?'

He nods. 'That's where I hit my head when I fell off my horse.'

'You fell off no horse. Come with me.'

Isehar follows Dainefin into the castle's drying room. It is a vast, high-ceilinged room, lit exclusively by long, narrow windows. Bundles of herbs and flowers hang from wooden beams. One of the walls is taken up by a large sideboard covered with trays of stiff muslin, where more leaves and flowers have been placed to dry. Herbs are arranged on the top shelf, meticulously labelled in glass jars and set out in alphabetical order.

He wonders how anyone can live with all these scents mixing together. His nostrils are starting to itch and he feels a headache coming on.

He sees Dainefin pick out three of the jars and pour a little of each of them into a mortar. He is mesmerised by the sight of her pounding the herbs, then infusing them in a liquid that smells of alcohol. She leaves four or five leaves out and strains the mixture into a glass.

'Sit down, please.'

Isehar does as he is told and Dainefin hands him the glass.

The concoction smells familiar, but that familiarity does not make him feel safe. The more Isehar tries to remember where he's smelt this before, the tighter the knot in his stomach gets. He takes another sniff, and wishes he'd never followed the Priestess to the drying room.

The quicker he gets this over and done with, the sooner he'll be back with Fayrem.

'Do I drink it slowly, or all in one go?'

Dainefin's answer is a whisper. 'A tiny sip.'

Isehar takes a sip of the mixture, then stares at her in horror.

'Have you drunk something like this before?' asks the Priestess.

He nods, and grasps the edge of the chair. He feels faint. He can hear the whooshing of his breath in his chest. He can't slow his breathing; he can't seem to get enough air into his lungs.

'Stop,' Dainefin warns. 'Do not try to remember. Listen,' she shakes his arm, forcing him to look at her. '*Listen.*'

She sits next to him and takes his hand.

'A long time ago, I too suffered from the same illness that Lyria has now. I communicated as she did and, like her, I had visions that I wasn't always able to understand. A long, long time ago,' the Priestess repeats, 'before you were even born, Reydn was my foster brother, and my best friend. We grew up together, just like you and Fayrem.'

Dainefin explains how she dreamt of what Reydn had done, how he'd erased Isehar's memories.

Isehar bends over sideways and vomits. Dainefin supports him, holding his forehead. He flops against the back of the chair, letting his legs slide under the table, feeling hollow, like a puppet.

Dainefin picks up one of the leaves and hands it to him.

'Chew this,' she says.

Isehar chews, pressing his palms against his temples. All the things he hasn't been able to remember are now emerging from the miasma of his memories, flooding his mind all at once.

'Stay with me,' says Dainefin. After she had the vision, she tells him, she nearly destroyed herself trying to figure out a way to stop Reydn – she didn't even know if she *could* stop Reydn or if she'd seen something that had already happened.

Isehar tries to focus on the Priestess instead of letting himself be swept away by what's going on in his head.

'Why me?' he manages to ask.

'I don't know,' she admits. 'I think at some point, he planned on "finding" you and returning you to your family for some kind of reward.'

Isehar still doesn't understand. What kind of reward could his family offer? How does the Priestess know Reydn?

Isehar is still confused and overwhelmed, but he's breathing normally now.

'Reydn must have changed his mind when Anur started visiting Murihen's court regularly. It must have been easier to pull his strings than King Hervin's.'

'King Hervin . . . ?'

Dainefin ignores the question.

'This,' she says, pointing at the still-full glass, 'is a sacred beverage. If taken regularly for long enough, it helps you forget the past. I can't believe Reydn stooped this low,' she adds, shaking her head.

'And these,' she says, pointing at the leaves she asked him to chew on, 'will help you remember. A little at a time – not all at once. I'll help you. You're safe now.'

Her voice fades as memories crowd his mind, all jumbled together like the smells of the drying room. Anguish is receding, and a sense of completeness he has never felt before is growing inside him. He feels like something he never knew he'd lost is being returned to him.

'And here's the best part,' says Dainefin.

He looks up, into her eyes.

'I know who you are. And tomorrow I'm going to take you home.'

I woke the next morning with a sigh of relief.

Chapter 25

Anur stops at the crossroads within sight of the city walls. What's the point of going on? He backtracks and dismounts, slapping Dek's flank and watching him gallop away through the expanses of blooming amaranth.

The red of these fields will be even redder soon. And not just because the sun is about to set.

Was that my thought, or Anur's? How was I seeing this? I was in bed, but not asleep. I'd been awake and fully conscious when I'd had that vision, I was certain of it. For a moment, I'd been in two places at once: on my pallet in Kolymba's house and also somewhere just outside the capital city.

I wanted to know what happened next, but my flash of awareness had interrupted the vision. How could I bring it back? I could feel it calling, but how was I to get back to it?

What had Dainefin said? That time is written on

the same page over and over again – my Empathic Aura could show me anything that had happened, was happening or was yet to happen. Mana Yan agreed, but Mana Yan wrote that visions could not be controlled. The Empathic Aura chose what to show me. Could I ask a vision to show itself?

I tried lying down, counting my breaths, relaxing. But it didn't work. Instead, I felt it moving further away. I knew where I needed to be, but not *when*.

Was it possible for me to think of my own past, and make it coincide with Anur's? To go back in my mind to that afternoon, that day, that week . . . . No, I was making the situation worse.

The vision called to me one last time and I strained to remember what I had just seen – endless swathes of blood-red amaranth.

I honed in on that one detail, recalling the awareness of the present my first Luminous Thought had given me. I cleared my mind of everything except Amarantha surrounded by endless swathes of flowering amaranth, swathes of red, flowering amaranth. Amaranth . . .

Anur turns to the north, the direction from which Murihen's army will march. Reydn knows that Father is aware an attack is coming, so he is doing something unexpected – charging from the north with hordes of good-for-nothings picked from the Separatists' ranks. The mountain passes north of the lake are a snowfield even in the summer, but it's the faster way around. It doesn't matter to Reydn that at least half the men will die of exposure. Reydn doesn't care about them; it's timing that's important. He'll give his troops two days to recover, and then they'll be set loose – they can burn the city down, raze it to the ground, do anything they want.

And no one will be there to defend the capital. Anur would bet his last coin that the Valiant and his men are in Hatablar where Reydn's *other* army is waiting for them.

Myrain may have more men, his cavalry may be armoured and trained, but Reydn has a different approach to war. He plays by his own rules and has no mercy. He offers the Separatists a way to channel their frustration, and frustration is the only lever he needs to pull for chaos to follow. That is the language Reydn knows best: chaos.

Anur can't work out what Reydn is hoping to achieve by joining forces with the Separatists – other than chaos. They are people he has repeatedly looked down on, people he claims he has nothing in common with. Anur is not convinced. Reydn acts aristocratic, but it seems fake.

In the beginning, Anur never questioned him.

Reydn is the only one with whom he could share certain ideas, ideas that none of his family would approve of. He'd tried to talk to Dainefin – to test the waters – but she insisted on defending Father's decisions, despite their ruinous consequences.

Anur knows that his father made a mistake with the Salterns' Edict, drawing all those refugees to Amarantha when it would have been so much better for them to stay where they lived ....It only led to discontent at the border.

Dainefin had been shocked when he brought that up, as if he'd said something monstrous. It's not like he suggested the people die . . . . But there was no point trying to explain himself. It was obvious that Dainefin didn't understand, and with her on the Council, ruling Amarantha would be a constant struggle – always calling votes, always compromising.

That's why Reydn's idea to get rid of the Priestess had seemed perfect. She'd been poking her nose into matters that didn't concern her for far too long; it was right to teach her a lesson. But the idea had been to keep her away from the Council for a while, not to kill her.

He'd never meant to kill anyone. Reydn had said the infusion would just make her forget who she was for a few weeks. When his mother had accidentally drunk it and died, he'd been horrified. What else could he do but run away to Murihen? At least there he wouldn't be surrounded by reminders of what he'd done.

But then his uncle suddenly became ill and died, having named Anur as heir to Murihen's throne. And Reydn had reappeared, whispering in Anur's ear . . .

Anur will reign over Murihen. But will he ever be free?

He pictures his life by Reydn's side. Every day, Reydn will be there, his hand controlling every decision.

Reydn and Dainefin are not so different. They both act out of self-interest, and the rest of the world has to go along with it.

Yet Dainefin is just – every decision she makes is morally superior to anyone else's. Which is why Anur can't stand her. She's even corrupted his own sister, turning her into a know-it-all too.

I tried not to be distracted by the thought my brother had just had about me. I needed to stay in the vision. Just a little longer . . .

Reydn, though. Reydn is chaos. He does whatever he wants at any given moment. Reydn acts purely on whims. Anur liked this about him at first, liked him because of that. Reydn's life looked so easy compared to his.

Anur wants an easy life. He wants to be free. He wants a life where no one dares to contradict him. It doesn't seem so much to ask.

He turns his back on the amaranth and walks away. A few metres from the edge of the cliff, he takes a run-up and jumps.

Chapter 26

There was still time.

I clung to that thought, because otherwise the Empathic Aura would have annihilated me. I would have stopped existing because there was no room in the world for my soul as well as everything I was feeling.

My fist clenched the corner of the cotton sheet. The darkness in my room thickened somehow, even though it must have been four in the morning and the sky was already fading to indigo along the horizon. I found the dark stifling, unbearable.

I dragged myself to the window, banging my thigh against the frame. I gulped down the fresh air.

There is still time, I repeated to myself. *It hasn't happened yet.*

My only hope of getting through the night was to distance myself from my feelings so I could dissect everything rationally.

I began at the beginning.

My brother had killed our mother. By mistake, but

he'd done it. I remembered him waiting with me, Sonni and Father outside our parents' bedroom door. He had glared at the Priestess as if it had been her fault. I suppose that in Anur's distorted world view, she was at fault. The poisoned infusion had been meant for her, not Mother.

It was typical of Anur. He was incapable of taking responsibility for anything.

I let rage triumph over all other emotions. How could he be so selfish? How dare he think of himself as the misunderstood victim! It may have been Reydn's idea, but Anur had gone along with it.

I felt betrayed – not just because of what he'd already done, but because of what he planned to do.

He hadn't even considered what his death would do to any of us!

I needed to let out the awful thoughts, to vent my anger so I could move past it and find a way to stop this from happening.

If Anur jumped, I would lose a brother. Not only the brother I had now, but the future version of him. I realised now that I'd always thought time would soften the edges of our personalities, that one day we would find balance and grow closer. Now that the hourglass had been overturned, I understood that the responsibility of building that relationship was mine, not Time's.

It would have been easy for me to let Anur disappear from my life. One less person who hated me and who I sometimes hated back.

My mother's voice echoed in my head: 'You can't hate him. He's your brother.'

She was right. He was my brother. I couldn't hate him, and I wouldn't waste my last chance to tell him that in person.

The afternoon before I left, Mana Tar invited me over to his house along with Kolymba and Syleanh – who had now recovered enough of her strength to walk, with a little help.

I had always known I would leave at some point, but the last vision had made my departure so unexpected that it still didn't feel real. I was leaving Cloch. I was going home.

There were no words to make our goodbye a little less heart-wrenching. Not for me, or Mana Tar, or Kolymba or Syleanh.

The herbal scent in the Mana's house was even stronger than usual. He had prepared a sweet infusion, which we sipped by the crackling fire in the hearth. As the day wore on, the brew in my cup became saltier. My tears were not for Cloch, but for them: Kolymba, Mana Tar, Syleanh.

Cloch, for me, was just an island. A place I had visited but would never return to. I didn't belong here.

I belonged with the people I loved. The people who, at that very moment, were silently drinking to my health. I cried because I couldn't take them with me, because I'd tried – and failed – at bringing all the Maír home with me.

Mana had a blissful, faraway look on his face, but

Kolymba appeared restless.

What are you thinking about?

'I want to go with you,' he said. His eyes darted to the Mana for permission.

Mana Tar gave a small nod.

Really?

'I can't let you go by yourself,' he said.

'And,' said the Mana, 'this way he'll have something new to teach us on his return.'

Until then, the Maír who had left Cloch hadn't fared too well, so I was touched by Kolymba's bravery. It was also comforting to know I wouldn't be doing the journey by myself.

Syleanh tugged on the Mana's sleeve. She handed him her graphite stick. He sharpened it and returned it to her.

What are you drawing?

'It's a picture for you. To remember the Kymirama . . . and me,' she signed.

The Lyria in Syleanh's drawing had little in common with the mental image I had of myself. She had drawn a tall, slender figure in a floor-length robe, holding a disproportionately small Syleanh by the hand. If not for the unmistakeable garland of curly hair on my head, I would have believed that she'd drawn my own childhood: an afternoon spent reading with Dainefin in the library.

It's beautiful, Syleanh.

Now that I thought of it, the Kymirama was the only place on Cloch where I had really spent time other than Kolymba's house. I'd gone there every day until Syleanh got hurt. I had met new people on the way there and back, but I couldn't say that I had got to know any of them well. I had read, rather than becoming a part of the community. Had I wasted my time here? What would Dainefin say?

'Don't worry,' said the Mana, ruffling Syleanh's hair. 'As soon as she's back home, she'll remember all our quirks.' He turned to me, 'But should you need to jog your memory, you can take this with you.' He handed me the Maír history book.

I can't accept this . . . . It's too much.

'Take a little of us home with you now,' said Mana Tar. 'You can always give it back when we return to Lyr.'

I took the volume with reverence. I had something to give him too.

I handed the Mana my jar of blue honey. It was still half full.

Thank you. For everything.

I wished with all my heart that the Mana was right, that one day he and Kolymba would bring their Maír brothers and sisters back home. I knew Syleanh would never stop trying to convince everyone either.

I vowed then and there to make sure my people would welcome them with open arms.

It would take a lot of work, but I would ask Sonni to help. Together we could lay the groundwork so Amarantha would bloom again, more beautiful than ever. Mana Tar, Kolymba, Syleanh and I would finish what Sari had begun.

Next, I gave Syleanh the seashell bracelet Sonni had made me and Cam's painting of Amarantha castle.

Syleanh was beside herself with joy. Her hands full, she gazed at Cam's painting, enchanted, and said, 'Home. Lyria. Home.'

I nodded.

E mana yendor . . .

Kolymba and Mana looked at each other.

'Said. Ancients. What?' asked Syleanh.

'They said many things,' the Mana answered with a smile, 'but they were right about that: "There are only two ways, the wrong way and the way back home." *Koinéi ama-tha.*'

'*Tha*. Ama. Koinéi,' echoed Syleanh. She set Cam's painting on the floor above her own paper and went back to drawing.

We sipped our infusion in silence. It was late by the time Mana Tar reminded us we had to get up early tomorrow.

He hugged me long and hard at the door and whispered, 'Safe, happy journey home.'

Kolymba and I each held one of Syleanh's hands. We had to stop every now and then so she could catch her breath – walking was still an effort for her. After crossing the square of the Kymirama and cutting through the lanes, we turned into her street, and stopped in our tracks.

Look at that!

On every doorstep, white-blue flames quivered in tiny earthenware bowls. There was something about their dance, and the way they'd been placed, that made me think of a choir, or the singing procession I'd seen in Denhole.

The trail of light led all the way to the end of the street.

Syleanh's eyes opened wide, and she limped faster, tugging on my and Kolymba's arms.

What makes the flames that colour?

'*Káori* wood and a blend of herbs.' Kolymba spoke quietly to preserve the magic of that moment.

When we reached Douk and Teira's door, Syleanh threw her arms around my neck, and I squeezed her tight. 'I love you,' we both signed at the same time.

Douk opened the door and grinned at us. He hugged first Kolymba and then me without a word.

Kolymba and I soon saw that the trail of lights accompanied us zthe rest of the way to his house.

'I think they're for us, Lyria,' said Kolymba.

Kolymba's house shone like the sea beneath a full moon. Dozens of little braziers surrounded it: on the ground, the windowsills, the garden. But one solitary flame lit his doorstep.

I was so moved that even the Empathic Aura was

speechless for a moment.

'I think they're wishing us luck on our crossing,' said Kolymba. 'And saying thank you.'

Who?

'The Lyrién.'

Just before drifting to sleep, I thought I heard a noise. No, not a noise, a vibration. Like a brief and barely perceptible earthquake.

I felt a current tug at me, gently, as if setting me ashore. I instinctively knew it was the Ata Mahari saying goodbye.

Goodbye. Thank you.

The Ata Mahari fell silent and I fell into a deep, peaceful sleep.

Chapter 27

SIX DAYS LATER

We'd had an unremarkable crossing but as soon as we set foot on land, Kolymba had been overwhelmed by emotion. He was touching the soil of what most Maír still considered a mythical land. I stood silently by his side while he adjusted to this new reality before we continued our journey.

Now, Shamabat glittered a mile down the road.

'Are you sure you're okay to continue on your own?'

Go. You have your own Path to take.

Deep down, I would have liked Kolymba to stay with me, to see Dainefin again, get to know the capital, learn my language even. But I knew it was time to part ways.

'One day,' he said, 'not too far into the future, I will come back. But I must return to Cloch first, as I promised Mana Tar.'

Before I let him go, I surprised him with the gift I had been working on in secret every night since he'd finished building the boat.

It's not perfect, but everything you need should be there.

Kolymba looked through the notes I had prepared for him for whenever he wished to return to the continent. It was plain paper, but I'd sewn the pages together as neatly as I could. There were hand-drawn maps, directions, notes and landmarks . . . pictures too. All the writing was in Maír, in the best calligraphy I could manage.

'Not a single error,' he commented with a smile, lingering over the page about Hatablar Forest.

Maybe not in the notes, but the maps . . . you may be better off navigating by the stars!

We laughed together and hugged. Again, his gaze fell to my Hatablar notes.

Hatablar's not that far from here you know. You could visit before you go back to Cloch.

'Then I really would have a story to tell,' he said with a smile.

'Good evening, Your Highness,' said Master Lohm when he opened the door, holding a green ceramic candle holder in his hand.

I thought he'd ask me lots of questions, but he just let me in as if I'd come for supper after a day's fishing.

As I stepped into the kitchen, Móiras leapt up and wrapped me in a briny hug. He'd somehow become more tanned since I last saw him, but his huge smile was exactly the same.

The table wobbled as he sat his massive body back on his stool.

There were dirty dishes and empty glasses on the table, and a mouth-watering seafood aroma rose from a saucepan. Lohm served me a huge helping of pasta, apologising that there weren't many clams left.

'I didn't want them to go to waste and we obviously didn't know you were coming.' Móiras poured me a glass of red wine. 'Every now and then this old man gets it into his head to cook enough for four.'

'Just in case you and Dainefin came back,' Lohm said to me.

Dainefin's absence loomed, but neither Lohm nor Móiras asked me any questions.

Where is everyone? The village seemed empty . . .

'They're expecting an invasion at any moment,' said Móiras. 'But I'm sure there won't be one,' he hastened to add.

Lohm whistled a verse of *Farewell, the Hills*, an old wartime ballad often sung at village fairs and the Foundation Feast, especially by people who'd had a little too much to drink.

Móiras talked over him. 'We're lucky. We're so far away from everything,' he said. 'The unrest is further inland.'

Móiras then told me that the Valiant was recruiting

youths from all over the kingdom. 'Rumour has it he's going to lead the army to wherever the Separatists are hiding out soon. That's why,' Móiras concluded, 'I won't let you travel by yourself.'

I don't need—

'I know. But I insist. You'll be more comfortable on the cart and some rest will be good for you.'

I couldn't argue with that.

What's happening in the capital?

'You know the phrase "no news is good news"?'

I nodded, though I'd always found that no news made me anxious.

Master Lohm was still whistling *Farewell, the Hills*. He tugged on my arm to make me stand up and improvised a dance of tiny, tiptoeing steps, twirling me on the spot a couple of times.

'*My love is not to wither in the snow…*'

On our arrival at the inn of Saint Josef's crossroad, Móiras and I were both exhausted. Between Shamabat and the inn, we had only stopped to sleep three times. But he was more tired than I, since he'd been the one driving. I had dozed in the back of the cart, amongst the crates of books that Lohm had asked us to deliver to the capital.

Móiras went straight to his room for a pre-dinner nap, but I needed to eat something sooner rather than

At a table by the fireplace, I spotted the last person I was expecting to find at the inn: Uncle Noalim. He was braiding wheat as he sat waiting for food, or perhaps for someone to join him. I looked around hoping to see . . .

'You won't find him,' said a familiar voice, 'but I'm so happy to see you!'

Reya threw her arms around me and hugged me tightly.

What are you doing here?

'We're headed to the capital to wait for Cam.'

Reya didn't pause for my next, obvious question. Her voice broke as she said, 'He went to war.' She took a deep breath. 'Sorry. But you're the only one who understands how I feel . . .'

Cam was gone, and Reya hadn't had anyone to talk to about it. I remembered how cruel the serving girl had been when Reya and I had gone for orzata.

Have you heard from him?

She shook her head, on the brink of tears.

Let's sit for a minute.

I didn't want to keep Uncle Noalim waiting for too long, but Reya and I needed to have this conversation in private. We sat at a table by the door.

Tell me how it happened.

Like many other young men in the village, Cam had received the Council's call to arms. But instead of joining up, he simply packed a haversack and headed to Hatablar, alone, on foot.

To Hatablar?

'Yes,' said Reya. 'That's what Old Bedevilled said when she came to tell my folks.'

Cam may have heard about the Separatists in the forest. But what could he do by himself, unarmed? **Why did he go?**

Reya couldn't answer that, but she appeared more worried than ever.

Don't worry, I tried to comfort her. **If he really is in Hatablar right now, I doubt anything will happen to him.**

I couldn't be certain of that, but from the last vision I'd had of Anur, I'd got the impression that Myrain had Hatablar well under control. Reya did seem comforted, but I had to fight hard to control my anxiety.

Cam's flight was perplexing. He didn't seem the type to abandon Uncle Noalim and go looking for trouble. But what tormented me was that he may have wanted to profess loyalty to my family. I hadn't hesitated to advise Isehar and Fayrem to ask Myrain for positions in the army. But Cam wasn't Isehar or Fay-rem. He didn't have anyone else to rely on.

'I can't blame him,' said Reya. 'I would have done the same myself.' She wiped at her tears with her fingers. 'We can't do anything about it now,' she concluded, sniffling. 'We'll just have to wait for him to come back.'

I nodded uncertainly. Could I really not do anything about it? Once I was back in the capital and my father knew about Reydn's plot, it would take no more than one order from me to have someone look for Cam and escort him back to Denhole, whether he liked it or not. Lyria, Princess of Amarantha, would do that.

But would Lyria, Cam's friend?

We'll wait.

I sensed that it was now my turn to tell my own story, but it would take days to tell Reya about the whole Maír saga, and the things that happened on Cloch. I also felt the urgency to go and talk to the other person who was having as hard a time as we were.

Reya understood.

'I'll leave you two alone. Look, his order is ready.'

A steaming plate of stew and a small jug of wine with two glasses had appeared on the counter.

Are you not eating?

'I haven't been hungry for weeks now,' she said.

Are you travelling comfortably?

'Yes, Noalim is showing me his favourite places along the way. At this rate, it will be another month before we reach the capital, but I'm enjoying taking it slowly.' She said this with a small smile.

I hugged her, we said our goodbyes and I took the tray to Uncle Noalim.

As I placed his meal in front of him, I noticed that his face was even more wrinkled than I remembered. I gently took the ears of wheat from his hands and signed my name on his palm.

'Doll,' he said, beaming.

It took me a while, but I signed one letter at a time on his palm to tell him I had brought his dinner and that Reya would join us later.

Uncle Noalim poured us both half a glass of wine. He cut his food into tiny pieces and put each one into his mouth incredibly slowly. At the end of the meal, he drank a sip of wine and wiped his mouth with a crumpled handkerchief that he kept stuffed up his sleeve.

I felt the despair in his every gesture, as if what he wasn't putting into words was seeping through of its own accord.

'He's gone.'

I took both his hands and signed a promise that I wasn't sure I could keep, but I felt I needed to make it to that old man with glistening eyes, who braided ears of wheat. One eye as blue as the sky, the other green as grass.

'He'll be back.'

On the day we reached the capital, the sky was a clear blue but the breeze brought a chill. Autumn was creeping in.

'You really want me to leave you here by yourself?' Móiras asked for the third or fourth time.

I do.

I was dying to see Sonni, Dainefin, my father, but I had to be here for Anur. I had to be ready. I squashed the small part of me that said I was being a coward, that I'd selfishly abandoned my family when they'd needed me and it had all been for nothing because the Empathic Aura was still there.

'As you wish. Don't do anything silly though. As

soon as you're out of provisions, get yourself straight to the castle.'

I hugged Móiras tight, then watched him ride through the city gates.

I turned my eyes to the west. The amaranth had bloomed, but hadn't yet turned the fields deep red. That was the only detail I remembered from the vision: the thickly flowering amaranth. I set out, looking for a place to camp until Anur showed up.

I found shelter in an abandoned stone hut, not far from my favourite cove. I made myself a bed by piling up fresh sand and laying my seven white tunics over top of it.

Summer may not be over just yet, but that first night, I thought I would freeze to death.

My warm clothes – the woollen tunics, trousers and stockings – were all still in Ama-Tángaor. When I'd packed for my escape, I'd decided to bring the tunics Kolymba had made me instead – Cloch had been so hot. I regretted not taking one of the blankets from the cart.

I lay on my sand bed – which, once compacted down, wasn't as comfortable as I thought it would be – trying to decide whether it would be wiser to bury myself in sand, or shake out the tunics and wear them all at once. In the end, I did neither. I just passed a sleepless night telling myself the sun would eventually rise and warm that cursed icebox.

I spent ten nights in that hut. Every morning I would stroll along the foreshore, picking up shells and letting my toes sink into its salty puddles. I would sit for hours, gazing out to sea.

Fear was my constant companion: fear of what would happen when I saw my brother Anur again, fear that I would fail and my vision would come to pass. I fought to keep the tragic thoughts at bay and focus on the rhythmic tempo of the waves. Occasionally I would come across a Luminous Thought, an instant of awareness.

I spent the afternoons reading the Maír book. I had almost learnt it by heart, as I had Aur-Lee's journal. Little by little, I noted down translations in the margins of my blue notebook, which was now full to the brim. I could not allow Maír to fade into the dark corner of my mind that housed rusty, unused scientific equations.

I stopped only when my stomach protested. I was thrifty with my provisions, allowing myself little more than a few bites at a time. I drank even less because my water was gone and I only had two flasks of orzata – which made me more, rather than less, thirsty.

When I wasn't meditating or reading the Maír book, I thought about Cam constantly. And Fayrem and Isehar, Kolymba, Mana Tar, Syleanh.

Then, as the sun made towards its westerly bed, I would go to the promontory and wait.

I had recognised the cliff from my vision – a rock wall that Anur often climbed down when the three of us went swimming. At the bottom was a tiny beach enclosed by boulders. On his way back, Anur would swim around the rocks and run up the other side of the promontory, which wasn't as steep.

I'd always sat with Sonni, watching Anur's feats and envying his physical prowess. But after my journey to Cloch, I didn't feel as inadequate as before. I got less tired on long walks – even enjoying them, in fact. I may have even been able to climb down the wall myself now, but I didn't try it. I had to be there when Anur arrived. The fear was worst when I sat there, scanning the fields for a horse approaching.

Every day, the red of the amaranth flowers deepened, while my provisions dwindled.

On the eleventh day, having drunk the last drop of my orzata, I decided to go home to resupply. It would take most of the day to walk there and back, and I knew I had hours of explanations ahead of me when I reached the castle. I also needed to warn my father of the impending attack from the north, even if I didn't know how or when it would take place. Without Anur, I wasn't going to be that much help.

As I left the beach hut behind, I couldn't help but feel anxious. What if Anur arrived before I returned and I didn't make it back in time?

But as I discovered upon reaching the crossroads, I needn't have worried. Anur was already there.

As soon as he saw me, he made to turn Dek around, towards the cliff.

'Wait!'

It wasn't an overwhelming wave of emotions unleashed by the Empathic Aura. It was a whisper. An actual whisper. It was my voice.

Anur froze, staring at me.

'I crossed the kingdom because of what you did.' My voice was getting stronger with every word. I fought the Empathic Aura's attempts to regain control – I wouldn't let it. 'Now I've just crossed it again – *for* you. I've been waiting here eleven days. Please just listen to what I have to say.'

It wasn't a long speech, but my throat was killing me.

Anur looked puzzled and a little scared, but he hadn't ridden off.

I thought I'd be afraid at that moment, but I felt oddly calm. I knew everything, perhaps even more than my brother did.

'Reydn tricked you,' I said. 'He killed her on purpose.'

I had assumed that our family had been turned upside down by Reydn's badly-executed revenge. But now, the pieces clicked together: Reydn's plan had always been to murder our mother. He'd used Anur so that Anur would flee to Murihen, where our uncle would mysteriously die and name my brother king. And who would be there for my brother to lean on? Who would be his sympathetic friend? Reydn. That's who.

Anur's jaw clenched, his muscles tensing in his neck.

'It was a mistake,' he said.

'No,' I replied. 'That's what he wanted you to believe. But the poison was always meant for Mother. Reydn killed her so you'd run away to Murihen.'

'He said Dainefin—' Anur started.

'Was the target, I know,' I said. 'And she was, but not in the way you think. Reydn never wanted to kill Dainefin. He wanted to make her suffer.'

'You're making this up,' he said.

'Dainefin and Reydn grew up together,' I continued. 'Just like Mother and Father. Reydn was the child of servants and Dainefin was a princess, but Dainefin spurned him.'

'But—'

'Listen to me,' I said firmly, my heart beating fast at the bluff I was about to say. 'I crossed the continent so that I could tell you this before you jump. I can't stop you from killing yourself, but at least this way you'll know how things really stand.'

I had played my best card, but it was costing me everything. Saying something so cruel to a person who had decided to take his own life went against my every instinct. I wanted to tell him I understood him and he wasn't alone. But I knew that it wasn't true. I *didn't* know how he felt. And my compassion would just make his burden feel even heavier.

I could see Anur's brain racing to understand how I could possibly know all this; how I could know he'd been planning to jump. I stayed one step ahead of him, quoting his own thoughts.

'You know Reydn. He thrives on chaos. Acts only on whims.'

My brother paled. It had been weeks since my vision, but only minutes, perhaps seconds, since he'd thought those exact words.

'And,' I went on, 'when others won't do as he says, Reydn gets his revenge. Reydn killed Mother to hurt Dainefin. He wanted to frame her because she never returned his feelings. But it wasn't just about Dainefin. Reydn envied our mother. She had got what he had always wanted most: power. Mother was a peasant's daughter – a nobody before she married Father – just like him. Her parents served at court, just like Reydn's. But Mother ended up marrying the heir to the throne of Amarantha. Reydn didn't. And for that, he envied her enough to kill her.'

'But Dainefin . . .' said Anur.

'Dainefin is the first princess of Amarantha,' I replied. 'It's complicated, but just believe me for now.'

'You really think Mother was Reydn's target all along?' he repeated.

'I know she was,' I answered.

'But why use me then? I just wanted Dainefin out of the way for a little while . . .'

'I think Reydn wanted you to go to Murihen.'

'But why?'

'I don't know,' I lied, sparing him the humiliation of knowing Reydn was after someone he could work like a puppet. Someday I would tell him the truth. Someday I would tell him about our cousin too. But now was not the time. I'd already dropped a lot of new information on Anur and I needed to convince him that Reydn was more at fault than he was. I had to be quick.

I was worn out from the effort of speaking again after months of silence, but I gathered whatever voice I had left and said, 'If you jump off that cliff, your problems will be over – but Reydn will get away with this. Please, Anur. Please don't jump. Come home with me.'

Anur looked thoughtful.

'Come on,' I said and held out my hand, 'let's go home.'

Chapter 28

I peeked into the Council Room and the Hall of Audience before finding my father and Sonni in the Dining Hall. I'd forgotten it was dinner time. Anur was resting in his room.

'I'm back,' I announced at the door.

My father leapt up and held me tight. He smelt of cologne and roast meat and home. I took a deep breath.

Sonni was next, giving me a hug before holding me at arms-length and looking me up and down.

'How are you? Have you eaten? Are you thirsty?' he asked.

We sat down, all in our usual seats. Me next to Sonni, Father at the head of the table. Anur should have been sitting at the other end, and, if they'd been there, Mother and Dainefin would have been in the empty seats opposite Sonni and me.

'Where's Dainefin?' I asked.

'She's in Murihen,' said Sonni. 'She went and came back; then she left again.'

'She's supporting your aunt. Poor Rehena has so much to think about now,' said Father.

I was disappointed, but not surprised, that I couldn't see her straight away.

'You can talk again,' Sonni observed.

And did I.

My father and brother were expecting me to tell them what had happened to me over the last four months, but instead I started at the beginning; my story began two hundred and fifteen years earlier, with Aur-Lee landing on the shores of Lyr. I told them everything up until Anur and I got home.

Neither of them interrupted even once, and by the time I had recounted my conversation with Anur, their faces had grown grave, the joy from earlier extinguished.

Several things – Aur-Lee, the Maír, Dainefin, the Isle of Cloch – I would tell them about in more detail over the next few days. That day, we all cared about just one thing: Anur.

When I'd told them about his hand in Mother's death, the way Reydn had manipulated him, Father stood abruptly and gripped the edge of the table. Sonni avoided our eyes.

'What's going to happen to Anur?' Sonni asked.

'The Council must decide whether to put him on trial,' Father answered darkly.

Considering who was on the Council, a trial was practically guaranteed. Its outcome, however, was not. I felt torn. I'd told Anur it wasn't his fault Mother had died, and it wasn't entirely . . . but he *had* been Reydn's accomplice. I didn't think that Anur should be imprisoned for life, but he did have to be held accountable for what he'd done.

'If he helps us catch Reydn, he may only be sentenced to heavy labour. But if he doesn't, he may spend a while in the dungeons.'

'Can't you pardon him?' Sonni asked.

Father shook his head, his face hardening even more. 'Even if he didn't mean to kill Levith, he did. And he acted from a place of selfishness and greed. He owes the kingdom a great debt.'

I could see Sonni struggling with the same feelings as me. We were torn by our love for our brother and the anger and hurt of his betrayal.

Father sighed. 'No point in putting off the inevitable. You two, go fetch your brother. I will summon the Council.'

On our way upstairs, Sonni looked at me as if seeing me for the first time.

'You look . . . good,' he said. 'Less . . . short?' he added, as if he found it embarrassing to pay me a compliment.

'Thank you,' I replied, savouring the way words felt in my mouth.

When we reached Anur's room, we found it empty.

He was gone, but he'd left a folded note addressed to Father, Sonni and me. My brother and I took it to Father and we read it together. Anur wrote that he had gone to find Reydn to make him pay. He explained everything he knew about Reydn's plan to invade Amarantha and warned us to be prepared for anything. He also asked for our forgiveness.

Sonni and I waited for Father to say something.

'I will forgive him,' he said. 'I only hope he returns to us.'

Chapter 29

Hatablar Forest, 5 September

Lyria,

Things have calmed down now, so we can tell you about everything you missed. Fayrem, Myrain, Cam and me are all fine. I'm telling you that now, so you don't have to worry.

Fayrem was the one who insisted we write to you, he's standing next to me, correcting my verbs. (He couldn't write this because his handwriting is too girly.) Without this pighead, Lyria, I would have gone crazy a long time ago. I know who I am now. In theory. I'm still all over the place inside my head. I'm trying to combine two different pasts, the one I thought I'd forgotten for good, and the other one that began after

No it's not!
v

396

the accident. Which wasn't an accident after all, it turns out.

I imagine someone must have told you already, but in case you don't know yet, guess who's back from the dead? Remember your cousin Ambar? Well ... that's me.

Dainefin made my memory come back. I remember what Reydn did to me — it was him, by the way, he's the one that took me. My memories ... I really don't know how to describe them. It's the worst thing that's ever happened to me. Dainefin reckons that Reydn kept me prisoner for two years before giving me to Fayrem's parents. Seeing my real mother — Queen Rehena — was definitely brilliant. But everything else ... I don't know, maybe I would have been happier not knowing. So that's what I mean when I say that Fayrem's holding me together, because he's the one who reminds me that even if Reydn messed up my life, it didn't turn out so badly for me after all. I have a brother who is also my best friend (he's blushing right now), I have my family, the one that brought me up, and my birth mother and family. And friends like you, of course. Well ... I guess you're family too.

I remember you, you know. I mean from before. You're in one of the first ever memories that came back to me, a stupid memory but you know what? I think about it most days. Remember those games of marbles on the beach at Murihen? We played them so often, but I remember this one in particular. It was when me, you, and Sonni formed an alliance against Anur, because he kept winning. I remember that moment so clearly. When that marble crossed the finish line — it was the same colour as your eyes, a present from your father, I think — we were so happy.

I don't know why I remember that so well, but it means a lot to me. I like it because it's familiar. It's peaceful. It has you and Sonni. I remember the two of you so clearly. You might remember less, you were little, you must have been five or six. Now that you're grown up, you look a lot like Dainefin — has anybody told you that?

When I met her, I couldn't help thinking of you. It's not the way she speaks — so strange to think that the last time I heard you speak was during that game of marbles — it's the things she does. It's like the decisions she makes are the same you would make, I think.

She's the one who took me home, not long after we returned from Cloch. When we got to the castle, she took us to talk to Myrain, like you suggested. We both signed up, but Fayrem got to start his training sooner because Dainefin insisted I visit

Murihen first.

I was so nervous. I'd never met the Queen before when I was just plain old Isehar and now I was going to be alone in a room with her ... as her son. I was so worried she wouldn't believe me, that she'd send me back. That I'd feel like a stranger. But she knew me straight away. And I did feel at home with her, even if it's going to take a lot of getting used to.

Dainefin also let me stop and visit my other parents on the way back. They were probably more shocked than I was by the news. They think me and Fayrem are doing the right thing, by the way ... even if they weren't exactly happy to hear we'd signed on with Amarantha's army. Anyway, Dainefin's the one who helped me to remember, and I'll be grateful to her forever.

When I saw her again in Amarantha a month ago, she told me she'd gone looking for Reyen. She didn't find him. He'd already left with his army.

I can't tell you if Dainefin was disappointed by that. I don't think she was really up to seeing him again, after what she told me about their past. They knew each other. Maybe you know that already. Well, Reyen was nowhere to be found. Perhaps it was better for her this way.

The rumour going round is that Reydn is commanding the Separatists from the border village Burgios.

When we came across their army yesterday, here near Hatablar, with Myrain and our five thousand, they had less than a thousand left — the others must have been on their way still or had deserted. Myrain expected more. Imagine, Lyria, five thousand against eight or nine hundred. The Separatists ran when they saw us, but some of them stayed. About a hundred, according to Myrain. And they were rabid, determined to fight to the last.

So Myrain, he sent two hundred of our own to meet them — I was there with Cam and Fayrem. Cam trained with us by the way! — and we outmatched them by far.

They were all wretches, Lyria, you should have seen them: they could barely lift their swords and handled them like sickles. They hadn't been trained for battle at all!

It was obvious that the Separatists were incapable of getting past us to the capital, so before we went in, Myrain ordered us to only fight to wound. We followed orders, but it wasn't easy. Reydn's men were determined to kill or die trying.

It was all over by midday.

We lost seventeen. They lost twenty-one. Many more would had died on both sides, if it hadn't been for Cam. He's incredible, you know that?

When we returned to camp after the fighting, we couldn't find him anywhere.

We were worried he might have been wounded, so Fayrem and I went back to the battlefield and found him there. But he wasn't hurt.

He was looking after them, Lyria. He was treating the wounded, from both sides, with hata honey. He'd spent the night before the battle collecting resin, can you believe it? He went from one man to the next, putting resin on their wounds. They were screaming at him that they'd rather die on the field than be treated by someone from Amarantha, but Cam obviously didn't hear them — I don't think he would have stopped if he could have.

When he finished on the battlefield, he returned to camp and helped our physicians. Fayrem got nicked by a sword on the arm, and now he's only got a little cut that looks like it will be gone soon. Says he's never felt better.

Cam's great. The Murihenians owe him a big favour.

All right, I'm going to stop talking about Cam because I'm starting to sense someone's getting jealous here. Not true!

As for the future, we're not sure what will happen to us now. My mother wants me to inherit my father's throne, but Myrain wants to promote us with merit and keep us around.

For now, we'll start by going to Amarantha. We got your letter, Fayrem and Cam are already making arrangements so that everything you suggested goes without a hitch. I can't help with that yet — I promised Sonni I'd stay by his side 'til this is all over.

I don't think there will ever be a king as worthy as your brother, Lyria. But I promise you that I'll try.

We'll see each other soon,

Isehar & Fayrem

Chapter 30

On the day of the attack, there was no attack. The Separatists reached the capital and found it empty.

The gates, open.

The drawbridge, down.

The streets, deserted.

The whole city immersed in silence, waiting.

The invaders felt their blood turn to ice in their veins as they walked the streets of a ghost town.

They proceeded cautiously, expecting an ambush at any moment. They were well aware they would be dangerously outnumbered, since they'd lost three-quarters of their number to cold and hunger.

The Separatists who had made it to Amarantha were gaunt and tired. They'd been sent north just as an unseasonably cold storm front had hit the mountains. The few that remained knew they didn't stand a chance, but they had their orders. They would fight this last battle.

Except that battle never took place.

Nothing even indicated that they weren't welcome.

The Separatists paused outside the great arch into the walled city. There, the arguments began. A few deserted, believing they were about to walk into a trap. Some left because it made no sense to assault an empty city. Others ran away just because they could.

The remaining twelve entered the city.

They got to the castle and inspected the ground floor. Empty.

They climbed to the second floor, and heard voices. Calm voices. They followed the sounds to the Audience Chamber.

There sat King Uriel, Prince Sonni, Dainefin, the Amarantha Council and Isehar, the future King of Murihen.

The twelve entered, and my father pointed to some empty chairs set in a semi-circle in front of the commission.

'Take a seat,' he said.

'Let us talk,' Dainefin added.

On the day of the attack, there was no attack.

Only a group of people, discussing, arguing, and compromising in the Audience Chamber of King Uriel's court.

I know all this because Sonni and Isehar reported it to me afterwards. I didn't witness it because on the day of the attack, I wasn't there.

Anur's note had confessed everything he knew about Reydn's plans. The Valiant had already left for Hatablar Forest three days before and there was no way to move his troops quickly enough to get them back in time. A few individuals riding hard though? They could make it.

Together with Sonni, Cam and Fayrem, I organised the evacuation of the city. We divided the people into groups: Cam would take Amaranthians to Denhole and the surrounding villages, while Fayrem's group would seek asylum in Sidera, on the coast. Cam and Fayrem each took nearly forty thousand people. I had the smallest group of two hundred families to escort to Shamabat. They were families with elderly grandparents, young children or the ill. We were the last to leave, waiting for some of the carts to return from the other villages. We filed out of the deserted capital the day before the assault.

On our journey, I spoke to every single person. I calmed and encouraged them with my words – words I was able to choose, to control the register of. Both nights that we stopped to make camp, I announced how far we were from our destination and what time we'd leave in the morning. Finding myself at the centre of attention no longer distressed me. In fact, public speaking now left a pleasant tingle in the pit of my stomach.

Shamabat was hardly the most hospitable of villages, but when the local women found out that the Princess of Amarantha was with the refugees, they opened their doors to all with no complaints.

We stayed there for a week, to give the Councils of Amarantha and Murihen the time they needed to conclude negotiations with the Separatists. It turns out that all they had ever wanted were fewer taxes along with some very reasonable requests – such as better roads that wouldn't flood in the winter.

During that week, I took care of evacuee families, making sure they had everything they needed. And when I was called on to resolve a dispute, I made an effort to disperse unpleasantness and boost morale. I helped serve food at mealtimes and organised readings in the square to entertain everyone. The rest of my time – the early hours of the morning, and those after dinner – was spent translating the Maír book.

I would rise at daybreak and only go to bed when I couldn't stay upright any longer.

It had all really happened. Lyr, Hatablar Forest, the Ata Mahari, the Isle of Cloch, my own adventures finding them all.

And now that I could speak again, I told anyone who was prepared to listen about Cloch and the real people who lived there.

Mana Yan had written a colossal book. Colossal, but incomplete. There was no mention of Dainefin, Reydn, Kolymba, the Rebels. No mention of Mana Yan's death or Syleanh's dedication to get to Lyr. The story of the Maír was still being told.

For the moment, I simply translated what had already been written, completing the last few chapters the evening before our return to the capital.

I would have done the same for the Maír if I could,

but there hadn't been time to make Kolymba's notes this thorough. How could two civilisations live so near without knowing the first thing about each other? I decided I would try to translate Aur-Lee's journal into Maír, even though I would most probably fail in the attempt. The longer I waited, the harder it would become to remember the Maír language. It would be my way to thank the Maír for all they had done for me, and their immense gift to me, and to the whole continent.

When we returned to Amarantha, we found it as we had left it. Fayrem's and Cam's groups had been back two days already, and the city was teeming with life. We were home.

Murihen's Council had announced that an operation for Reydn's capture was under way, and my father sent all his people to their assistance, including some of our own Consuls. My aunt, independently of the Council, promised a reward for any information that led to Reydn's capture.

Anur was still missing, and the Valiant set out to look for him. A week later, two messengers brought the same news to the courts of Amarantha and Murihen, a few days apart – Anur had beat everyone to the chase and found Reydn at the fjords of Styr. But neither of them had made it back alive.

The tide brought their bodies back to shore, washing them up on an inlet not far from where

Dainefin and I had set off for Cloch all those months before. They were found by a man who had been intrigued by the sight of a nobleman's horse wandering alone at the top of a cliff. If it hadn't been for Dek, we may never have known what happened.

A messenger was sent to catch up to the Valiant. Myrain didn't want anything to happen to Anur's body, so he rode to Styr to collect him personally and bring the Prince of Amarantha back to his family with the respect he deserved. Myrain's kindness spared us another funeral with an empty coffin.

And when he returned to Amarantha with Anur's remains, we learned there'd been signs of a struggle on both bodies.

We would never know the truth, but I couldn't help thinking that my brother had avenged Mother of both her killers. I kept that thought to myself though.

We gathered every Sunday to remember Anur, Mother and Uncle. We left the speeches to the bishop. To us fell the humble gesture of forgiveness.

Only once did Sonni and I allow ourselves to voice – for each other's ears only – our regret at missing the chance to bond with our older brother.

The Empathic Aura fed on all this pain and came back to torment me. It had never really gone. Like Kolymba, I had recovered the power of speech but didn't have complete control over it. I was still powerless to express intimate emotions, or those that I myself did not fully comprehend.

Until I found my own Reason, like Dainefin and Kolymba had, the Empathic Aura was part of me. In the meantime, I played music, wrote, read – I received crates of books from Master Lohm by anonymous or improbably-named authors, making me suspect that they were all his own work – and spent time with my friends.

I loved to surround myself with the new people in my life who filled gaps I hadn't known were there. Cam, Reya, and Noalim lived in the city now, but I also kept in touch with those I couldn't see in person: Móiras, Master Lohm, Isehar and Fayrem.

I was protective of the moments I spent by myself, but I also made an effort to show my face in the city a little more often.

I often walked through the central square, where a monument had been erected in memory of the seventeen who had fallen in the war. Only three had been soldiers. The others were traders and artisans, people who had never imagined they would die in battle.

Every citizen in Amarantha – myself, Father and Sonni included – attended their funeral. For days afterwards, the square was scented by the candles and flowers left at the foot of the monument.

Then the candles burnt out, the flowers wilted. They were taken away and fresh candles and flowers left in their place, to burn out and wilt in turn. They were refreshed again and again, fewer each time.

People stopped talking about the battle, and no one ever paused to think of the crisis that had been averted. Life was too short to dwell on 'what if's.

Every night before going to bed, I gazed out my bedroom window at the fields of nearly-spent amaranth, and dwelt on that very thing. I knew all too well what would have happened 'if'.

Sonni found me in the library late one night and begged me to write something for his coronation speech.

I sat at Aur-Lee's writing desk waiting for him to at least have a stab at it, so I could help him rephrase – or correct his grammar. But no, Sonni just sat next to me, his mind as lost as his gaze.

I passed him the quill.

'Write and I'll dictate.'

He heaved a sigh of relief.

'Today we hold both joy and grief in our hearts,' I dictated. 'We have lived through a time of grief; now begins our time of joy. Before I, with all of you, give in to the feelings of hope that this, more than any other day . . .'

I yawned.

'Infuses . . . ?' Sonni suggested after a few moment's pause.

'. . . infuses in our hearts, I would like to dedicate a thought to those who have not been as fortunate as we, and . . .'

He stopped writing.

'What is it?' I asked. He passed me the sheet of paper in reply.

'It's terrible,' he said.

I read through what I had just dictated.

'Really disgusting,' I concurred.

We burst out laughing.

'What were you expecting, it's three in the morning!' I pointed out. I took back the quill and made to cross it all out and start afresh, but Sonni stopped me.

'No, leave it as it is. It's my coronation speech. They're expecting something pompous.'

With the visible effort he was making to keep a straight face, it was hard to take him seriously. But he was the one ascending to the throne.

'As you wish, Your Majesty.'

I returned the quill and went back to my dictation.

I began an homage to our mother and brother, but Sonni stopped me.

'It's not fair to speak only of the people we've lost.'

He showed me a roll of parchment on which he had got Myrain and Father to list the names of the victims of the battle of Sidera. Including the ones from Murihen.

'This is why you're going to be a great king,' I said.

Three weeks later my brother was crowned. Sonni's speech was a triumph, and my father placed the crown on Sonni's bowed head himself. When Sonni rose, the citizens of Amarantha exclaimed, 'Long live King Sonni!'

And I joined them, at the top of my voice.

Late that evening, after everyone else had retired for the night, Sonni came to find me in the library again, as had become his habit. We talked about what he'd do in the days to come, and shared a good laugh about all the pomp and ceremony of the day.

'I have something for you,' I said eventually and went to the shelf that held the largest volumes.

When I had imagined this moment, I thought I would say something epic to my brother. But all that came out of my mouth was:

'Here.'

I placed in his arms a brand-new volume, fresh from the Shamabat print shop.

'What's this?' he asked, opening to the first page.

'A book,' would have been a reductive answer. Old Lohm had created a work of art. The cover, the same colour of the leather binding on Aur-Lee's journal, bore the gold-engraved title - *Maír* - followed by Mana Yan's name and the monogram of my initials.

As for the content, not only had my draft been corrected and typeset, but the volume had been enriched by new material, provided by the people I cared most about. Cam had copied a few drawings from the original and made new ones representing every corner of Hatablar forest. He'd also developed the map of the Isle of Cloch that I had sketched from memory. The final chapters were filled in by Dainefin: her story, and the rebellion of Reydn and his followers.

'It's my coronation present,' I said. 'A present for the whole kingdom, actually, but I wanted you to be the first to see it.'

'I can't wait to read it,' said Sonni, embracing me.

Dainefin and I sat in her study, a small alcove next to the castle drying room.

'You need to start thinking about what you want to do with your life,' she said, trying to sound encouraging.

I had thought that once everything was settled after the coronation, Dainefin and I would once again resume our classes.

Dainefin was not of the same mind. School was over, real life was beginning.

I didn't know what I wanted to do with my life. Even if I'd done nothing but ask myself that question for weeks.

'There's no need to decide now,' she reassured me. 'It will come to you.'

I had thought everything was all right as it was. I read, played music, gazed out to sea. I took care of my family and friends, and let them take care of me. I did miss Cloch, but I didn't yet feel able to return. It was a life lived by halves, divided between two homes.

'You are already living your life by halves,' Dainefin reminded me.

Without even realising, she had quoted Kolymba's words to me, and I was struck by a pang of nostalgia. I stood up, searching for distraction on the wall where she kept her herbal stores: dozens of little jars containing dried leaves, flowers and fruits of all shapes and colours. I picked out three that I found inspiring – elderflower, blue chamomile and eucalyptus – and made an infusion.

I served it to the Priestess.

'You did learn something on Cloch,' she smiled.

'Yes, I did,' I replied. 'I learned that serious discussions flow better when you wash them down with a hot drink.'

Another pang.

I miss everyone there so much.

'So do I,' said Dainefin.

'Why don't you go back to Cloch?'

'Lyria, I don't belong there anymore. Nor do the Maír. They're frightened of returning, but they can't stay there forever.'

'Why didn't you ever tell anyone about the Maír? Why not tell us the truth?'

'You don't know how many times I nearly did,' she sighed. 'But then, with time, I convinced myself I didn't have the right.'

'The right to reveal the existence of the Maír?'

'Yes. And to turn your family's life – the whole kingdom – upside down,' she added.

I paused to think.

Do you think it's a mistake that I'm telling everyone about the Maír?

'Absolutely not,' she said. 'I'm so glad you are and that you had Lohm print your book, Lyria.'

But then why didn't you tell us everything sooner?

'In truth, it never felt like my place.'

We sipped our drinks.

414

'You know,' she said, after a while, 'when I left Cloch, I assumed the effects of the Ata Mahari would gradually fade away, that I would start ageing like everybody else.'

'Why did you think that?'

'I was back in Lyr,' she explained. 'I no longer had a reason to age so slowly. When I discovered that was not the case – that there was nothing I could do about it – I resented the Ata Mahari, and Cloch, and even Mana Yan. I wanted nothing more to do with the Maír.'

Mana Yan got it wrong?

I thought of my Maír friends, who still believed the ritual was a gift so they could return home to Lyr.

'I don't know,' Dainefin answered. 'Perhaps if everyone returned . . .'

We fell silent again.

'Lyria, I'm sorry . . . I advised you to steer clear of your visions, because I had lost trust in Mana Yan's, and then my own. Those visions of the little boy abducted by Reydn tormented me for years . . . they stopped long ago, but I still should have recognised Ambar. I should have . . . '

'When did you stop seeing him in your visions?' I interrupted.

'Two years after Cloch,' she replied.

'No, I mean how long ago?' I specified.

'One hundred and fifty years and counting.'

'And you're surprised that after one hundred and fifty years you didn't make the connection? I can't imagine how you can even hold all that time in your memory,' I added, to distract her from the thought of Ambar. 'Do you remember . . . everything?'

'Almost. Let's say I've allowed myself a little help.'
She gestured to her herbarium.

I thought you wanted to forget.
Dainefin shook her head.

'Those who forget risk making the same mistakes all over again,' she said.

We finished our infusions and I was struck by the feeling of having just caught up with the Priestess, after chasing her for years. Since Cloch, things had changed. I knew who I was, who I belonged with. I knew where home was.

There were so many things I wanted to ask Dainefin. Did she regret not being able to confront Reydn in person? Did she believe I could overcome the Empathic Aura one day, or that I'd remain like this forever? Did she think the Maír would ever come home?

And what about her life? What had she done with herself in those centuries between Cloch and Shamabat? I wanted to hear everything – nothing left out. She read my mind. 'It's a long story.'

'We have time,' I replied. 'And we have infusions.' I nodded at Dainefin's immense herbarium.

'In that case . . .' she said with a smile.

She stood and wiped the damp residue from our cups to prepare a fresh infusion. She reached up to the shelves, but before making her selection she turned back to me.

'What would you like?'
'You choose,' I answered. 'I trust you.'

Epilogue

I decided to walk down to the sea in search of peace and solitude after a restless night. The Empathic Aura had made an exhibition of itself from the moment I had laid my head on my pillow – a couple of hours after sunset – to the moment I had given up and angrily kicked off my covers – an hour before sunrise. I had not slept a wink, and my mind was more active than ever.

I glanced out my window. It wasn't long before dawn, there wasn't a cloud to be seen, and I consoled myself by anticipating the colours the sky would take on as the sun rose, on this day of almost-spring.

I tiptoed along the castle corridors and down the steps. The smell of freshly baked bread was already wafting up from the kitchens – the boy who worked for Cam and Reya must have dropped by with the order. I let the warm scent draw me down into the kitchens. They were empty of people, but a basket of bread was sitting on the counter. My piece was on top, wrapped in a cloth embroidered with my monogram. I grabbed it to take with me. Shame the bakery boy had already been and gone. He was a good lad, and a quick chat with him always put me in a good mood.

I resolved to call on Cam and Reya on my way home. Their bakery was near the city gates, and on a day like this I would relish listening to the rhythm of Amarantha rising from its slumber on the long stroll back. I slipped out the kitchen door and headed towards the sea.

The steps running from the side of the castle down to the foot of the promontory were still damp from the rain of a couple of days before. I slipped on a muddy step and ended up on my knees on a little natural platform jutting out of the rock face. The impact was cushioned by grass thick and soft enough to spare me a nasty injury. I leaned over to check how high over the cove I was. High enough, it turned out, to have split my head in two if that platform hadn't broken my fall.

I sat back on the grass and checked my knees. Barely grazed. My hands had a few more scratches and were grubby with soil.

I rubbed my palms clean on the grass, and that was when I noticed a blot of an unusual colour an inch from my hand: the blue of the sea when there isn't a single cloud in the sky.

I recognised it. It was a *lyr* flower.

I sat staring at it, resisting the temptation to pick it. I sniffed it: the scent was neither sweet nor bitter, sharp nor musky, fruity nor balsamic. It wasn't so much a smell as the feeling that everything made sense – even if I couldn't make sense of everything.

When I looked up, the sun was a shining thread stretched along the horizon, reflecting off the water all the way to the shore. I had missed the moment it peeked over the sea.

The sunrise lit the sky and the sea in so many colours that it would be pointless to count them. I was enchanted by a string of pink clouds stitching the sky, filtering the rays of the sun to fire them off in all directions.

And then, suddenly, I saw them.

Three ships on the horizon.

They were still very far away, but I somehow knew what writing they bore on their gunwales: the same words Kolymba had carved onto the boat he'd built to bring me home. *Koinéi ama-tha.*

Koinéi ama-*tha*.

Glossary of Maír Words

ama (**ah**-mah) – home
ama-cóir (**ah**-mah **co**-eer) – graveyard
ata (**ah**-tah) – time
dainefin (**die**-nay-feen) – chief's daughter
hari (**ah**-ree) – water, river, rain, sea, brook,
     lake, sap, mirror, dew, to weep, to drink,
     to flow, wet, damp, liquid, transparent,
     blessing
hata (**ah**-tah) – tree
inu-dhearma (**ee**-new dee-**ear**-ma) – herbal
     infusion for forgetting one's past
kóinei (**ko**-ee-nay) – way, road
kymirama (kee-me-**rah**-ma) – library
kymiron (kee-**me**-rone) – book
lyr (leer) – blue mythical flower
mahari (Mah-**ah**-ree) – river
maint-uri (Ma-**eent oo**-ree) – offspring
Maír (Mah-**eer**) – survivor, survived
mana (**mah**-nah) – elder
pamau (pawm-**ow**) – faithful
tángaor (**Tan**-gah-or) – rebellious
yuvidestra (You-vee-**dest**-rah) – awareness

Character Name Pronunciation Guide

Name	IPA	Pronunciation
Ambar	'am.bar	**ahm** - bar
Anur	'a.nur	**ah**-noor
Aur-Lee	'aːur 'liː	owr lee
Cam	'kam	cahm
Catam	'ka.tam	**cah**-tahm
Cesa	'tse.sa	**cheh**-sah
Dainefin	'dai.ne.fin	**die**-nay-feen
Dek	'dɛk	deck
Dill	'dil	deel
Douk	'duk	dook
Fayrem	'fej.rem	**fay**-rem
Feyal	'fejal	**fay**-yahl
Fran	'fran	frahn
Gaudrot	go'droʊ	**gohd**-row
Hervin	'ɛr.vin	**er**-veen
Isehar	'aj.zi.ar	**i**-se-ar
Kolymba	ko.'lim.ba	co-**leem**-bah
Kyriann	'ki.rjen	**kee**-ryen
Levith	'le.vit	**lay**-veet
Lumio	'lu.mjo	**loo**-me-oh
Lyria D'Aur	'liːrja 'daːur	**lee**-rya d-owr

Mana Kathún	'ma.na ka'tun	mah-nah kah-**toon**
Mana Pun	'ma.na 'pun	mah-nah poon
Mana Suppur	'ma.na 'sup-pur	mah-nah **soop**-poor
Mana Yan	'ma.na 'jan	mah-nah yahn
Marahn	'ma.ran	ma-**rahn**
Maya	'maja	ma-ya
Móiras	'mɔi.ras	moy-ras
Noalim	'nɔ.a.lim	noh-ah-leem
Phinnean	'fin.ne.an	feen-nay-ahn
Rehena	re'iːna	ray-ee-nah
Reya	'reja	ray-ya
Reydn	'rej.den	ray-den
Rila	'ri.la	ree-lah
Myrain, Roy	'mi.rain, 'rɔi	me-rah-een, roy
Ruthven	'ri.vən	ree-vn
Sama Kas	'sa.ma 'kas	sah-mah kāhs
Sama Tar	'sa.ma 'tar	sah-mah tahr
Sari	'sari	sah-ree
Sayd	sa'id	sah-**eed**
Sonni	'sɔn.ni	sohn-nee
Syleanh	'si.le.an	see-lay-ahn
Teira	'tej.ra	tay-rah
Lohm, Thelonius	lɔm, te'lɔ.njus	lom, te-**loh**-nius
Eugenius	ew'dʒe.njus	eh-oo-**jay**-nius
Uriel	'u.rjel	oo-ree-ayl
Yodne	'jod.ne	yod-nay

Place Name Pronunciation Guide

Amarantha	a.maˈran.ta	ah-mah-**rahn**-tah
Ata Mahari	ˈata maˈa.ri	**ah**-tah mah-**ah**-ree
Burgios	ˈbur.d͡ʒos	**boor**-joes
Cloch	ˈklɔk	clock
Denhole	ˈdɛn.ol	**den**-ol
Hatablar	ˈa.ta.blar	ah-tahb-lahr
Hóir	oˈiːr	oh-**eer**
Maír	maˈir	ma-**eer**
Murihen	ˈmu.rjen	**moo**-reeh-ayn
Serra del Lárr	ˈsɛr.ra ˈdel ˈlar	**sayr**-rah dayl lahr
Sidera	ˈsi.de.ra	**see**-deh-rah
Styr	ˈstir	steer

Acknowledgements

A community of friends, colleagues, collaborators and fellow literary citizens is responsible as much as I am for this literary creature who now also lives in the anglophone world. (If I forget anyone, please let me know. I'll bake you my signature pizza.)

To my mum and dad and my brother Marco for trusting I knew what I was doing (when I most definitely did not).

To my earliest readers and closest friends: Matteo Furlanetto, Dario Carbone and Elisabetta Traficante. To my friends and supporters, here: Agnese Brasca, Irene Lucca, Sara Tamburello, Alessandra Volonté, Rob Will Shaw, Simone Busnelli, Erika Dugnani, Monica Consonni, Mattia Pozzi, Giulio Barbiera, Anna Busciglio, Valentina Broggi; and there: Alessandra Lacaita, Gemma Nanni, Elena Gessi, Maria Solinas, Paola Colombo, Danielle Prostrollo and Hannah Riches. And to my writing mentor and friend, Elizabeth Haynes.

To all the artists involved in the recording and performing of the Amarantha soundtrack: Mell Morcone, Marco Rimondo, Lucia Picozzi, Luca Rapazzini, Luca Crespi; Eleonora Romano, Benedetta Oltolini and Agnese Brasca; and to Cinzia Farina for lending her voice to Lyria.

My deepest thanks also go to all the supporters of the crowdfunding campaign for future performances.

To my former colleagues and managers at Lush and at Norfolk Library and Information Service (there's so many of you!) for making my day jobs not just "not unpleasant", but also inspiring, motivating and a lot of fun.

To Ella Micheler, Leah Tanaka and Marinella Mezzanotte for co-creating the English translation of Amarantha. Ella and Leah, you are two of the most talented and humane literary professionals I know. Thank you for believing in this project as much as you have.

To the places of Amarantha and their people: Sicily, Ireland, Rapa Nui and Aotearoa New Zealand.

To the Norwich literary and music community for offering me a taste of what a creative life looks like, and to the city of Norwich in general. To Dave, who made it a home, if only for a moment.

About This Translation

Amarantha is a translated novel with a twist...

Usually, a translator will work on a book alone and it then goes straight to an editor. For *Amarantha* however, we took a different approach: the author (E. R. Traina), translator (Marinella Mezzanotte) and the editors (the Kurumuru Books team) worked on the story together in a creative collaboration. To learn more about our unique process, visit: *www.kurmurubooks.com*

We, the publishers, would like to thank E. R. Traina for allowing us to publish her novel in this way and for working so closely with us to create the wonderful story you have just read. We would also like to thank Marinella Mezzanotte for her commitment to the translation over the past two years.

If you, the reader, are interested in finding out more about literary translation or want to read more translated books, we recommend starting with World Kid Lit. You'll find lots of resources on the blog and on social media at #WorldKidLit all year round, or #WorldKidLitMonth in September, when there's a month-long celebration of translated books from around the world. We also recommend the Stephen Spender Trust, who can bring multilingual creativity courses to your school.

Sincerely,
    The Kurumuru Books Team

E. R. TRAINA is an Italian poet, author and translator. She was born in April 1990 to a Sicilian family in Brianza, a place she endured for more than twenty years thanks to frequent trips to her local library and to Milan, where she fell in love with poetry, literature and theatre.

She sings and plays guitar and the accordion, inspired by Irish folk, Mediterranean and South American music. She wanders around, following her projects or the changing seasons; sometimes she leaves Europe, but she usually comes back.

She loves islands and ports, and beginning her sentences with "but". But she hopes people don't mind.

MARINELLA MEZZANOTTE accidentally became a literary translator while she was an artist's model trying to become a writer. She now translates Italian fiction into English, while still writing and modelling, and wondering where the next accident will take her. Her story *Yesterday's Pies* appeared in the 2013 Bridport Prize anthology.

KURUMURU
BOOKS

Increasing diversity in children's, middle-grade, and young adult literature.

Our mission (and yours, should you choose to accept it!) is to bring more diversity to children's, literature. We specialise in translated, bilingual, and global books because we believe that reading about other cultures is key to building empathy and understanding. Plus, nobody should ever feel left out, so we want our books to help make everyone feel included and represented in literature.

We invented the word *Kurumuru* based on the German 'kuddelmuddel', which means a joyful, colourful, swirling mix of everything – and that's exactly what we stand for. Our mascot Jack is part rabbit, part deer (or maybe antelope), and part bird. He comes from all over and loves to travel. (Sometimes he even visits the moon!) He's always on the lookout for his next favourite book.

To find out more and to join our newsletter visit
www.kurumurubooks.com